LOOKING FOR CASSANDRA JANE

looking for

 Tyndale House Publishers • Wheaton, Illinois

cassandra jane

MELODY CARLSON

Visit Tyndale's exciting Web site at www.tyndale.com

Edited by Kathryn S. Olson

Designed by Zandrah Maguigad

Scripture quotations are taken from the *Holy Bible*, King James Version.

Library of Congress Cataloging-in-Publication Data

Carlson, Melody.
  Looking for Cassandra Jane / Melody Carlson.
    p. cm.
  ISBN 0-8423-4098-X (sc)
  1. Abused children—Fiction. 2. Children of alcoholics—Fiction. 3. Adult child abuse victims—Fiction. I. Title.
PS3553.A73257 L65 2002
813´.54—dc21   2001007060

Printed in the United States of America

05   04   03   02
5   4   3   2   1

To CHRISTOPHER
my "hometown sweetheart"
With love,
MELODY

ACKNOWLEDGMENTS

Thanks to . . .

SARA FORTENBERRY
for seeing the "beauty"
in Cassandra Jane;

REBEKAH NESBITT
for believing in the project;

and KATHY OLSON
for her polishing touches,

as well as everyone at TYNDALE
whose efforts worked together
to make the story into a book!

chapter one

MY DADDY USED TO SAY I had the devil in me. My grandma said it was only because I was a highly spirited child, yet as time went on I figured my daddy might've been right after all—especially seeing as how he and the devil were already on a first-name basis anyway. I was fifteen years old before anyone told me that Jesus loved me— and even then I didn't believe it.

I can still recollect my daddy's face reddened by whiskey and rage. "I'm go'n' to beat the devil outta you, Cassandra Jane Maxwell!" he'd bellow in a slushy voice. Then with his usual drunken awkwardness he'd yank off his leather belt and come after me.

Of course he only did this after the empty Jack Daniel's bottle went spinning across our cracked linoleum floor, and that bottle gave me the advantage because it's not that tricky to elude a drunk—especially if you're fast. And I was fast. But even to this day I still sometimes see my daddy's face when I hear a TV evangelist going on and on about the devil and evil and all.

This is not to make it seem that my daddy was a truly wicked man. The fact is, I mostly loved my daddy. And when he was sober he was a fine-looking and well-mannered gentleman. He liked wearing a freshly pressed shirt with a neatly knotted bolo tie and he believed in polishing his shoes. And his dark hair, like his shoes, would gleam in the sunlight, combed through with Brylcreem (just a little dab'll do ya). And when my daddy walked through town he'd hold his shiny head up high, almost like a cocky rooster strutting through the chicken yard, and seemingly oblivious to all those quick side-glances or knowing nods coming from our fellow townsfolk.

Maybe this was his way of making up for all that was wrong in his life, or more likely he was telling himself that he would do better that day, that he wouldn't give in to his weakness again. And like his hair and his shoes, my daddy talked real smooth and slick too, when he wasn't under the influence. He sold top-quality used cars at Masterson Motors on Main Street, and on a good day he could easily best any other salesman on the lot. My grandma said Clarence Maxwell could charm the stripes right off of a snake—and she meant it as a compliment. But his life was full of sorrows. And his escape in those days was always the bottle.

My daddy used to say that I killed my mama. Of course he only said this when he was under the influence, but my best friend, Joey Divers, told me that whiskey never lies. And I suppose in some ways it was true, because if I hadn't been born my mama wouldn't have died. But then I never asked to be born and there were plenty of times when I surely wished that I hadn't been. Although my grandma said that's like wishing you were dead and it's an insult to your Maker.

My mama died when I was only three days old, and years later I overheard my grandma saying that if my daddy hadn't been out drinking he might've taken my poor mama to the hospital before she bled herself to death. But I would've never dreamed of saying that my daddy killed my mama. Truth is, I know firsthand how bad it feels to lug *that* kind of guilt around with you. I would never wish *that* upon anyone, no matter how pitifully wicked they were.

Since my daddy was pretty much useless after my mama died, my Aunt Myrtle looked after me some. I guess I was a real fussy baby and I suspect I was fairly trying for poor Aunt Myrtle, but I reckon the reason I was so cantankerous was because my mama was dead. To be honest I don't remember that far back, although I've heard said that hidden somewhere deep in our subconscious we do remember such things. I do, however, remember my Aunt Myrtle looking at me with those pale blue eyes. The corners of her lips might turn up into something of a smile, but her eyes were cold and hard like the surface of the park pond those few times it froze over. And her smile, like that brittle veneer on the icy pond, was deceiving. As kids we always knew that even though the pond looked like it might support your weight, you never could count on it and only a plumb fool would go out beyond the edge. One year an unsuspecting deer wandered out and the ice gave way and the poor, confused animal went right down into the freezing dark depths below. And that's about how I felt around my aunt.

Aunt Myrtle usually came over to our house to take care of me. She always had her hair fixed up and lacquered with Aqua Net hair spray you could smell before she even walked in the door. I think she fancied herself to be a Donna Reed look alike wearing all those shirtwaist dresses and high-heeled shoes, but now that I think about it those outfits don't seem like the best kind of housekeeping clothes. She'd tie one of my dead mama's aprons around her thick middle and do a little cleaning and cooking if it suited her. But mostly she just watched the television (shows like *As the World Turns* and *Search for Tomorrow*) or else she just walked around the house like she had a corncob stuck somewhere inside her anatomy. And I knew to stay out of her way.

My earliest memory of Aunt Myrtle was being scolded and pushed away from her long full skirt. My hands were probably sticky or dirty and she was afraid I'd muss her all up, but even when I was squeaky clean she always kept me a good arm's length away. I don't think she was ever real comfortable around kids, and although she did eventually marry, she never bore children of her own. Back when I was little I thought maybe she hated me because I had killed her only sister by being born. But later on I learned that my mama was only her stepsister and no blood relation at all. And as it turned out, my Aunt Myrtle never really liked her much anyway, and I figured that was why she didn't like me either.

Joey Divers told me that his mama told him that my Aunt Myrtle had been in love with my daddy at one time. I couldn't understand this because my Aunt Myrtle seemed like an old woman to me—almost as old as my grandma I thought when I was little. But one day I asked Aunt Myrtle how old she was, and she told me she was almost exactly the same age as my daddy and that they had even gone to school together as kids! The way she said this to me was strange, with those pale blue eyes of hers looking almost dreamlike. It made my skin feel creepy and I wondered if Joey hadn't been right all along.

About that time I became fearful that she might actually be in love with my daddy still, and even though she'd been my mama's step*sister,* I didn't for the life of me want Aunt Myrtle to become my step*mother.* But perhaps her infatuation for my daddy might explain why she put up with me all that time, since I knew she could hardly stand me. And I remember how she'd go on and on, talking like she had my best interests at heart, but in the next breath she'd be telling me how I was a *bad little girl* and how I'd never amount to anything. I know she'd heard my daddy say I had the devil in me and naturally she believed him. But for all her hard work and self-sacrifice it never got her anywhere with my daddy. And I must credit him with that. In fact, although I know he was "involved" with a few women here and there, he never actually fell in love or remarried. In his own way I believe he remained true to my mama's memory. And perhaps that was the main part of the reason for his sorrows.

My grandma would've taken care of me more of the time if she could've, but she had her little grocery store to tend to. Her first husband, my mama's daddy, had built that store with his bare hands from scratch just before the Great Depression. It was an old, boxy wooden building not much bigger than a small house, but with a little apartment above. Situated on a corner downtown, its only windows faced the street, reaching from the ceiling clear down to the floor, and it was all shadowy and dark toward the rear. The store had the smell of oldness to it, as if the bygone years of apples and pickles and sliced bologna had somehow soaked right into its wood plank floors. But it wasn't an unpleasant odor, and it always made me feel comfortable and right at home, like it was a part of me and my history. It was usually nice and cool inside, even on a hot summer day.

Grandma said they used to rent out the apartment before my grandpa died, but it was a real blessing for her to have it when she and my mama were left alone and the Depression set down upon them like a hungry, old bear. She said that little one-bedroom apartment gave her and my mama a safe haven and a roof over their heads, and I think those were happy times with just the two of them. I never quite understood why she upped and married Myrtle's daddy just shortly after the Depression ended—just when things were finally looking up for her. And the saddest part about that "blessed union" was the way her second husband just emptied her cash register till, as well as her two bank accounts, and then ran off and left old Myrtle behind. But my grandma was a good woman and believed that the good Lord would see her through these fiery trials, and I never once heard her complain about getting stuck having to raise her stepdaughter.

Sometimes my grandma would tell me stories about my mama, and when I was five years old she gave me a framed photograph to keep as my very own. And I would look into those dark soulful eyes of the black-and-white photograph and think she must've been the most wonderful woman in the whole wide world. Her skin looked as smooth as my grandma's favorite cream pitcher, and her hair was thick and dark and curly. And even though her dress is all out of style with those big, puffy shoulders, and no one ever wears their hair like that anymore, I know with a certainty in my soul that my mama would still be a knockout if she suddenly appeared on the street today. I used to think I'd grow up to look just like her. But like so many other dreams, it hasn't really come true.

My grandma said that my mama's daddy died when Mama was just a little girl, and that Mama never really got over losing him. It seemed to comfort Grandma that at least the two of them were up there in heaven together now.

However, I found no consolation in this. I'd have much preferred to have her down here on earth with me, because I'm pretty sure my mama and I would have gotten along real well. Naturally I came to this conclusion from looking at her photograph. I'd pretend to have these long, wonderful conversations with her, and she always said really intelligent things (like she'd been around some to know about the world instead of just growing up in Brookdale where everyone is pretty average and normal).

And since she was sort of exotic looking, I liked to imagine she'd been a princess from the Far East, kidnapped at birth and sold to my grandparents because she was so beautiful. She was sure lots prettier than old Aunt Myrtle. I suppose that's why my daddy liked my mama better. My grandma told me I resembled her, but I still can't see it. When I was little I'd climb up onto the bathroom sink and look into the murky mirror in front of our medicine cabinet, but all I saw was a pale, pinched face with two dark holes for eyes and a mop of black hair sticking out all over. My grandma said the black hair and dark eyes came from my mama's daddy. He was full-blooded Cherokee, which makes me one-quarter. The first time I saw an old photo of my mama's daddy, I was sadly disheartened. He didn't have long braids or beads or feathers or anything that looked the least bit like a real, true Indian. Instead he had on an old-fashioned soldier's uniform. My grandma said that was because he'd been in the army and fought in World War I a long, long time ago. I thought it would've been much more exciting if he had fought against Colonel Custer at the Little Big Horn, and I even told Joey Divers that he had. And Joey actually believed me—until he told his mama, that is, and of course she set him straight.

Joey then pointed out that I was a liar, and I didn't argue with him on that account, but in my defense I did tell him that I had what my grandma called a very fertile imagination. Now I wasn't exactly sure what *that* meant just then, and neither was Joey (although he did look it up later) but it seemed to smooth things over just fine. And Joey forgave me, which wasn't surprising, because I was, in fact, the only friend he had.

Joey Divers was what my grandma called "a poor lame duck." He had suffered from polio when he was just a baby and consequently had a useless left leg and was forced to wear a stainless steel brace connected to an ugly black shoe. And therefore he couldn't run and play with the other boys, and sometimes they even teased him about it. But not when I was around. That's because I was never afraid of them. In fact, I don't think I was afraid of hardly anything—except for my daddy, that is, but only when he was drunk. Anyway I would stand right up to those stupid boys, fists doubled, eyes squinted up real mean, and I would tell them that I was one-quarter Cherokee Indian and that my grandpa had whupped Colonel Custer at Little Big Horn, and that I could beat up every single one of them!—one at a time, of course. Fortunately they never took me on. I suspect they thought they might get in trouble for fighting with a girl, especially when the fight was due to the fact that they'd been picking on a little lame boy. And I guess I was mostly relieved that they didn't want to fight with me. Although I did get a reputation for being pretty tough and, I suppose, pretty weird as well.

That reputation helped me to get through a lot of hard times. After all, it wasn't easy having a drunk for a father in a small town like Brookdale where everyone knows everything about everybody. And besides that, sometimes being tough is all a girl's got anyway.

chapter two

I CAN HONESTLY SAY I was a child of the sixties. Before starting first grade in 1960, I was like that little ant who wanted to move the rubber tree plant, and I had *high hopes*—high in the sky, apple-pie hopes! But it didn't take long before I realized that life for me wasn't going to be easy. And it seemed to start out with those ugly, brown, lace-up shoes that Aunt Myrtle insisted I needed for school.

Actually they were quite expensive (which in my opinion was an unfortunate waste of good money!). I can still remember how the young pock-faced salesman claimed they would "help" my feet (like he was a medical expert), but for the life of me, I couldn't see any reason my feet needed help—why, I'd been walking on them just fine for at least five years! On the way home, I pouted in the front seat of Aunt Myrtle's car, saying that those orthopedic shoes looked just like Joey Divers's polio boots. Well, she told me I could just count my blessings and thank the good Lord that at least I didn't have a stainless steel brace to wear with them. Leave it to Aunt Myrtle to find the sunny side of things. Anyway Joey liked my shoes just fine. In fact, I suspect it was those blasted shoes that really solidified our friendship back in the very beginning. And that was only because of Sally Roberts.

On the very first day of school Sally Roberts walked right up to me. And for a brief, hopeful, and slightly delirious moment, I thought she was going to invite me to be her friend. But then she looked straight down at my shoes and laughed. "You look just like Minnie Mouse." She turned to her friend Lucy Marsh. "Just look at those skinny legs sticking out of those clodhopper shoes." And they both laughed long and hard.

I turned and walked back to my desk, holding my chin in the air and trying to act like I didn't give a whit about Sally Roberts or her friends, but all the while wishing that the knothole in the wood floor beneath my desk would just open wide and swallow me up whole so that I could simply disappear altogether.

By recess time I'd decided the sooner I could wear out those horrible shoes, the better off I'd be. So I climbed onto the merry-go-round, and when it got to going real fast, I let my feet hang down over the side, dragging my shoes *thumpity-thump*, *thumpity-thump* over the top of the rough blacktop. I hoped that by the end of the week I'd need a new pair of shoes—maybe something in patent leather with little silver buckles, or maybe even white saddle shoes. (As it turned out those orthopedic shoes were tougher than steel, and they lasted until I finally outgrew them the following spring.)

Joey Divers stood nearby watching my little shoe-scraping exhibition with wide-eyed interest until he finally came over and spoke to me. "Do you know that you might be wrecking your shoes?" he asked. Sheepishly I told him what Sally Roberts had said about me that morning.

"I think your shoes are very nice," he said seriously as he leaned into his crutches. "I think they make you look intelligent." I wasn't sure if that was good or bad, or if I even wanted to know. So I just stared at him and said nothing. Then he told me that *intelligent* was just another word for "really smart."

Well, at the ripe old age of six, being pretty still seemed preferable to being smart. And when I looked over to see Sally Roberts playing hopscotch surrounded by a group of admiring girls, her blonde curls bobbing up and down as she hopped along in a fluffy pink dress, I felt seriously jealous. Of course I knew that her daddy was an important person at the First National Bank and that was probably why Sally's shoes were shiny and black with straps so dainty you'd have thought all that hopping and jumping would just bust them right off. Those were the kind of shoes you wore to Sunday school or birthday parties (that's if you were lucky!). It just didn't seem fair that she was so rich she could wear them to school for everyday if she wanted to; and even her anklets were clean and white, trimmed with delicate lace along the edges. It was enough to almost make me cry, and crying was something I tried not to do much of, even back then.

I later asked my Aunt Myrtle if I could get some lace-trimmed anklets, and she just laughed. Then she told me I better learn to appreciate plain and sensible clothes because it wouldn't be too long before I would need to take care of the laundry all by myself. Which of course turned out to be exactly true. The following summer, my Aunt Myrtle went off to work as a teller at the very same bank as Sally's daddy. Naturally she could no longer help me or my daddy with our mundane household chores since she had to get herself really dolled up to go stand in that little caged box and hand money out to important people.

To tell the truth this was something of a mixed blessing. It did get Aunt Myrtle out of my hair, but at the same time it suddenly seemed that my daddy expected me to do all the cooking and cleaning and everything. And *that* seemed like a whole lot to ask of a seven-year-old girl, although my daddy told me more than once that he did as much when he was a boy (he'd been taken in by a farm family who'd only wanted a slave child). So I tried real hard not to complain, at least not when my daddy had been drinking—I knew better.

It wasn't long until I got this notion that if I did everything just right, just perfect even, then maybe, just maybe, my daddy wouldn't drink so much, and maybe he and I could finally be like those happy families that I saw on my grandma's TV set (*Father Knows Best* and *My Three Sons* and *Leave It to Beaver*). Of course it never worked out that way, but that didn't stop me from trying and hoping. I even wore one of my mama's old ruffly aprons tied around my waist (it reached to the floor).

Getting everything done just right became a sort of superstitious game for me. I thought if I got all the dirty dishes washed up and the floor all swept and supper started by five o'clock, then my daddy would come home by six and be sober. Once in a while, it worked. Most of the time it didn't. After a while I just gave up altogether and learned to do the minimum of work, and then just lie low. That's when my daddy started calling me lazy and mean and wicked. He could get himself all fired up mad about things *not* being done just right around the house, but I soon came to realize that he'd get just as mad when things were done perfectly too—if he was drunk, that is. I finally figured if I was going to catch his wrath no matter what, why bother trying to be perfect all the time? And the less I did around the house, the more reason he'd have to get mad anyway. And that always gave me a real good excuse to just clear out of there.

It was during those years that I started my secret club in a shed in the backyard out behind our house. Our house was just a rental (we weren't the sort of folk who could actually own a home) and I suppose I didn't have any real legal right to use that old shed, but since nobody said I couldn't I figured it must be okay. I can still recollect that sweet musty smell of old damp wood mixed with the lawnmower smell of old cut grass and gasoline. And that shed had lots of neat stuff inside it too. I knew they weren't my daddy's things, and I guess they belonged to our landlady, but since she was about a hundred years old and confined to her wheelchair I didn't expect that she minded much that we borrowed them. Besides, it was just me and Joey in the club most of the time anyway, and usually we were real careful with everything. That is until we burnt the whole place down. But that was purely an accident, involving candles and a science experiment that went awry.

When we first started meeting in the shed, we cleaned it up as best we could, sweeping out decades' worth of dust and thick spiderwebs. I told Joey that black widows lived in there, and it scared him so badly he wouldn't come back inside until I swore on an old Bible that we'd found on a shelf that I had lied to him about the spiders. Then we set up an old wooden card table and two rickety chairs in the center of that dark, dank space. And for some reason we even put the Bible on the table. It's not that we were religious or anything, but it just seemed like a good thing to do. And it looked nice sitting right there next to our dues jar, which was most often empty.

Of course we didn't know exactly what the purpose of our club was to start with, but we both knew we needed a place to get away from our troubles. It wasn't that Joey had a truly bad family or anything. In fact, his daddy went to work almost every single day, long hours too, and sometimes even on Sundays, although Mrs. Divers said it was a sin to work on the Lord's Day. Anyway, Mr. Divers built small houses and additions and fences and such for people in Brookdale, and he hardly ever got drunk—just once in a while like on New Year's Eve, and Joey said he never got mean-drunk, just goofy-drunk is all. Mr. Divers was a big, barrel-chested kind of man, with muscles that bulged right through his T-shirts. He'd been a Marine in the war and he walked with a swagger, and I'm sure no one in town ever crossed him. And I'm just as sure that he loved Joey in his own way, but I don't think he ever knew how to show it real well, leastways not back then, when it really counted. I think Mr. Divers felt worried that Joey was such a fragile boy that he might actually break if he was handled too roughly, and so he reserved all his wrestling and roughhousing for Joey's younger brother, Randy (a healthy child who was born after Dr. Salk invented his famous polio vaccine).

Unfortunately what Joey missed out on in attention from his daddy was more than compensated by Joey's mama. Mrs. Divers babied and coddled him to the point where Joey said it sometimes actually felt like he couldn't breathe (which even caused Mrs. Divers to suspect he might have asthma, although he did not). She didn't want him to go to school, or to play with other children, or even to go outside much. Consequently, Joey started school later than most kids, but at least he'd spent a lot of time reading books and making models of cars and airplanes in his room.

So if our club had given itself a name, it might have been called the Misfits Club. We never called it that, at least not out loud, although I'm sure we both thought it from time to time. I suppose in some ways it was similar to what people these days might call "group therapy," and in all likelihood it might've saved me and Joey from some additional psychoses in our later lives. Not that we sat around and whined about our problems all the time, but if we needed an ear we always found it in each other.

Most of our time was spent pretending and daydreaming. Maybe that's what misfits do to escape the sad realities of their pitiful little lives. Our favorite dream was that we would one day invent something extraordinarily brilliant and consequently become rich and famous. And then people would point to us and say, "I remember when I used to know them back when they were just nobodies." And because of my deprived economic state, we also spent a fair amount of time and energy on moneymaking ventures that would increase our club treasury (which we stowed away in an old canning jar that we kept hidden under a loose floorboard in the shed).

We had no pride when it came to making money, and we sold everything from hand-squeezed lemonade to All-American greeting cards. And we quickly learned (due to the stainless steel leg brace and the consequent empathy factor) that Joey made the best salesman by far. Folks would take one look at his limp and quickly shell out money for whatever it was we happened to be peddling that day, whether they wanted it or not.

The funny thing was, we never knew exactly how to use our earnings. Mostly we just squandered them on sweets and movies, and then we'd have to come up with some whole new capitalistic scheme and start all over again. One time we even sold stolen produce door-to-door. We'd sneaked into old Mr. Bernstein's orchard and picked two of his peach trees clean (actually, I picked while Joey gathered). Somehow my grandma got wind of this, and we had to turn all our earnings over to Mr. Bernstein as well as work in his orchard for several days as restitution. Turned out he was a pretty nice guy, and he invited us to stop by and visit whenever we liked. After that, my grandma began giving us odd jobs in the store to make extra money, and our life of crime was narrowly averted for a while.

All during this time my daddy and me just drifted further and further apart. I stayed away from home as much as possible, slipping in and out like an evening shadow. Once in a while, if my daddy was on a really bad rampage, I would sneak out and sleep in the clubhouse, but I didn't like it because I knew lots of spiders still lived in there. (Despite my promises to Joey, I wasn't totally sure about my black widow theory. Somehow spiders and bugs just seemed to be everywhere in the darkness and I would imagine them creeping all over my face.) But I'd just pull my blanket tighter around myself and console myself with knowing it was better than facing my daddy's rage.

For a long time, I never told my grandma about any of this. It seemed she had so much on her mind just trying to keep her store afloat, without any help from Aunt Myrtle anymore, and if I ever hinted at any kind of trouble her face would get all squinched up and anxious-looking. And I just didn't like to worry her with my troubles.

My daddy was an orphan. He was born right after the big stock market crash in 1929. My grandma thought his folks must've come across some awful hard times, what with the Great Depression and all, and probably were so impoverished they had to give him up. She told me how lots of families got split up back then, and some folks were so poor that they just couldn't keep their kids.

I'm sure that explains some of my daddy's problems. It's one thing to have your parents die on you, but it's something else when they just up and give you away like an old, worn-out piece of furniture. I used to think that if I ever had a baby of my very own it wouldn't matter how poor I was—even if I had to scrub toilets or sweep the gutters—I wouldn't give up my baby for nothing. But like my grandma always says, you shouldn't judge a person until you've walked a mile in his moccasins. (I used to think my grandpa, the Cherokee Indian, made that one up.)

One night when my daddy wasn't drunk, and we were sitting on the couch together watching *Gunsmoke* in a nice, congenial fashion, I asked him why he didn't ever try to find his family.

"What family is that you're talking about, Cassandra?"

"You know—the family that gave you up for adoption." That week's episode happened to feature a little boy who'd been separated from, and then reunited with, his birth family. And when it ended everyone all seemed pleased and happy.

His face darkened with a frown. "I don't know anything about those people."

"Well, they might still be alive," I said hopefully. "Even if they're pretty old by now. And you know, I wouldn't mind having an extra grandma or even a grandpa around." I was thinking it might even mean getting more Christmas and birthday presents, and things were pretty slim pickings most of the time.

"Well, the fact of the matter is, Cassandra, if my parents didn't care enough to keep me with them, then I sure as spit don't care enough to go out of my way looking for them after all these years."

Now I thought that was just a mite ungracious on his part. I mean, what if they had no idea where he was or even if he was alive? But I didn't venture to say so.

"But what if you have some brothers or sisters?" I persisted, thinking I might have some aunts, uncles, or maybe even a cousin or two out there somewhere.

My daddy just laughed and said, "Well, if they're anything like me, then who'd want to know them anyway?"

I thought about that for a minute or two and figured he had a point, and yet I still longed for more family and felt a mite curious at what might be out there.

I knew my daddy didn't like to talk about his childhood. Usually he didn't like to talk much at all, leastwise not to me, or so it seemed. So sometimes I'd slip behind the long, thick window drapes in the front room and listen while he was talking to someone else. Usually the best eavesdropping times happened when

Charlie Fox and my daddy had both downed a couple of drinks but weren't falling-down drunk yet.

I suppose Charlie was the closest thing my daddy ever had to a best friend, but even old Charlie got fed up with him sometimes. Surprisingly, Charlie was always real nice to me. I think maybe he felt sorry for me, probably 'cause he knew my daddy better than most. But the older I got, the less I liked Charlie. I figured if he really, truly cared about my daddy he wouldn't always come over and drink with him. I mean, it wasn't like everybody in town didn't already know my daddy had a drinking problem. Seems to me Charlie could've done his drinking with someone else. But as Grandma often said, "Birds of a feather flock together."

It was later on when I realized that Charlie had a troublesome drinking problem himself. It took a little longer for it to catch up with him, but it finally did. When I was in junior high school, Charlie's wife took his three kids and moved off to Florida. Poor old Charlie never got over it. Just one year later he drove off in one of Mr. Masterson's brand-new Pontiacs—drove that 1968 Firebird straight into the levy and sunk it clean to the bottom. The town called it a drunken driving accident, but my daddy said that Charlie killed himself on purpose, and we kids didn't swim in the levy that whole summer.

I always knew Grandma would help me if I ever *really* needed her. She was like my ace in the hole, my insurance policy. In the meantime I went about life carefully, staying out of the way most of the time, and when I didn't, I ran fast. Looking back, I suppose I should have gone to Grandma, but I guess I thought that underneath it all, she must've known what my life was really like. I figured everybody in town must've known how my daddy got all ugly and mean when he drank too much. If only he'd been more like old Charlie or even Mr. Divers—those goofy sort of silly drunks—I think we could have gotten along just fine. In fact, later on in life, I used to wonder why Charlie's wife had even run off like that in the first place. Sure, Charlie might've been an alcoholic and all, but it seemed to me that he never really hurt anybody. Not like my daddy, that is.

chapter three

WELL, THE DAY FINALLY CAME when I needed my ace in the hole. But it was almost too late. The doctor said that if Joey hadn't found me when he did and called for help, I would've died for sure. At the time, I thought that might have been a good option—then I could be with my mama and the grandpa who was the Cherokee Indian. But later on I was thankful for Joey's loyal intervention.

It was the summer of 1964, just before my tenth birthday, and my daddy hadn't sold a car in weeks. Our rent was two months overdue, and the landlady, even from her wheelchair, was threatening to throw us out on the street. Just the same, my daddy could still afford a cheap jug of wine.

It had been one of those hot, lazy days in August. Joey and I had been out on his front porch, drinking homemade root beer and playing Monopoly until almost nine o'clock at night, but then his mama came out and fretted over whether Joey might catch a chill out there (although it must've been eighty degrees!). Since those were the days when I was still in the good graces of Mrs. Divers (she knew I provided a handy diversion for her poor lame child, and friends were in short supply just then) I wisely decided not to wear out my welcome. I thanked them for their hospitality, and after promising to meet Joey the next morning at eight, I left.

I remember that night as if it were yesterday, standing out in the shadows of their boxwood hedge, watching their little two-story house with the darkness all around me. From where I stood, their windows glowed just like amber, with white curtains moving ever so slightly in the evening air. I could hear the sound of *The Ed Sullivan Show* playing inside, and I wished, not for the first time, that my daddy hadn't bashed in our worn-out TV. Sure, its picture tube might've been a little fuzzy, but if you sat far enough across the room it didn't look too bad, and the sound worked just fine. Anyway, I fought back feelings of envy as I watched Mrs. Divers through the kitchen window, her aproned back to me as she stood before the stove making what I felt certain, by her fast jiggling arm, must be popcorn. My stomach rumbled with hunger. I had been careful not to come over to Joey's house until after their dinner hour had passed that evening. Just a few days earlier, I'd overheard Mr. Divers say, "Doesn't that child ever eat at her own home?"

It was well after dark when I slipped quietly into my house. I wasn't overly worried that my daddy would be in a drunken state since his bottle of cheap wine had been nearly empty that morning, but out of habit I was still cautious to catch the kitchen screen door before it slammed loudly behind me. From the streetlight outside I could see a shiny object on the table and thought with dismay that it was an empty bottle of booze. But upon closer examination, I discovered it was a canning jar . . . and then I recognized the long jute string around the neck, tied there so we could pull it up from its hiding spot beneath the loose floorboard. It was our club treasury jar—and it was empty!

Just a few days ago Joey and I had counted our accumulation of wealth, and it had been well over twelve dollars, all honestly come by, mostly from working at my grandma's store. We had planned to sell Kool-Aid and earn eight more dollars in time for the Porter County fair next week, which would make ten dollars apiece to spend just as we liked on rides and cotton candy and maybe even some of those spin-art pictures where you squirt on the paint as the card twirls round and round.

Now the jar was empty. I suddenly noticed my daddy looming in the darkened doorway that led to the front room. Just a few feet away from me, swaying back and forth with a bottle dangling from his hand. Not a wine bottle this time, but the long-necked, square-shaped kind of bottle, suggesting something strong like bourbon or rye.

"You been holdin' out on your ol' man," he said in a slurred voice, unsteadily shaking his forefinger at me.

I knew this meant trouble, and I shook my head in silent denial as I slowly started to back away, but not quickly enough. With amazing speed—for a drunk that is—he lunged forward and grabbed me by my sleeveless cotton shirt, pulling it so hard I heard the buttons snap off in sharp, angry pops.

"Where'd you get that money, Cassandra Jane?" he sneered. "You been stealing from your ol' man, have you? Sneakin' money outta my pockets when I'm not lookin'?"

Again I mutely shook my head, trying to pull away from his iron grasp, wishing my tautly pulled shirt would simply split in two and like Peter Rabbit I would gladly flee away and run half-naked down the street until I reached my grandma's store. But he had hold of my arm now and gave me a hard shake, and I thought I heard something in my neck pop. Then his twisted face came so close to mine that I could smell that sweet, putrid aroma of alcohol emanating from him like a poisonous vapor.

I knew this was a very bad situation. And if I didn't get away fast, it would likely turn worse. If only his grasp would weaken, just momentarily. I knew I could be out of there in a flash and he'd never catch up with me. I'd bang on my grandma's apartment door and tell her everything, and of course she'd take me in. But his grip was like a vise, and the next thing I knew he was swinging his other fist at me, with the bottle still in it, just like I was his punching bag.

I closed my eyes and held my free hand up to protect my face, but it was useless to try and duck the blows. The sound of my own skull cracking rang in my ears and I was pretty sure that it was all over with right then, although I do remember hitting the floor, too. I felt just like a limp rag doll as I collapsed onto the hard linoleum. But that was the last thing I remembered until the next day when I woke up in the hospital with my grandma at my side, holding my hand gently in hers.

"It was your little friend Joey Divers who found you," she explained as she stroked my hand. "Poor boy, he was fairly shook up, but somehow managed to place a call to the police."

"Joey called the police?" I watched her face curiously, still seeing the edges blurred with a double image, a result of the concussion.

She nodded. "Joey told me you two had planned to meet."

I groaned. "The fair. We were going to make some more money for the fair. But Daddy took it—" I felt hot tears streaking down my face.

"Hush, child," soothed Grandma. "The fair's the least of your worries right now."

Then in a quiet but firm voice she told me I'd never have to go back to live with my daddy again. "I don't have much to give you, child, but at least you'll be safe."

I remember drifting off to sleep again after that, all the while clinging to Grandma's promise like it was my only lifeline. I suppose, at the time, it was.

And Grandma almost managed to keep her promise. For the next few years, I enjoyed something of a normal life. Well, as normal as can be for someone whose dad was locked up for nearly killing his only daughter. But living with Grandma seemed a fitting reward for the pain and suffering I had endured over the years, and while she didn't baby and pamper me too much, she did make sure I got decent food to eat, had presentable, if not stylish, clothes on my back, and a clean place to sleep.

And she loved me. Although she was never given over to emotional displays of affection, I felt certain she loved me. I know I loved her. And she brought a sense of real security into my shaky little world. Even if I did sleep on a cot in the corner of her tiny living room (in the little apartment above the store) it was still *my* space—my corner—and no one was allowed to disturb a thing there. I kept the old photo of my mama taped to the wall, right where I could see it every night before I went to sleep with the sound of *The Tonight Show* playing quietly on Grandma's television. I even used to pretend Johnny Carson was my real daddy as I felt myself slipping off into a dream world that was most often better than real life. Later on I would add a picture of the Beatles to my wall space next to my cot. And from time to time I'd tape up a picture that I'd drawn myself— usually it was a horse or a little house in the trees with smoke coming out of the chimney and a rainbow overhead. But that's where I drew the line in decorating. I wasn't about to slather what little space I had with lots of dumb pictures. For the most part, Mama and the Beatles were plenty for me.

My tenth birthday came not too long after I'd moved in with my Grandma, and to my surprise, Joey's mom dropped him by to help me celebrate. At first I thought maybe Grandma had invited him over, but as it turned out Joey had remembered my birthday all on his own.

"The fair wasn't all that great this year," he told me as he casually handed me a small, neatly wrapped box (he'd used the Sunday comics as gift wrap). "You didn't really miss much."

I figured he was just trying to be nice since I'd been laid up with my broken arm and a couple cracked ribs during fair time. "What's this?" I asked, giving the box a small shake.

"It's for your birthday, silly." He rolled his eyes and made a goofy face.

I carefully unwrapped the box to discover a small transistor radio inside. "Wow, Joey, this is really cool."

"See that?" He pointed to a funny-looking wire wrapped in plastic. "You put that plug into your ear and you can listen to music without bugging your grandma."

"Thanks so much, Joey. This is the best gift I've ever gotten!"

Then he looked down at his feet, and I wondered if my gushy appreciation had embarrassed him, or maybe he was just feeling uncomfortable about my unfortunate situation. And then I wondered if perhaps he hadn't bought what seemed an expensive and slightly extravagant gift to me because he felt sorry for me. And as much as I wanted and needed his friendship, I couldn't bear to think it was based on pity.

"Hey, can I sign your cast?" he asked suddenly.

"Sure."

Then he pulled a blue felt-tip pen out of his pocket. "I came prepared."

I laughed and stuck out my arm and watched as he took his time to artfully pen his name in big balloon letters: *The Amazingly Awesome Joey Divers!*

For the remainder of the summer, Joey came to visit me when he could, which wasn't often because he had to ask his mama to give him a ride. I suspected she'd been secretly relieved that my nasty incident with my daddy had landed me on the other side of town where my less-than-wholesome influence might be a little more removed from her precious son, but I did appreciate her bringing him by sometimes, and I always enjoyed his visits.

"I've got this idea for how I can adapt a bicycle," he told me one day as summer was coming to an end. Then he pulled a folded paper from his shirt pocket. It turned out to be a complete mechanical drawing of his plans.

"Joey, that's great."

"Yeah, I figure I can get around town better on this, and I won't always have to ask my mom to drive me around."

I hoped that meant he could come over and visit more often.

"Of course my mom's not too crazy about this idea, but I think I can talk my dad into it." He then explained how the bike would work technically, with one pedal removed and a hand-braking device and all sorts of other things. And I think that's when I first began to realize Joey's mental superiority, and I wondered if he might not actually be a genius like Mr. Albert Einstein.

If not for Joey's visits and my transistor radio, it would've been a bleak summer. Like Joey had said, I could insert that little earplug right into my ear and listen to my favorite popular station without disturbing Grandma with "all that noise they call music" as she liked to say. But whenever I was alone I'd crank that little radio up as loud as it would go. Still I could barely make out the words of some of the songs with all the static and crackling that was on the air in those days. As a result, I mixed up a lot of the lyrics, and I actually thought the Beatles were singing "Lucy in *disguise* with diamonds. . . ." Of course it made perfect sense to me, and I still like the image it brings. I see this bag lady who's all dressed up and dripping in diamonds, and I think, *What a great disguise!* And maybe my misunderstanding of those lyrics actually brought out some hidden creativity in me, because I'd just sing right along with the radio, making up my own version of the words when I couldn't quite make them out.

The downside of listening to the radio so much was coming up with funds to replace those expensive little transistor batteries. Finally I finagled a deal with Grandma to mind the store for her in trade for batteries. I knew Grandma wanted to do more for me, but she was barely getting by just then with her little store barely holding its own. But at least we had peace and quiet and good food to eat, and that's a lot more than I can say for living with my daddy.

While I tried real hard not to think about him too much, he came to mind fairly often, and my thoughts about him were somewhat confusing. Sometimes I even felt guilty, as if it were my fault that he'd beaten on me and gotten himself locked up. I thought that if I'd maybe handled things differently he'd still be a free man. But then in the next moment, I'd have to admit that I felt much safer knowing he was behind bars. He sent me a number of letters, all eloquently written and amazingly apologetic, and each time he begged me to write back to him and tell him that I'd forgiven him. Naturally since he was locked up he was forced to remain clean and sober (I knew they weren't supposed to drink liquor in there) but he promised over and over that he would never go back to the drink. I just wasn't sure what to believe, and as a result, I never did answer his letters. Over a period of time, he ceased to write to me altogether. Which I suppose was for the best.

By the time I hit fifth grade, I'd pretty much given up on ever being the kind of girl that went off to slumber parties or giggled with her friends at recess or had money in her pocket to go buy soft-swirl cones at the Dairy Maid after school. My grandma took me shopping for clothes at places like the Goodwill Store, and I would try real hard not to pick out pieces of clothing that I'd previ-

ously seen on my classmates at school (since I knew from experience what happens when someone like Sally Roberts recognizes
you wearing an old green-and-red-plaid skirt that used to belong
to her). And yet finding an item of clothing that no one would recognize seemed near to impossible in a town as small as ours. One
time, I literally begged Grandma to drive me all the way to Lambert
to do my shopping there, but she thought that would be a waste of
both time and gasoline when we had a perfectly good thrift store
right here in town. I never had the heart to tell her exactly why I
wanted to make the trip. But as a result of wearing those pieces of
cast-off clothing, often recognized by my classmates, I made giant
strides in the continuation of my tough act during those wonderful
preadolescent years when girls can be so snide and cruel.

I don't mean to make it sound as if Brookdale was such an
awful town to grow up in, all full of miserable people and sadness
and the like, because that really wasn't the case. Sure, it's true that
my daddy seemed to attract trouble the way a cookout attracts yellow jackets, but there were many fine and upstanding folks in our
town—or at least I thought so when I was too young to know any
better. There was something good about being a kid in the sixties—
something simple and laid-back, something you just don't see
nowadays.

The truth is, I don't think our sleepy little southern town was all
that much different from the rest of the little towns spattered across
the country, especially at that time. We had a number of small business and retail outfits on Main Street, several eateries that pretty
much tasted all the same (no one in our town had even heard of fine
cuisine or "ethnic" style foods back then). We had four grade
schools, two junior highs, and one high school that could draw half
the town to a football game on a Friday night. We had the right side
of the tracks and then, of course, the other side (where I usually

lived). And I think for the most part, people in Brookdale were having a pretty good time (or so it seemed to me since I was always on the outside looking in). Curiously enough, we didn't have much trouble with the civil rights movement since the "town fathers" had always seen to it that very few blacks were able to comfortably locate into our town. (Fortunately that all changed during the seventies—after some sharp ACLU lawyers made some interesting discoveries—and today I'm proud to say that Brookdale boasts a much more mixed and integrated population.) But back when I was a kid, the "fine citizens" of our "fair" town thought they had the world by the tail, and for the most part, I think they considered themselves pretty well off, or maybe it was simply a form of blissful ignorance.

The sixties were like that for a lot of folks, living in their modern ranch houses, eating their TV dinners, and driving their gas-hog cars. There seemed to be a general oblivion to the suffering that happened to other people. And in some ways that oblivion might've sustained me too, as if I were playing right along with them, pretending that my life was no different from theirs. But in the same way I knew I was wearing dirty underwear beneath a neatly pressed dress, I knew that my life was not like theirs.

Even as a kid I knew a hardened exterior was my best protection against the hateful remarks that people like Sally Roberts and her kind so easily tossed my way. And during these difficult times, it brought me great comfort to know I could always count on Joey Divers to listen to my woeful tales and show some honest sympathy. Plus he always had something witty and clever to say about those ignorant people who mistreated others, which made us both feel better. And together we would vow that one day we would make them all sorry that they'd ever treated us in such a fashion, for we still believed that the day would come when we'd both be rich and famous.

I'd gotten so attached to my little radio that I took it with me almost everywhere. And I knew (or sort of knew) all the words to the top twenty pop songs. And I thought I had a fairly good voice too, and naturally Joey agreed with me, and even put up with me singing "Up, Up and Away" loudly and somewhat obnoxiously in public.

That's when he first started calling me Cass (like Mama Cass from the Mamas and the Papas). I hadn't yet seen a photo of Cass Elliot and felt honored and slightly elated to share the name of the woman with the sweetest, most honey-coated voice this side of heaven. Later on, I saw her photo on a record album and felt slightly dismayed, but by then my loyalty to Mama Cass had been set like cement on a hot day, and I wouldn't go back on her just because she had something of a weight problem. I knew that would make me no better than Sally Roberts, and if there was one thing I was determined not to ever become like, it was her! (I still remember the day Mama Cass died—I felt personally aggrieved to learn of her loss. They played her hits on the radio for a full week, and I sang along faithfully. I still get a little misty-eyed when I hear her sing "Dream a Little Dream.")

Somehow Joey managed to get his daddy to buy him that bicycle, and as planned, he worked it over so that he could pedal with his right foot while his left leg hung limply at his side and brake with his hands. He even had a special saddlebag to hold his crutches. Now he was able to ride over and visit me as well as to work at Grandma's store. Even when things got so bad that she couldn't afford to pay him, he still came.

"It's okay," he told her one day after she explained her financial dilemma. "I just like being here. And besides, this will look really good listed on my resumé as my work experience."

"What's a resumé?" I asked, pausing from restocking the candy section.

"It's something you write up on a piece of paper, for when you're ready to look for a real job."

"What kind of job would you want to get?"

"I don't know. But I plan on getting a work permit as soon as I turn fifteen."

Then I remembered that Joey was a couple years older than me, and as strange as it seemed, for him fifteen wasn't all that far off!

Grandma had always trusted Joey in her store, perhaps even more than she trusted me. Not that she thought I would steal from her, but Joey was so completely trustworthy and dependable, and so smart he knew how to work the cash register when he was only twelve. So by sixth grade, it got to be a regular thing for Joey and me to have the run of the store on afternoons and weekends. It wasn't terribly busy, because by then most people were shopping at the big supermarkets (another one had come to town) but we felt grown-up and proud to be running the store on our own just the same.

Of course the only time customers came into our store was when they were in too big of a hurry to drive over to the larger ones, and usually they'd only purchase an item or two and then get cranky if we didn't give them their change fast enough to suit them. And the whole while, I always figured they were looking down on us or feeling sorry for us. I'm sure they wondered how we managed to stay in business at all. But just the same, I think Grandma really appreciated our help, and I suppose that she actually needed us around more than we knew, due to the fact that her health was failing. Looking back now I'm sure she knew her "little tired spells" were a warning of some sort, and I think even then she suspected she wouldn't be around for all that long.

I can't imagine what life would've been like without Joey to keep me company during those years. I began to appreciate more than ever how smart he was, and getting smarter every day. He was just like a sponge when it came to soaking up information and knowledge and important facts. He subscribed to all kinds of science and mechanical magazines, and sometimes I thought Joey Divers knew absolutely everything there was to know about everything.

Sometimes he even got a little cocky and silly and acted like he did, but not very often. It just didn't seem to be in his nature to be full of himself like that. In fact, I think he actually went out of his way sometimes not to make me feel dumb. And it's not that I was stupid, because I got pretty decent grades in school (now that I was getting regular food and a good night's sleep) and I was in the top classes for reading and math, but somehow I just never felt quite as brilliant as I believed Joey to be.

To be honest, I think I envied his intelligence a little. Then I'd tell myself it was only fair that since Joey hadn't been blessed with a healthy body, he should at least be blessed with an extra-smart brain. But I think there were times when I would've gladly traded my healthy body for his smarts—and maybe he would've agreed to the trade, for it seemed that more than anything else, Joey still wanted a pair of good, strong legs. I never quite understood why his handicap bothered him so much, because in my eyes Joey could do anything he put his mind to, and he put his mind to a lot!

I soon discovered that while I remained a misfit and (I felt certain) the most unpopular girl in school, Joey was slowly coming up in the world—this primarily due to his intellectual capabilities. By the middle of sixth grade, teachers began to respect him more, and there was talk of moving him up a year in school. Of course I was happy for him, but I prayed every night that it wouldn't happen. I wasn't sure what I'd do without Joey Divers as my best friend. And even though we became too embarrassed to sit together at lunch anymore as sixth grade drew to a close (primarily due to the insensitive teasing of our classmates—I still cringe inwardly when I hear kids chanting, "Two little lovebirds sitting in the tree, K-I-S-S-I-N-G . . .") we continued to nurture our friendship in private. (Not with any kissing, mind you! The thought never even crossed my mind back then, and I'm certain it never crossed Joey's, either.)

By the end of sixth grade, the fatal decision had been made. Mr. Garret, our grade-school principal, announced that Joey Divers would start the next school year in junior high as an eighth grader. An eighth grader! Why, that sounded almost like moving to another planet. Just going into junior high and starting seventh grade seemed like a pretty big leap to me, but eighth grade was unimaginable! And I felt completely devastated by this news. I believed this would prove the final blow that would end my one and only true friendship.

As it turned out I was mostly right. Oh, not so much because Joey got moved up a year, but more because of the way that silly boy-girl thing in junior high intensified so greatly. It's as if everyone had suddenly been bitten by the love bug and could think of nothing but pairing off. I'm sure it must've started with Sally Roberts and Jimmy Flynn, and I heard she's the one who asked him to go steady. But whatever the case, the trend was begun, and nearly everyone in seventh grade just fell right into line. Well, except for me, that is. Naturally no one would want to go steady with the nerdiest, most unpopular girl in the entire school. And although the thought did occur to me that Joey and I could pretend to go steady (as a guise to cover our friendship) I found the whole idea somewhat disgusting. And so, as a result of all this romancing going on, even the thought of continuing my friendship with Joey became an uncomfortable option—if it was even an option at all.

Because, for instance, how could I possibly tell Joey Divers that I needed a training bra but was afraid to ask Grandma lest she think me presumptuous? Could I possibly explain to him how terribly embarrassing it was to dress down in PE, or how I always tried to hide in the corner because I was the only girl still wearing an undershirt instead of a real brassiere? Or how could I tell him how I was scared to death that I might get my first period right just as I was standing in front of the class to give a book report? Because I knew from last year's "Mother's Tea" that menstruation (a word I couldn't even bear to say aloud) was inevitable for young ladies of my age. But I ask you, how could a boy, even one as smart as Joey Divers, possibly understand and relate to these feminine secrets and womanly things?

And so Joey and I parted ways. Oh sure, we still chatted with each other on occasion, and he still came to work in the store sometimes, but not nearly as much as he used to (since he was lots busier with school now). And I'd noticed how he was quickly developing his own sort of social life—somewhat anyway. Moving up a grade had proved good for him. It gave him something of a fresh start, I think. He joined the chess club and got himself on the honor roll and would even make a solid campaign for class president before leaving Brookdale Junior High. Why, he was almost popular! I think it had to do with the sixties movement and the way our generation was just starting to develop more compassion for others. Well, some others anyway—not for me. And Joey's stainless steel leg brace became something of a real status symbol, I think, although I'm sure Joey never saw it quite like that. Anyway, it was never the same for Joey and me once he got moved up. We could never go back to the way it had been before, back when we were both just kids and rattling around the old neighborhood. And, oh, how I missed that.

chapter four

IN SOME WAYS, those years living above Grandma's store should've been considered the "good years." And in many ways they were. Maybe it's just that they ended too soon. For when I look back, they feel like a brief blur of contentment sandwiched amidst what was a trying and difficult childhood and an adolescence that always felt like it was going just slightly sideways, or worse.

My grandma had her first stroke when I was thirteen and a half. Fortunately, by then, we'd already had the training bra conversation and covered the details of getting my first period (having raised two girls, Grandma was surprisingly well versed in the ways of a woman). But just the same, I was completely devastated to see her laid up and suffering in the hospital.

"You'll get better, Grandma," I assured her with all the thirteen-year-old confidence I could possibly muster.

She pressed her pale, thin lips together and nodded. She was still unable to speak, but she squeezed my hand as if to assure me she was trying her best. And within a few days she made considerable progress and was able to speak again with just a slight impediment. Still, it gave me hope. And I tried to be strong for her sake.

"You're doing better, Grandma," I said as she showed me her daily progress, sitting up in bed, moving her fingers and toes, and finally getting up and shuffling behind a walker a little. Still the doctor seemed concerned about her recovery and refused to release her from the hospital just yet.

"You be all right," she mumbled to me one day after school.

"Yes, Grandma, I'm all right." I studied her face, noticing how the left side looked loose and slack again. The nurse had already explained how she'd had a bad spell and that I could only visit with her for a few minutes today.

"You . . . be . . . good . . . girl," she said, taking care to form the words so that I'd understand.

"Of course, Grandma," I promised.

"You . . . make something . . . of yourself . . . someday."

I nodded, fighting to keep the tears from forming. I knew that she thought she wasn't long for this world, but I didn't want to believe it. I wasn't ready to say good-bye.

"You . . . good girl . . . Cassie."

I leaned over and kissed her cheek. "I love you, Grandma," I whispered in her ear. "I'll see you later."

I stood by the door and listened as Grandma talked to Aunt Myrtle. "You . . . take care of . . . Cassandra Jane." She struggled to say my whole name.

"Of course, Mama." I heard Aunt Myrtle shift in her chair.

"You . . . promise me," said Grandma with a surprising firmness in her voice that almost gave me hope.

"I promise you, Mama. Cassandra will be fine."

"Good."

Grandma didn't die straightaway, but suffered a couple more strokes that left her completely debilitated. For three sad days, she lay confined to her bed. I could tell by her eyes that she felt something awful about leaving me on my own like that. I tried to keep up a strong front for her sake, talking like everything would soon be right back to normal, but all the while I figured the end must be near. And it was. After a week of suffering, she died, the doctor said, "peacefully and in her sleep." I know I should've been relieved for her, but I was shattered. I knew I would be completely lost without her. My ace in the hole was gone.

As it turned out my daddy was released from jail just the day before her funeral. (I suspect he may have used her death as a sympathy plea or something of the sort). To everyone's surprise, Mr. Clarence Maxwell (also known as the town drunk, child beater, and now jailbird) actually had the nerve to show up at her burial service, all dressed up in a navy blue suit and looking like he was on top of the world. I avoided him by dashing back to the big limousine that was driven by Mr. Parsons, the undertaker. I pretended to be so grievously devastated as to be unable to converse with my daddy or anyone for that matter (which wasn't too far from the truth).

Later on that afternoon, he came by Aunt Myrtle's, where I'd been deposited just days before, and apologized up and down and all over again for all he'd done to me and all he'd put me through. He swore, once again, he was on the wagon, for good now and that he would never, ever drink again. The perpetual salesman, just as charming as ever.

I remember vaguely wondering why some authorities (like the county or something) would allow this to happen. But then, why should I matter to them? Later on, I learned that I was just one of those many cases that fell through the cracks. Maybe that's the story of my life—the girl who fell through the cracks. Who fell and fell and fell . . .

Anyway, I took one long, weary look at my daddy and then turned to my Aunt Myrtle, still dressed in her new black sheath dress (she'd bought it special for the funeral, but already it pulled tightly across her midsection). With God as my witness, I wasn't quite sure which one of them would be worse. I actually considered flipping a coin right then and there, but I figured that wouldn't place me in a very good light with either one of them. It was plain to see my Aunt Myrtle was already taken in by Daddy's neatly pressed suit and sugarcoated words, and she quickly settled the question for all of us.

"You go on home with your daddy now, Cassandra Jane." And then she had the nerve to quote my grandma as if to solidify her point. "You know your grandma always used to say *Blood is thicker than water,* and your daddy is your only blood relative right now. Besides, I happen to think kids should be with their parents." Then she winked at my daddy as if they'd hatched this crazy scheme earlier today (maybe they'd come to an agreement while standing over my dead grandma's fresh grave, totally ignoring the promise Aunt Myrtle had made just days earlier at her deathbed).

Of course I don't know why I should've been surprised by any of this. I knew that Aunt Myrtle had never liked me as a child, and I'm sure she despised me even more as the gawky teenager I was quickly becoming. I think she'd even disliked me living with Grandma during the last few years. To her I was nothing more than an aggravating nuisance that she'd just as soon not think about, let alone have living under her own roof. Already she'd complained about my long, straggly hair, threatening to cut it all off before the funeral except there hadn't been time. And so I told her good-bye and packed up my paisley canvas bag (the one Grandma had found for me last year at the Goodwill for only two bucks "just in case I ever needed to go somewhere . . .") and off I went with my daddy.

Naturally, he didn't have a car or anything yet, so we had to walk across town on foot, and I felt certain that every single soul in Brookdale was staring right at us as we went. I'm sure they were thinking, *There goes that good-for-nothing, child-beating, drunk-ard of a car salesman and his skinny, hopeless daughter with her stringy black hair.* I don't know exactly why, but for some reason I felt horribly embarrassed and miserably ashamed as we walked down the street. Me, in my old brown coat that used to belong to Cindy Walters, carrying my little, worn suitcase, and my daddy fresh out of jail and walking with his chin up as if nothing whatsoever had ever gone wrong in his life.

What a pitiful pair we made! And it's not like I had any illusions of grandeur or any reason for pride of any sort. Goodness knows, I knew better than anyone that I was just a nobody—a scrawny, piti-ful, little nothing. And in some ways I'd always considered myself the next thing to invisible. But not that day, oh no! On that day I felt painfully and glaringly conspicuous. It's as if someone had aimed a high-powered spotlight straight at me, taking me in from the top of my straggly head clear on down to my toes that were painfully rub-bing the ends of my penny loafer shoes (a half-size too small, but I'd liked their looks when I found them at the Goodwill shortly after Christmas, and I'd tried to ignore their worn-down heels that had the tendency to make me walk slightly pigeon-toed if I wasn't care-ful).

I'm quite sure my cheeks were just blazing, and I think I must've had real tears in my eyes (even though I'd become quite adept at holding back tears by then). Oh, maybe I was being overly melodra-matic, or maybe I was missing my grandma. Or maybe it was simply the result of being thirteen and a half and the way everything in my life just suddenly seemed sadder and worse and more hopeless then ever before. But I'll never forget the humiliation I bore on that gray afternoon in early February. And I think something inside of me just snapped during that long walk across town.

Somehow my daddy, without a cent in his pocket, had managed to secure us a tiny, furnished two-room hovel in a shabby apartment complex on Main Street directly across from Masterson Motors, where Daddy felt certain he would be able to get his old job back. Actually, I think the place was more like a motel, because the tenants seemed to come and go weekly, but I believe they called the place "The Manor Apartments," which seemed slightly ridiculous. Daddy kindly let me have the one and only bedroom and he slept on the couch. The nasty place smelled like old cigarette butts, bad booze, and God only knew what else. I hated it there.

And I suppose that's when I began to go truly wrong. That must've been about the time when those words from my daddy started to ring true in me. Because that's when I first began to believe that I really did have "the devil in me" after all. And the funny thing was, my daddy was staying true to his word back in those days. Why, he did manage to get his job back at Masterson Motors, and he did stay on the wagon, for a while at least. So I really couldn't blame my actions and misbehaving on him or his drinking. Well, not directly anyway.

chapter five

MY GRANDMA LIKED FUNNY SAYINGS, and she seemed to have one for just about everything. When I was younger, I actually thought she'd been making all this stuff up as she went along. I later learned they were simply colloquialisms (which is a fancy word for funny sayings). One of these funny sayings stayed with me for many years, because for whatever reason, I thought she was talking about me. My grandma used to say, "As the twig is bent, so grows the tree." And while I didn't know exactly what it meant back then, I somehow knew it had to do with me. But I could never quite tell if it was good or bad or somewhere in between.

Being generally insecure, as time passed I naturally began to assume it was bad. I reckoned I was the twig, and it seemed no big secret that I was getting fairly well bent up by all my unfortunate circumstances with my daddy and his drinking ways. So I figured by the time I grew up I'd probably be one twisted-up, good-for-nothing, crooked old tree. And if you ask me, that wasn't a very hopeful picture, so I tried not to think about it too much. Especially when it seemed I was getting more and more bent with each passing day.

It's not as if things went immediately bad for me (at least not so as anyone might notice) but inside me—deep down, in this secret, hidden, tucked-away place—everything just started to change after my grandma died. I suspect the only thing that kept me from changing right off the bat was her memory and those promises I'd made shortly before she died. But unfortunately, those restraints only lasted about six months, during which time I started getting as hard on the inside as I already was on the outside (or so I tried to convince myself at the time). Looking back, I can see how things might've gone better for me right then—except that I was in something of a trap—the trap of believing I was nothing.

I didn't start smoking cigarettes until the end of seventh grade. It wasn't hard to get money from my daddy back then since he was still on the wagon and pulling in some pretty wages from old man Masterson by selling those used cars. Besides that, it was easy to lay a guilt trip on him. He was always ripe for the picking, and I picked him as much as I could, while I could, that is. I figured he owed me.

Because of my impoverished lifestyle while living with Grandma, I had learned how to shop thrift stores—and I soon discovered that thrift-store finds, combined with my own natural creative ability of sewing on colorful beads and tapestry braiding, resulted in some pretty cool threads. Especially back in 1968, when patchwork jeans and smock tops made from old linens were the epitome of fashion chic. Well, for the cool, that is (or so I told myself). Square people like Sally Roberts still settled for crispy store-bought clothes—probably from places like JCPenney or Montgomery Ward.

And so in a strange sort of way, I became somewhat hip in our little podunk town ('course, it took them a few years to figure this out). I tried to put on an air of confidence, and on a good day I imagined myself to be a *trendsetter with attitude.*

It was that same spring of 1968 that I pressured my daddy into getting me a used guitar and shelling out twenty bucks a pop for guitar lessons. (Amazing what guilt can do to a man.) Every week I walked over to Fourth Street to be tutored by Pete Jackson (who just happened to be the coolest musician at Brookdale High and the first person I ever met who actually smoked marijuana). And right there in his parents' two-car garage (thickly insulated for acoustics, he explained) Pete would teach me a few new chords each week. He also told me I had real musical talent. And I suspect if he hadn't already had a girlfriend who liked dropping in on him, unannounced, he might've even hit on me. Or so I liked to think. So, in some ways, Cass Maxwell was sitting on top of the world. In a matter of speaking, that is. She just didn't know it.

I turned fourteen in August of 1968, and I know for a fact that that is when I first acquired my own "reputation." I suspect it originated with my private guitar lessons with Pete and the way I often hung around to hear his band practice afterwards. And it didn't hurt that I wore the shortest miniskirts in town (only allowed due to the endless guilt trips I habitually tossed at my daddy and the turning up of my waistband when I was out of his sight) or that I had "developed" and required more than just a training bra. I think my long mane of black hair may have turned a few heads as well.

The funny thing is, I didn't fully realize this at the time. It's only in retrospect that I have truly begun to understand such things. To be honest, at the time I mostly saw myself as a social reject who wore secondhand clothes and had a nose that was overly large for her face (of course by then I had started to idolize the likes of Cher, Joan Baez, and rocker Janis Joplin—for whom I also grieved deeply a couple years later when she overdosed on drugs). Suffice it to say that, at the time, in 1968, a lot of these things went right over my head.

When Pete's friend Kurt Laurence asked me out I flippantly agreed, but at the same time I felt completely terrified. Why, I was only fourteen. I knew that good girls didn't date at that tender age (especially not boys who were going to be seniors in high school!). But I had that tough exterior so polished by then that I'm sure Kurt never suspected what was truly going on inside me. In fact, I doubt he even knew that I was only fourteen.

As I recall, we went to a drive-in movie, although I can't remember what was playing. My memory is somewhat blurred due to the fact that Kurt smoked a joint, or maybe two, in his '62 Ford Mustang. He offered me a drag, but for some reason I still can't quite put my finger on, I declined. Nonetheless I believe his secondhand smoke most assuredly affected me, at least somewhat. Unfortunately for Kurt, it didn't affect me enough to get him what he wanted. And when he dropped me off at home (we were living in a little rental house on Oak Street by then) he seemed a little put out. Needless to say, Kurt didn't ask me out again. But that certainly didn't mean that he told any of his buddies that our date was a failure. No, of course not. What seventeen-year-old boy would admit such a thing?

My daddy wasn't overly thrilled that I had gone out with a high-school boy, and it was about this time that I began to fear my guilt trips were wearing a little thin on him. So in an effort to preserve what was actually turning into a somewhat tolerable lifestyle, I decided to lighten up on him a bit and, in essence, clean up my act.

As it turned out my behavior (whether good or bad) had little effect on his, because he eventually fell off of the wagon anyway. His first plunge occurred late that fall. I was in ninth grade and acting somewhat mature and responsible at the time. But as a result of his drinking, I soon returned to my old ways of creeping around, sneaking in late after he'd passed out on the couch, and trying to remain invisible to avoid any unnecessary unpleasantness. But I knew I was living on borrowed time. I needed a better survival solution, or at least a friend I could turn to in a time of need.

By then Joey Divers was little more than a far-off childhood memory for me, and besides he was already in high school—another world, it seemed. I longed to be in high school too. I felt I was too mature for the shallow superficiality of junior high, where girls like Sally Roberts and Cindy Shelton lived for "game days" when they got to wear their blue-and-yellow cheerleading uniforms and bounce down the halls like celebrities who owned the school (which, in most ways, they did).

I felt there must be something more to life than popularity and cliques, and certainly I *wanted* something more. Or so I tried to make myself believe. I suppose in all honesty this might've simply been my way of protecting my constantly wounded ego. Because if the truth had been known (and believe me, I would rather have been tortured and died a thousand deaths than to admit this back then) I secretly longed to be one of them. And I knew I could've pulled it off, too, if only they'd have given me the chance—which would never have happened in a billion years.

Sometimes, when I was alone and safe from prying eyes, I would imagine myself actually dressed like them, talking like them, going home to a ranch-style house like the ones they lived in, with a patio and barbecue in the backyard, and where two parents lived—and maybe they even fought from time to time (I mean I wasn't completely delusional) but in my fantasy my parents would always make up and then take us all out for ice cream afterwards. Sometimes I'd get really carried away with my fantasy and pick out furniture for the living room, the kind of clothes my make-believe mama would wear, and even my bedroom, which was sometimes pink with a canopy bed but more often pale blue with an eyelet bedspread and matching curtains. But like I said I would've rather had my eyes plucked out than to admit this to anyone.

It was just after Halloween when my daddy fell off the wagon.

And surprisingly, it didn't seem all that bad—at least not at first. The next day he kind of apologized, then told me that it was no big deal. "I can control myself with alcohol," he explained from where he sat on the sofa, bent over, holding his throbbing head between his still trembling hands. "It's not like it used to be, Cassandra, I promise you. I'm in control now and I'll only drink socially."

I think I almost believed him, and I suppose in some ways this made me feel less guilty for the way I'd been manipulating him so much. Still, I worried what would happen if he went back to his old ways and drunken rages. Because you just never can tell with a drunk. It's best to just stay on your guard.

So I was back to tiptoeing around so as not to upset him in any way, and I got and installed a lock on my bedroom door. Still, I never felt completely safe in my house.

I even briefly considered the possibility of going back to Aunt Myrtle and begging her to take me in, although I suspected that she was involved with "some man" just then, since I'd noticed a large blue Buick parked out behind her house where not too many could see it, and on something of a regular basis, too. Naturally, I was well aware of her "philandering ways," as my grandma used to say to Aunt Myrtle when she thought I was well out of earshot. (I had to look up the word but discovered it had to do with illicit love affairs.) Now why anyone would want an illicit or any other sort of love affair with my old Aunt Myrtle was one of the great mysteries of life, but having seen a number of cars parked in the back of her house over the years, I suspected my grandma had her pegged just about right.

So, anyway, it didn't seem that Aunt Myrtle could offer much of a haven if my daddy suddenly decided to go off the deep end and become violent again. I grew greatly troubled trying to think what I might do if this were to happen, and as a result it became some-what difficult to concentrate at school, but I tried just the same.

I'd heard about kids going into foster homes, and in some ways that almost seemed preferable to being beaten, but what if the fos-ter parents were square and conservative and made me start wear-ing my skirts down to my knees? I'd seen girls like that in school. They walked around clutching their notebooks tightly to their chests with their shoulders slumped over, eyes cast downwards. Why, they looked downright miserable to me. And at this stage of my life I felt fairly certain they had it even worse than me. (Of course time would prove me wrong on this, as well as many other things.)

The bottom line for me was, at that stage of life, I felt too old and too grown-up to be treated like a child again. I'd seen too much of the seamy side of life. And I was used to my own independence and didn't particularly want anyone telling me what to do or how to do it. . . . well, that was, unless I might possibly find that perfect subur-ban family (the one from my fantasy) but I was smart enough to know that wasn't a reality-based dream. Not for me, anyway. Finally, I came up with a plan. I decided I should try very hard to make a friend (and I knew I couldn't be picky) who might be willing to take me in, at least temporarily, should a crisis arise.

As fate would have it, Brenda Tuttle moved to Brookdale in mid-November. I noticed her right off because of her distinct style of clothing. For starters, her skirts were even shorter than mine. And she wore long, hoop earrings that reached almost to her shoul-ders. Her lips were painted a pale shade of whitish-blue, and she wore thick, black eyeliner all the way around her eyes (not just on the upper lids, but on the lower ones, too). I'd never seen anyone or anything like her, and quite frankly, I was fascinated. Just the same, I decided to play my cards carefully—I'd been rejected enough times to know how to protect myself. At the end of her second day, I hung out by the entrance that I'd seen her use the previous day and offered her a Camel.

"Thank God," she gasped as she took the cigarette from me. "I was worried sick that no one in this moronic junior high school smoked. What a moronic bunch of Goody Two-shoes!"

"That pretty much describes it," I said as I let out a long, slow puff.

"I'm Brenda," she said, glancing over her shoulder back toward the school. "You s'pose we should go 'cross the street? My mom'll kill me if I get into trouble on my second day here."

I nodded. "Sure. I'm Cass."

"Nice to meet you." She smiled. "And I like your name. I've been trying to think of a cool nickname for Brenda, but haven't gotten too far."

"How about just Bren?"

She thought about that for a moment. "Yeah, maybe so. Maybe with a *y*, though. *Bryn . . .*" She said it slowly. "Yeah, that sounds kinda cool."

By now we'd reached the other side of the street and were standing in the Baptist church parking lot—where my grandma used to go to church (when she did, which was rarely). I knew there were people inside who might recognize me, but I didn't really care if they observed me smoking. In fact, I rather liked the idea that it would bother them.

"Groovy top, Cass," said Bryn. "You get that here in town?"

I laughed. "Not hardly. I made it myself from an old tablecloth. You can't find anything worth wearing in this stupid backwater town."

She laughed too. "I figured as much. I still can't believe my mom made us move here."

"Your mom?" I thought this was curious, since it was usually the dads that seemed to run things back in those days—at least in our town.

She flicked her ashes onto the ground and rolled her eyes. "Yeah, my mom's a divorcée, and she got this job at the chemical plant that pays her almost as good as a man."

By now our cigarettes were both burned down to almost nothing. "What do you like to do after school, Bryn?" I asked, suddenly wondering how it was that one made a friend—especially a girl-friend. I'd never had a real friend other than Joey, and the things we used to do to fill the time seemed pretty juvenile and silly now.

She frowned. "I don't know. I just kinda hang out. My mom works graveyard, so she doesn't like me making any noise while she sleeps during the day."

I nodded. "That makes sense. Well, do you want to go get a Coke or something?"

"Sounds cool."

And that was pretty much how my friendship with Bryn began. It didn't take long to learn that she wasn't the brightest porch light on the block—at least not when it came to academics. But she was clever in some ways—like boys and smoking and drinking, stuff like that. I guess you'd say she had street smarts.

I'm sure she was what my grandma would have called a "bad influence," but I figured I'd already started to go bad all on my own by then. It just turned out that Bryn was already going in the same direction. I remember when I first met her mom. It was about a week after they moved to Brookdale. Mrs. Tuttle was a large, buxom, peroxide blonde, but not the kind men are necessarily attracted to. Oh, maybe some, but she was more that loud-mouthed, tough, bossy type—the kind who could easily hold her own in a bar full of men or down at the chemical plant. But I liked her. In some ways I trusted her more than I trusted Bryn. And I think she actually liked me, too. Ironically, I think she even thought I was a good influence on her daughter. And maybe, in some ways, I was. You just never quite know about these things.

chapter six

I REMEMBER MY GRANDMA SAYING, "You can't squeeze blood out of a turnip," and since that sounded fairly obvious, I had to ask her what she meant. "Well," she'd said, "it means that you can't expect something from somebody when they just plain don't have it to give to you." And I suppose that pretty much describes my friend Bryn.

By Christmas vacation of ninth grade, we'd become fairly good friends, relatively speaking, that is. It bothered me that she wasn't a bit like my old friend Joey Divers. Of course who was I to be picky? Still, the truth is, I never felt completely close to or even very comfortable with her. I'm sure this was partially due to her habitually deceitful ways and partially because she was so hopelessly boy-crazy. Her obsession over boys made it hard to really know who she was—or what worried me even more was that maybe that *was* simply who she was, that that was all there was to her. And I suppose it didn't help that I knew she used me some. But then, of course my original plan had been to use her, too. And since that's how I'd started this odd friendship in the first place, who was I to point fingers at anyone? Kind of like the pot calling the kettle black, as my grandma used to say, which is just another way of saying, "Don't judge." She'd explained that to me one day when I told her how Aunt Myrtle had been gossiping and putting down one of her coworkers at the bank.

Anyway, my goal with Bryn had been to find a place where I might crash in the event my daddy's drinking habits got out of hand, which they were rapidly starting to do. And it came in real handy that Mrs. Tuttle worked graveyard, too. I always knew I could sneak out of my house whenever I needed, and then just wait until eleven to go knocking on Bryn's door. I had a system all worked out where I'd bolt my bedroom door, then grab my bag and slip out the window. Naturally I only did this when my daddy came home yelling and cussing and knocking stuff around.

Bryn always welcomed my unexpected visits, for they afforded her the opportunity to sneak out too, and then she could stay out as late as she liked, knowing that I was there to cover the phone for those unexpected nights (mostly on Fridays or Saturdays) when her mom might call after midnight to check up on her. I usually made up an excuse like she was in the bathroom or already asleep. And Bryn didn't hesitate to tell her mother she was spending the night at my house when she was really out partying with her latest wild and crazy boyfriend.

I suppose if the truth were told, it was Bryn who really managed to nail down my reputation as a "fast girl," even if it was mostly a case of guilt by association. It didn't matter much to me, though, since I was quickly reaching the place where I no longer cared much about what anyone thought of me. Other than my grades, that is. I still cared about my education.

Sometimes Bryn would tease me for taking my classes too seriously. Maybe it was Joey's early influence on me, or just my own personal pride, but I still wanted to get good grades. I suspect the reason it irked her so was because even if she'd really tried I don't believe she had the brains to cut it. Her memory was appalling. So she put her energies into other things—primarily her appearance, which grew increasingly colorful, and then boys, of course.

And when it came to boys, Bryn just took for granted that I was doing the same as her. It never even occurred to her that I was still a virgin, and I certainly didn't make any effort to straighten her out on this account. In fact, I preferred her to think I was sleeping with guys—even if my head count would never appear anywhere nearly equal to hers. Whose was? And sometimes I even concocted wild stories (based loosely on the trashy magazines I'd discovered lying around the Tuttles' house) just to convince Bryn that I was really "doing it" when she grew suspicious that I might've been holding out on her.

Oddly enough I was still getting asked out by boys—mostly ones in high school and never any that I cared much for, and mostly, I think, because they'd heard overblown rumors about me and Bryn and how we had these "reputations" for being wild and easy and all. I have to laugh now when I think how these things get started. For instance, I can just imagine Kurt Laurence (the first guy I went out with) lying to some other guy about how willing I was. I mean, what was he going to say? That I wasn't? That he, a senior who played in Pete Jackson's rock band, couldn't even get any- where with Little Miss Nobody? Of course not. Guys love to brag about these kinds of conquests, even if their conquests are only a mere figment of their hormone-driven imagination and ability to spin a lewd and outlandish tale.

I would go out with these older guys, and while I'd make out and stuff, I never, ever went all the way—and, oh, did that tick some of these guys off. And occasionally it would give me a real scare, too. Like the time Rick Stone simply would not take no for an answer. He started getting really rough with me, and I swear if I hadn't been the daughter of an abusive drunk I might not have been able to defend myself in the manner in which I did. Oh, the things that Daddy never realized he taught me in the ways of self-defense. All the same, it was a long and chilly walk home for me that night. (And as a result I slowed down that whole dating business after that.)

I must give my daddy some credit, though. He completely avoided alcohol for several months right after the New Year. I think he could've almost died after a serious binge on New Year's Eve. He'd gone to some party with an open bar, and I suspect he'd taken full advantage of all the free booze. Someone brought him home in the early morning hours, just dumping him on the couch like a big, old sack of potatoes. I remember standing there and staring at him, white-faced and limp like he was half dead. And I suppose he almost was. I even considered calling for an ambulance when he didn't regain consciousness for the better part of the day. But I was afraid if I did, he might get mad. I knew that we didn't have any health insurance coverage and ambulances were fairly costly, even back then. And so I just hung around and waited. Finally, I saw him move, and I made him a pot of coffee and encouraged him to take a shower.

It was after that when he really did *try* to give up drinking. Every single week he tried, always on a Monday. And sometimes he'd actually make it until Saturday before he'd go out drinking again. Fortunately for me, he somehow managed to preserve his job at Masterson Motors, but he wasted so much money on liquor that we just barely managed to pay the rent and keep a little bit of food in the fridge. And most of the time it was pretty slim pickings at my house.

I remember how shocked Bryn was the first time she saw our barren kitchen. She went through all the cupboards and the fridge and then finally turned to me and said, "No wonder you stay so skinny, Cass. You guys must live on air around here." I considered making up some big old tale about how it was shopping day that day and how we'd just cleaned out our cupboards last night. But too many times I'd witnessed her twisting and turning in some crazy whopper she'd gotten herself caught up in, and I simply decided to stick to the truth.

"Well, I guess this is what comes from having a drunk in the family, Bryn." I smirked at her and pointed my finger in mock accusation. "Just let it go to show you that if you keep up your wild-thing drinking ways this might happen to *you*, too."

She threw back her head and laughed. "Oh yeah, I'm so sure. I can just see me at an AA meeting now. Hi, my name is Bryn and I'm an alcoholic." Then she got serious. "Is that why you won't drink none, Cass?"

I shrugged. I usually tried not to make a big deal about it when I refused a beer or whatever the going thing might be, but I suppose she was partially right. "I just don't like the taste of alcohol," I admitted, which was not untrue.

She laughed again. "Ya don't hear me complaining none. That just means more for the rest of us. Hey, where does your dad hide his booze, anyway?"

I showed her one of his secret little hiding spots beneath the bathroom sink and watched as she poured herself half a glass of amber liquid. I didn't really care if she emptied the entire bottle, didn't care if he noticed it missing or not.

By then he and I were like ships that passed in the night, anyway. I made sure I only spoke to him when I stopped in to see him at work when he was mostly sober—and then it was always just to say "hey" and joke around before I'd hit him up for some cash. I'd found that was my best chance of obtaining money during those on-again, off-again drinking days. If I waited for him to come home at night, his head would often be swimming and his pockets empty. But when I caught him on a payday, every other Friday, he'd usually give me enough for groceries and then some. Problem was, he sometimes got a draw on his check, and I could never tell exactly when that might be.

As a result I ate at Bryn's home quite a bit. And here's one more thing I'll have to give Bryn—she may have been a liar and way too loose with the boys, but she had a most generous and giving spirit. And so did her mother, Mrs. Tuttle. In some ways, looking back, I see those Tuttles almost like angels in disguise. Okay, so maybe the disguise was laid on a little thick, but I'm not quite sure what I'd have done without them. Or maybe things would've just unraveled all that much sooner.

By the time I turned fifteen (the summer before entering high school) I was already feeling somewhat old and frayed and worn down in my spirit. And, I suppose, just slightly jaded, too. Life no longer seemed to hold much promise or sparkle. Not that it ever had, but at least when I was a kid, I'd had Joey around, and together the two of us weren't afraid to dream big, and in those days we could even believe in those impossible dreams. And dreams could carry you a long ways back then. But more and more now I felt just like a kid standing outside and gazing longingly through a candy store window. I saw others living the kind of life that I knew I could never have, and I suppose it was finally getting me down. For years, I'd tried not to pay much attention to those other girls—the ones like Sally Roberts and the like. And you'd think it might've gotten easier over time, but it never really did. In fact, I'm sure it only became harder. And for some reason the summer of '69 pushed me to the limits.

Sure, I still had Bryn. She and I still hung out a lot of the time (at least when she wasn't with her new boy-of-the-month). I knew she was better than nothing—and better than being the town's social outcast all on my own little lonesome. And her home really did provide a handy haven from my daddy's fits of drunken rage, which had been coming on more frequently and with more regularity once the warm weather came upon us. For some mysterious reason, my daddy thought summertime was drinking time.

The honest truth was I liked Bryn's company less and less as time went by—and even *that* made me feel bad. More and more, I found myself wanting something more, something beyond all this. I just wasn't exactly sure what it was or how I could possibly get it.

Shortly after my fifteenth birthday, I followed Joey's example and got myself a work permit and—after several rejections at classier joints—a job at the Dairy Maid. It was smelly and hot and nasty in there, but at least I now had money in my pocket and a good excuse to stay out late at night. The rub was that kids from school often came in and naturally couldn't resist poking fun of me and my silly little Dairy Maid uniform with its perky white hat and matching apron (a sharp contrast to my usual hippy getups of embroidered smock tops and beads and such). And unfortunately, I lost some of my usual hardness and confidence in this somewhat humiliating situation and ridiculous attire. I guess I felt sort of like a sitting duck—like suddenly it was open season on Cass Maxwell.

After one particularly long and tiring day—it seemed that every Little League team in Brookdale had come in, and every single boy wanted some sort of specialty sundae, and they weren't exactly being patient—I was getting ready to close out the till and call it a night when I looked up to see Sally Roberts and two of her girlfriends walk in. I could've kicked myself for not having flipped over that Closed sign just a minute earlier, but it was too late now. All three girls had flopped down at the counter. And to make matters worse, it looked as if they'd spent an enjoyable day out the lake (since they had on bikini tops and cutoffs and were sporting some pretty dark tans). My tan had faded considerably since joining the working ranks.

"Sorry, you guys, we're closing up now." I smiled, trying to sound far more cheerful than I felt. I knew it did no good to put on my usual tough act while wearing that ruffled Dairy Maid hat. The two were just too incongruous to be believable.

"Oh, come on, you've got time to make us a little old banana split," said Sally. "It's not quite ten yet."

I glanced up at the clock over the counter, silently watching as the second hand slowly made its way up to the twelve. "Well, it's ten now," I announced as I swiped a damp cloth over the plastic-laminate countertop.

"Yeah, well, we got in here *before* it turned ten," said Sally with a familiar glint in her eye. The other girls giggled. "And you better serve us our banana split."

I turned around and narrowed my eyes at her. "We're closed, Sally."

"Where's the owner?" she demanded hotly. "Where's Clint? Does he know what kind of retarded girl he's hired to work for him here? Come to think of it, you're probably not even fit to serve food, Cass Maxwell. I'll bet you don't even know how to wash your hands properly."

I took in a deep breath, then pressed my lips together as I glared at her. Ironically, I had just discovered exactly whose blue Buick had been parking with such regularity at my Aunt Myrtle's house, and I now felt sorely tempted to reveal my findings, which would be of particular interest to Miss Sally Roberts. But Clint was in the back cleaning up just then, and I didn't really wish to create a problem that might threaten my job. So I bit my tongue. "Fine," I snapped at her. "What do you want on your banana split?"

Naturally, it took them at least five minutes to make up their minds, and then they just ended up choosing the traditional pineapple, strawberry, and chocolate combination. "Fine," I snapped again as I went over to the big stainless steel ice cream machine, which I unfortunately had not cleaned out yet or I would've had a legitimate excuse not to serve them. Thinking murderous thoughts about Sally, I ripped my knife through a banana and slapped it into the dish, then quickly heaped in three sloppy mounds of ice cream, adding topping, nuts, and whipped cream with a vengeance. It might not have been the most beautiful banana split, but at least it was quick. I thumped it down on the counter before Sally and turned to go clean the machine.

"That's not what we ordered!"

I spun around in time to see Sally wink at her friends.

"We wanted hot fudge, marshmallow, and caramel toppings," she said with a sly smile. The other two nodded in agreement with her, now starting to giggle. "I think she really is retarded," Sally spoke to her friends as if I wasn't there. "But then, what can you expect when her daddy's such a lush and all? Most likely his drinking habits messed up her genes long before she was ever born."

I felt just like the pressure valve on the deep-frying cooker after it had been left on High too long. I leaned across the counter and looked Sally right in the eyes. "Yeah, Sally, well, speaking of daddies, it's too bad yours isn't a little more discreet when he goes sleeping around. And I can't say much for his taste in women, either." I forced a harsh laugh, then added, "Does your mama know about this?" I paused for drama's sake, thoroughly enjoying the shocked expression on her face. "Or maybe that's your daddy's whole problem in the first place—maybe your mama is a cold fish just like her little girl! Poor, poor man!"

Sally picked up the spurned banana split and chucked it straight at me. It hit me square in the chest, then slowly slid down my uniform front in an elongated sticky streak of yellow, red, and brown. "You big, fat liar!" she yelled.

Despite my dripping chest and the sticky mess now at my feet, I kept my calm. "No, Sally, it's the honest truth. And if you don't believe me, why not ask your daddy why his car's always parked out behind Myrtle Brown's house during weekday lunch hours and then again on certain evenings, usually around eight o'clock." At this point, I didn't even mind that I'd incriminated my own aunt—what had she ever done for me anyway? Besides, I figured most folks in town already knew all about this little affair by now.

Sally's perfect Noxzema-girl complexion flushed deep red with anger, and maybe some embarrassment, too. And her two cohorts appeared appropriately and uncomfortably speechless, with Donna Moore tugging urgently at her elbow and nodding toward the door. But to my surprise, two fat tears began to roll down Sally's smooth cheeks. I must admit I felt a slight trace of remorse just then, at least for a few seconds, anyway. But I smothered any compassion in my renewed anger as I realized the mess I now had to clean up due to her banana split–throwing incident. Fortunately for me, Sally said nothing more as she allowed her faithful friends to guide her out to the parking lot, where I'm sure they licked her wounds and said all sorts of horrible things about me.

I was just flipping over the Closed sign when Clint emerged from the kitchen. "What on earth's been going on in here?" he demanded, eyeing my soiled uniform and the broken banana split dish still splattered across the floor.

I shook my head and rolled my eyes. "These rude girls came in after closing time and ordered a banana split. And then after I gave it to them, one of the girls threw it at me and they ran off."

"*Kids!*" he muttered as he turned back to the kitchen. "Don't know why I don't just sell this whole blasted business and go off and live on some quiet deserted island somewhere!"

chapter seven

JOEY DIVERS WAS NEVER ONE to let anything go to waste, and he hadn't wasted any time putting his experience from Grandma's store to good use. True to his word, as soon as he'd turned fifteen, he'd gotten himself a job at Saunders Stationery, and there he'd worked full-time for the past two summers (and part-time during the school year). I often spied him through the large plate-glass window as I hurried down the street to my own job. He always looked so studious and frightfully grown-up standing behind the counter at the office supply store, diligently serving his customers.

The Dairy Maid was just a few doors down the street, so Joey stopped in for lunch occasionally—although usually not more than once a week, and even then he always ordered frugally, usually a grilled cheese sandwich and iced tea. Sometimes I teased him about being a tightwad, but he assured me he was simply doing his best to save up for college.

"*You* saving for college?" I said as I refilled his iced tea (on the house, as long as Clint wasn't looking). "You're so smart, Joey, I'll bet you'll get all sorts of scholarship offers and things—they'll probably pay you to go to school."

He chuckled. "Oh, I doubt that. But you, better than anyone, should know that you can't always count your chickens before they hatch."

I laughed, remembering how my grandma used to say that to

us whenever she'd catch us trying to calculate our weekly earnings from her little store, and she was usually right. "I suppose not."

"Are you looking forward to going to high school this fall?" he asked as he adjusted his black-rimmed glasses. I still couldn't get used to the idea of Joey in glasses. It did make him look older and slightly intellectual, even if it was in a somewhat nerdish sort of way.

"Yeah, but it kinda feels like I should've been there already."

He frowned. "Yeah, I guess dating all those older guys makes you feel pretty grown-up."

I could tell by his cynical tone that he didn't approve of my personal life. And while an old, small part of me actually appreciated his concern, the larger, brassier, mouthier part felt judged and insulted. "Nothing's wrong with me going out with older guys."

He shrugged. "I guess not. That is, if you don't care what people think of you or your reputation."

The place was getting busier now and so I just rolled my eyes at him and strutted off to take the order at the next table. Still, his words burned like iodine in an open cut and I couldn't shake them as I clipped the order onto the wheel and gave it a spin. Then suddenly, it occurred to me. *Maybe he's just jealous! Maybe he wishes he were one of those guys taking me out.*

From where I stood at the front counter, I glanced over to where he sat all alone at the little table, dressed in his usual neat white shirt and straight dark tie. Then I shook my head as I mentally tallied a tab. *No way!* Joey Divers was way too square and sensible to be interested in a wild thing like me. If Joey had a girlfriend (and for the life of me, I couldn't imagine that he ever would, but if he did) she would probably be the type to wear a pleated skirt, not too short, matching knee socks, and shiny penny loafers—someone like Ali McGraw in *Love Story*. Not someone like me.

Joey looked slightly sheepish when he came up to the cash register to pay his bill. "Cass, don't get me wrong," he said. "I still think you're great. I just want you to be careful—watch out for yourself, you know?" He smiled apologetically, a small flush creeping into his cheeks.

"I know, Joey. Thanks for caring." I handed him his change and smiled in an overly bright way. "I'll be just fine."

On Labor Day weekend, just days before school started back up, I learned (by eavesdropping on a conversation between a couple of high school teachers who'd come into the Dairy Maid for the "best burger deal") that Joey Divers had been moved up another year! He would start school as a senior the following week—now two years ahead of me. Mrs. Sparks, an English teacher, said, "With Joey's test scores, he could've gone straight on to college, but he opted to stick around Brookdale High another year."

"Probably due to that bad leg of his," said Mr. Lawson, a science teacher who also coached football. "I'm sure that makes life tough for him."

I felt a sharp mixture of pride and disappointment. This meant Joey would only be around town for one more year. I wondered why I even cared, since our paths crossed so seldom these days. But for some reason I did. It seemed like no matter what, Joey Divers was always leaving me behind.

I'd been thinking on his words some lately, and I suspected he was right. I did need to be careful. It seemed the only way to make any real change in the direction my life appeared to be heading would be to break off my friendship with Bryn. And even though there were things about her that drove me totally nuts sometimes, I didn't know what I'd do without having her place to crash at when my home life was less than ideal. I honestly couldn't think of anyone else that would take me in. And so I felt caught between a rock and a hard place—the rock being Joey and the hard place, the Tuttles' apartment.

And yet, when I made my first appearance at Brookdale High, it was with Bryn at my side. I'm sure we must've looked like a couple of hookers in our micro-miniskirts, colorful hosiery, snug-fitting tops, and flashy jewelry. It's too bad the dress code at the high school prohibited pants for girls, or I'm sure I would've dressed a little more modestly in my embroidered bell-bottoms or even my OshKosh denim overalls. As it was, when it came to school, I simply fell into the habit of dressing like Bryn—almost as if it became a competition to see who could get their hemlines the highest. I'm guessing I might've won, but I had the advantage with longer legs. I'm sure we turned quite a number of heads—and not just the students', either. By then, Bryn was dying her hair blonde, and I must admit it didn't look half bad on her in a trampy sort of way. We didn't have too many classes together since I, as usual, leaned more toward the academics, whereas Bryn chose her classes based on what she assumed she had the best chances of passing. Naturally, she had no intention of going on to college, and her mother often said it'd be a major miracle if she made it through high school with diploma in hand.

As it turned out her mother was right. Bryn got pregnant in the winter of our tenth grade year. To make matters worse, it wasn't with one of her numerous boyfriends. No, it turned out to be her math teacher, Mr. Walker. He'd been tutoring her after school (well, that and other things . . .). Naturally, it was quite the scandal, since Mr. Walker was "happily" married with two young children. But then it was those "if it feels good, do it" kind of days— "Make love, not war" and the like. So, what could anyone expect? Of course Mr. Walker got fired, and Bryn got sent to live with an aunt up in Connecticut right after spring break just as she was starting to show.

About the same time Bryn was getting herself into trouble, another interesting phenomenon was occurring at Brookdale High. A revival of sorts had hit, and it seemed that kids throughout the school were turning into Jesus freaks right and left. Bryn and I would make fun of them, not so as anyone could hear, of course, but just between ourselves as a form of entertainment. But with Bryn gone, I must've suddenly looked alone and vulnerable—a sinner just waiting to get saved, ripe pickings for the more evangelistic types. And so I soon found myself on the hit list of every fanatical Christian kid in our school—including Joey Divers!

Yes, it seemed that even my old buddy Joey had been sucked into this new Jesus-freak fad. Apparently he'd gotten himself pretty involved in some sort of nondenominational youth group that seemed to be growing daily. It all seemed pretty weird to me. At first I tried to ignore the kids who came up to me and asked questions like: "Do you know Jesus?" I mean, how stupid is that? Doesn't everyone know who Jesus is? Or else they'd say, "Do you know what's going to happen to you when you die?" "Well, who on earth does?" I'd toss back at them.

I thought I was a pretty hard nut to crack, and I extracted a smidgeon of pride from it, but at the same time I suspected that Joey had made me into his own personal mission—save Cassandra Maxwell or bust! And despite my stoical vow to remain cynical and aloof, Joey's regular attempts to break me were wearing me down some. And to be honest, what with Bryn gone now I suppose I enjoyed the attention.

"Look, Cass," he explained at lunch one day. "I know it's hard for you to believe that Jesus really loves you—I know, probably better than anyone, what your life's been like. And I'm sure it doesn't feel much like Jesus loves you. But really, he does!" He peered at me through his dark-rimmed glasses, and his big brown eyes seemed more sincere than ever. Almost convincing.

"It's just so hard to believe all this, Joey," I countered. "I mean, if I believe in Jesus like this, then doesn't it mean I have to believe in the whole Bible as well? And I don't think I can swallow all that. I know Grandma believed all that hooey, but I just can't handle all that stuff about Noah putting a bunch of animals in a boat or Moses parting the Red Sea. I mean, who really believes all that crud?"

He looked at me for a long moment—not like he was irritated or intimidated or anything negative—just thinking, kind of mulling it all over. "You know, Cass, I totally understand where you're coming from. I'm a fairly scientific person, and I had some serious doubt and hang-ups. But then a guy explained that it's all about faith—that you make a conscious choice to believe in Jesus, like taking a step of faith. And then slowly it becomes more real, and your faith grows."

"And so has yours? Grown, I mean?"

"I'm sitting here telling you about this, aren't I? Look, Cass, you can trust me—you know I wouldn't be telling you all this if I didn't completely believe it myself. It's changed my life."

"Changed your life?" I scowled at him.

He nodded. "Yep. I actually became a Christian a while back. Back when I first started high school."

"Last year? You're kidding me, Joey. Why've you been so quiet about it?"

He smiled. "I guess I was just learning a lot of stuff and trying to figure things out for myself. But I know that having Jesus inside—" he tapped his chest—"*really* inside me, has made all the difference. I wouldn't be who I am now without Jesus."

I felt stunned and slightly wounded. "Well, then why didn't you tell me about it sooner, Joey? I thought we were friends."

He looked down at the table between us. "You were off doing your own thing, Cass. I didn't think you wanted to hear what I had to say. But you know I kept praying for a chance to say something to you. And sometimes I'd almost think it was the right time, and then something would happen, or you'd say something that'd stop me. I don't know, it just never seemed to happen."

I still felt hurt, but my hard shell cracked just slightly. "I've been through so much in the past year, Joey. If you really had something that was real, that really and truly changed your life—well, then why wouldn't you offer it to me, too?" I saw him swallow hard as he looked into my eyes, and I could see I'd hurt him now a lot.

"I'm sorry, Cass."

I stood up. I felt betrayed and upset, and I wasn't even sure why. "Yeah. If what you say is true, Joey, then it's like you've been walking around with a pile of money in your pocket and your old best friend is out begging on the streets and you don't even offer her a penny." I started to walk away.

"Cass, wait—"

But I just kept walking. And for the rest of the day I avoided Joey and every other crazy Jesus freak in that stupid school, and finally I hurried straight to work. (I was still working part-time at the Dairy Maid then.)

With each step I reluctantly mulled Joey's disturbing words over and over in my mind, not sure I understood a bit of it, but interested just the same. Yet, at the same time, I knew this Jesus stuff was taking up too much space in my brain. I reminded myself that I had bigger problems to think about just now. Like where was I going to land the next time my daddy got out of hand?—which could be any day now. Bryn was gone, and I still hadn't lined up anyone else to take her place. Working was some consolation, and

I'd managed to save up a little money—not in a glass jar this time where my daddy could get to it, but at the Citizen's Bank (not the National Bank where my aunt used to work before Mr. Roberts fired her over some "personal indiscretion" last summer).

Anyway, I went straight to work scrubbing down the tables with all these troubles just bouncing around in my mind until it almost felt as if my whole head might simply explode and splatter all across the black-and-white-checkerboard floor Clint had put in a few months ago. I was so distracted with my troubles that I scarcely noticed how the time had passed and I'd forgotten to flip over the Closed sign, and now a late customer had entered and sat down at the counter just a couple minutes past ten.

"Cass?" I heard as I slowly swiped a bleach-soaked rag along the countertop.

I looked up in surprise, then paused in the middle of a long wiping stroke. It was Joey.

"Can we talk?" he asked.

"I'm working." I bit my lip and continued to wipe down the counter.

"Yeah, but it's closing time. Maybe I can give you a lift home."

"You have a car?" What else had he been keeping secret?

He grinned and shook his metal crutch. "Yeah, an automatic."

"Okay, but I'll warn you, I'm in a pretty foul mood tonight."

"It's all right; I'm sure it's partly my fault."

I hurriedly cleaned up and closed out the register, then yelled good-bye to Clint in the back. Joey was already in his car, a large, sensible blue Chevy.

"Nice," I said as I slid into the vinyl seat.

"It's okay. Someday I'll have something even better. Want to go over to Nellie's and get a cup of coffee?" Nellie's was an all-night café on the other end of town.

"Sure, why not?" I leaned back into the seat and sighed deeply, thinking I'd rather just go to sleep. I felt so tired, so weary.

After getting seated at Nellie's and being served a couple mugs of stale, thick coffee, Joey didn't immediately bring up the Jesus stuff. Instead he made a little small talk; he asked me how I was doing.

"You mean me, personally? Or me as far as living with an unpredictable jerk who may or may not go into a drunken rage at the drop of a hat sometimes?"

He grimaced. "Yeah. I guess that's what I mean. How's it going with your dad these days? I really haven't talked to you about that in ages. I guess I just assumed he's all straightened out now, especially after that last episode that landed him in jail."

"I guess a lot of people assume that. Maybe they should check out the Eight Ball Tavern some evening. He spends most of his time and money down there."

"I'm sorry. It must be hard."

I exploded with a swearword I wouldn't normally have used. "You'd better believe it's hard, Joey! And I haven't had anyone to help me out—other than Bryn and her mom—and even they're gone now. And I'm freaking out over what's going to happen the next time. I mean, I've been trying to do the right thing, working hard in school, saving up money, but it's all just getting so hard. Sometimes, like right now, I just feel like giving up—just totally giving up."

He nodded, folding a napkin into a neat triangle. "Don't give up, Cass," he said softly.

I looked over at him. I could feel my eyes filling with tears, and I really didn't want to cry—at least not here in public, and not in front of Joey. Maybe it was because he was being nice to me and I wasn't used to that. Or maybe I was just tired. "Then what, Joey?" I asked in my old sarcastic voice. "Should I take one of your miracle faith pills and just call you in the morning? You really think if I believe in Jesus that everything's going to simply change overnight?" I could see my cynicism hurt him, and I felt unexpectedly bad. "I'm sorry, Joey. I shouldn't make fun of your religion. It's great if it works for you."

He shrugged. "It's okay. I think I deserved some of that. Your words really got to me today, Cass. I mean I'd never looked at it that way—like I was walking around with something you needed and not even offering it to you. I'm sorry."

I waved my hand. "Oh, you know me, I was just being all melo-dramatic. I shouldn't have said that. I didn't mean it."

"But you were right. I did have something that was changing my life, and I didn't try very hard to share it with my old best friend." He reached across the table and took my hand. "We used to be so close, Cass. Don't you miss that sometimes?"

Now I could feel tears actually running down my cheeks, and I knew I couldn't trust myself to speak. I swallowed hard and looked down at the table, everything blurred.

"Cass, listen to me—Jesus is real. He really is real. He wants to come into your heart. He wants to take all the ugliness that's in your life and make it beautiful. He has a plan for you. He really does. You know me, Cass. It might've taken me too long to tell you this, but you know I wouldn't lie to you."

Now I forced myself to look up, fully aware that I was actually crying in public, me, the tough chick—the one no one could hurt. "But—but—I don't know, Joey . . . I don't know how—what to do. It all sounds so strange—and unbelievable."

He nodded. "I know. I felt the same way. And it's something you have to do on your own, Cass, when you're ready. It's a per-sonal thing. But honestly, all you have to do is ask Jesus to come into your life, and he does it."

I'm sure Joey continued, saying a bunch of other things too, but I never really heard them. I was too weary and upset to listen, and finally I just asked him to take me home. As Joey quietly drove to my house that night, I kept tumbling all his words around in my mind, and I think something was almost starting to make sense.

But when he parked in front of my house, I could see all the lights were on inside, and my heart started to race. This was not a good sign.

"Thanks for everything, Joey," I said in a flat voice, my eyes focused on the little rental house as I wondered what my daddy might be up to tonight.

"You okay, Cass?" he asked. And I could tell by his voice, he meant it. He cared. But what could he do to help?

I turned and looked at him in his dimly lit Chevy, sitting there looking so grown-up, so . . . together. Suddenly I just wanted to grab him, to hold on to him, to cling to him, and to beg him to take me with him, to love me, to marry me, to . . . *anything!* Anything that would get me out of this crazy mess called my life.

But instead I just pasted on my good-old-girl smile and said, "Sure, Joey, I'm fine," and climbed out of the security of his blue car. I slipped the strap of my oversized bag over my shoulder and put on my brave face as I turned and waved over my shoulder. "Thanks for the ride, Joey. See ya round!"

chapter eight

As it turned out I didn't "see Joey around" for a long, long time after that night in April 1970.

I had a feeling I was heading straight for trouble when I walked up to the little rental house. All the lights were still on inside, our little house just cheerfully glowing like a jarful of fireflies, and I suspected my daddy was in there getting himself all worked into a lather about something or other. I went real slow waiting for Joey's car to finally pull away. When I felt certain Joey was out of sight, I ducked around back, deciding to just lie low for a while. It wasn't the first time I'd done so, and I felt relatively certain that my sober persistence would outlast my daddy's inebriated state. And once some of those lights went out and my heart rate slowed down some, I'd quietly make my way inside.

So I sat down on an old willow stump that had already started growing itself back into a tree and watched our house from the tiny, weed-infested patch of grass we called a backyard. Even though it was spring, it was still cool at night, and my skimpy, polyester Dairy Maid uniform was anything but warm. I pulled my school clothes out of my shoulder bag and wrapped them around my legs for insulation as I sat and shivered there, waiting for some sign that it was safe to go in. Part of me still wanted to ponder upon

Joey's words, to consider his claims that Jesus really loved me, but the rest of me was too overwrought and worried about what might lie ahead for me. Not just tonight, because I could wait this one out, but what about the next night? And the next?

I briefly considered walking over to Aunt Myrtle's place on the other end of town, but I still felt a little guilty about her losing her good bank job as a result of my mouthing off to Sally Roberts last summer. Now Aunt Myrtle worked as a clerk at an automotive store, and the few times I'd walked past and spied her back there, her mouth had been drawn in a tight line, and I didn't think she enjoyed her work much. For all I knew she might even know that I was the one who blew the whistle on her. I hadn't actually spoken to her in well over a year now. For that reason and a lifetime of others, I was unwilling to walk halfway across town, knock on her door, and then risk her fiery wrath. Besides, if my daddy were truly drunk, he'd probably pass out before too long anyway. I could just wait him out.

Finally it was well past midnight, and the lights were still burning like a Christmas tree. Suddenly I became worried. What if he'd had an accident or something? For all I knew he could've stumbled, fallen, and hit himself in the head—he might be unconscious and bleeding himself to death right there on the kitchen floor. It's ironic now to think that it was this empathetic sense of concern that made me quietly open our back door and tiptoe into the brightly lit kitchen.

To my relief, he was not bleeding on the floor there, and I silently turned off the lights and made my way back toward my bedroom, deciding to skip using the bathroom (at least for an hour or so) until I could be sure that all was quiet and safe from behind the security of my bolted door. I turned off the hall light and tiptoed in absolute silence.

Just a few feet from my bedroom, I heard my daddy's drunken

voice, and he appeared before me as if out of nowhere. "Wha'sha think yore doin' sneakin' round like this until all hours of the night?"

He stepped directly in front of me now and I could see his outline silhouetted by the faint light coming through my bedroom window. Already I was poised to turn and run, but I never even got the chance.

It's amazing, the strength of a drunkard's grip sometimes. You expect them to be all sloshy and relaxed—like they couldn't hurt you even if they tried. And sometimes it's just like that, too, but not always. And not on that night. I can remember my voice screaming bloody murder the first time he hit me, and then yelling for help again and again and again—I hoped that someone in the neighborhood might hear me and call the police. That's about all I remember until waking up, once again, in a hospital bed.

The next few days were kind of a blur for me with police taking statements and a lady from the county named Mrs. Johnson interviewing me. *It's about time,* I was thinking as I answered her inane questions. She informed me that Aunt Myrtle, my only living relation (besides my daddy, who was now incarcerated) was unable and unwilling to take me in. Aunt Myrtle, of course, was not actually related to me by blood, but I kept these thoughts to myself. Then Mrs. Johnson began describing the county's foster care program to me.

Despite my earlier assumption that, being almost sixteen, I was too mature for a foster home, I now welcomed the idea of having someone—anyone—take care of me. Especially in light of my broken nose, fractured wrist, and concussion. At the end of the week, an older couple came by the hospital to pick me up. Their name was Crowley, and they lived on a small farm near the neighboring town of Snider. Did I mind leaving my old high school? they asked me. I just shrugged and said, "I guess not."

The Crowleys drove an old pickup, and I remember jostling painfully in the seat between the two of them, each jolt feeling like a fresh blow to my bruised and battered body. But I kept my lips pressed together and my eyes straight ahead. And I tried not to judge this couple by appearance. After all, here they were willing to take a perfect stranger into their home. How bad could they be?

"Just don't understand a man who'd do that to his own daughter," said Mr. Crowley as he gripped the big steering wheel with two rough and calloused hands. It wasn't the type of comment that demanded a response, but I felt, in light of the fact that they were rescuing me, perhaps one was deserved.

"My daddy's a troubled man, sir." I spoke quietly, careful to use *sir* since these were older, country folks and probably expected me to act like a mannerly young lady. "And he's had a drinking problem for quite some time now. But when he's sober he's a completely different person—you wouldn't think he could hurt a fly."

The woman made a *tsk-tsk* sound. "Well, you won't have to worry about that no more, dear. You'll be safe with us from now on."

I turned and looked at her, wondering if what she said was really true. She wore a plain housedress under a faded corduroy car coat and white, cuffed, cotton anklets and sturdy brown shoes with dust around the edges. But her clear blue eyes looked sincere to me, and despite all I'd seen in my life I really wanted to trust her. I needed to trust her. "Thank you, ma'am," I said.

Their farm was one of those old-fashioned types where they grew a little of this and that and kept a few hogs, cows, and chickens. About eighty acres, Mrs. Crowley explained as she showed me to my room upstairs. "It belonged to my husband's father before us, and we'll most likely pass it on to our son."

"You have a son?" I asked. For some reason I'd assumed this couple to be childless, kind of like that Kansas couple, Auntie Em and Uncle What's-His-Name who took care of poor Dorothy before the tornado whisked her away.

"Yes. He lives in town with his wife and baby—works at the feed and seed."

"Do you have other children?"

"We did. Our oldest boy, Roy Crowley, Jr., was killed in Vietnam about a year ago—just days before he was to have come home for good."

"I'm sorry."

She nodded. "Yes, dear, so are we."

Downstairs in the living room, Roy Jr.'s photo and medals were displayed on the mantel as something of a memorial to their son. He wasn't all that much to look at with his short-cropped dishwater blond hair and somewhat nondescript features, but something in his eyes appealed to me, and sometimes I would find myself standing there in front of the fireplace just staring into his face and wondering what he was thinking about now. Now that he was dead.

The Crowleys were very good to me, and especially patient during those first few days. They treated me kindly but made it clear they expected me to pull my weight around the place as my health returned. After a day or two, Mrs. Crowley wanted to wash my clothes for me. I explained to her that I'd always done my own laundry, but she wouldn't hear of it, at least not until I was feeling a lot better and she could give me a lesson on how to use her old cantankerous wringer washer. I told her I'd used a wringer washer before, but still she insisted. I remember feeling embarrassed as I handed over my strange-looking and worn items of clothing.

"Goodness," she said. "It looks to me like you don't have nothing but rags to wear, child." She held up a miniskirt and frowned. "And surely there's nothing here that you could possibly want to be wearing to school."

I just shrugged. At that point in time, with my nose all swollen and discolored, and a large brown and yellow lump on my forehead, I suppose I no longer cared what I looked like or wore to school—or anywhere else, for that matter.

"Well, we'll have to do something about this."

By the following weekend, my bruises had faded considerably, and Mr. and Mrs. Crowley decided to take me into town to do some errands and shopping. It was the first time I'd seen the town of Snider, and I felt surprised that it was much smaller than Brookdale. An agricultural town supported by the local farms, it had about two blocks' worth of businesses. Mr. Crowley dropped his wife and me at a small JCPenney store on Main Street and said he'd be back to pick us up around noon. I cringed just slightly when I saw the scanty racks of women's clothes we had to choose from. This store didn't even have a junior section. But I could see by Mrs. Crowley's face that this was a real treat for her—a woman who'd never been blessed with a daughter, suddenly buying school clothes for a girl. "How about this one?" she asked as she held up a flowered dress in somber shades of blue and green.

I swallowed hard as I glanced over the rack. "It's nice," I said in a flat voice. It didn't take us long to pick out a few outfits (two dresses and a skirt and blouse) and some underthings and socks and "sensible" shoes, which really weren't so bad considering that "sensible" shoes were coming back into fashion these days. Then we were picked up by Mr. Crowley and treated to lunch at Stanley's (the town's only diner).

I expressed my appreciation to both of them for taking me in and buying me the clothes and everything, at the same time hoping desperately that I'd be able to stick it out with them without freaking out and running away or something equally stupid. And I kept telling myself that I could and should change myself as an act of self-preservation. Somehow I had to make what seemed like a bad movie—or maybe just the opening scene in *The Wizard of Oz*—work. And if I was lucky, I'd someday be able to click my heels together and find my way back home—to a real home and real family—wherever that might be.

"Your social worker tells us that you're a hard worker and a good student," said Mr. Crowley as he sipped his coffee.

"Yes, and Mrs. Johnson said you're a good artist and a good musician, too. And I've seen that guitar you've got," said Mrs. Crowley. "But I haven't heard you play once. Don't you like to play no more, Cassie?" They'd taken to calling me Cassie, which like everything else felt strange and foreign, but somehow fitting in this new life I'd so recently slipped into.

"I don't know." I took a sip of my chocolate shake, surprised that it tasted better than the ones I'd made at the Dairy Maid.

"Well, you'll be starting school on Monday, and maybe that'll help cheer you up some," said Mr. Crowley. "Being round kids your own age, and all."

Mrs. Crowley laughed. "Yes, I s'pect it ain't easy being with a couple of old folks like us."

"No, no," I said. "You guys are great. I guess it's just a lot to get used to all at once."

She gently patted my hand. "Well, just you take your time, then. Get used to things slow and easy-like."

I wore the navy blue skirt and light blue blouse to church the next day (the least objectionable of yesterday's clothes purchases). Everyone seemed to know everyone in the little country church, and people came over to greet the Crowleys and meet me when the service was over. And it had been a nice service too, quiet and dignified with no yelling or accusatory finger-pointing from the pulpit going on.

But my mind had difficulty focusing and holding on to the preacher's words. More and more, it seemed my thoughts were sort of jumbled and scrambled, and I felt seriously worried that my daddy's recent blows to my head might have permanently damaged my brain some. And since intelligence was still important to me, this possibility concerned me a lot. To think, I'd been so careful to avoid things like alcohol and drugs to preserve my faculties, but more than likely what little sense I'd possessed had been knocked out of me at the tender age of fifteen. Like most things in life, it just didn't seem fair.

After church, the Crowleys' younger son, Tim, and his wife and baby came over for supper. I liked his wife, Suzy. In fact, she didn't seem all that much older than me, and she immediately began joking with me about the tragic shopping conditions in Snider, scandalized that her mother-in-law had actually taken me to that "sorry JCPenney store" to get school clothes. "You should've called me, Mom," said Suzy. "I'd have driven Cassie over to Dayville and done some really good shopping there."

"Well, I s'pose we could take all those things back," said Mrs. Crowley uncertainly.

"Oh, that's too much trouble," I said, feeling sorry for the older woman.

"Well, sure, why not?" said Suzy. "I could leave little Timmy with my mom and go pick Cassie up from school tomorrow and then we could take those old-lady clothes back to Penney's and get her some new things." So it was settled, and Mrs. Crowley didn't even seem to mind—not too much, anyway.

Suzy picked me up after school the next day as promised. "How'd your first day go?" she asked as I climbed into her car.

"Okay, I guess." I slumped down into the bucket seat, longing to disappear from the planet altogether.

"That bad, huh?"

I glanced over at her. "How'd you know?"

She laughed. "Well, it wasn't that long ago I was going to school there, and I know how it is with new kids. And I don't s'pect it helps any that your face looks like you got hit by a truck."

I reached up to touch my nose, no longer so badly swollen, but still discolored some. "I guess not."

"But I also remember that kids forget stuff and things can change. So maybe if you just hang in there, everything will start to look better before long. And you've only got about six more weeks of school, anyway. Things might look a whole lot different by next fall."

I nodded. "Yeah, I suppose so."

Suzy took charge of our little shopping expedition, and to my surprise I found myself actually relaxing a little and almost having fun. She reassured me that her in-laws were really good people, just a little stodgy and old-fashioned.

"Maybe that's what I need," I said, only partially realizing the truth at the time. "I just hope I don't let them down."

"Well, just work hard and don't act too disrespectful, and everything should be fine."

And so I did. And somehow I managed to make it until the end of the school year without embarrassing myself too badly. Well, other than being relatively stupid when it came to simple things like caring for and feeding livestock, but the Crowleys (and their animals) were patient with me. When Mr. Crowley read my report card (whether it was the mercy of my new teachers, or being in a smaller school, I had somehow maintained my four-point average) he was so pleased that he took the three of us out for dinner, something they almost never did. And that evening, they invited me to call them Eunice and Roy, and in some ways we were feeling almost like family.

chapter nine

LOOKING BACK NOW my time spent living with the Crowleys, even though it was brief, seems like a much-needed vacation from the troubles of my strange and crooked little life. And it was a complete departure from my wild and wicked ways that could've led me who knows where. For the first time ever, I almost felt like a normal girl.

Almost.

Perhaps the only thing that disturbed me much during that era was my unwillingness to pick up my guitar. For some reason, whenever I looked at my poor old Martin guitar, I thought of my daddy and a lifestyle I wanted to put completely behind me. So finally I just tucked the sorry instrument into the darkened back end of my narrow little bedroom closet and spent my free time sketching pictures or reading from the Crowleys' large selection of Reader's Digest condensed books. I don't know how many books I read "just part of," but it bothered me some. Maybe it just seemed too much like the way I had lived my life in the past years.

During that summer, one of the happiest of my youth, I went to church gladly and regularly, and surprised myself and everyone else by going forward after the salvation sermon one hot and humid Sunday when I'm sure everyone else would've just as soon heard the benediction and gone on home to their cold ham and potato salad. I'm still not sure that I knew exactly what it was I was doing, or even if it really "took" at the time. But the following Sunday, I was baptized down at the river with three other young people, and then we had ourselves a big celebratory picnic.

To this day, I can still recall that wonderful, cleansing feeling as the chilly, albeit muddy, waters washed over my head. When I stood up, I truly felt like a brand-new person—inside and out. And I don't think it was all my imagination, either—I truly believe that God got ahold of me that day.

After we got home, I briefly considered calling up Joey Divers to tell him the good news. But I didn't. I think part of me was still enjoying the luxury of leaving all my past back there in Brookdale and everything and everyone right along with it. I had become Cassie of the Crowley farm down High Banks Road—that nice girl who gets the best grades in Snider High's sophomore class and gladly goes to church every Sunday. Why mess with something that was working?

Eunice and Suzy put together a nice little birthday party for me when I turned sixteen, inviting friends and relatives and young folks from church. I wore a pale blue dress (hand sewn by Eunice) and flat sandals. Eunice and Roy surprised me with a brand-new Bible. They spent a lot of time reading their old, worn, leather one, and they thought I might like one of my own, after being baptized and all. I still have a faded Polaroid photo that Tim took of me at that party, holding a broad pink cake with wobbly blue letters that read: *Happy 16th, Cassie!* It was a happy time indeed.

But all this goodness came to a swift halt one sultry afternoon shortly after my birthday. Roy was out in the west field, preparing the soil for winter wheat, when he ran his tractor just a little too high on the small hill that bordered their farm—the very thing that Tim remembered his daddy had always warned him about when he plowed that field. The old John Deere tractor hit a bump and just rolled over sideways, pinning Roy underneath. Killed him instantly, the doctor reassured us later. We didn't even know it had happened until suppertime when he hadn't returned to the house on time.

"Run out and see what's keeping Daddy," said Eunice as she set a plate of fried chicken on the table.

I remember the sky was a strange shade of yellow that evening—kind of like tobacco-stained teeth. I figured it had to do with the high humidity and heat plus the dust in the air, but it gave me an eerie feeling just the same. And the closer I got to the west field, the more I began to sense that something was really wrong.

When I saw the overturned green tractor, my eyes filled with tears, and I began to run with all my might through the soft, rich, upturned soil. But as soon as I saw him, lying there lifeless with both eyes still open, I knew I was too late. I can't really remember all that much after that—how I got back to the house or told Eunice the bad news. The rest of that day just sort of blurs in my memory now. I think God is kind to us in that way—the way our memories mercifully fade into oblivion when something horrendous happens. Sort of like a protective amnesia.

Eunice was never the same after that. The woman I'd thought was the definition of strength itself just went totally to pieces after losing Roy. She'd lost Roy Jr. the year before, and losing her husband was just too much for her. I tried to comfort her as best I could, but it was almost as if she didn't know me anymore. And I suppose since I was such a recent addition to their family, in her eyes it may have seemed as if I'd never been there at all. I tried not to feel too hurt over that. And I know she meant me no harm.

At first Suzy and Tim talked about having me come live with them, but I worried it was more Suzy's idea than Tim's. They were going through a struggle of their own just then, with Tim feeling they should move out and take over the farm and Suzy determined not to give up her sweet little house and life in town. Finally, Mrs. Johnson (the lady from the county) made the decision for us with one short phone call. "Based on your successful adjustment with the Crowleys," she explained to me, "I've found a very nice family back in Brookdale who'd like to take you in."

Within the same week, Tim sold the farm and Eunice went down to Florida to stay with her sister Louise. And as I packed my bags once again, I wondered whether God was real or not.

I wanted to pray, and I really tried, but the words just wouldn't come out sounding right. What I really wanted to say was: *Hey, God, how come you let this happen? Why did you have to go and let Roy die just when things were getting good for me?* But I suspected that would be disrespectful and rude, not to mention selfish. And, thinking I was able to intimidate God, I kept my thoughts and my doubts to myself.

As I dragged my dusty guitar out from the back of the closet, I discovered my old paisley canvas bag, the one my grandma had gotten me at the Goodwill. I unzipped it to find it stuffed full of all my old clothes—the ones I'd scavenged from thrift shops and re-designed and decorated and then discarded when I'd come to live my new life with the Crowleys. On top of these strange-looking pieces, I now laid the new Bible that Eunice and Roy had given me for my sixteenth birthday. I felt it might be better off there for the time being.

Suzy took a break from packing up the Crowleys' belongings and sat with me on the front porch as we waited for Mrs. Johnson to pick me up. "Sounds like they're real nice people," she said with her ever-positive outlook. "And you're such a good kid, Cassie. I can't imagine how things shouldn't go just great for you from here on out."

I nodded mutely, not entirely convinced, but wanting to remain strong. "I guess so. I just feel a little worried about going back there—to Brookdale, I mean."

"But you're a new person now, Cassie." She grabbed me by the shoulders and looked right into my eyes. "Why, just look at you— you're beautiful—on the inside and out. You're smart. You're a good girl, Cassie. Don't let anyone tell you otherwise."

I nodded again, this time trying to hold back tears as I ran my fingers up and down the dusty frets of my guitar. More than anything else right then, I wanted her and Tim to change their minds about everything. I wanted Suzy to say: *"Don't worry, Cassie, we've decided to keep the farm, after all, and we want you to live out here with us. You're a part of our family and you always will be."* But of course those words never came. And I remembered how my grandma used to say that "charity begins at home," and I guess the Crowleys needed to be taking care of themselves right now, not looking out for someone who wasn't even kin. But oh, how I wished I were kin.

It wasn't long before that familiar dusty station wagon pulled into the driveway, and Suzy helped me load my guitar and bags into the back (I now had two suitcases besides the old canvas bag) and then we hugged, with tears. "You just call me if you run into any trouble, Cassie." She looked me in the eyes again. "I mean it. You hear?"

"Yeah, thanks," I muttered as I climbed into the station wagon.

I know Mrs. Johnson kept a constant chatter going as she drove to Brookdale, but for the life of me I can't remember a single word she said. Finally, she pulled to a stop, on the *good* side of town, and I looked out my window to see a rather nice-looking, stucco split-level before me, fully fenced and landscaped—respectable. "Is this it?" I asked weakly.

Mrs. Johnson smiled with satisfaction. "Yes. And if I'm not mistaken that's Mrs. Glenn coming right now." Just then a white, shiny, late-model Cadillac pulled into the immaculate driveway and a small, neatly dressed woman climbed out.

"Hello, there," called Mrs. Johnson.

Mrs. Glenn turned, as if caught by surprise. "Oh yes. I forgot the time. Come on in. I've just been at the store."

We entered the house, and at once I could tell that it was air-conditioned, although I'd never lived anywhere that was air-conditioned before. I looked around the corner of the entry to spy a sunken living room. It looked like something right out of a movie set, with big potted plants and art on the walls, and a long, low, pale three-pieced sofa, connected by blond end tables in the corners, each with a large pottery lamp in its center. Everything looked expensive and new, and matched perfectly. It was beautiful! Almost too beautiful to use, I thought.

Apparently Mrs. Glenn thought so too, since she led us right past this showroom and into a smaller, less formal, but nicely furnished room (what they called a family room, although they never had family over). It was situated near the kitchen with what looked like a real bar toward the back. From the big floor-to-ceiling windows in this room, I could see directly into the Glenn's backyard, and there, shining like a giant blue gemstone, was a sparkling swimming pool with a wide terra cotta patio all around, and padded lounge chairs clustered here and there!

About then, I thought maybe I'd done died and gone to heaven. I'm sure my jaw was hanging clear down to my chest. Suddenly and unexpectedly cheered, I wondered if this was God's way of rewarding me for how hard I'd tried to be a good girl while living with the Crowleys. *Well, okay, then,* I thought, *let's bring it on!*

I'm afraid I didn't listen very well as Mrs. Glenn and Mrs. John-

son conversed over iced tea, or I might've started to figure things
out a little sooner. But as soon as Mrs. Johnson departed, I was
shown to my room (or my "quarters," as she called it). She took me
downstairs to the basement and showed me a small windowless
"bedroom" with its own tiny bath and what appeared to be a kitch-
enette (a card table, chair, old refrigerator, and hot plate). It wasn't
really all that bad, but slightly disappointing after what I'd allowed
myself to briefly imagine to be a dream come true. "Naturally, we'll
provide you with groceries," she was saying, "but I'll expect you to
take care of your own meals as well as the cleaning and laundry and
such."

I nodded dumbly, unsure if she meant my own cleaning and
laundry and such, or that of the entire household. I soon figured
out it was the latter. As it turned out I had been taken into their
home to be something of a live-in maid (only I wasn't to expect to
be paid). Of course I'd get to attend school and have my basic
needs provided for, but in exchange I would be expected to do
"chores."

After recovering from my initial disappointment, I listened as
Mrs. Glenn went over the house rules, droning on about how I
wasn't to use the pool except during specified times, or to have
friends over (which I knew wasn't a problem) and a whole list of
other tawdry details. Trying to stay positive, I convinced myself this
situation wasn't so bad after all. Oh, sure, it wasn't my fairy-tale
dream—that had only lasted a few minutes. But maybe this was a
way for me to live in a safe place and still have my independence.

It was clear this couple (with grown children who rarely visited) had no desire to be involved in my life on a personal level. I
was simply there to "help out." But I started thinking, maybe I
could get my old job back (or a better one) and if I had enough
money in my savings account, perhaps I could get a car, too. Then

I'd just come and go as I pleased. I'd already noticed that my "quarters" had a separate exit, which Mrs. Glenn expected me to "use primarily, especially when we're entertaining."

She handed me a couple of very specific lists, then although she didn't say it in exactly these words, I understood that she expected me to become her "invisible maid" who helped her immaculate household to continue functioning perfectly with a whole lot less effort from her.

"You see, my husband is an important man in town," she said somewhat apologetically, "and he often brings home clients, and all the cocktail parties and whatnot can be pretty wearing on me. As I already said, our children are grown and, goodness knows, I have no desire to be a mother again. But we're happy to provide for a good girl, as long as she can help out and live up to our expectations." She looked me up and down carefully as if assessing both my character and physical strength. "Does that sound agreeable to you, Cassandra?"

I looked around my dismal quarters and smiled weakly. "I think so."

"Well, time will tell." She headed for the stairs. "Oh yes, the groceries in the car are for you. Please go and get them directly."

Keeping a nice house like the Glenns' in top-notch working order took more effort than I'd imagined, but in the next few days I began to get the hang of it, and Mrs. Glenn seemed fairly pleased with my progress (although she never hesitated to point out my many flaws and shortcomings—she did so with little notes slipped under my door at night). Still, I wasn't sure how it would go once school started up the following week. Would I be able to maintain my grades (still important to me at that point) while keeping house, as well as hold a part-time job? It seemed, for the moment, the job might have to wait.

On the Friday before Labor Day, I finished my chores earlier than usual (it was just past noon) and decided to walk into town. It was the first time I'd been in Brookdale proper since that night my daddy had beat me up. Surprisingly, the town seemed bigger and livelier than I recollected, but I quickly figured this must be due to my last five months spent in and around the tiny town of Snider.

I felt just slightly conspicuous as I walked down Main Street, but then wondered if anyone even recognized me in my rather normal-looking Wrangler blue jeans (no beads, fraying, or embroidery) and ordinary-looking blouse—and as usual, of late, my hair was pulled back into a long tail, hanging neatly down my back. But I began spotting kids I'd known from my old school, and they looked different, too. To my amazement, many now wore clothing that looked strangely similar to my old "hippy rags" as they used to call them back when they liked to tease me. Why, I even spotted Sally Roberts and Shelly Sinclair in front of the post office—both wearing, of all things, bib overalls! Here it was, 1970, and it seemed that Brookdale had finally been hit with the trends of the sixties.

I know I should've seen the humor and irony here, but the truth is I felt personally affronted by this turning of the tables. As usual, it seemed that poor ol' Cassandra Maxwell was on the outside looking in! Now you'd think with all the troubles and conflicts I'd experienced of late (death, displacement, and the like) clothing would be the very least of my concerns. After all, I'd almost convinced myself while living with the Crowleys that how a person dressed was rather superficial and insignificant. But somehow this whole weird experience of seeing Sally Roberts in bib overalls just really freaked me out. I still remember how I turned around (did a one-eighty right there on Main Street) and headed straight back to the Glenns' house (a twenty-minute walk) and dug out my old canvas suitcase.

I unzipped the bag and noticed my new Bible sitting right on top and was immediately assuaged with a mixture of confusing feelings. Guilt mixed with hope, faith with doubt, sorrow with sweetness, and finally I just had to set the leather-covered book aside.

I quickly changed into a wrinkled summer smock top and a pair of faded bell-bottoms trimmed with ribbons of tapestry tape at the hemline. I grabbed my old beaded shoulder bag and slipped out my exit again, this time being careful not to be heard or noticed (I sensed that Mrs. Glenn would definitely not approve of my appearance) and then hurried back toward town. And it was weird, but as soon as I was a block away from the Glenns' house, I suddenly felt like myself again—free and alive and young! But it was strange, because at the same time I felt just slightly guilty, too. I figured it might have to do with church and God, but to be honest, I wasn't even sure why.

My destination, I suddenly realized as my steps quickened, was the stationery store. For some unexplainable but deeply compelling reason, I felt I must see Joey. I just knew that if I explained everything to him—what had happened at the Crowleys, how I was feeling right now—he, of all people, would understand. I knew that Joey would be able to straighten me out. But when I reached Saunders Stationery store, Joey was nowhere in sight. Finally, a young woman asked if she could help me, and I inquired about Joey.

"Oh, Joey went off to college over a week ago," she said, as if I should've known this important and obvious information already.

"Oh . . ." was all I could think to say as I stood stupidly before her. I wanted to ask exactly where it was he'd gone off to college at, but didn't sense she wanted to continue her conversation with me. Besides, a man who looked to be a real customer had walked in by then, and I figured I could always go to Mrs. Divers to ask for an address. If I wanted to, that is.

Feeling fairly dismayed and just slightly lost, I continued to walk through town in something of a daze, not really seeing anything or anyone specifically. *Joey is gone*, I kept telling myself. *Joey is gone.* I suddenly felt like that "ship without a rudder" that Pastor Henry back in Snider had preached about not too many Sundays ago.

Finally I stopped at the Dairy Maid—slightly comforted by the familiarity of the old place. Then I asked for Clint, thinking I'd say hi and maybe even see about getting my old job back. The girl at the counter just laughed at me. "Clint Campbell? Why, he sold this place months ago and went down to Mexico to live."

I blinked, then ordered a soft-serve cone. I continued walking through town as I slowly licked the soothing, cool ice cream. I felt like a completely displaced person—like some of those sad-eyed Vietnam refugees you saw on the news. Or maybe I'd just stepped into some sort of twilight zone—maybe this wasn't really Brookdale at all, or maybe I wasn't really Cassandra Jane Maxwell. At one point, I honestly considered stopping by to see if my Aunt Myrtle still lived in town, but I figured with my luck, she probably did.

chapter ten

I WAS STANDING ON A CORNER next to the five-and-dime trying to decide whether or not to cross the street when I noticed something that finally made me feel like I had a real connection in Brookdale. It was a lime green poster stapled to the telephone pole announcing that Pete Jackson's band would be playing at the annual Labor Day dance on Saturday night in the park.

Pete was the guy who'd given me guitar lessons a couple years earlier. I knew that he'd graduated ages ago, and I was somewhat surprised that he was still around. Not that he was the kind of guy to be college-bound, but then who would choose to stick around a podunk town like this after high school? Not me.

I pondered whether or not I had the nerve to show up at a dance all by myself, then thought, what did I have to lose anyway? And yet at the same time I wondered how I would've felt about all this a few weeks earlier—back when I was committed to being a good, straightlaced, church girl. But that was before God had let me down by disrupting the quiet little life I'd worked so hard to create. What did it matter what I did or where I went now? Who really cared about me anyway? Who even knew I was alive? I stopped by the Citizen's Bank, where I still had my savings account, to withdraw a little pocket money before I headed back to the Glenns.'

Within minutes Mrs. Glenn was knocking on my door telling me I needed to come upstairs and help her get things ready. *Ready for what?* I wondered as I quickly changed my clothes. Turned out they were throwing a "little party" that night and I was stuck in the kitchen slicing cheese and cold cuts and making dips out of dried soup mixes and sour cream for the next couple of hours. I finished just as the guests began to arrive and was finally dismissed for the evening.

Trying to suppress my feelings of being left out (left out of what? I asked myself with ire—a stupid grown-up party?) I went downstairs to my little underground home and sat on my bed. In an attempt to block out what was going on upstairs I tried to work on a pencil drawing that I'd started back at the Crowleys'. It was a picture of the horse in the corral next to the barn. But for some reason I just couldn't focus. I couldn't even remember what the roof of the barn looked like.

And besides there were too many thoughts tumbling through my head, just going round and round like clothes in the dryer. I had doubts about God and myself and even the world I lived in.

Finally I picked up my Bible and ran my hands over its smooth, supple leather surface. I lifted the book to my nose and inhaled its fragrance—it reminded me of the saddle that had hung out in the Crowley barn. Roy had promised to give me riding lessons on Old Mary in the fall when the weather finally cooled down a bit. I would've liked to have felt the power of a horse beneath me. I really think I could've learned to ride and maybe even been good at it. If I'd just had the chance.

"Why, God?" I asked suddenly. I could feel big tears gathering in my eyes—the first ones since that day I'd found Roy under the tractor. But no answers came to my short prayer (was it really a prayer?) and so I set the Bible aside and picked up my guitar and

played loudly and badly until my fingers became sore and tender—
I'd have to work to get those calloused fingertips back. I felt no concern about making too much noise that night since it was clear the
Glenns' party and music were much louder than anything I could
produce.

Finally, bored with my stuffy and windowless quarters, I slipped
outside and looked into the backyard from behind a rhododendron.
I watched, at first with voyeuristic fascination and then later disgust,
as a group of adults (some of the respected leaders of our fair city)
acted just like a bunch of drunken, crazy kids around the pool.

One lady wearing a hot pink halter dress kept pushing fully
dressed men into the pool, then laughing loudly as they sputtered
to the surface. Finally a couple of guys sneaked up behind her,
jovially picked her up, and tossed her into the pool. She emerged
with an angry face, makeup running and drippy hair, but it quieted
her down some.

The laughter and pranks continued, and from where I stood in
the darkened protection of the shrubbery I suddenly felt jealous of
their lighthearted fun. It seemed so unfair and upside down from
what I thought life should be. And then I realized that tomorrow I'd
be the one responsible to clean up all their messes in the yard and
house, and so, feeling disturbingly like Cinderella, I turned away
and slunk off to bed.

Before I fell asleep I thought of my daddy and his drinking
escapades, which I felt certain had never included parties anything
like the Glenns liked to throw. Then I wondered what he'd think of
me, living as a servant girl, here with these strange people? But as
quickly as the thought came, I dismissed it. What did I care what he
would think?

Knowing I most likely had a full day of cleaning before me, I got
up early and slipped into my bikini and cutoffs. I suspected the

Glenns would sleep in, and probably be seriously hungover after their late-night partying, and I planned to catch some sun as I picked up the backyard, then possibly take a quick dip in the pool (during my official "pool time," which was limited to the mornings on Saturdays). I put my little transistor radio in my pocket, with the earplug stuck in my ear, and bebopped to the music as I toted a garbage bag around the yard, picking up empty beer cans and drink containers and other various bits of garbage littered all about and even in the pool.

At first I felt somewhat stunned to discover signs that pot had been smoked, along with some even more disturbing items related to other "recreational" drug usage. Could it really be that these "responsible adults" actually used the same kind of crud that Bryn and her boyfriends had been into? I shook my head in disgust. What was life coming to, anyway?

"How's it going?" called a man's voice from behind me.

I jumped, dropping a beer can loudly on the terra cotta tile as I turned to see Mr. Glenn standing in the doorway, wearing a navy blue bathrobe. I'd only met him a couple of times before and then only briefly. But my first impression was that he might be a little nicer than his no-nonsense wife. "Oh, hi," I said, suddenly feeling self-conscious and even somewhat intrusive—although I was doing exactly what I'd been told to do.

"Sorry, I didn't mean to startle you." He lit a cigarette and inhaled deeply. "Man." He whistled out a stream of smoke as he looked around the garbage-strewn yard. "Looks like we really trashed the joint last night. You need any help out here?"

I mutely shook my head, embarrassed to realize that I still held the twisted butt of a smoked joint in my hand. I dropped it into the garbage bag and swallowed. "No, I'm fine," I finally said. "I just thought I'd better get an early start on this."

He chuckled. "And to think I thought Kelly was crazy when she said we were getting paid to keep a maid, but as usual it looks like she was right."

I frowned over at him, suddenly realizing how he must think it was some sort of great joke to take advantage of me like this. And who knew what other advantages he wanted to take? That's when it hit me—a plan that might get me some real bargaining power. Or perhaps it was just plain blackmail.

I opened the garbage bag, pulled out the partially smoked joint, and held it up. Then, using an innocent voice mixed just slightly with cynicism, I said, "You know, Mr. Glenn, I don't think CSD would be too happy to find out they've placed a poor homeless kid in a foster home where illegal drugs are being used."

He squinted into the sun, reaching up to rub his chin, as if pondering my words. Then he looked back at me, and I felt his eyes traveling uncomfortably up and down, not so much as if he was checking out my body (although I'm sure he probably was) but more like he was checking me out, adding me up. I suddenly wished I had thrown a T-shirt over my tangerine string-bikini top, or that my faded and frayed cutoffs were not quite so short. It wasn't exactly an outfit I'd planned to wear in the presence of my new "foster parents." But keeping my cool, I held my ground, not even flinching.

Then he chuckled. "Well, you don't exactly seem like the kind of kid who'd get too bent out of shape over some old fogies smoking a joint or two, now would you?"

I shrugged. "Well, you just never know, do you? Like my grandma used to say, you should never judge a book by its cover."

He scowled darkly. "What're you getting at, Cassandra?"

I was surprised he actually knew my name. "Well, this is supposed to be a *foster home.*" I said the words as if they should mean something dignified, respectable.

He frowned and snuffed out his half-smoked cigarette in a nearby ashtray that I'd already emptied. "Don't you like it here?"

I shrugged again. "I can take it or leave it."

Now he looked defensive. "You could've done a lot worse, you know."

"I don't know. Right now I feel like I'm pretty much a slave around here. And to be honest, I don't really like that."

"Yeah, I suppose it could seem like that." He scratched his head. "Well, let's talk then. Is there anything we can do to make it better for you? Kelly seems pleased with you. She says you've been doing a really good job."

Now I laughed. "I'll bet she does." I glanced around the yard and sighed deeply. That's when it occurred to me that maybe I should just be up-front with this guy. "The thing is, Mr. Glenn, I don't think I can keep all this up and expect to get good grades, too. Besides that, I wanted to get a part-time job and start saving up for a car or college or something. And I'd kind of like to have a life too, you know."

He nodded, realization sinking in. "Yeah, that seems fair enough." He picked up an empty soda can and tossed it into my bag. "Okay, how about this then—how about if you don't take that part-time job, just for now anyway, but maybe we could let you keep the CSD money—that is, as long as you keep doing a good job with the housecleaning. That sound fair to you?"

I kept my face blank, unwilling to reveal just how good it did sound. "I guess so. Just as long as the housework doesn't interfere with my school." I paused, suddenly realizing that I held all the cards here. "And as long as I can have a little life of my own, too. I don't want to spend every free hour cleaning up this place."

"That seems fair enough."

"And you'll explain all this to Mrs. Glenn?"

He nodded, then stuck out his hand. "Deal?"

I shook his hand, not entirely sure what I was agreeing to, but fairly certain that for once in my life I had the upper hand.

I wasn't too sure what God thought about blackmail—or about me, for that matter—but I felt I was on my own in those days, and once I took matters into my own hands, it seemed that things began to look up. As expected, it took most of the day to clean the house and yard, and when Mrs. Glenn finally got up she was in a grumpy mood and didn't seem to even notice how greatly the appearance of her home had improved. I wished I'd taken "before" and "after" photos, but at least her husband had noticed, and he seemed to appreciate my efforts.

Finally, it was nearly five, and everything was pretty much back to normal, so I slipped back downstairs to clean myself up and get ready for the dance, no longer feeling so intimidated for going solo. All day long I'd looked forward to this event, and I played rock tunes on my little transistor radio as I tried on a number of outfits, finally deciding on my old fuchsia-colored, tie-dyed shirt and my bib overalls with the embroidery across the front. I slipped in some big hoop earrings and let my hair just hang loose for a change—it was past my waist now. I slipped on my sandals and decided I'd stop to pick some flowers to put into my hair (I'd noticed an empty lot just a few blocks away that was overgrown with weeds and wild-flowers).

Just as I turned off my radio, I noticed my Bible again and felt a strange little twisting in my heart—as if my recent actions were somehow a deliberate choice to turn away from God. Although that's not exactly how I felt—I felt more like I was trying to find out who I *really* was—and if God was really real and wanted to take me for who I really was, well, then that would be just fine. But I was tired of playing games.

I stopped by the Dairy Maid and ordered myself a burger basket and Coke, then sat down at an outside picnic table to leisurely eat while I observed others coming and going, ordering sundaes and dipped cones and corn dogs.

A tall guy with shaggy, light brown hair caught my attention as he ordered a large Coke from the outside window. Something about him seemed familiar, but I couldn't put my finger on it. Finally, I realized he was Jimmy Flynn, a boy who'd been fairly popular back in junior high (he used to go with Sally Roberts) but had moved away in ninth grade. Sally had been brokenhearted and pined away for him—for at least a week—until she started going steady with Tom Morrow. I noticed Jimmy looking my way and decided to grace him with a smile.

"Don't I know you?" he said as he carried his Coke over to my table.

I laughed. "Probably not. But I think I know you. Aren't you Jimmy Flynn?"

He smiled, a really great smile with white teeth framed in a tanned face. "I mostly go by Jim now. But who are you? You look familiar."

"Just a nobody. I'm sure you don't remember me."

"Mind if I sit?"

"Hey, it's a free country." I flipped my hair over my shoulder—an act of nonchalance, or so I hoped. "My name's Cass Maxwell, and if you remember me at all, you probably wouldn't be sitting here for long."

His eyes lit up. "Yeah, I do remember you. Didn't your dad try to kill you once back in junior high school?"

I forced a grin to my face. "Yep, that'd be me. And just for the record, he tried to kill me again, just last spring. But here I am, alive and well. Sort of well, I guess." I frowned. "Now I'll excuse you if you want to politely stand up and leave. And don't worry, I'm used to it."

He frowned and shook his head. "No way, Cass. I'm not leaving. In fact, I think you're interesting." He smiled again. "And a lot more real than most girls I know."

At first I thought he might be putting me on, but his smile seemed authentic. Still, you never know. It was my experience that kids could be extremely cruel. Especially the popular ones. I decided to keep my guard up—just a little. "So," I began, "didn't you move away back in junior high?"

He nodded. "Yep, but this summer my mom and me decided to move back here."

"Just your mom and you?"

"Yep. My parents split up last year, and my brother Bill's in college, so it's just me and my mom, and since her sister lives here in Brookdale, we decided why not just come back."

"That's cool. I'll bet Sally Roberts is flying high—you guys used to be quite an item. Does she know you're back yet?"

He grinned. "Yep. I've seen her a couple times."

"You guys back together then?" I dipped a fry in ketchup, thinking how Sally would react if she could see her sweet Jimmy sitting with me now.

"Not really. I kind of wanted to just hang out for a while, not get too tied down, you know?"

"Yeah, I know. I'm used to being a pretty free spirit, too." I watched him from the corner of my eye as I picked out the onions from my burger (so much for requesting no onions). But I could sense him checking me out and I wondered what he really thought.

He reached across the table and touched the daisy I'd tucked into my hair. "Yep, that's just what I thought when I first saw you sitting here by yourself."

"Why's that?" I tried not to look as uncomfortable as I was starting to feel.

"Well, a girl has to be pretty sure of herself to sit all by herself and eat at the Dairy Maid. I can't imagine Sally ever doing that. She doesn't go anywhere without her little throng of worshipers."

I laughed. "I guess I never thought of it that way. But you could be right. The truth is, I really do like being with people, but I'm used to being alone, too. And I suppose I kind of like being alone sometimes." I looked at him. "But not always."

"So what're you into then, Cass?"

"Into?" I thought for a moment. "Life's been so crazy lately that I don't know if I'm even sure anymore. But I do like doing art, sketching and stuff. And I really like music. I play the guitar and make up songs and stuff." I glanced at my watch. "In fact, I was going to go hear Pete's band play at the dance tonight."

His brows lifted. "Want any company? Or is this one of those things you'd rather do by yourself?"

I laughed. "No one really wants to go to a dance alone, do they? Truth is, I've only been back in town about a week. And I feel like I don't know anyone around here anymore. I'd love to have company, that is—" I stopped myself.

"That is, what?"

"Well, I'm not exactly the Sally Roberts type, if you know what I mean."

"That's cool with me."

And that's how it came to be that I showed up at the Labor Day dance with Jimmy (or rather, Jim) Flynn. And for the first time in my life, I felt more than subhuman in my own hometown. Of course Sally Roberts and her girlfriends snubbed me something terrible. But Jim treated me just like an equal, and pretty soon some of his old friends joined us, and they treated me just fine, too. Toward the end of the dance, Tom Banks asked us if we wanted to come to a kegger down at the levy, but to my pleased surprise Jim announced that he didn't drink. "You go ahead if you want, Cass," he said.

I shook my head. "No thanks, I don't drink either."

"Oh, please, don't tell me you two are Jesus freaks?" teased Tom.

Jim just laughed, and I felt guilty for not speaking up. But what could I have said? That I'd gone forward in a little country church and been baptized in a muddy river? What did all that really mean in the end? Where had believing in God gotten me? And did I even believe anymore? So I didn't say anything.

Jim asked me if I wanted to get coffee after the dance, and so we went to Nellie's, which brought back a flood of memories from that last conversation I'd had with Joey. I remembered his concern and realized how he was right. And in that moment I missed him more than ever.

I suppose I was being pretty quiet, and finally Jim spoke up. "You okay, Cass? You look kind of sad."

"I was just thinking."

"About what?"

And then to my complete amazement, I sat there in Nellie's Diner and told Jim Flynn all about my life of late—living with the Crowleys and my "God" experience, then Roy's death, my doubts, and finally living as a servant with the Glenns.

"Man, and I thought my life had been kinda rough last year," he said after I finished.

I made myself laugh. "I'm sorry, Jim. Talk about a blabbermouth. I can't believe you didn't just excuse yourself and slip out the back exit."

"No, I think it's interesting. I feel honored you told me all that. I feel like I really know you now. Man, Cass, you've been through a lot."

I shook my head. "Yeah, and that's just the recent stuff. Sometimes I feel like there's this old woman underneath my skin—like I've really been living for about a hundred years, but I just happen to look like a sixteen-year-old."

"Yeah, I know what you mean. But maybe it's just the times we live in. You know stuff is going on all over the world that just doesn't make sense. Sometimes I wonder why we all don't just tune out and turn on."

Now that made me laugh for real. "So, what's your story, Jim? I was surprised that you don't drink. I assume that means you don't do drugs, either. What makes you want to be straight?"

He shrugged. "Well, for one thing, I promised my mom I wouldn't. I got into trouble before we moved here—for drinking. I guess I'm trying to make a fresh start. I might even go out for football."

Now this surprised me. With his long hair and fringed leather vest, Jim didn't really seem like the jock type. "You play football?"

"I used to. My mom really wants me to take it up again. She thinks it'll keep me out of trouble."

I laughed. "That just shows how much parents know about jocks and sports."

"Yeah." He nodded. "That's when I first started drinking, you know, celebrating after the games."

"Well, Jim, I hope you do what *you* want to do—not just what your mom wants you to do. We've got to be real and become our own people, you know. In the end, that's all we've really got, anyway."

He held up his coffee mug as if to make a toast. "Yeah, here's to becoming our own people."

I grinned as I clicked my cup against his.

chapter eleven

RETURNING TO BROOKDALE HIGH wasn't nearly as bad as I'd antici-
pated that day when I'd sat with Suzy out on the Crowleys' front
porch. My friendship with Jim proved a real icebreaker during
those first few days. And while we weren't exactly dating, I sensed
the relationship was building into something more. But by the
end of the week Jim announced that he'd decided to go out for
football.

I don't know exactly why this disturbed me so greatly, but it
did. I asked him if it was because of his mom, but he insisted it was
just something he wanted to do and the coach had agreed to let
him come try out even though the team had been practicing for a
month already. Naturally Jim made the team—he was actually
pretty good. I figured this meant he and I would be history now.
And wasn't it handy that Sally Roberts was a varsity cheerleader?
She'd be right out there on the fifty-yard line jumping and screaming for him to S-C-O-R-E at every single game.

But during the second week Jim still showed no interest in Sally
Roberts and continued to seek me out at lunchtime and after
school. Toward the end of the week he asked me if I was coming to

his first game. "Sure," I said, wondering why, since I'd never really liked football that much before.

His eyes lit up. "And then afterwards maybe we can go out for a bite to eat."

"Sure," I said again, halfway expecting him to change his mind by then, mentally preparing myself to see Sally Roberts hanging on his arm after the game. I went to the game and watched the Brookdale Bullets narrowly defeat the Harris Cowboys, cheering for Jim from the stands, and to my surprise almost enjoying it.

Afterwards I stood outside the locker room (along with a bunch of other girls—none of whom spoke to me) waiting for Jim to come out. I must confess, I felt silly and out of place and almost left before Jim came out and even then I felt stupid and self-conscious and didn't know if I could do this again. But then we went out for pizza and when I was with Jim people treated me like I really was someone. Even though that was a welcome change I didn't like thinking that the only reason they were nice to me was because of him. The whole thing troubled me a lot.

The weirdest thing about that evening was when several kids who were well known as "Jesus freaks" came over to our table and started trying to evangelize us. I knew that some of these kids were the same ones Joey had hung out with last year but I pretended not to recognize them. Finally one of them, a tall, gangly boy, pointed his finger right at me. "Aren't you Cass Maxwell, Joey Divers's friend?"

Well, I couldn't very well say no, so I just nodded mutely.

"Oh, go on, you guys," said Jim good-naturedly. "Go on and convert someone else tonight."

"Joey Divers had us all praying for you last spring," said the guy, with an earnest look in his eyes. "Hey, Sara, Mitch, you guys," he called over his shoulder. "Remember how we were all praying for that Cass Maxwell chick last spring? Well, this is her—she's right here!"

And then about five of them came over and stood before our table, all staring at me as if I were some sort of sideshow freak in a circus.

"You guys need to just lay off," said Jim, suddenly standing up. A couple of the other football guys at our table stood too.

I instantly felt a mixture of gratitude and shame. Grateful and proud that Jim was standing up to defend me, but embarrassed that I was spurning these religious friends of Joey who had actually prayed for me. "You guys really prayed for me?" I said, surprising even myself.

"Yeah," said the girl named Sara. "Joey was real worried about you. One day we all got together and prayed around the clock—all night too."

"Really?" I said, feeling a strange little twist in my heart.

"Okay, that's just great," said Jim sarcastically. "Cass really appreciates your concern. Now can you just clear out of here and let us finish our pizza in peace?"

As they started to back off I looked up into their faces and said, "Thanks."

"Man, what a bunch of jerks," said Scott Taylor (one of Jim's football buddies). "Those Jesus freaks are really starting to get out of hand."

"Yeah," said Jim. "But you gotta admire their nerve."

"Nerve?" said a girl named Tammy. "Don't you mean *nerd*?"

Everyone laughed. Everyone but me.

Jim drove me home that night in his mom's car, parking just down the street a ways from the Glenns' house—as I'd asked him to do. "You okay, Cass?" he asked as we sat in the darkened car. "You seem pretty quiet tonight."

I shrugged. "I guess I'm just feeling a little out of place and try-ing to figure some things out."

He slipped his arm around my shoulders and slid me over next to him. "That's one of the many things I really like about you, Cass. The way you give me an honest answer and think about things more deeply than other girls."

I turned and looked into his eyes—I could feel his breath on my face and suddenly felt a strange but not unpleasant shiver run through me. "It's the only way I can be," I said softly.

He pulled me closer and then covered my mouth with his in a long, slow, intense kiss. And then just as slowly he pulled back and a pleased smile crept over his lips. "Was that okay?" he asked.

I sighed. "Actually it was better than okay." And then we kissed some more, and by the time I got out of his car I no longer remem-bered exactly what it was that had been upsetting me earlier.

All I knew was that out of all the boys who had kissed me before (and there'd been a few) no one had ever made me feel quite like that. And while the feeling was warm and wonderful and amazing, it also struck me that it was just slightly dangerous. Still I refused to think about that. I would only remember the comfort and security of being gathered into his arms—and that kiss!

Jim and I dated steadily for the next several weeks. And it was blissful, mostly. But the pressure was building between us. Before long Jim was pushing me to have sex with him. And I was consider-ing it too. Why shouldn't I? Everyone else was doing it. And who cared what I did? My daddy was in prison. My mama and grandma were dead. I was nothing more than a live-in maid to my foster par-ents. And it seemed my only real friend in the entire school was Jim, and other than this sex thing it seemed we'd been getting along just fine. So why not give in? It'd probably be fun.

But still something deep down within me—like this quiet

urgent voice—kept warning me not to. Was it God? Was it me? Was it the ghost of my long-lost mama? Or maybe it was just the memory of my old friend Bryn, who'd gotten into trouble not that long ago.

Finally I felt like I might actually be going crazy—didn't they lock up people who heard voices? Okay, so it wasn't an actual voice, but it seemed pretty real just the same.

And then one afternoon at school, between choir and geometry, I just totally lost it. I ran into the girls' rest room and locked myself in a stall and sobbed quietly. *What should I do?* I kept asking myself—or maybe I was praying—I'm still not sure. But the next thing I knew, I heard a voice from above. And I looked up to see a head of blonde curls bending down over me.

"Are you okay?" asked the girl hanging over the side of the bathroom stall.

I recognized her as one of the Jesus freaks who'd confronted us at the pizza restaurant that night after the game. I just shook my head.

"Want to talk?"

"I don't know."

"You're already late for seventh period. I've got a car—we could just skip."

"Skip?" I looked at her incredulously. "I thought you were supposed to be a Jesus freak."

She laughed. "Just because I believe in Jesus doesn't mean I'm perfect." She tossed back the hair from her eyes. "And besides, Jesus might rather I spent time with you than snooze through biology. So how about it? Wanna go talk?"

"Sure. Why not?"

Her name was Sara Hanson and she drove a yellow Volkswagen bug. "My daddy got this for me on my seventeenth birthday," she said as she slipped it into gear and pulled out of the school parking lot. "He's just so glad that I've finally straightened out." She laughed. "I used to be really screwed up. I was into drugs and boys and whatever trouble I could find. But then I found Jesus and now I live for him."

"You were into drugs?"

She nodded. "Yeah, what a mess. And then we moved to Brookdale last year and these kids all started witnessing to me—especially Joey—"

"Joey Divers?"

"Yeah. In fact he's the one who really got to me. He's really smart and what he said made sense. And finally I just decided to give it a try. And well, here I am."

She parked her bug down at the park and we sat there and talked for a long time. I told her all about Jim and how he was the only friend I had and I thought I might be in love with him, but I just wasn't sure that I was ready for sex. It's funny, I never told her about the voices at that point or the other things that had been confusing me. Instead we just talked about sex and she told me why she believed that Jesus had told her to stop having it. "I know it sounds strange," she said, "but I really believe that Jesus wants me to love him with all my energy. Now that doesn't mean that I'm having sex with him. I mean that would be pretty twisted, wouldn't it? But it's like I'm supposed to love him with all of me, and I can't do that very well if I'm having sex with every guy who comes along."

I'd never heard anyone say anything like that before. It sounded slightly fanatical, but it sort of made sense too. "So will you ever have sex then?"

She laughed. "Sure. At least I think so. But not until I get married. And I feel really sure that Jesus has some guy all picked out for me to marry. I'm thinking it might even be Joey Divers."

"Really?" A strange jolt of jealousy ran through me, but I quickly dismissed it.

"Yeah, I think I'll go to the university too."

"Is that where he's at?"

"Yeah. He got a full scholarship there. He's such an academic."

I nodded, fighting the lump that was growing in my throat. "I know. He used to be my best friend."

"I thought you must've been pretty special to him. I mean why else would he ask us all to pray for you night and day like that?" She studied me closely. "Were you his girlfriend?"

I forced a laugh. "No, nothing like that. We were always just friends. Good friends."

"That's good. We should all be good friends. That's what Jesus wants." She reached over and touched my arm. "But how about you, Cass? Don't you want to give your heart to Jesus too?"

I shrugged. "I don't know."

"I think you do. I think that's why you're thinking about all these things and getting so frustrated. I think it's just because Jesus is reaching out to you—calling you to himself."

I had the strangest sensation just then. Not exactly like when I went forward at church, but similar. A compulsion really. It's as if I couldn't resist, or maybe I just didn't want to anymore. "You know Sara, you may be right. You see, I sort of gave my life to God last summer, but then everything just fell apart and I figured God had let me down and so I think I sort of reneged on him, if you know what I mean."

"I know. But sometimes even when things are looking totally hopeless, we just need to keep trusting him anyway—and then he just turns everything around. But he can't help you if you don't let him, Cass. And he can't show you which way you're supposed to go if you just keep pushing him away from you. He wants to be your best friend, you know. You wouldn't just push your best friend away now would you?"

I didn't tell her I hadn't had much experience with best friends as a rule (well, other than Joey—and I suppose in some ways I did push him away, eventually). "I don't know."

"Well, I know you wouldn't. You seem like a good person to me, Cass—not that it matters 'cause Jesus takes us no matter how bad a shape we're in. But I think if you really gave your heart to him—well, I think you'd be true to him."

And for the second time that day I began to cry. "I don't usually act all soppy like this," I sputtered. "I don't know what's wrong with me today—I wonder if I'm going nuts or something."

Sara just laughed. "It's Jesus touching your heart, Cass. Just sit here real quiet for a minute and see if you can't feel him touching you now."

And so we just sat in silence in her little car parked down by Oak Grove Park where the trees' leaves had all turned brown and red and gold and I tried to see if Jesus was really touching my heart like she said he was. And to be honest I truly think he was, and so right then and there I silently asked Jesus to really come into my heart. And it was as if this heavy load was instantly lifted from me. Finally after a long while I turned and told Sara, almost afraid to speak and risk losing what seemed to be going on in me. And she was so happy she hugged me.

"You're my sister now, Cass," she said with wet eyes. "I'm so glad for you. I can't wait to write and tell Joey. He'll be so pleased."

As she drove me home I felt pretty certain that Jim wouldn't be quite so pleased. But I knew I had to tell him all about this. And perhaps Jesus was calling on him too. It could happen. And so like grasping a little lifeline I held on to the slim hope that Jim would ask Jesus into his heart too—after all, hadn't he given up drinking and such? Maybe he was ready for something like this. I prayed for Jim during the remainder of the day while I did my chores at the Glenns' and then got ready to go to the football game that night.

Of course, I thought to myself as I walked back over to the school where I would catch the activity bus that would take me to the football game in a town twenty miles away. *Why, of course, Jesus wants to save Jim too—that's probably why the two of us became such good friends in the first place. And then after Jim sees the light* (as I remembered hearing Pastor Henry say) *Jim and I can continue to date and have a good time together.* And this is exactly what I prayed for as I walked through town. Yet even as I said these prayers I sensed a shadow of doubt hanging all about my words. That would be just too good—too amazing and unbelievable! Especially for someone like me—someone who always seemed to come by everything the hard way. Why should anything change now?

And as it turned out I was exactly right.

chapter twelve

MY GRANDMA USED TO SAY you can't make a silk purse out of a sow's ear and I suppose that's a little how I felt that night when I figured out Jim and I were history. At the time I probably tried to flatter myself into thinking it was simply the result of me becoming a Jesus freak, but underneath all that I felt like a social failure—sort of like Eliza Doolittle gone wrong.

It was almost Homecoming week and naturally Sally Roberts had been nominated as one of the contestants for Homecoming Queen (I heard she nominated herself). But as fate would have it (that very day, during seventh period, while I was sitting in Sara's car turning myself into a Jesus freak) Sally Roberts had somehow coerced Jim into agreeing to be her escort at Homecoming next week. I came by this information quite innocently enough during halftime in the girls' rest room (behind a closed stall door) as Sally and her cheerleading buddies adjusted their makeup and sprayed on perfumes that smelled like a rancid mixture of overripe strawberries and lilacs and chattered like magpies in front of the big mirror above the sinks. Just before I opened the door I heard Sally's high-pitched little-girl tone that always made my skin crawl. "And Jimmy Flynn's going to escort me!" she squealed with delight. My fingers froze on the little latch that held the flimsy plywood door closed and I sucked in my breath and waited.

"How'd you talk him into that?" asked head cheerleader Julie Miller.

"I consider it a mission of pure mercy," said Sally in what had suddenly turned into a haughty tone. "Don't you know I'm saving him from turning into poor white trash just like that Maxwell nerd he's been seen with late—"

Well, that was all I could take. I threw open the door and stepped out, then instantly wished I hadn't. Their conversation ceased as I walked past them, my jean jacket brushing against the blur of their red-and-gold uniforms. I headed straight for the sink. Focusing my eyes on the water I quickly washed my hands, not even glancing up into the mirror, not wanting to see their perfectly made-up faces reflected there. Other than the sound of water and a toilet flushing, the room was hushed, but I could feel their eyes burning mean, dark holes into me. I saw Sally toss a challenging look my way as I moved past her. But she said nothing, only smiled smugly, victorious, as I exited the stuffy, perfume-saturated room.

I never did return to the stands that night. Instead I walked around the somewhat deserted town that didn't look all that different from Brookdale and wondered what was the real meaning of life. I did believe that I'd given my heart to Jesus that day—but for what reason? I wasn't entirely sure. Why did Jesus need my heart in the first place? And now it seemed somewhat defective—what would Jesus want with a broken heart?

After circling the town I found myself back at the high school parking lot and the game still only in the beginning of the fourth quarter. So I slipped into the activity bus, went clear to the back, curled up on the cold, hard, vinyl seat, and cried myself to sleep. When the bus finally returned to Brookdale High, I walked straight home—not bothering to wait outside the locker room for Jim. I wondered if he'd miss me. I hoped he would. Still as I walked toward the Glenns' house I felt strangely and unexpectedly encouraged. For some reason it no longer felt as if my life were completely over. Something had changed in me. And although I felt slightly mystified by all this, I wondered if it might actually be Jesus. Could he be doing something in my pitiful little life? It seemed possible.

Now if I'd been a normal girl, living a normal life, I might've thought up excuses to hang around the kitchen the following day expecting the phone to ring. But as it was I had no phone of my own and wasn't allowed to use the Glenns' phone for incoming calls (sometimes I could sneak an outgoing call if Mrs. Glenn wasn't around) so Jim didn't even have my phone number.

Maybe this was a relief of sorts, for I felt no distraction as I went about my Saturday chores, only a sort of hopeful numbness. And when I got done I returned to my room to do my homework and play my guitar. I even had the clarity of mind to write a little song about Jesus coming into my heart that even to this day I still sing sometimes.

Did I feel bad about being dumped for Sally Roberts? Well of course! But I now realized it wasn't going to be the end of my life. I think for the first time I really understood deep down in my soul (well, maybe it was just a brief and fleeting glimpse) that I couldn't fully depend on earthly people. Somehow I figured that eventually everyone would let me down in one way or another, maybe not intentionally, but sooner or later it would happen. After all I'd had a rather full history of being let down—why should I suspect anything would ever change?

But during this same flash of insight I also realized that Jesus would never let me down—somehow I just knew that I could count on him. And I think I really believed it—at least during that moment in time. Unfortunately we don't always grab on to and really adhere to the things we truly believe. Or perhaps we simply grab on to them too tightly, and then, like grains of sand in a doubled-up fist, they trickle through our fingers and disappear altogether. Sometimes faith can be kind of slippery like that I think.

On Sunday afternoon I went outside to rake the soggy maple leaves from the parking strip along the street (the last activity on my weekend "chores list") when I noticed a bright yellow car coming toward me. And then I saw someone waving from inside and realized it was Sara in her VW bug. She parked in front of the Glenns' house and climbed out. "I was hoping I'd catch you," she said. "I forgot to get your phone number and when I tried one from the phone book, it was disconnected." She glanced up at the Glenns' house. "Nice place, Cass."

I suddenly realized that she really didn't know anything about me and was just assuming that this was where I lived with my family. So I leaned the rake against the tree and sighed. "This isn't really my house, Sara, I just live here and do housework for them." I couldn't bring myself to use the term *foster home* since it hardly seemed a fitting description of the arrangement we had going on here.

"Oh." She looked slightly puzzled. "Well anyway, I came by to see if you want to join us tonight—for what we call a rap session."

"What's that?"

"Oh, just a bunch of us that get together and talk about Jesus and God and spiritual things and stuff. It's not related to any church or anything. And it's pretty laid-back. We all bring pop and chips and stuff, and then we sit around on the floor and just rap together for as long as we want. It's at my house tonight. Want to come?"

I shrugged. "I don't have a car. Do you live very far from here?"

"I'm only about six blocks away. But I can pick you up if you want."

"That's okay. I'm used to walking pretty much everywhere." So she gave me her address and phone number and I promised her I'd come.

"So are you doing okay, then?" she asked me, concern showing in her blue eyes. "I mean, now that you've got Jesus in your heart, are things going okay for you? You seem a little down."

I shrugged again. "Well, it hasn't been exactly easy. Jim and I are broken up now—well, at least I think we are. I haven't actually seen him in a couple days."

"That's probably for the best, Cass. Especially since he was pushing you, you know. Now you can just get all that much closer to Jesus." She smiled brightly, reminding me of an ad for toothpaste—the Colgate girl.

But I sensed despite the perky smile she was sincere. "Yeah, I was kinda thinking the same thing," I tried to sound more positive, "and I even wrote a song about Jesus, and I can play it on my guitar and . . ." I looked down at the leaf-covered ground, suddenly wondering why I was going on like this, telling her all about the song that was so personal to me.

"Cool," she said. "Maybe you can share your song with the group tonight."

"Oh no, I don't think—"

"Oh, come on, Cass, you're not supposed to keep your light under a bushel basket, you know. And it'd be really neat if you sang—everyone would love it. We always sing songs in the beginning. Some kids bring their guitars and we really get down sometimes." She tugged on my arm. "Now listen, I want you to bring your guitar and your Bible—you do have a Bible, don't you?"

I nodded dumbly.

"Okay, then, it's settled. And on second thought I think I should swing by and pick you up. No sense in you walking and lugging your guitar six blocks when it's supposed to rain again tonight. I'll come by around six-thirty."

I explained to her about the Glenns and my "no visitors" rule, then showed her my back entrance where she could knock on the door.

"Cool!" Then she turned and waved. "See ya then!"

I finished raking the mushy leaves and returned to my room, where I practiced my little song again and again, worried that I'd make a complete fool of myself in front of this group of Jesus freaks. Why I was so worried about impressing these kids that I had only six months ago completely put down and disdained was a pure mystery to me. But for some reason it mattered now.

Sara picked me up as promised. "Now let me warn you, my parents aren't exactly saved. I know that probably seems weird since I'm having this thing at my house, but I figure the influence will be good for them. But I just want you to know that they smoke and drink and cuss and stuff—and so if you think you're coming to some goody-goody churchy home, then you'd better be fore-warned."

This actually made me laugh. "Well, I doubt there's anything your family could possibly do that would shock me. I've pretty much seen it all. My dad was well-known as the town drunk and now he's in prison—or maybe he's out by now. But it was his second time, so I don't know."

"Wow, what did he do?" She actually seemed impressed.

"He beat me up while he was under the influence."

She glanced over at me as she pulled into the driveway. "Man, I knew your family had some problems, Cass, but I didn't realize it was anything like that. That sounds pretty exciting."

"Exciting?" I felt my brows arch. "It's pretty gross, if you ask me."

"Well, I know. But it's just not your everyday small-town story."

"I guess 'everyday' people should be thankful for that."

I had to admit the rap session was pretty cool. I couldn't believe how warm and friendly and genuine the kids seemed—it's like I suddenly had this huge group of friends who accepted me just as I was. I didn't even mind playing my song for them, and everyone said they really liked it.

It was so strange—kids from all walks of life were gathered in this one place and yet there was this unity. I knew that only Jesus could do that. And for the first time ever, I think I felt almost completely at home. It was amazing.

A guy who'd graduated a couple years ago and was now taking a correspondence Bible course was obviously leading the group. His name was Scott Jones but his friends all called him Sky. (Sara said it was because his eyes were sky blue, but Joe Allen, a guy with a witty sense of humor, jokingly said it was because he was such an airhead.) Anyway, Sky directed the group during the discussion and his deep spiritual beliefs and religious convictions became increasingly apparent to me. You could just tell that Sky really wanted to serve God.

I stayed late to help Sara clean up and asked her about Sky and how he'd come to be such a strong Christian. "Oh, you and Sky have some things in common," she said as she placed a tumbler in the dishwasher. "His dad's an alcoholic too, and there's been a lot of violence in his home."

"Does he still live at home?"

"No. He's got a place of his own—a dumpy little trailer over by the railroad tracks. But he says he'd rather be there than living in his parents' home where they fight all the time."

"Yeah, I can understand that."

"Well, I should warn you that half the girls in the group think they're in love with Sky." She laughed. "I try not to be one of them—although he is awfully good-looking, don't you think?"

I shrugged, unwilling to commit myself one way or the other. "So do any of the kids in the group date each other?"

"Yeah. Mitch and Cindy have been going out for a while now. And there's a few others too. Sky says he doesn't want to date anyone because it might get in the way of his taking care of all of us."

"So does he see himself as being kind of like a pastor or something?"

Sara nodded as she closed the dishwasher. "Yeah, he's sort of like our shepherd, I guess. We're not exactly a church of course, and some of the kids do go to churches with their families and stuff. But some of us think of this group as our church. And Sky says that's how churches first got started back in the early Christian days. Kind of cool, huh?"

I nodded. "Yeah. It seems more real than those churches where you go and sit in pews and read prayers from books and stuff like that."

"So you want to keep coming?"

"Sure."

"We meet on Wednesday and Sunday nights. And it looks like we'll be meeting at my place for a while. Cindy's folks said she can't have it there until her grades improve."

And so I guess that's how I became a Jesus freak. A boy broke my heart and Jesus fixed it.

It's funny to think of now, but Jim and I never really "officially" broke up. Maybe it's because we never really "officially" went together. The next conversation I had with him was the following Monday, when I told him I knew about this thing with Sally Roberts. He seemed somewhat apologetic and said he'd been talked into escorting her. But I told him it didn't matter anyway since I'd given my heart to Jesus and was now an "official" Jesus freak.

"You kidding me, Cass?" He looked at me as if he actually thought I was pulling a fast one and he was all ready to crack up laughing.

I shook my head firmly. "Nope, I'm serious. This is for real, Jim. And it's just what I needed in my life."

He blinked. "You're really serious?"

"Yep. And if you ever want to know more about giving your heart to Jesus, just feel free to ask." I forced a bright smile to my lips (because the truth was, I still hurt a little inside, especially when standing face-to-face with him like that). "I'd still like to be your friend, Jim, but my heart belongs to Jesus now."

"Well, okay, then." He stepped away from me as if I might have some contagious disease and then he nodded and just kept walking. I felt like someone had punched me and yet I simultaneously felt something like a martyr too—like I'd given up something important just so I could serve Jesus.

Never mind that Jim had already sidestepped me to escort snooty Sally Roberts at Homecoming, which I later heard she won although I didn't attend that football game—or any others for that matter. Suddenly football games not only seemed "carnal" (a new word I learned from Sky the following Wednesday) but silly as well. *Carnal* meant something was opposed to the ways of Jesus. It was like sin or something. And it seemed according to Sky that most things in life were fairly carnal.

But for some reason I didn't mind hearing this news. In fact I think I was eager to embrace this sort of teaching. In a weird way it was a relief for me to find out that so many things were wrong and bad and sinful and "worldly" (another word Sky liked to use that meant the same thing as *carnal*).

Somehow all these classifications made it easier for me to make choices because everything was either right or wrong, black or white—clear-cut and straightforward. It's almost as if I no longer needed to think for myself. And the truth was, my troubled mind had already been abused and exhausted with all the thinking I'd been doing and I felt more than ready to give my brain a little break . . . or as it turned out a rather long one.

So for week after week I did little more than school, homework, chores, and then rap session and Bible study. (Wednesday was called Bible study, although it seemed we listened more to Sky than to the Bible. And Sunday was rap, where Sky would lead us in group discussions.) When I wasn't busy with these activities I was either scouring my Bible (which I began to mark and underline like I'd seen Sky do) or making up new songs on my guitar.

To my amazement I soon became something of a leader myself in our little group. It seemed my musical abilities were a little more accomplished than the others and Sky started calling me his "right-hand girl" when it came to leading our worship time. And I must admit that I greatly enjoyed his attention although at the same time I constantly repented of my "carnal" nature lest I enjoy his favor a little too much.

It was during those weeks that I began to come down hard on myself for every little thing I did that seemed wrong (which seemed to be mostly everything). I would get down on my knees before Jesus in the privacy of my little windowless abode and beg and plead for his forgiveness, and after that I might even deprive myself of things like food or my guitar as a form of penance.

Sky talked about penance a lot. It was a way for us to show God how sorry we were when we blew it (which seemed to be most of the time in my case). I had problems using the "bad words" I'd picked up during junior high with Bryn. And I sometimes told lies, mostly to the Glenns. And my thoughts were just always running away to some carnal place. It just seemed I could never get myself to be quite good enough to really please Jesus. But it was a good challenge for me and I never wanted to give up trying.

Just before Christmas our little group decided to launch an all-out campaign to spread the good news about Jesus to our entire town. We devised a plan where we would go door-to-door in pairs and tell every single living soul in Brookdale about Jesus and how he wanted them to repent of their sins and to understand the true meaning of Christmas.

Sara and I were partners, and with less than two weeks before Christmas we began to work out "our district's plan for salvation." Sky had warned us, quoting from the Bible how many would ridicule us for our faith but that we were to simply shake the dirt from our shoes and continue on to the next house when this happened.

I suppose in a way this ridicule and rejection was something of its own reward (for it proved to us that Sky once again was exactly right-on). But to my surprise there were actually some people who welcomed us into their homes and they actually listened to our little speech, and some even asked us what church we attended. When we said "none" there were some who appeared slightly taken aback and concerned.

"You girls don't attend a church?" said a sweet old lady with blue-tinted hair. I must confess I liked her. She had soft, powdery-looking cheeks and a cozy old-fashioned home with crocheted doilies on every armrest. And her homemade snickerdoodle cookies just melted in my mouth. I liked her so well that I briefly imagined "adopting" her as a surrogate grandmother and I'll bet she'd have been willing. But of course I did not.

"Well, we don't go to a regular church," explained Sara. "But we all meet together to pray and stuff—just like a church, only better."

The woman frowned. "But you girls need to be in a real church too, with a real pastor who's trained to preach God's Word and to watch over you."

Sara and I smiled knowingly. How uninformed and stodgy some of these elderly folks could be. But we were polite and tried to humor the old woman.

"We have a nice youth group leader at our church." She tried again as we walked toward the door.

"Now don't you worry about us," I assured her. "We meet at least twice a week with our brothers and sisters and we're more devoted to Jesus than most people who go to regular churches. Thanks for the cookies, ma'am."

Still she seemed unconvinced and kindly invited us to come to her church for the Christmas service. "We have candles and a living Nativity scene and the choir's been practicing for weeks."

Once again we declined and she said she would be praying for our spiritual well-being. We thought this highly amusing since it seemed perfectly clear to us that we were living far more spiritual lives than she and most likely everyone else in her fuddy-duddy little church, but we thanked her anyway.

We met several more like her, but for the most part people just turned us away, and then we would dramatically stand on their walk and pretend to be shaking the dirt from our shoes before we walked on to the next house, usually even laughing as we went. But the most amazing thing was when we actually came across some poor soul who had never heard the news that Jesus could forgive sins, and like ripe fruit just waiting to be picked they listened to every word and then even allowed us to pray with them. The only slightly frustrating thing at this point was if they asked us what they should do next. Like one particular woman with young children who seemed to be trapped in a horrible marriage.

"You girls are a real godsend to me," she said after we finished praying. "But what should I do now? My husband is a real mess and my mama keeps telling me to leave him and come live with her. But I've got these little kids, and I don't know. . . . I think I just need someone who is wise about these things—someone I can talk to." Her eyes lit up. "Can you give me the name of your church—so that maybe I could call up someone there? A pastor or something?"

So once again we explained our situation to her but then we didn't really know quite what to say. We took down her phone number and told her we'd ask our leader to give her a call. But I'm sure he never did. We were all pretty overwhelmed with our "reaching the town" mission just then and the most important thing seemed to be hitting every household with our gospel message. What came after that? Well, no one really seemed to know.

As we tramped from house to house Sara informed me that Joey Divers had come home from college for Christmas vacation and I asked her why he hadn't come to any of our meetings or joined us in our citywide crusade.

"I invited him to come," she said as we walked away from another unbelieving doorstep, pausing to shake the pretend dust from our feet, "but he didn't want to."

"Oh dear," I said. "Do you think Joey has fallen away from Jesus?" I felt proud to be using all this new terminology—phrases like *falling away* or *getting saved* or *washed in the blood*—it was all like a brand-new language to me but I took to it like a duck to water as my grandma might say.

"You know, I was thinking the same thing, so I asked Joey about his spiritual condition. He assured me he was doing just great."

"Well, what's his problem, then?" I asked, feeling mildly irritated.

"I think he's jealous of Sky."

I stopped walking and turned to her. "Jealous of Sky?"

She nodded, her lips pressed together as if she'd just used a bad cussword (one of the last bad habits of my flesh that still gave me trouble from time to time).

"But that's awful," I said quietly. "Jealousy is a sin, isn't it?"

She nodded again. "We'll have to be praying especially hard for poor Joey."

"That's for sure," I agreed as she knocked on yet another door.

Our mission continued right up until Christmas Eve day, and all during that time I never once saw or spoke to Joey Divers. I felt just slightly bad, though, because even if he was committing a grievous sin by being jealous of his brother and our spiritual leader, Sky, I still felt a childish loyalty toward my old friend Joey. I must admit I struggled with it some, fearing it might actually be a part of my "old sinful nature" trying to veer my spiritual allegiance away from Sky. And so as a result I made no attempt to see Joey during that time. Somehow I felt it would be wrong—sinful, even.

chapter thirteen

THEY SAY A PROPHET is never accepted in his own hometown and I suppose that was the case with us and with Sky.

Shortly after Christmas (after the completion of our crusade) the local newspaper ran a mean-spirited article about our group's "insensitive and somewhat crazed evangelistic efforts" and how we Jesus freaks had "literally assaulted the entire town" with our fanatical beliefs. The editor even accused us of being a cult! Not that I knew exactly what that meant, but it surely didn't sound good to me.

Sky was extremely upset and affronted by these wild accusations. He actually seemed quite depressed as he held a somber meeting just after Christmas. He carefully explained to us that this was a sign of the times and we were being persecuted for our religious beliefs, and then he read aloud a strong rebuttal letter that he'd written and sent to the paper, although he said he doubted that they'd dare to print it. But to everyone's surprise it appeared in the paper the morning before New Year's Day. And on that same day I just happened to be in town picking up some last-minute groceries for Mrs. Glenn when I ran into Joey Divers in the produce section.

I noticed him over by the orange bin before he saw me. His cane had caught my attention. (He'd exchanged his metal crutch for a sturdy wooden cane during his last years in high school. I suspected it was a little less dependable but it probably made him feel better. And if you didn't look too closely at him you might not even notice the shiny metal of his leg brace beneath the neat hem of his pants.) All in all Joey looked good—and surprisingly collegiate—in his dark gray sweater and tan cord pants. He'd replaced his heavy black-rimmed glasses for smaller wire-rims and had allowed his hair to grow some. It now fell in dark waves just above his collar line.

He saw me as he turned around to set a bag of oranges in the cart. "Cass!" he exclaimed. His face broke into a huge smile, and for the first time in my life I felt that Joey Divers was actually quite handsome (funny I'd never noticed before, or perhaps it was something college had brought out in him). Those unexpected feelings caught me off guard and I felt my cheeks blush as I realized I would surely need to kneel and confess the sins of my carnal flesh in order to become clean again.

"Hey, Joey," I said soberly, hoping my eyes wouldn't betray me.

"It's so great to see you!" He walked over to me and looked as if he was about to hug me—although we'd never hugged before, or at least not since we were quite small. But then he hesitated (probably due to my dour expression) and extended his hand. A confusing mixture of disappointment and relief washed over me as I took his hand, enjoying the strength and warmth for a long moment but knowing I'd have to repent of this as well later. What was wrong with me?

"How're you doing, Joey?" I tried not to look into his eyes.

"Great. College is great." He released my hand, then reached out and put his hand on my shoulder, leaving it there for just a moment. I knew it was meant to be a gesture of kindness. "How's it going with you, Cass?"

"It's going really good," I finally said, stepping back just far enough to cause his hand to fall away from my shoulder. Then I looked down at the bunch of bananas hanging limply in my hand. "I got saved, you know." I looked up at him then, waiting for some sign of approval—approval was critical to me in those days, almost an addiction I suppose.

"Yeah, Sara told me all about it in a letter last fall. That's so cool, Cass. I'm really happy for you. I pray for you all the time."

I frowned. "You do?" Did he think I was some sort of troubled case to be in need of his prayers? And then I remembered how I'd told Sara we should pray for him—for his jealousy problem with Sky. "Well, we're praying for you too, Joey."

He smiled again. "Thanks, I appreciate it."

"We've been doing this citywide outreach thing," I said as I placed my bananas in the cart. "It's really been great."

His brow creased slightly. "Yeah, I've been reading about it in the paper."

"Well, don't believe everything you read," I warned him. "You know how newspapers are all so worldly and carnal. They twist everything around to make us look bad just because we're trying to serve Jesus."

He didn't say anything for a moment, just pressed his lips together as if he was thinking hard about something. "You know, I think it's cool you're trying to serve Jesus, Cass. I really do. . . ." He paused again, as if judiciously considering each word. "But I just want you to be careful."

"Careful?" I eyed him with suspicion. Who was he to tell me to be careful?

"Yeah. I know how Sky seems like this really great guy and all. And I know he really seems to love Jesus too. But there's just something about him that I think you should watch out for—"

"Joey Divers!" I pointed my finger at him. "I can't believe that you of all people would talk like—"

"But, Cass—"

I firmly shook my head. "Now listen, Joey. I don't want to hear you slandering your brother in front of me."

"But you need to be careful—"

"Joey," I said warningly, "I'm getting seriously worried about you. I don't like the way you're talking about Sky. It's unchristian-like."

He held up his hands in surrender. "Okay, Cass. Just one thing, though."

"Yeah?" Suspicion laced all through my voice.

"Just make sure you're reading the Bible for yourself and don't let anyone else do your thinking for you."

I frowned. "Joey, since when have I ever let anyone think for me?" I thought about Sky but then reminded myself, *That's different.*

He shrugged. "I don't know, Cass. But just promise me you won't. Okay?"

I nodded. "Except when it comes to Jesus. We're supposed to let him rule in us, you know. His mind is supposed to be like our mind."

"Yeah, well, just make sure you're hearing from Jesus then, Cass."

I wanted to remind him that Jesus sometimes talks to us through others but instead I just said, "Sure."

"Well, I've got to get back," he said. "My mom's been under the weather lately and she was craving some fresh-squeezed orange juice this morning."

"Give her my regards." I looked at him for a long moment, suddenly wishing things were different, that I had spoken to him in the old familiar way. But it was too late. I had changed—was changing. "And you take care now, Joey."

"You too, Cass. And be careful."

As I walked home I felt a little sorry for Joey that he couldn't see what a great thing God had brought into my life. But looking back now, maybe I was just too afraid to think about what Joey was implying. Besides, I had other things to think about just then.

I quietly put the groceries away back at the Glenns' hoping to avoid any direct conversation with Mrs. Glenn. I'd been trying to lie low, hoping to appear more helpful and available around the house since I knew she was none too pleased with how much of my time and energy had been taken up with what they both now called my "Jesus freak group" during the holidays, especially since they'd done a little entertaining and had found themselves slightly "shorthanded" one evening last week. (In my opinion their form of entertaining was extremely wicked and carnal and quite honestly disturbing to my spirit). And naturally the more enlightened and spiritual I became the less and less I felt inclined to cater to their worldly and sinful ways, not to mention that of their friends! I'd performed my regular chores and, when it was required, some of the prep work for their parties as well. But afterwards I'd always just clear out, not showing my face until the next day when it was time to clean it all up again.

Tonight was their big New Year's Eve bash and Mrs. Glenn had informed me early on that she wanted me to stick around for much of the evening. "I don't want you slipping off to your room tonight, Cassandra," she warned me.

"I have a prayer meeting—"

"I don't care. I need you on hand in the kitchen. At least until ten—you got that?"

I nodded, knowing that any argument would only work against me. And I suppose I felt somewhat unwilling to rock the boat since I knew that this week would be my "payday," and the amount they paid me was somewhat unpredictable and quite frequently based on the way they felt I'd "performed" in the days just prior to when the CSD check arrived in the mail.

Initially Mrs. Glenn had balked at her husband's idea to "pay" me but finally she agreed. Although she insisted they shouldn't just hand over the entire check, and as a result the amount varied each month. But still it was better than nothing.

I'd managed to accumulate a nice little nest egg in my savings account and at this rate I thought my chances of going to the university had improved greatly (plus I'd been keeping my grades up at school and even had hopes of scholarships). So in some ways my future was looking brighter than ever.

All this I felt was thanks to the way Jesus was taking care of me now. As Sky would say, "His hand was upon my life and he was taking my ashes and turning them into beauty!" And so I cheerfully promised Mrs. Glenn that I would remain "on hand" until ten o'clock—at which time I planned to run on down to Sara's, where my friends would be in the middle of an all-night prayer vigil for the city of Brookdale.

I was stuffing celery with Cheez Whiz around nine o'clock when I first noticed the sickening sweet aroma of marijuana mixing with the acrid cigarette smoke that had already filled the air. I rolled my eyes in disgust as I continued filling the celery sticks with the bright yellow spread and sincerely prayed that Jesus would just make them all sick to death of their nasty and sinful ways.

The blaring music out in the living room was so loud my head actually throbbed and as usual the house was filled with rowdy guests who acted more like teenagers than teenagers (at least the ones I currently ran with). I felt like a can that said Contents under Pressure, and the pressure seemed to be increasing by the moment. Still I just bit my lip and continued to pray—Jesus could get me through this. But when I noticed a guy huddled over the counter in a corner of the kitchen with a suspicious little pile of white powder, I knew I'd had enough.

"You know that garbage is going to take you straight to hell," I said loud enough to be heard over the din of music as I banged the enameled plate of stuffed celery right next to him and shook my head in obvious disapproval.

He glanced up with a dark scowl, then slowly broke into a crooked smile. I'd guess he was pushing forty but like so many of the Glenns' friends was trying to act younger. His hair was below his ears but slightly thinning on top and he wore a burnt orange turtleneck and bell-bottom jeans as if he thought he was still in college. Without blinking an eye he carefully scooped his powder back onto the piece of waxed paper, folded it, then slipped it into his pants pocket. "I thought you kids liked getting high," he said, moving closer so I could hear him better.

"Maybe some kids." I turned from him to rinse my hands in the sink. "But not me. I'd rather get high on Jesus." I dried my hands, then leaned against the counter, folding my arms and looking at him evenly, waiting for his reaction.

"You one of those Jesus freaks I been reading 'bout in the paper?"

I forced a smile and stuck out my hand. "Yes I am, as a matter of fact. The name's Cass, and my heart belongs to Jesus." This was the line I'd used on our recent door-to-door campaign.

He grinned and shook my hand. "My name's George, and I'd like to hear more about this, Cass." He moved closer and I could smell alcohol on his breath. A little alarm went off inside me as I was suddenly reminded of my own daddy and I felt sorely tempted to just pull back and run the other away. But then I sternly reminded myself that this poor excuse of a man was just another sinner in need of hearing the good news about Jesus and how to be saved.

"Really?" I poured potato chips into a big wooden bowl, then wadded up the bag and tossed it into the garbage.

"Yeah, I think this sounds real interesting."

Suddenly I envisioned myself leading a repentant and kneeling George in the sinner's prayer right there on the Glenns' fake brick linoleum kitchen floor. I could just imagine Sky's smiling approval as I told him and the others about the amazing conquest I'd made on New Year's Eve. "Now you're sure about this?" I asked him, remembering Sky's words about not casting our pearls before swine—a warning he gave us about trying to talk to people who weren't inclined to really listen to our views.

"Yeah, tell me more." He leaned forward with what I felt was sincere interest and without hesitation I launched myself right into God's plan for salvation. I kept one eye on the kitchen clock as I paced myself in telling the gospel message—so as not to be overly late for tonight's prayer vigil. I wound it all up at just a quarter till ten. "And so you see, that's about all there is to it," I said with a satisfied, maybe even smug, smile.

"That simple, huh?"

I nodded, then glanced at the clock. Not wanting to show up at the prayer meeting smelling like French onion dip, I still hoped to take time to scrub off the effects of playing scullery maid all evening. "The rest is up to you, George—'cause you're the only one who can choose which way you'll go." Then despite my hurry to be done and out of there, I forced myself to wait one more full minute, just in case he wanted me to pray with him or something.

"Well, thank you for telling me all that," he said, his face just inches from mine. "It's been right interesting."

"Okay, then if you'll excuse me I've got to get ready for a prayer meeting we're having tonight."

He chuckled. "You goin' to go pray for us sinners, are you?"

"You bet we will." I nodded with spiritual pride and confidence, then waved as I ducked down the stairs to my quarters below. In the last month or so I'd actually grown to appreciate my little windowless dungeon and in some ways it had become something of a sanctuary from all the noise and din above, although I could still hear the loud beat of the bass thumping from the eight-track stereo system just above the ceiling of my bedroom. Just the same it was relatively quiet and peaceful down there, and I sang happily to myself as I quickly showered, a feeling of spiritual pride rising in me as I mentally replayed the words of truth that I'd so boldly shared with that poor sinner George upstairs. It would be fun to tell the group tonight—maybe we'd even say some special prayers for George's salvation.

But when I came out of the steamy bathroom and turned the corner to enter my bedroom there was George, sitting as bold as you please right there on my little twin bed, a big Cheshire cat grin playing across his pudgy face almost as if he thought I might've actually been expecting him.

I felt my heart slam like a rock against the inside of my chest, but I tried to remain calm as I pulled my skimpy pink towel more tightly around my body. "Please leave!" I said in what I hoped was a persuasive tone, although I could hear my voice trembling like a little girl about to cry.

"Aw, now don't you be sending me away so soon, angel girl," he said. "I just wanted for us to do some more talking about all this God and Jesus stuff." He patted the bed beside him. "Come on over here and tell me more."

"Not now!" I spoke loudly and with more strength, moving

slowly back toward the bathroom where I knew there was a lock on the door.

But just as I turned to run he leaped up and grabbed me by the arm. I screamed as he pulled me toward him.

"Dear Jesus!" I cried, the words no more than a hoarse whisper, "Dear Jesus, dear Jesus, save me! Send your angels to protect me!"

What actually happened directly after that prayer is little more than a fuzzy blur in my memory, but this is what I think may have happened. I suspect that when George heard me utter that prayer, something in him suddenly lost interest in the horrible sinful act he was about to commit against me. And after a few unimaginable, horrifying, and humiliating seconds, he released his death hold on my neck, backhanded me across the face, and shoved me away. As I tumbled to the floor I grabbed the blanket for cover, and clutching it toward me, cowered in the corner until he finally stumbled back up the stairs, cursing all the way, slamming the door behind him. Still in a shocked state of horror and disbelief I whipped on my jeans and sweater and without any shoes dashed out my back door and across the frozen lawn and then ran and ran until I reached Sara's house. I pounded on her door, crying and screaming hysterically, until she finally came and opened it up. I then collapsed in her arms, sobbing uncontrollably.

I don't remember telling Sara exactly what happened, although I must have. By then I felt so exhausted and confused and hurt and humiliated it was hard to think straight. And to be perfectly honest I suppose I even wondered if I might not have brought the whole atrocious thing upon myself. Was it something I'd said? The type of clothing I had on? Perhaps in some way I'd enticed that horrible nasty man down into my room and I didn't even know it. I kept those troubling thoughts to myself—between me and God.

The next thing I knew Sara had taken me up to her bedroom, wrapped me up in a warm, fuzzy blanket, and gone to get help. I wasn't exactly sure what kind of help she meant to fetch. The police? Her parents? What? And I remember sitting there shaking uncontrollably and just wanting the whole dreadful business to go far, far away—to be completely gone. Or maybe I could just disappear instead.

"Oh, Jesus," I prayed, "can't you *pleeease* just come and get me right now—just take me home?" But to my dismay, before Jesus removed me from the planet, Sara returned.

I was relieved to see she'd brought neither her parents nor the police. (Apparently her parents were out partying at the Elks Lodge and it never even occurred to her to call the police.) Instead she had Sky in tow, which in its way was humiliating enough.

He sat down next to me on Sara's fluffy pink bed (the kind I used to fantasize about having) and looked into my eyes. "Are you okay, Cass?"

His words felt like a sword that just cut right through to my soul, and I felt tears of shame filling my eyes. And I was too embarrassed to return his gaze. Had Sara told him of the humiliation that had befallen me? And if so, what would he think of me now? Did he know that I had just minutes ago been struggling with a man who'd been intent upon having sex with me? (It's strange to think of this now, but the word *rape* never even entered my mind just then.) All I cared about at that moment was: What did Sky think of me? Did he think I was a horrible sinner?

"Cass," he said again, only this time he lifted my chin with his hand and forced me to look into his clear blue eyes, "are you okay?"

Tears were spilling down my cheeks now and my chin trembled as I shook my head. But still no words would come.

"Sara says that someone tried to hurt you."

I nodded my head vigorously.

"She said a man tried to take advantage of you in your bed-room. Is that right?"

I could feel my face twisting with emotion as I nodded again.

Sky's brows drew together and he exhaled loudly. "Poor Cass."

Those two sympathetic words just made me crumble and I began to sob all over again. "I don't know what to do," I cried. "I don't know what to do."

Sara was sitting behind me now, stroking my hair and telling me not to worry and that Jesus was going to make everything okay. Sky was still frowning. It honestly seemed that he was as troubled by all this as I was, and that was somewhat comforting.

Finally he spoke. "Cass, did this man force you to fornicate with him?"

Now I wasn't entirely sure what that word meant, but I strongly suspected it had to do with sex. And as far as I knew I didn't think I'd actually "had sex." Still I wasn't totally sure about this word. "I—I don't know for certain what you mean," I said. "But if you mean am I still a virgin—well, yes, I think so."

Sky let out a sigh of relief, but Sara said, "You're kidding, Cass, you're still a virgin?" I looked at her from the corner of my eye and nodded stupidly. Then she laughed, sort of nervously, like she wished she hadn't said that.

"Still, what that man did was wrong and sinful," said Sky in a stern voice. "Do you want us to pray for you, Cass?"

I wasn't exactly sure why he wanted to pray for me (I mean it seemed they should be praying for that awful sinner George) but I just nodded and sat there in silence as the two of them "covered me in prayer." And the fact is, I truly did feel better when they finished and even said a hearty "amen" myself.

It did seem like Jesus was healing me and making me clean

again, just like Sky had asked him to. Now I wasn't exactly sure about the how or the why of it, but I did feel something positive happening inside. And I began to feel hopeful that what had happened to me that night (as horrible as it seemed) might not, after all, turn out to be the end of the world as I knew it.

But then I'd been wrong about these sorts of things before.

chapter fourteen

SARA AND SKY AGREED THAT I should not return to that "den of iniquity" (the Glenns' New Year's Eve party). Sky decided I would spend the night at Sara's following our prayer session.

About a dozen of us were there that evening (only the most devout) and we piously hit our knees and bowed our heads (while others in town drank, danced, and exploded fireworks). Our plan: to pray for the city of Brookdale until well after midnight and into New Year's Day. As much as I wanted to participate in this important vigil I shamed myself by drifting off right there, facedown on the Hansons' avocado green shag carpeting.

I realize now that my unfortunate experience back at the Glenns' had probably drained what little strength and energy I'd had left, but when I awoke the following morning to find the sun already up, I felt like a miserable failure in the area of prayerful petitioning and I silently repented and begged God to forgive me.

The other kids were all gone by then and Sara said we should probably tiptoe on up to her room and keep quiet because her parents had come home somewhat plastered last night, and apparently her dad hadn't been terribly pleased to see their family room filled "with a bunch of praying fanatics" as he'd loudly called them, and she expected her dad might be slightly disagreeable if not fairly well hungover by the time he got up. And so she and I just crashed on her bed and slept much of the day away.

Sara was right about her dad. He was in a foul mood that day and he seemed to have his sights set on our little fellowship group. "What's this nonsense I've been reading about in the paper?" he demanded when he discovered us making sandwiches in the kitchen. He waved the newspaper in her face. Apparently it contained an editorial rebuttal to Sky's letter on the previous day. "It sounds like you kids are nothing but a flaming bunch of lunatics. Just how far do you plan on taking this crazy Jesus freak business anyway? Next thing I know you'll be off joining some group of holy rollers and speaking in strange languages."

"Oh, Dad!"

"Don't you 'oh, Dad' me, young lady," he snapped right back at her. "I don't like the way you and your little Jesus freak friends are turning into such raving fanatics. I think that editor's hit the nail on the head. You kids probably are starting a cult!"

"*Dad!*"

"You better keep still and listen to me, missy!" He shook his finger under her nose. "All this religion nonsense isn't healthy. Good night, Sara Louise, it wasn't all that long ago that you were barreling down the road into some other kind of serious trouble." He glanced at me as if he were concealing some deep, dark secret, although I already knew all about Sara's speckled past. "And now here you are, going off half-cocked and head over heels into this crazy religious crud. Why, I think you'd fall for just about anything that came down the—"

"No!" I could hear the hurt in her voice. "This is *real*, Daddy!"

"Oh, and how in tarnation do you know what's real and what isn't? For pete's sake, Sara, you're just a kid."

"Jesus said we should all have faith like little children," she retorted. "And it sure wouldn't hurt you any to—"

"Yeah, and that's the other thing that really steams me. I swear, every time I turn around I find you looking down your nose at me and your mother. As if you suddenly think you've turned into Saint Sara or something."

"Well, Daddy," she said quietly but firmly, "it's not as if you guys are exactly living a great life."

"Don't you go telling me how to live, missy!" He shook his fist at her and I cringed. "Don't you go forgetting that I'm the one that works all week long just to pay for the food you and your Jesus freak friends are always shoving in your face. I'm the one putting a hanged roof over your head. If you think I'm such a big ol' sinner then why don't you just try getting by without me?"

She slapped her sandwich down on the counter. "Fine, Daddy, if that's the way you want it, I will!"

He laughed. "Yeah, let's just see how long you can make it on your own out there—you think this Jesus of yours is going to feed and clothe you and put gas in your car?"

"Yes, as a matter of fact, I do!"

I set down my sandwich too, then backed away, wishing I could just disappear into the bright-colored poppy wallpaper that decorated their kitchen wall. Their argument had completely diminished what little appetite I'd had. I mutely followed Sara up to her bedroom, where she began throwing clothes into a large suitcase.

"What are you doing, Sara?" I asked with wide eyes.

"I'll show him," she said. "I'm almost eighteen. I can make it on my own."

I blinked. "Really? You really think so?"

"Sure. Why not?"

I watched as she haphazardly threw a few things into her bag.

I suspected though (by the way she was packing) she wasn't really serious about leaving. After all, I knew what it meant to pack your bags to really leave—you have to do it more carefully than that. But I kept these thoughts to myself and in just minutes she was finished and I followed her downstairs, wondering exactly where it was she planned to go.

I knew she sure couldn't stay with me. In fact I wasn't overly eager to go back to the Glenns' myself. For one thing I knew there'd be a huge mess to clean up. And then I wondered if I should inform the Glenns of their creepy friend George's advances toward me last night. Although to be honest that whole episode seemed a little like a foggy dream by then and I could almost convince myself that it had never happened at all. Anyway, that's what I wanted to believe. And it's funny to think that's exactly what we do sometimes— believe what we want.

"Where are you going?" Sara's mother called. She stood by the front door, shaking her head with a firm mouth, as we reached the bottom of the stairs.

"Daddy wants me to move out," said Sara in a wounded voice.

"Oh, of course he doesn't."

"Yes he does. He said that I'm a religious fanatic and that I should go live on my own." She sniffed. "And I'm almost eighteen. So I'm going now."

"Oh, don't be ridiculous, Sara. Your father's just upset because all of those cars were blocking his driveway last night and he couldn't even get our car into the garage and then . . . well . . . you know how he gets after an evening of—" she glanced over at me with curiosity—"well, you know what happens when he—uh, over-indulges. He's always a little cranky the next day, but you know it'll blow over before long and then he'll apologize to you about the whole crazy thing."

"But he's putting down my beliefs." Sara's lower lip protruded slightly.

"Now you know how he can be about religion." Her mother shook her head, then reached for her purse. "Just go put that silly suitcase away, dear. Here, I'll give you a few bucks, and you and your friend—uh, what's your name, dear?"

"That's Cass, Mom. You've met her a dozen times."

"Oh yes, Cass. Anyway, maybe you two can go take in a movie or something."

Sara took the money, then scowled. "Mom, I already told you we think all movies are a sinful waste of both time and money."

Her mother laughed. "Oh well, whatever. You girls just go and have you some fun and let your poor father get some rest."

And so Sara left her bag sitting next to the stairway and we headed out to her car. "Do you want me to take you home?" she asked after starting the engine.

I just shrugged. "I don't know. I'm trying to decide if I should tell the Glenns about what happened last—"

"That's right!" She smacked herself in the forehead. "I almost forgot all about that stupid jerk friend of theirs trying to force you to—" She made a face then groaned. "Oh, Cass, it's too gross to even think about! How're you doing, by the way?"

"Okay I guess. But I still feel kind of creepy about the whole thing. And kind of confused too. I mean, I know Jesus is healing my heart and everything but I wonder what I should do about it. Or maybe I shouldn't do anything. I just don't know."

And then to my embarrassment I started to cry again. Not that loud sobbing like last night but just silent tears running down my face. I looked down at my lap. "I just feel so—so stupid."

"Let's go talk to Sky," she said suddenly, throwing her car into gear. "He'll know what to do."

I'd never been to Sky's place before but I felt curious to see where our saintly leader actually lived. As it turned out it was rather disappointing. Just a trashed-out little trailer parked next to the railroad tracks.

"Sky told me he's taken a vow of poverty," explained Sara as she parked next to an overflowing trash can. "And he thinks all worldly possessions are sinful."

"Wow," I said, unsure as to whether I was impressed or just surprised.

Sara knocked on the thin metal door and after about a minute Sky opened it. He looked rumpled and sleepy—and to my dismay, not terribly spiritual. "Huh?" he said. "What're you two doing here?"

"We need some advice," said Sara, taking the lead as usual. "Can we come in, Sky?"

He frowned slightly, then opened the door wider. "Sure, come on in. Welcome to my humble abode."

I tried not to stare at his stark, yet somewhat messy, habitat. I found it incongruous that this "together" spiritual leader lived in what appeared to be such a chaotic and shabby dwelling. So as not to judge him, I told myself it was only because he was serving God, not man, that his place was in such a state. And I focused my eyes on his large Bible and various other study books scattered throughout the room.

"I'm not much of a housekeeper," he said as he cleared a place for us to sit on a lumpy, mud-colored couch. Then he flopped down into an orange vinyl beanbag chair, mended with duct tape in the shape of a cross. "Now what can I do for you ladies?"

"This is really about Cass," said Sara. "She's still pretty upset over last night, and she's wondering what she should do about her living conditions at the Glenns'. And I got to thinking on my way over here that she really shouldn't return to that evil place. I mean, think about the drugs and alcohol and sex and who knows what else goes on there. In fact it wouldn't surprise me if those horrible Glenns might not be secretly worshiping Satan. Cass says they actually listen to music from Black Sabbath and Grateful Dead—and we all know that's the devil's music."

Part of me wanted to defend the Glenns because despite all their flaws I didn't really think they were Satan worshipers, but on the other hand, you just never knew. And Mrs. Glenn did seem to wear a lot of black . . .

"And," continued Sara, "I would consider having Cass come stay with me for a while, but my parents have really been picking on me lately because of my—my religious beliefs." She turned to me. "Why, Cass even witnessed my dad persecuting me just today. So I don't really think that's an option either. In fact I came this close—" she held her thumb and forefinger together—"to just moving out of there myself today."

Sky nodded slowly, taking this all in as he rubbed the golden stubble on his strong, squared chin. Obviously he hadn't shaved yet. Finally he spoke. "This is really interesting."

"Interesting?" I felt a bit confused.

He smiled. "Well, lately I've been praying about this *thing* . . . ."

"This *thing*?" I leaned forward with interest.

"Yeah. It'll probably sound a little weird at first. But you see, about a week ago I had a vision."

"A *vision*?" I could hear the spark in Sara's voice. "What kind of vision was it, Sky? Can you tell us?"

"I wasn't planning on telling anyone just yet—not until I knew for sure—but suddenly it's all starting to make perfect sense." He studied us both carefully, as if measuring us up, perhaps trying to determine whether we could be trusted with such precious and perhaps holy information.

I attempted to appear as mature and spiritual as my sixteen and a half years and various life experiences could afford me.

"Come on," urged Sara. "Tell us."

He nodded with satisfaction. "Yes, I sense that the timing is right."

"Right for what?" I asked, suddenly wishing he wouldn't be so mysterious but get straight to the point. Yet at the same time I silently chastised myself for my obvious impatience that reeked of immaturity. So I leaned back into the dusty couch and folded my arms, determined to play it cool. I wasn't a child anymore.

He smiled. "Well, about a week ago I got a letter from my grandma, my dad's mom. She lives in California, out in the country, a little ways from Carmel. Anyway, she's got advanced diabetes and is going blind and she'd heard that I was at 'loose ends' as she put it. She asked me if I'd consider coming out there and taking care of her and the place for a while. At first I thought no way, I can't go out there when I'm needed here." He looked imploringly at us. "I couldn't just up and leave my little flock behind." Then he frowned. "But about that same time we started getting all that flack from the newspaper. And at one point I thought we should just shake the dust from our feet and move on—we should just leave Brookdale behind and—"

"*Go to California?*" said Sara eagerly.

He nodded. "Yes, we could all go live on my grandma's property in California. And then I could really teach and disciple everyone in the ways of our Lord. And we could grow our own food and take care of ourselves and—"

"And no one would pick on us for our beliefs," said Sara.

"And we could live just the way that Jesus wants us to," added Sky.

Sara sighed. "Wouldn't it be wonderful . . ."

I wasn't entirely sure what I thought. Quite honestly it seemed a little extreme and just slightly scary. "What about school?" I asked tentatively, instantly regretting my words when I saw their expressions.

"School?" Sky sighed deeply. "Don't you yet understand, little one, that the learning of man is mere foolishness to God?"

"And besides, Cass, think about the kinds of stuff they teach us in school," added Sara. "Evolution and sociology and all sorts of ungodly things."

I nodded slowly, hoping to appear wise. Perhaps they were right about these things. "What about money?" I asked. "How will we support ourselves?"

Sky smiled tolerantly at me as if he really believed I were a small child. "God will provide, Cass."

"That's right," said Sara with enthusiasm. "Like I just told my dad, God will take care of us." She turned to me, beaming now. "Doesn't it sound exciting, Cass?"

I still wasn't totally convinced, but when I considered my options they didn't seem so hot either. I studied Sky carefully. "Do you really think this would work?"

He chuckled and then held up his hands. "Where is your faith, little one? If God wants us to do this thing, then who are we to question his ways?"

I nodded, a slow smile breaking onto my face. I wanted to believe him. I wanted to think it was possible for us all to go someplace safe and wonderful and live happily ever after. Maybe it could happen. "Actually it sounds pretty cool. I mean, it'd be nice not to have anyone telling me what to do—to be treated like a grown-up. But in some ways it just sounds too good to be true."

Sky nodded. "Isn't that how God is? He seems too good to be true, but there is none truer—no, not one."

"Oh, Sky!" cried Sara. "When can we go?"

"Let's pray," said Sky.

So we all bowed our heads and prayed. Well, mostly Sky prayed, but Sara and I nodded our heads in agreement and we both said "amen" a lot and with enthusiasm. Sky asked that God would show us his divine and perfect will and lead us in the way that we should go. And when he finished Sky picked up his big Bible and flopped it open. I could tell by where the pages fell apart that it was the Old Testament (I was familiar enough with the Bible to know that much by now).

Sky closed his eyes and plunked his finger down onto the page. Then he opened his eyes and read. And this is what he read: "'And I have said, I will bring you up out of the affliction of Egypt unto the land of the Canaanites, and the Hittites, and the Amorites, and the Perizzites, and the Hivites, and the Jebusites, unto a land flowing with milk and honey.' Exodus 3:17."

To be perfectly honest, when I heard all those names like the Jesubites and Parasites, well, I just didn't fully get it at first. I thought maybe he'd gotten the wrong verse or something. But then Sky reread it, slowly this time, and leaving out all those something-ites parts, and suddenly it made perfect sense.

"Listen," he said, "'I will bring you up out of the affliction of Egypt.' Can't you see that Egypt is just like Brookdale? We're all in spiritual oppression here—just like slavery. And then it says that God will deliver us 'to a land flowing with milk and honey.' Don't you see? That has to be my grandmother's farm. We can raise our own milk cow and bees to make honey and we can grow our own food and everything. Doesn't it all make perfect sense?"

The next thing I knew we were all singing and marching around his tiny little trailer singing about how God was going to deliver us from the bondage of Brookdale. And that's when I became totally sold out to Sky's "vision." At last we were going to be delivered—our troubles would all be over!

Finally we all collapsed back onto the sofa, laughing so hard we were almost crying.

"All right then, when do we go?" asked Sara with her usual eagerness.

"As soon as God provides what we need for our trip," said Sky.

"What do we need?" I asked.

"Well . . ." Sky grew thoughtful. "I have my VW bus and I think that'll get us there. But I'm a little short on funds right now."

"I've got some money," I piped up.

"Enough to get us clear to California?" asked Sara skeptically.

"Yeah. I think I've got about eight hundred dollars in my savings account."

"Wow!" Sky was impressed. "Where'd you get all that?"

I grinned. "I guess God provided."

He gave me a high five. "Way to go, sis!"

I felt a slight twinge of remorse when I considered how hard I'd worked to save up for what I'd considered to be my college fund. But how could you argue with the ways of God? And so it was decided that sooner would be better.

"We shouldn't tempt God," said Sky. "If he's calling us to do this thing we should do it straightaway—to wait is to doubt, to doubt is to sin."

"But I can't get my money out of the bank until tomorrow," I said, realizing in dismay that today, New Year's Day, was a holiday.

"Well then, let's wait until tomorrow," said Sky, his eyes bright. "That will give us time to rest up and prepare."

"What about the others?" asked Sara.

"Let's get the word out that everyone's invited to come along. Then we'll just pray and see what happens."

We talked some more about the trip and what we'd do once we got there, but it was that dreamy kind of talk where everything works out just perfectly and I don't for a minute think that any single one of us really knew what we were getting into—what we were creating in that moment. All we knew was that we believed God was leading us—and who wanted to question the leading of God?

We also decided that I would return to the Glenns' house that day—so as to avoid any unnecessary suspicion. So I went back and began cleaning up the remnants of last night's party, my one consolation being that I would never have to do it again! With my domestic responsibilities taken care of, I was then picked up by Sara and we went over to Cindy's house, where an impromptu meeting had been called—a meeting of great urgency, Sara had informed everyone by phone. Almost everyone in our little group attended.

Sky explained exactly what it was we were embarking upon, and as he told the story it seemed to grow even more wonderful and spiritual and exciting by the moment. It was as if we were these spiritual pilgrims going off to discover the new country and true spiritual freedom and God only knew what else. Maybe we'd even write a book about it. Sky mentioned the possibility that God might be calling some of us to be prophets or who knew what else.

It amazes me now to think that not one among us questioned any of this at the time. While a few quietly decided not to join in, no one said anything negative about Sky's plans. And most of the group really wanted to come.

In the end there were seven of us that would go at first and almost everyone else promised to join up with us later. The original seven would consist of Sky and Sara and me, plus Cindy and Mitch (who hoped to be married soon), as well as Linda Farnsworth and

Skip Holmes (a couple of kids I didn't know that well, but who also came from troubled homes and were eager to escape to "The Promised Land").

When I finally got back to my quarters (which once again seemed to be my dungeon—symbolic of the bondage I'd soon be delivered from) I carefully packed up my things and then fell into bed utterly exhausted. I think one of the most amazing things about that entire New Year's Day was the way I almost completely forgot about that horrible episode with George the previous night. With so much else on my mind it was as if that unfortunate and ter- rifying event had just been completely wiped away. And so I slept soundly that night. In fact I can't even recall if I prayed before I went to sleep or not—but then we'd been praying a whole lot lately and I was feeling pretty spiritually elevated just then.

The plan was to rise early (before the Glenns awakened) and to quietly load my stuff into Sara's car. (She and Sky had decided just this evening that it was God's will for her to take her car as well. I wasn't sure what her daddy would think about all this but figured that was for God to sort out later.) With any luck, and God's help, all the parents (and the Glenns) would just assume we were at school as normal. And we'd be far, far away before anyone actually began to notice our absence.

I can still remember the chill of excitement that ran down my spine as I stood next to the Glenns' modern split-level house in the gray, predawn shadows, expectantly waiting for Sara's car to pull up. I had my things piled behind the protection of the laurel hedge as I looked hopefully down the street, watching for her yellow bug.

And oddly enough, in the silence of that moment I thought about Joey Divers. I'm still not sure what exactly brought him to mind—maybe it was thoughts of how I was once and for all leaving Brookdale. But for whatever reason, I thought of him and I remembered his last words to me, right there in the produce section of the supermarket. *"Be careful, Cass,"* he had warned me.

What had he really meant? Wasn't I being careful to "go where God led me"? How could a believer be any more careful than that? Surely if Joey really understood everything I'd been through—especially lately—he'd support me wholeheartedly in this brave decision to go forth into the Promised Land. (That's what we were already calling our destination in California, "The Promised Land.")

My heart fluttered with excitement when I finally spied Sara's car approaching and thoughts of Joey's concern vanished. We'd soon be on our way! Now if only I didn't have to wait until the Citizen's Bank opened up at nine o'clock in order to empty out my savings account.

But at least I could be thankful that I had such a gift to give. Everyone in the group was treating me with the utmost respect because of my contribution. Even Sky had refrained from calling me "little one" after he'd learned of my nest egg. I told them that we should view the money as God's provision for all of us—not just from me personally.

Naturally Sky had agreed and I could see that he'd been impressed when I said this—I could tell by his eyes. And sure, I knew it was a pretty big sacrifice on my part. But I also knew that I was doing it wholeheartedly for God (and for the group). I believed I was being a cheerful giver! And I think that I truly believed that God would take care of me from that day forward. Of course Sky had assured me that I could count on that. And he'd also said that God would surely reward me for my generosity. Sky told me that God's Word promised that I would be rewarded generously and sufficiently—and in due time! Whenever that might be. And so I had no reason to doubt.

chapter fifteen

I'M SURE IF MY GRANDMA had been looking down upon me (from her front-row seat up there in heaven) she'd have been thinking that Cassandra Jane Maxwell had jumped right out of the frying pan and straight into the fire. And I'll admit that thought actually did pass through my mind, be it ever so briefly, but I immediately convinced myself that it was simply one of those deep, dark doubts that needed to be dismissed. And so I did.

"Look in that bag," Sara told me after I'd thrown my things into her backseat and was sitting safely next to her as she cruised a nearly deserted Main Street. I could see she was suppressing giggles as I opened the brown paper bag to see about a dozen cans of spray paint—in a rainbow of different colors.

"What's this for?" I asked as I examined the hot pink color on one plastic lid.

"We're going to anoint my car for the trip!" She laughed as she turned on the street that led toward the railroad tracks.

"You're going to spray-paint your car?" I was incredulous. How could she bear to mess with the beautiful yellow paint job on her VW bug?

She nodded. "Yep. And then I'll head on out of town ahead of you guys. Sky said we'll meet up again in Sedgewater."

"Why's that?"

"Less conspicuous, I guess."

I wondered how inconspicuous a psychedelic bug would be, making its way out of the conservative town of Brookdale, but kept these thoughts to myself. And so Sara parked her car next to Sky's trailer and the seven of us all grabbed a spray can and just really whooped it up. With inspired creativity we "anointed" Sara's little bug with wild stripes and rainbows and flowers and fishes and crosses until you could hardly see a speck of the original yellow paint.

"Good thing you don't have any neighbors," said Mitch as he put the finishing touch on a large purple cross that stretched across the hood of the little car. "They might call the cops on us for vandalizing or something."

Sara laughed. "Oh yeah, sure, vandalizing my own car!"

I tried not to think about what her father might say about all this. In fact, I found it quite irritating that my mind seemed to be plagued with so many doubtful thoughts in the first place. I knew those kinds of thoughts would just deflate my faith and so I decided I must keep them at bay, or as Sky would say, "take them captive," which meant, he'd explained, that if your thoughts impaired your belief in any way then you should simply disregard them altogether. This became quite common practice among us as time went on, almost as if we were disengaging our minds entirely. Because how could we trust our own thoughts—weren't they human and sinful? In other words when you enter "The Promised Land" you'd better just check your brains at the door.

Finally Sara's car was properly "anointed" and after a prayer for God's blessing it was decided by a coin toss that Mitch and Cindy would ride with her and the rest of us would follow along with Sky after I'd collected my money from the bank. We remaining four passed the next hour by "anointing" Sky's van in a similar fashion—more rainbows, doves, crosses, fishes, flowers, and trees, until the spray cans were all emptied with only the rattling sound of the mixing ball going *clickity-clack.*

I thought the van looked rather beautiful in a psychedelic sort of way and not entirely unlike numerous other vans and buses that we would later see along our cross-country trek. But just as we were finishing up, a horribly frightening thought crossed my mind again and try as I might I couldn't "take it captive."

I never told a soul that day or even thereafter, but it occurred to me that morning that perhaps something would go wrong at the bank—perhaps the teller would refuse to let me take out my money! I can't even begin to describe the horror this filled me with—I worried about Sara, already on her way in her "anointed" automobile, with less than twenty dollars in her pocket. And Sky didn't have much more. Between the seven of us we had maybe fifty bucks—barely enough to get us to the next state. What would I tell everyone if something went wrong now? What would Sara's daddy say about her car if because of me she was forced to drive it back home and park it in the driveway?

My palms were sweating and I could feel the heat rising up my neck and into my face as I walked into the nearly empty bank that gray winter morning. And I swear I felt just as guilty as a real-life bank robber when I approached the teller clutching my purse between both hands.

I sensed everyone's eyes on me and felt certain they suspected the very worst. I wouldn't have been too surprised if they had already alerted the security guard or maybe even the police. I felt sure I was just seconds away from crumbling and confessing to the teller that I was only sixteen years old and about to run away with a bunch of other kids.

I held my little passbook in my trembling hand as I forced a smile to my lips. *You can do this, Cass,* I told myself firmly. *It can't be any harder than growing up with a drunk for a dad.* As ironic as it may seem, that crazy thought strengthened me inwardly somehow. And the next thing I knew I was informing the teller that I wanted to close my savings account.

"You want to close it completely?" She eyed me with curiosity.

"Yes." I took a breath. "You see, I'm buying a car today and it's going to take every penny in there plus all the money here in my purse. But I just really need this car."

She nodded. "Yes, I can understand that, but have you considered getting yourself an auto loan from our bank and then you could keep your savings—"

"Thank you, I know how that works. But you see I just don't believe in owing people money." I smiled again. "I promise I'll reopen my savings account just as soon as I can."

"Well, okay, then. How do you want the bills?"

"Oh, I don't know. How about twenties?"

"Twenties?" Her brows lifted. "That'll be a lot of bills."

I smiled again, trying to mask how ignorant I felt just then. "Oh, that's okay. It might be kind of fun to see that much money all at once."

So she counted out *forty-one* twenty-dollar bills and a ten, a five, and then sixty-five cents. I slipped the thick wad of money into my oversized purse and thanked her, then walked out of there feeling just like Faye Dunaway in that *Bonnie and Clyde* movie that had come out a couple years earlier, right after the first time she'd helped Clyde to knock off some bank. It was all so thrilling and exhilarating that it took every ounce of my self-control not to just run out of there and into the parking lot screaming like a banshee.

Instead I walked slowly and deliberately, attempting some deep breaths in order to suppress my excitement.

"I did it!" I cried after the van doors were safely closed. I turned to Sky from the front passenger seat of the van (reserved, I suspected, for the most generous contributor to the trip) then reached into my purse and pulled out the huge wad of cash.

I held it up and proudly fanned the bills as I showed my fortune to everyone. I'd never actually handled that much money in my entire life and it felt kind of invigorating. Everyone else seemed to like it too, because we all just whooped and hollered and screamed as Sky pulled out of the Citizen's Bank parking lot and drove down Main Street and out of town.

We all began to sing a rowdy worship song—loudly praising God for his mighty provision! I felt so thankful and relieved right then that the thought never occurred to me that this pile of money had actually been my little nest egg, my college fund, my future.

No, quite honestly, I only saw those green bills as my ticket to freedom—my means of serving God within the comfort of this "family" that he'd so graciously given me—I was going to live with my brothers and sisters in blissful harmony from now on! And I think I was almost completely happy as Sky drove out of town. Euphorically happy even. Honestly, although I didn't actually know it at the time, the high that day was even better than drugs. And it lasted me all the way to Sedgewater, where we met up with Sara, and beyond. I'm sure it kept me high for at least twenty-four hours. Well almost, anyway.

Despite the fact that only three of us were actually licensed to drive (Sky, Sara, and Mitch) we all took turns at the wheel in order to continue our round-the-clock trip. All except for Linda that is, for we all knew she was a little high-strung and too easily freaked out to drive. Not wanting to be killed in a wreck we didn't pressure her any.

Sky felt it was imperative to reach California as quickly as possible and so our colorful caravan of bus and bug began its beeline to the West Coast. Sara and Sky drove for most of that first day. After a long day we had a late dinner at a McDonald's in town just outside of Oklahoma City and after running around the parking lot and acting crazy for about five minutes (we definitely had ants in our pants) Sky, the ever responsible one, told us it was time to pack it up and move on. Mitch took over driving for Sara and I took over for Sky. The plan was to take turns driving and sleeping and to stop only for gas, food, and bathroom breaks.

Other than those few rare times when Mrs. Glenn had asked me to drive her Cadillac to the grocery store (she didn't know I only had a learner's permit) I really hadn't driven all that much. My first driving experience came while living with the Crowleys. Fortunately Roy had taught me to drive his truck, which was a stick, and so I was fairly comfortable driving Sky's manual drive van. But due to Roy's untimely death I'd never had the chance to get my driver's license.

I swallowed back the lump in my throat as I thought of the Crowleys and Roy's accident with the tractor. Like so many other segments of my life, that comparatively happy time spent on their farm seemed far removed now—almost another lifetime away—as if I'd lived a number of varied and different lives in my short sixteen and a half years. And although the era with the Crowleys contained mostly good memories, I tried not to think of them as I drove. I didn't want to consider what the Crowleys might think of my "spiritual pilgrimage" if they knew, which of course they did not.

This was just one more thought I forced myself to "take captive." Like so many other things, I simply wouldn't think about it. *It's all in the past,* I told myself—*all in the past, all in the past*—I repeated these four words over and over in my mind as I drove in the darkness. Matching the beat of the words to the rhythmic sound of the tires, I directed the van down the long, dark strip of highway. I kept my eyes straight forward, focusing all my attention on keeping the van just to the right of the white stripes that ran down the center of the road. *Just keep going,* I told myself, *just like those white stripes, keep going, keep going—for God is leading the way.* And that was enough to sufficiently occupy my attention as the others tried to catch some shut-eye.

Skip had leaned back in the passenger seat next to me, a pillow wedged between him and the window. He appeared to be sleeping soundly—at least he was snoring. Before we'd left Brookdale, Sky had taken a mattress from his trailer—well, it wasn't exactly *his* trailer. I later learned it actually belonged to a friend of his mother's. Anyway, he tossed the dusty mattress into the back of the van and this, combined with all our various sleeping bags, suitcases, and pillows, made for a lumpy although not unwelcome bed. As I drove, I knew that Sky and Linda were sleeping back there.

While I would never admit this to anyone (not anyone in our group anyway) this bothered me some—even back then. I couldn't be entirely sure but suddenly I imagined that Sky and Linda were making out back there. It shamed me to think such thoughts, and almost as quickly as these evil imaginings entered my mind I knew that it was horrible and disgusting and sinful for me to think this way about my sister and brother—my brother who was giving up everything to "take his flock to the Promised Land." How could I be so base, so carnal?

And riddled with this awful guilt I actually began to wonder if perhaps George's attack on me on New Year's Eve had somehow warped my way of thinking about such things. Would I always be suspicious of others from now on? Had I been soiled by the sins of the flesh? What could I do to repent of this evil way of thinking? And then I realized this was another one of those "thoughts I must take captive." I couldn't allow myself to entertain such vile suspicions. So while I drove I earnestly prayed that God would forgive me and cleanse my mind and my spirit and protect me from such sinful thoughts. And the road grew blurry as real tears streamed down my cheeks and I imagined Jesus cleansing me and making me whiter than snow. I wiped my eyes and took in a deep breath and I knew everything would be okay. I began to hum "Amazing Grace" and before long, all was quiet and peaceful and my earlier enthusiasm about the trip returned to me, because after all we were on our way to the Promised Land!

Sometime around 2 A.M. Skip awakened and told me it was his turn to drive. So we pulled over and, trying not to disturb Sky and Linda in the back, quietly switched seats. We waited as Mitch did the same behind us in the little VW bug, this time letting Cindy drive. "There's room for you back here, Cass," whispered Sky. "Why don't you come lie down for a bit?"

But for some reason that I'm still not entirely sure of, I declined to join them back there. Maybe I was still a little frightened of my own sinful nature. "It's okay; I'm fine up here," I told him. "I'm not really that sleepy right now anyway, and I'll keep Skip company for a while."

Skip turned and smiled. "You mean you're going to keep me awake?"

I laughed. "Yeah, that's probably what I mean. All those white lines can be a little hypnotic if you don't watch out."

And so I sat up front next to Skip, fairly wide awake now and trying to make sure that he didn't fall asleep. We chatted together and for the first time I really began to know him better. He was a senior that year—would've graduated in the spring. But he said he'd had no plans to attend college anyway and would probably just get drafted into Vietnam. Besides that, his parents' marriage of nearly twenty-five years was on the rocks and he suspected that they were both having affairs and would soon be divorced.

"I guess it was a good time for me to leave," he said quietly, but I could still hear the pain in his voice.

"Yeah," I agreed. "But I'm sorry. That must've been hard on you."

"I suppose, but you know what they say about God moving in mysterious ways. I suppose if my parents weren't such a mess I might not have come—and then just think what I would've missed out on."

"It's really exciting, isn't it?" I began to get dreamy again. "I mean, to think in just a couple days we'll all be living together in the Promised Land—spending time before the Lord and working together to take care of each other—it's going to be so neat!"

"Yeah, kinda like heaven on earth." He sighed. "And I've heard the weather is really great in California too."

And then we got a little silly, probably tired from all that driving, but we began singing every old California tune we could think of. Songs like "Do You Know the Way to San Jose?" and "California Dreaming" (one of my personal favorites) and the one that starts out, "If you're going to San Francisco . . ."

Finally I felt a little guilty for singing such worldly songs when we were supposed to be following God to a more holy life. "Uh, maybe we should sing something a little more spiritual," I suggested.

"Yeah, I suppose you're right."

So then we began singing some of the choruses and praise songs that we'd learned from Sky and before long, both Sky and Linda sat up and began singing with us. Sky dug around until he found my guitar, and right there in the middle of the night, plummeting seventy miles an hour down some Midwest highway, we had ourselves a pleasant little songfest—worshiping God together in unity as we headed toward our spiritual destiny. I'm certain I even got goose bumps.

After we finally ran out of wind, Sky took over the wheel for the next shift. At this time I went ahead and climbed into the back, and feeling completely, but happily spent, I flopped down on the mattress next to Linda. I tried not to envy her (aware that she'd spent the entire night in relative comfort back there and had most likely gotten the best night's rest of everyone) for I knew that it was sinful and wrong to envy and by then I was working harder than ever to keep my heart pure for Jesus.

My thinking back then seems strange to me now, but at the time it made perfect sense. And the further we proceeded on our journey, the more important this line of thinking became to me. I actually began to believe that if I could just be good enough—free enough from sin—that all would go well with this thing we were attempting to do and that God would look down upon us with great pleasure and that he would abundantly bless us with all that we needed in life.

Underneath my thin and untested veneer of faith I still had my little shadows of doubt to contend with—I knew what it was like to be hungry and go without and I didn't particularly relish the idea of living like that once again. And so I began to convince myself that if I could just be good enough, righteous enough, holy and pious enough—then all would be well.

We stopped for breakfast in a small town west of Amarillo and I still remember the dour looks we got as we poured out of the van and bug looking all grubby and rumpled. I think we actually enjoyed our "hippy/Jesus freak" status and the attention it got us.

"Bring your guitar in, Cass," called Sky. "We'll sing some songs before breakfast." So I grabbed my guitar and the seven of us went inside and situated ourselves in a large corner booth and began singing praise songs. I halfway expected the manager to come over and shut us down but to our surprise we got no complaints.

"Well, that's right nice," said a middle-aged waitress. "But if you kids think you're gonna sing for your breakfast, you better think again."

"No," said Sky. "We're just hoping to share a little bit of the joy of the Lord with the people in this place."

"Now that's a new one." She laughed, then took our orders.

After she left Sky told us he had an important announcement to make and naturally we all stopped talking to listen to him.

I know it sounds just like that old TV commercial, but when Sky talked, people listened. There's no denying that there was "something special" about him. Some might say it was simply his good looks or his dramatic way with words—before they really knew him, that is. And I'll admit he was easy to look at with his shoulder-length, wavy blond hair. And his voice had this calming yet compelling authoritative quality to it. But there was something more, too.

Maybe it was the way he held his head at a certain angle, with his chin tilted just slightly upward, and the way he looked upon us with that even gaze that felt like he was meeting your eyes but was actually looking just a little bit higher, maybe about to the center of your forehead (as if he were reading your mind, which some people later on actually believed he could do). But those clear, blue eyes—just something about their bright intensity made you want to believe that whatever he said was truly spiritual, vitally important, even life-changing, and always, always well worth listening to. He just had that effect on you.

And so there we were, his six faithful followers, somewhat

worn and road weary, sitting in the corner booth, eyes and ears attentive to his "important announcement."

"I've had another vision," he said quietly, slowly, then pausing for effect. "It came to me while I was driving this morning. God told me that he is taking us to a *new* place and that he is making us into *new* people and that we shall all have *new* names."

"New names?" repeated Sara. "You mean I won't be Sara anymore?"

"That's right," said Sky. "We will take off the old and put on the new. You know, Jesus said you can't pour new wine into old wineskins. Therefore, we shall all have new names."

"Cool," said Linda. "I never much liked my name anyway."

"How about you?" asked Skip. "What'll your name be?"

"Well, as you know, I've already changed my name," said Sky. "Remember, my old name used to be Scott. But God told me I could change it to Sky because that's how big my future would be—as long and as wide as the sky."

"Yes, I remember," said Cindy. "But what will our names be?"

Sky closed his eyes for a moment, as if meditating.

Just then the waitress began bringing our drinks, noisily clunking cups of cocoa and coffee and glasses of juice and water onto the table. All the while Sky just sat there with his eyes closed, his face serene—almost trancelike. The waitress looked curiously at him, then just chuckled to herself as she walked away. When it grew quiet again, aside from the clanking of dishes in the kitchen and the chatter of other diners, Sky began to speak.

"Linda, your name shall be Moonlight."

"Moonlight." She sighed dreamily as she pushed back a strand of dishwater-blonde hair. "Yeah, I like that, Sky."

"Sara, your name will be Sunshine."

Sara smiled. "Cool."

He turned to Cindy. "You will be known as Breeze."

"Breeze?" Her face looked slightly puzzled for a moment but then she nodded. "Yeah, that's okay, I guess."

"Mitch, your name shall be River."

Mitch nodded. "Yeah, I can handle that."

"Skip, you shall be called Stone."

"Cool, kinda like Peter, huh? Didn't his name mean *rock* or something like that?"

Sky nodded. "That's right."

Now I waited expectantly, the last one to be renamed. I felt almost afraid to move or even breathe—what would my new name be?

"Cass, you will be our Rainbow."

"Rainbow." I repeated the name quietly as I imagined the beautiful watery strips of colors with the sunlight shining through. "I like it."

Now Sky looked around the table. "From here on out we will only refer to one another by these new names. Understand?"

We all agreed, playfully trying out our new names with each other but getting some, like River and Stone, switched around. By the end of breakfast we'd almost gotten it figured out.

"This is so cool," said Sunshine (formerly known as Sara). "I really do feel like a new person now!"

Sky went up to the counter to pay the bill. I'd handed my money over to him the previous day (as had everyone). But first we'd made a big pile and dedicated every cent of it to the Lord and asked him to bless it and—like the loaves and fishes—to multiply it. I wasn't sure where Sky had stashed it all but I wasn't concerned, just curious as to whether the bills had reproduced yet. But quite honestly I was no longer worried. Between God and Sky I felt we were all in good hands.

"Hey, Rainbow," called Sky. "I believe it's your turn to drive now. You ready?"

"Sure," I agreed, catching the keys as he tossed them my way.

"Wait, everyone," called Moonlight. "I'm getting out my camera. Let's all line up in front of the van and get some pictures."

And so we all posed ourselves in silly positions around the psychedelic van and bug while Moonlight took some shots on her little Kodak Instamatic. Then she practically assaulted a man who'd just climbed down from a semi that appeared to be hauling a load of livestock and somehow convinced him to snap a picture of all seven of us.

"Crazy bunch of hippies," he muttered after he took several shots then returned the camera to her. "What's this world coming to anyway?"

"God bless you!" Sunshine cried out in return.

"Jesus lives!" yelled Stone.

The rest of us pointed up toward the heavens and yelled, "There's only one way!"

The man just rolled his eyes and ambled on toward the diner.

As I climbed into the driver's seat and waited for the others to get in, it hit me once again that I was really on my way somewhere—somewhere important. And suddenly I imagined myself to be a new person, just like Sky had said. A new person who, from this day on, would be known by a new name—Rainbow! I thought about my new name, running it through my mind. Now didn't that mean something like hope or promise or something wonderful like that? I focused my eyes on the westbound highway and told myself that at last, I was going home!

chapter sixteen

IT TAKES A CROSS-COUNTRY VAN TRIP with a bunch of unwashed teen-aged friends to fully appreciate the sacrifices made during the hippy movement. It's not that our goal was to look and smell like a carload of farm animals exactly—it was simply inevitable. And although the next two days on the road were long and grueling and somewhat odorous we all remained in surprisingly happy spirits. On our second day of almost nonstop travel I asked Sky why we had to get to California so fast—so fast that we couldn't even stop to bathe or wash our hair. (Not that hygiene was my major concern.) But since I'd never been much outside of Brookdale I felt slightly dismayed that we couldn't take a little time to see more of the country as we traveled—and I suspected the Grand Canyon was somewhere nearby. Sky said he felt it best we get there quickly. "Partly because I'm concerned about the health of my grand-mother, and partly because we don't want to chance getting stopped."

"Stopped?"

"Well, you know, Rainbow— " he affectionately patted me on the head— "other than River and me, you guys are all underage."

"Oh yeah." I nodded, suddenly remembering that in the eyes of the law we might all be considered runaways.

Later that day Sunshine wanted to call her parents from a pay phone at a gas station. "Just to let them know I'm okay," she'd quickly explained after Sky had stopped her from dropping her dime in the phone (in fact, he confiscated her dime).

"No, Sunshine. No one calls anyone until we get there," he turned and announced to all of us. "We can't allow any single one of us to put the entire group at risk." Sunshine wasn't too happy about this and for a brief moment I considered how her mother might be feeling right now—I remembered how just days ago she'd shown such concern for her daughter and wanted to patch things up between Sunshine and her dad. I felt bad for her, but in the next instant I made myself forget these things—just more thoughts to take captive.

And that's when it occurred to me that if I was "captivating" these thoughts then I must be putting them somewhere. But where was that? So that's when I began to imagine some sort of big, gray prison cell designed to contain Cass's—I mean Rainbow's—errant and sinful thoughts. I must admit this image seemed almost humorous to me at the time.

It was on the second day, during a pit stop in New Mexico, that Sky announced we would call each other brothers and sisters from now on—since that's what we were in the eyes of the Lord. "Does that mean we have to say Brother Sky and Sister Moonlight?" asked Sunshine. "That's kind of a mouthful, you know."

Sky considered this. "Well no, I suppose that seems a little formal. Maybe for when we're meeting outsiders. For our own little family we can be more relaxed. But when you refer to the guys from now on you can call them the brothers, and the girls, the sisters. Does that make sense?" We all agreed that it made perfect sense. We would now be the brothers and the sisters—one big happy family.

And it was amazing how close we all became to each other during this grueling three-day trip. It's as if our spirits really were uniting. Even Moonlight, whom I'd felt the most distance from (and only because I had to keep chiding myself for being so horribly judgmental against her) began to feel more like a real sister to me. It was also on the second day of our trip, just after dinner, that Sky had announced that all the sisters would travel together in the van during the night. And the brothers would ride together in the bug. At first we wondered what this was about, but he told us that God had told him that we were to keep separated for the remainder of our trip to prevent impure thoughts. And that seemed to make sense and naturally no one argued with him. No one ever argued with Sky. Well, almost no one.

As a result we sisters enjoyed the feeling of sisterhood even more while being together in the van for those last two days. Sunshine took the lead among us, probably because she was just a natural leader anyway and also she was the oldest (almost eighteen). Since I'd never really had close girlfriends before (other than Bryn and that was always a strained relationship) this was new and rather fun for me. And for some reason it felt more relaxed and freeing than when the brothers were present where it often seemed we had the constant strain of vying for attention. I suppose it was mostly the sisters trying to get Sky's attention, but I think there was a little tension between the brothers too. And even River and Breeze (who were already established as a couple) seemed as if they needed a little break from each other.

"Hey, Breeze," said Moonlight, "will you and River get married in California?"

Breeze giggled. "Oh, I don't know. What makes you ask that?"

"Well, don't you think some of us should get married once we get all settled in and everything?"

Sunshine, who was driving, threw back her head and laughed. "So what are you saying, Moonlight? Are you wanting to get married or something?"

"Maybe . . ."

We all turned and looked at her (except for Sunshine who glanced up in the rearview mirror and continued driving). "Are you serious?" said Sunshine. "You really want to get married?"

"Well, it's probably better than living in sin." Moonlight poked Breeze in the arm.

"What're you saying?" asked Breeze. "Are you saying you think that me and River are doing it?"

Moonlight just laughed.

"Well, we're not, you know," said Breeze defensively. "We know that's wrong—that's fornication, you know."

"Yeah, we know you're not doing it, Breeze," said Sunshine soothingly. "Moonlight's just being silly, aren't you, Moonie?"

"*Moonie?*" she said indignantly. "Don't you go calling me Moonie, *Sister Sunny!*"

"Okay then, you better not go accusing *Sister Breezie* of things you don't know anything about."

"*Sister Breezie?*" She let out a hoot of laughter. "That's good."

By then we were all laughing and teasing and calling each other by these newly discovered nicknames. I even became Sister Rainy. "Well, we better not let Brother Sky catch us changing our names already," I warned as the laughter finally subsided.

"Yeah, it'll just have to be a sister thing," said Sunshine.

No more talk of marriage was heard during the trip, but I must admit I wondered if Moonlight might not be onto something. And I felt a confusing mix of emotions about the idea. Part of me knew that I was too young to marry, but another part was intrigued by the possibility. And naturally these were just some more thoughts I had to lock away in my captive dungeon. I wondered how many thoughts that place could contain without bursting out at the seams and embarrassing me.

We had a little celebration when we finally crossed the California state line. And to our delight it was a clear and sunny day. We actually got out of the vehicles and danced around and even kissed the ground. Then we made a little circle and Sky led us in a word of prayer before we climbed back into the car and van and prepared for the final hours of our arduous journey.

We reached Carmel late in the afternoon and stopped at a store to pick up some provisions. "I don't know what my grandmother will have on hand," said Sky as we filled a cart, "so we might as well come prepared."

I can still remember the rush I felt when we finally pulled to a stop on a little country road. The only sign that we were at the right place was a rusty old mailbox in front of a gravel driveway that looked fairly overgrown with weeds and grass. Sky stuck his head out the window of the bug and hollered, "This is it! We've reached the Promised Land!" Then we followed him down a long driveway until we came to a two-story farmhouse with a barn and a couple of small outbuildings tucked next to a low green hill. The place was thoroughly overgrown with briars and weeds and the leaning buildings appeared about to fall over, but to me it really looked like Paradise! We all jumped out of our vehicles and literally danced around, praising the Lord and shouting and laughing—and then we followed Sky's lead and kneeled right there in the driveway and prayed for God to bless this place as we dedicated it to him as "The Promised Land."

"You all wait out here while I go inside and have a quick word with my grandmother," said Sky.

Moonlight begged him to hurry since she really needed to use the bathroom. "Bad," she said as she hopped around. The six of us continued to sing praise songs to pass the time as we waited outside in the cool January air, and finally Moonlight couldn't stand it any longer and proceeded to relieve herself in the nearby bushes.

Then just as daylight began to fade Sky came back out and flipped on the porch light. A big smile lit his face. "Come on in," he called. "I haven't figured everything out yet, but Gram wants to meet everyone. I didn't exactly tell her that we would all be staying here. She thinks you're all just passing through. But I know that God is working this thing out for us. And we can't question his ways. We just have to take this thing one step at a time—kind of like when the Israelites took the Promised Land. So for now let's not mention to her that we're all going to stay here. Okay?"

Naturally we all agreed, but I remember chastising myself for the tremor of worry that passed through me. What if Sky's grandmother didn't want us? What then? But down to the dungeon I tossed these thoughts as I pasted a faithful smile across my face and stepped into the old farmhouse. The living room smelled like a bad mixture of cooked cabbage, dirty laundry, and stale cigarette smoke. And right off I could see that no one had kept house here in quite some time. Situated on a couch that seemed to be serving as a bed was an old woman who looked to be almost as wide as she was tall, and I'd guess she was maybe five feet tall at best. Next to her was a metal TV tray with an overflowing ashtray and several empty dishes that looked as if they'd been sitting there for some time. I don't actually remember how Sky introduced us to her but I'll never forget her response.

"What are you kids? Some kind of traveling circus or something? How'd you get those names anyway? Raincloud and Moonshine and why, I can't even remember the rest!"

"These are the new names that God has given us," said Sky in a solemn voice. But Sunshine and I had to irreverently suppress giggles over his grandmother's comments.

"God gave you names?" She hooted. "Now ain't that something! You think he'll give me a new name too, Scotty?"

"Actually I go by Sky now." This conversation was making him uncomfortable.

"Sky?" she looked up and over in his direction, but not right at him, and that's when it became apparent that she could barely see, and I remembered then how Sky had said she was almost blind from her advanced diabetes. "What's your mother think about you changing your name, Scotty?"

He sighed deeply. "You know, Gram, we're all pretty hungry and I'll bet you are too. How about if we start fixing some dinner? We stopped by the store and got some things." He turned to us. "Why don't you go get those groceries and bring them in?" Then he stopped me. "Rainbow, you know a little about cooking and cleaning, don't you? How about if you stay in here and get things going in the kitchen?"

"Sure," I said.

"Who do you want to help you?"

Now this was a new twist. I got to pick someone to help me? "How about Sunshine?" I suggested.

She smiled. "Okay, but you'll have to show me what to do. I'm pretty hopeless in the kitchen."

As it turned out the kitchen was pretty hopeless too. At least at first glance. Obviously Sky's grandmother had been challenged by her fading vision, to say the least, to fend for herself, and as a result the place looked chaotic with various dishes and pots and food items spread all over the counters. But Sunshine and I rolled up our sleeves and began to attack it. I put Sunshine to work washing dirty dishes (so we'd have something to eat from) while I tried to make enough space on the counters to prepare a meager meal of spaghetti, salad, and bread. Almost two hours later we all sat around the dining room table and ate. But before we ate I made sure to take a nice plate out to Sky's grandmother, reintroducing myself to her as Rainbow, not Raincloud, this time.

"Did you do the cooking?" she asked, sniffing the plate.

"Yes. I'm not the best cook," I said apologetically. "But I've had a little practice."

"How old are you?"

By now I knew that Sky had told her we were all college-aged, so as to avoid unnecessary questions. "I'm eighteen," I said quietly, choosing the closest legal age to my own. Somehow it seemed less of a lie to me at the time.

"Well, what're you doing tramping around the country with my grandson?" she asked as she shoveled a bite of salad into her mouth.

"We're all just good friends," I explained. "Like brothers and sisters. And Sky is like our big brother. We really look up to him. And he's a good guy."

She looked in my direction, and with her mouth still full of lettuce, smiled. Her eyes were a foggy gray. "That's nice," she muttered. "Well, if you like to cook, little Raincloud, then maybe you should think about sticking around here awhile. I could use some good meals."

I patted her thick, flabby arm. "Thanks, uh, Mrs.—" I paused, wondering what to call her. I didn't remember if Sky had mentioned a name or not.

"Aw, just call me Gram. I know I talk like a mean old broad but I'm not really so bad—not once you get to know me."

Most of us (the sisters and Sky) stayed in the house that night. There were two bedrooms upstairs and two down (one of which was occupied by Gram). Sunshine and I shared one of the upstairs' rooms and Breeze and Moonlight shared the other. Sky took the other downstairs' bedroom and the other two brothers threw Sky's old mattress down and camped in the loft above the barn (which they said was also inhabited with mice who liked to frolic at night). But everyone was so exhausted from the long trip that despite the conditions I think we all slept soundly that night.

The next morning I found myself in the kitchen again, attempting to fix pancakes, bacon, and eggs for eight hungry people. Sunshine tried to be helpful, but I quickly discovered that of the four sisters I was the only one who knew anything about cooking and that really wasn't all that much. After breakfast Sky came in with Breeze and Moonlight in tow, then said to me, "I want to talk to you outside." He turned to the other three. "You sisters finish cleaning up in here."

I wondered if I'd done something wrong as Sky walked me out to the backyard. I knew that the bacon had been a little underdone and some of the pancakes a little dark.

"Rainbow, I can see I'm going to really be needing your help here."

I sighed in relief. So I wasn't in trouble. "Yeah, that's cool."

"And I just don't want it to turn out that you're doing all the work. So we've got to make a plan."

"Okay." I looked at him, waiting expectantly. After all, he was the plan man.

He ran his fingers across his chin, which I'd noticed had gone unshaven for several days now. "I think what I want to do is to put you in charge of all the household."

I nodded, unsure as to what exactly this meant but willing just the same, anything to serve God and my brothers and sisters. "Okay," I said, waiting for him to explain.

"But I don't want you thinking that means you have to do all the work. I want you to fix it so that all the sisters do an equal share—no slackers, you know? Can you handle that?"

I frowned, thinking how the other girls were all older than me and had been Christians longer . . . I'd sort of looked up to them, especially Sunshine. "Oh, I don't know. . . ."

"Come on, Rainbow. I really need you to do this for me."

"Okay," I said again, at the same time wondering how I'd handle overseeing the other sisters, especially Moonlight. Would they even listen to me? What if they didn't respect me? But I kept these doubts to myself.

He smiled and ran his hand over my head, giving my long braid a gentle tug. "Thanks, Rainbow. I knew that when God sent you to us it was for a really special purpose. It's like your name suggests. Rainbow is the promise of hope."

The warm rush I felt with his words was unexplainable, but it was in that moment I felt I'd probably do anything for Sky, anything at all. "Thanks, Sky," I muttered, looking down at my feet and hoping my cheeks weren't blazing, giving away my thoughts like two red flags. I would of course repent later.

"Oh, and another thing," he said. "I think the sisters should all start dressing more modestly."

"More modestly?"

He nodded. "Yeah. No more jeans and overalls and cutoffs. I think you should all wear dresses from now on."

"Dresses?" I stared at him. "But this is a farm—"

"I know. But women used to wear dresses in the old days."

"Oh, you mean like *long* dresses?"

"Yes!" He smiled again. "Long dresses."

"But we don't have anything like that—"

"Can't you make some?"

"You mean *sew* them?"

"Sure, I guess so."

"Well, I used to do a little sewing—"

"Great." He smiled brightly. "Rainbow, you're amazing!"

I felt my blush deepening, but at the same time knew I needed to stay focused and be practical. "But, Sky, how can I sew dresses? I don't have any fabric—"

"Well, look around Gram's house. She used to sew a lot. And if you don't find anything to use, then I'll take you to town to buy something. But have faith, little one. I'm sure that God will lead you."

Although I was pleased at his attention I still felt a little overwhelmed and slightly confused, but I tried not to show it. Sky's approval meant everything to me. "Okay, Sky, I'll do the best I can."

"I knew you could handle this, Rainbow. You are a true gift from God to me."

And so it came to pass that I was put in charge of the sisters.

chapter seventeen

ON OUR THIRD DAY IN CALIFORNIA, almost a week after we'd left Brookdale, the seven of us gathered out at the end of the driveway just before sunset, right next to the road, to officially dedicate the farm to God's service.

The brothers had constructed a rustic sign made of twigs nailed and glued to an old barn board that announced who we were to all passersby: *The Promised Land*. First we sang praise songs as River and Stone set the posts into the muddy ground. Then we all got down on our knees, right there in the dirt and gravel, and prayed that God would richly bless us and our new home.

I don't think Gram ever knew that we had renamed the place, but then perhaps it didn't really matter since, as Sky so eloquently put it (during our little dedication ceremony): "In all actuality, this land belongs to God and God alone—and he is simply loaning it to us for this season. Let us pray that we use it for his glory."

To my surprise, the sisters didn't resent my new role of leadership—at least not at first. Well, other than Moonlight, that is, but then I think she would've resented anyone other than herself in this role. I suppose she made her objections fairly obvious by the way she ignored me most of the time.

Fortunately Sunshine and Breeze seemed to respect that I knew a little more about cooking and housekeeping than they did, but then I'd had most of my life to learn these things whereas they'd lived in "normal" households with mothers who apparently took care of all these troublesome domestic chores for them. As it turned out, other than me, Breeze was the only one who actually knew how to do laundry—and so I immediately appointed her head laundress. And since Gram's dryer was broken down, this was no easy task. The small clothesline quickly proved inadequate for the drying needs of eight people. Fortunately for Breeze none of us were overly consumed with cleanliness (back then we had a tendency to wear our clothes for days without laundering) but between sheets and towels and Gram's needs it was definitely a daily chore, and it wasn't long before the brothers got a bigger, sturdier line hung.

When I informed the sisters that we were to begin wearing dresses, and as soon as possible, I experienced some natural resistance. But I wisely suggested they take their grievances up with Sky. And he quickly set them straight on this issue, quoting by memory from the Bible about how women were to be modestly dressed and not to cut their hair, which wasn't a problem since we all wore our hair long and had no intention of cutting it anyway. So the new spiritual dress code was agreed upon.

I located Gram's sewing closet during that first week, and although Sky had told me to "appropriate" whatever I needed (because everything really belonged to God anyway) I somehow felt obliged to approach Gram first. I must admit to feeling slightly guilty about this, as if I was going behind Sky's back, but while everyone else was out working on the land—our biggest and most immediate challenge—I sat down to talk with Gram.

I suppose in some ways she reminded me of my own grandma,

although the two women were as different as night and day. Perhaps it was just her age that I felt respectful of. Whatever it was, I tried to befriend this old woman and probably spent more time with her than any of us, including her own grandson.

"How are you doing this morning?" I asked as I placed a fresh cup of coffee on her ever-present TV tray.

"Oh, I'm all right, I guess." She made a disgruntled face. "I just wish that darned TV of mine hadn't gone out like that. Land knows it'd been running just fine for years. And I really miss my good buddy, Bob Barker, on *The Price Is Right.*"

I patted her pale, flaccid hand, but kept silent about the fact that Sky had actually unplugged the "evil" television when the old woman had been asleep in her bed. He'd told us that television was the devil's tool and the way that Satan would eventually poison all the minds of the current generation, which may have turned out to be partially true. And so the next morning, when she tried to turn her TV on, we all just pretended to be surprised and to show concern, acting like we were trying to see what was wrong, and then finally Sky stepped in and told her that the picture tube had gone out since it was a pretty old television after all. He told her he'd take it into town to get fixed, but he had actually ordered the brothers to set it out in a corner of the barn and throw a tarp over it. It would be destroyed (along with a number of other things) later on.

"Would you like me to read to you from the Scriptures?" I offered. Sky had strongly recommended we try this approach whenever Gram complained about missing her television.

"No thank you! I've heard enough Bible reading of late to last me right up until I meet my Maker, which may not be so far off now." She ground out her cigarette and then coughed loudly, hacking into her ever-present handkerchief. "Just don't know what'll do me in first—diabetes, these lungs, or *pure boredom!*"

"So you really believe you'll see your Maker then?" I tried to change the subject back toward more spiritual things—Sky expected such from us.

She took a sip of her coffee, then slowly sighed. "Don't know why not."

"Don't you ever worry that you might not be living your life the right way?"

She laughed, but it sounded sarcastic. "Don't see how I could be living the *wrong* way—the good Lord knows I can't do much more'n move from this sofa to the bathroom to my bed—and sometimes I can't hardly do that. Don't see how that's hurting no one."

"But don't you want to live a life that's pure and holy and dedicated to God?"

"You know, honey, this is what I just can't quite figure out with you kids—what is it exactly you're trying to do? You act like a bunch of religious fanatics, like you think you're going to work your way into heaven or something."

"God wants us to live our lives set apart for him. He calls us to holiness." I'd been learning a lot lately, and Sky gave us regular Bible lessons several times a day—sometimes he could go on for hours. And we were required to take stringent notes (this as a result of River falling asleep once after dinner).

Gram slowly shook her head, then leaned back into the sofa, her nearly blind eyes gazing blankly toward the ceiling. "Well, I've never been one to put on any pretenses about knowing anything about religion. And although I went to church a fair amount as a little girl, I've been neglectful as an adult. But in the past few years I've grown painfully aware that I'm coming to the end of my life. Good grief, my doctor told me more'n a year ago to get my affairs in order—" she laughed— "whatever *that* means. But his warning did get me thinking about religion some, and I remembered what my own dear mother used to tell me back when I was just a small child. She used to say that Jesus Christ was our free ticket into heaven—that all we had to do was to *receive* him. Now that seems simple enough to me."

"Yes," I said, not disagreeing with her in principle. "I suppose it is that simple. But I guess what we're trying to do is to live a better life right now—while we're still here on earth. We want to serve God in the best way we can."

She smiled. "Well, I suppose that's not such a bad thing, dear, not really. Especially nowadays when so many kids are taking LSD and protesting and doing God only knows what else. I s'pect being overly religious ain't such a bad thing. Just you remember what my old granny used to tell me."

"What's that?"

"She used to say that some folks should watch out not to become so heavenly minded that they're no earthly good."

I thought about her words, and I knew I'd heard them before, probably from my own grandma, but to be perfectly honest, I wasn't exactly sure what they meant—at least not then. "Well, I don't think we need to worry about that, Gram. But speaking about earthly goods, I found a closet that's just full of sewing things."

She nodded. "Yes, I used to enjoy sewing. But then I got sick, and my eyes got too poor. I suppose I should just get rid of all that old stuff, maybe give it to the Goodwill or something."

"No, no . . . we don't need to get rid of it. I mean if it's okay, maybe I could use it."

"Sure, honey, you do whatever you like with it." She turned her face toward me. "You're a good girl, Rainbow—" Then her mouth twisted as if she'd just bitten into a sour lemon. "Tell me, dear, what's your real name?"

I thought for a moment, then looked over my shoulder to see if anyone was around before I answered in a whisper, "Cassandra Jane."

She patted my hand again. "Cassandra Jane. Why, that's a real pretty name. Much better than Rainbow."

"My mama gave it to me before she died."

Gram frowned. "Your mama died?"

For some reason, I just opened up to her then. I told her all about my past, about losing my mama and my grandma and how my daddy was in prison—or maybe he was out by now.

"Oh, you poor little thing. Why, I had no idea. Well, don't you worry, you can stay here with me just as long as you like, dear." She lowered her voice. "I just hope all those other kids will be heading on their way soon. I have to admit they're starting to wear on me some. But you are most welcome to stay on here." She smiled and I could see how yellowed her teeth had become from smoking. "And you're a good little cook, dear. That meat loaf you made last night was just perfect."

To my surprise, her sympathetic words actually brought tears to my eyes, and I thanked her for her kindness. It wasn't often in my life that anyone said anything very appreciative to me. I thought of the Crowleys. Even their words of praise had been few and far between.

But speaking of meat loaf reminded me that it was about time to start preparing supper again, and so I went back into the kitchen and donned my apron. It seemed I spent about half my waking hours in that kitchen. I didn't mind so much once I'd gotten everything all cleaned up and organized to my own liking—and of course I had Sunshine as my right-hand helper. But I knew that, more and more, they'd be needing her help outside, because there was lots to be done to get the farm in order. And so I knew I'd better learn to get along as best I could, all on my own, when it came to fixing the meals and working in the kitchen.

Fortunately, it was a pleasant, old-fashioned, country kitchen that reminded me some of the Crowleys.' I suspected that Gram had been a pretty good cook during her day, and I knew from talking to her that she had a particular penchant for sweets and desserts. And I tried to use her favorite recipes in order to accommodate these longings (of course I would later learn that this is just what a diabetic person does *not* need to indulge in, but she never once told me otherwise).

The kitchen had an abundance of tall cupboards, all filled with odd bits and pieces of stoneware and crockery. The cupboards were painted a nice pale shade of green. (I only discovered this after spending an entire day scrubbing them down with SOS pads—before that, they looked to be the color of old tea bags or tobacco spit.) Off the back porch was a good-sized pantry (full of old, empty canning jars). And I hoped to stock those shelves with my own home-canned produce in the upcoming summer. Gram had already told me of the fruit trees on her property that had once provided an abundance of apple, peach, pear, and plum preserves. But perhaps my favorite thing in that kitchen was the big picture window above the deep enameled sink. It looked out over what was soon to become a very fine vegetable garden.

In the center of the kitchen was an old wooden table with a bleached and worn surface that had seen many years of hard use. As spring drew near I enjoyed going out in the midmorning sunshine and picking a bunch of wildflowers, which I'd arrange in a pale green mason jar and set right in the center of the table—a pretty sight, if I do say so myself. But because the kitchen was my domain, I suppose I didn't really mind all the work that came along with it. At least not to start out with anyway.

It wasn't too long until I got the first garments of our "proper attire" sewn. In between meal preparations and Bible class, I'd set up the little Singer sewing machine on the kitchen table and sort through the stacks of old fabric. Most of the pieces were odd-sized leftovers from some previous sewing project, and none quite large enough to do anything substantial. So I started just sewing a colorful assortment of calicos, stripes, and plaids together to create larger pieces (long enough to make a skirt that could reach from waist to ankle). And then I gathered these "patchwork" lengths onto a waistband in order to create what I began to call "prairie" skirts. These colorful garments quickly gave us something modest to wear until I had time to create real dresses. And to my pleased surprise the sisters were completely delighted with their new patchwork skirts, and everyone thought I was quite clever. Yes, those were the good old days (as I remember them, that is).

And so, although it consisted of a lot of hard work, our first few months in "The Promised Land" passed fairly happily for the group. Looking back, I suppose it was sort of like a "honeymoon" phase—I know I still had great hopes and high expectations for all of us, and I believed that God was truly blessing us for our obedience to him.

Everyone worked hard to get the garden weeded and tilled and ready for spring planting. And the brothers made significant progress on the remaining acreage, mending fences for livestock, fixing an old chicken coop, cutting back wild berries and thistles. River was in charge of "agriculture" and tilled and prepared many acres for planting corn and beans and garlic (for our own use and to sell in town).

And all sorts of promising things were in the works. Stone turned out to be clever with tools and became our handyman. He was kept busy from morning to night. It seemed we were all working hard toward the same happy dream. And that in and of itself was fulfilling.

We started and ended each day with a time of prayer and Scripture reading—this always directed by Sky. But in the evening, after Gram had been escorted to bed, I would lead the group in praise songs, many of which I had written myself. After that we usually turned in early, pleasantly exhausted from our daily chores. The sisters continued to sleep in the house—and the brothers (except for Sky, who still occupied the downstairs bedroom) slept in the barn, where Stone had designed and built a more sheltered and rodent-free bedroom for them.

Occasionally Gram would query me as to how long the group planned to stay on. I think our presence in her house worried her some, probably more than any of us really knew. But her questioning decreased as time passed. I think she was grateful for the company, and it was plain to see that she needed someone to stay on and care for her. Perhaps she knew she wasn't long for this world, for it seemed her health was steadily failing. And so, for these reasons, I suspect she bit her tongue and kept her concerns to herself. Several times I asked Sky if we shouldn't take her in to see her doctor, but he insisted that doctors were all quacks and could do nothing to help her anyway, and that if we really cared about her we would lift her up in our prayers—which I did, usually on my own. But still she seemed to be fading fast.

I suppose the first real "trouble in paradise" came when River and Breeze were discovered "fornicating" together in the brothers' makeshift bedroom up in the barn one evening. Apparently it was Sky who caught them. And, after Gram had been tucked in, he made them both appear before the whole group (contritely, down on their knees), and he made them confess their sin and ask our forgiveness. Of course we forgave them. Then Sky told them that they must be married, to prevent this sin from occurring again.

Sky explained that the ceremony was to be simple, with no

frills—a wedding was nothing more than making a public vow to God. Just the same, I worked hard to finish up a pale yellow calico "prairie" dress that I'd been working on for Sunshine (but with her permission I quickly altered to fit Breeze, who was a little shorter). And that morning, Sunshine and I gathered a few wildflowers and some ivy, and these we braided into Breeze's hair. We knew how ashamed she felt for her "sinful act" and, while we did not condone her behavior, we were trying to encourage her. I even stayed up late the night before to bake a carrot cake, frosted with cream cheese icing tinted yellow to match her dress. This I also adorned with wildflowers. So despite Sky's "no frills" decree, we did manage to make things nice for River and Breeze.

And so on that sunny April afternoon, we held our very first wedding in "The Promised Land" (naturally, it was officiated by Sky). We all gathered outside, under the big oak tree, which would become our official "wedding location." And the words were spoken, and presto, River and Breeze were united in the eyes of God and man, and (according to Sky) the two became one.

Of course a honeymoon was out of the question (since finances were dwindling fast and a honeymoon was just a worldly thing anyway) but it was decided that Stone would now vacate the barn bedroom and come into the house to bunk with Sky, until other arrangements could be made. We knew that Sky wasn't too pleased with this new setup. For some reason he always had this strong need for his own space—apart from everyone else. And, naturally, we never questioned this. It seemed only right and fitting that our leader deserved something more—something better than the rest of us.

With Breeze moving into her new husband's quarters, Moonlight now had a room all to herself. This wouldn't have seemed like such a big deal, except that Sunshine and I both felt that Moonlight was not pulling her share of the weight around the place. In fact, if it wasn't a sin to speak evil of your sister, I would've publicly said that she was downright lazy. She was supposed to help with the house-cleaning and farmwork, but she seldom did. And in the rare event that she did, the job was never done right. (I tried to talk to Sky about my concerns once, but he insisted that I should handle it myself. This in itself should've given me a clue, since Sky was usually more than willing to correct a wayward brother or sister, but I was still somewhat naïve in those days.) Try as I might, I just couldn't seem to make Moonlight understand the importance of things like sweep-ing, mopping, dusting, and especially cleaning toilets.

In fact, I wasn't even quite sure how she spent most of her time—other than sleeping, that is. Usually if you wanted to find Moonlight, you would simply go look in her bed. Of course, I would later understand that she had a good reason to be so tired. But back then it seemed like nothing more than pure, sinful laziness to me.

And what made it even more frustrating was that when she wasn't sleeping, she was often bathing, washing her hair, and basi-cally just primping. Now you wouldn't think this would even be possible since sisters weren't allowed to wear makeup, perfume, or any other kind of toiletry or adornment. But somehow Moonlight always managed to look pretty good. Sunshine and I suspected that she'd held on to some items (like mascara, lip gloss, lotion, hair conditioner, whatever . . .) and kept them hidden somewhere in her private room, but we never actually got up the nerve to go in there and search.

Our way of punishing her came in the form of exclusion. With Breeze newly married and occupied with River's attentions, and Sunshine and me sharing a room and a quickly growing friendship, Moonlight was pushed right out of the sisters' circle. And for this I still feel a little guilty. I, of all people, should've known better.

Anyway, it should've come as no great surprise when Moonlight became the next one to marry. But the shocker was that she was "the chosen one." Moonlight had been picked to become Sky's wife.

Although we both kept our mouths tightly shut over this unexpected development, I suspect that Sunshine felt just as hurt as I that Sky had not chosen one of us. After all, we were the self-sacrificing, hard workers. I slaved all day in the kitchen and Sunshine not only helped me, but put in a man's day outside in the fields as well. And, of the sisters, we were the ones who most wholeheartedly followed Sky's teachings. We took our lives and our work seriously. And where did it get us? Plus it was no secret (between the two of us) that we'd both had similar feelings for our leader. Oh, certainly, we'd call these feelings "brotherly love, respect, and spiritual admiration," but I think we both had a serious crush on Sky. And to be perfectly honest, I'd always felt it was more likely that Sunshine would be the one to marry him, although I must admit to nurturing my own pathetic, little hopes (especially around the time when he chose me to be the leader of the sisters). And even though I was the youngest, it hadn't seemed entirely impossible that he might pick me.

But just as our kitchen garden began to put out real produce, it was announced that Sky and Moonlight would be wed.

chapter eighteen

MY GRANDMA USED TO SAY that the rain falls on the just and the unjust. And about the same time as Sky's big wedding announcement, poor Gram took a turn for the worse.

Confined to her bed, and with horrible open sores on her feet, it fell upon me (and occasionally Sunshine or Breeze) to care for her. Moonlight complained she couldn't handle it, insisting that the mere sight of Gram's swollen and discolored feet made her literally sick to her stomach. (And when I did the arithmetic—about six months later—I decided it must have actually been the morning sickness that had made her feel so puny just then.) But in Gram's final days, it took me and Sunshine and Breeze to care for her, almost around the clock. She was a large woman and her legs and feet had become nearly useless to her. And just the simplest bodily functions became overwhelming chores for all of us. It took all three of us sisters just to roll her over in order to change the sheets, which had to be done several times daily. Poor Breeze, she must've been doing four to five loads of laundry per day, but she hardly ever complained. And come to find out she was also with child. But fortunately for Sunshine and me, Breeze, unlike Moonlight, did not suffer from morning sickness, or if she did she never complained.

And although we three sisters followed Sky's instructions to a T and regularly "anointed" Gram with oil (a liberal greasing of her old gray head with Wesson cooking oil) and prayed, she never seemed to improve any. And finally, despite our fervent prayers and best efforts, she passed away on July 4 (which I suppose could be considered her own personal "Independence Day").

Unfortunately for Sky and Moonlight, it was also the day they'd chosen for their big wedding event (not that any great plans had been made or invitations sent). And naturally, it was merely coincidental that it fell on a national holiday because by this time we all agreed with Sky's theological thinking: All holidays were simply sinful excuses for commercializing pagan celebrations.

As fate (or God) would have it, I was the one to make the grisly discovery when I slipped in to check on Gram that hot July morning. Feeling strangely familiar with death by now (this was my third direct encounter) I simply swatted the bluebottle fly away from her forehead, then pulled the sheet up over her lifeless face and went to fetch Sky.

I felt only mildly surprised when Sky refused to call anyone in town about his grandmother's death. In fact, that was the very day that he decided that telephones were an invasive and unnecessary link to the sinful outside world and pulled them both from the wall. And that's how it came to be that we laid Gram to rest the same morning as the wedding.

Sky chose a serene and well-shaded spot out by the pine grove (and I truly think Gram would have appreciated the pleasant location). He then conducted a simple funeral service of reading Scripture, praying, and singing.

We didn't worry too much that none of her friends or family were informed or invited to attend her funeral, since she hadn't received one single visitor or personal phone call the whole time we'd been there (more than six months, by then). And we already knew that Gram had been estranged from her only son (Sky's alco-holic father) for years now. I know how it saddened Gram that their relationship had never been mended over the years. And based on some things she told me, I suspect that she'd expected her son to make the first move. But no move had ever been made, and now it was too late.

I wondered how this made Sky feel, since he and his father were on this same particular track of burned bridges. But then Sky had a habit of quoting Scripture at us about how we had to leave fathers and mothers to serve the Lord. And other than me, everyone in our group had left home and family behind—most without a backwards glance, or even a word that I knew of, although Sunshine told me in confidence later on that she had secretly called her mom shortly after our arrival in "The Promised Land" and assured her that she was safe. But naturally Sunshine didn't reveal our whereabouts to her mother since that would've put everyone at risk.

On the same day as the funeral, strange as it may seem, Sky and Moonlight were wed as planned. Once again we met under the old oak tree, this time late in the afternoon. There, River, being the second-oldest brother, performed the sober ceremony of matri-mony.

Sunshine and I both felt utterly exhausted after first "prepar-ing" Gram's body for burial, and then spending several hours scrubbing down her old room (the largest bedroom in the house and the one to be used by our current newlyweds). And as a result of these distracting demands this really did turn out to be a no-frills event. There were no special flowers or dresses or wedding cakes that day. And I'm fairly certain Moonlight never quite forgave us for this. But we figured she should've been pleased anyway—after all, she'd plucked herself the prize plum by managing to get hitched to our fearless leader. And we suspected the marriage, in and of itself, would elevate her position in our household considerably.

After Moonlight vacated her bedroom to take up residence with her new husband in Gram's old room, River and Breeze moved back into the big house and confiscated Moonlight's old room. And so we were just like one big happy family again.

Well, not exactly. I'm sure we were still slightly overwhelmed by the day's events, and I think Sunshine and I were both a little stunned by the marriage. I can still remember that first night (after Sky and Moonlight had wed). It was hotter than a firecracker upstairs and Sunshine and I were completely worn-out as we lay upon our bed with the window thrown wide open but hardly a breeze to stir the humid air. As weary as we were, we weren't too tired to speculate on which of us would be the next to marry. But perhaps the more disturbing question was which of us would remain the spinster of the household? After all, we both knew that only one available bachelor remained. And while we may have laughed and joked about the whole crazy situation, I know we both felt seriously worried that we would be the one that "no one wanted."

And so I remember praying silently and fervently that night as I selfishly begged God to have mercy on me and to help me through this difficult trial (although I knew I might need to repent of my selfishness later on; Sky was continuously warning us that selfishness and jealousy were our worst enemies). And while I never specifically asked God to let me marry Stone, I know that's exactly what I had in mind as I prayed so fervently.

Oh, it's not that I loved Stone, mind you, I just didn't think I could endure being the only one of our group who'd been, in essence, cast aside. Maybe it was because I already had such a rich history of having been cast aside—starting with a mama who (albeit innocently) had died and left me behind, and then a daddy who chose the bottle over me, a grandma who died, an aunt who shoved me off, and so on and so forth. . . . I just wasn't sure I could endure one more major rejection.

Perhaps with all this in mind, I began to act in a somewhat flirtatious way with Stone (another thing I would likely need to repent of, but later, I hoped—*after* we were happily wed). And although I felt guilty, it seemed as if Stone enjoyed my attentions (not to mention my berry crisp and zucchini bread). However, I knew my brazen ways were creating an awful barrier between Sunshine and me. And for this I felt true regret—because, out of everyone there, she had been the closest and dearest friend to me.

After a week or so of this silliness, I finally gave up my selfish pursuits and privately confessed the whole thing to Sunshine, begging her to forgive me. And then she told me that she'd actually been trying to do the same thing when they'd been working together outside! (But to no avail, since she felt certain that Stone was already smitten with me.) So then and there, we both solemnly promised that no matter what happened, neither of us would marry and abandon the other. There would be no "lone single sister." And so it was all settled. Or so we thought.

In late August, not long after my birthday (which, like all other holidays, went completely unnoticed, and I never mentioned it to anyone, except for Sunshine, and this only in passing to let her know I was now seventeen), Sky gathered us together to make another "important announcement." Without first consulting either of the parties concerned, Sky informed us that God had shown him in a vision that Stone was to marry Sunshine.

During the following days, I totally buried myself in the kitchen. Fortunately, all that produce that Gram had promised was now coming on like clockwork, and I could easily spend up to twelve hours a day in the steaming kitchen, poring over old cookbooks and working over boiling vats to can and preserve our bounty. I tried to hide my pain and put on a brave face as I told Sunshine that I was happy for her, and that she was free from our silly vow. After all, I knew that above everything else, God's will must be done. And in Sunshine's defense, I don't think *she* was all that pleased with her "arranged" marriage either. I know for a fact she didn't love Stone. But then, as one of my favorite old radio songs by Tina Turner used to proclaim, "What's love got to do with it?" Nothing, it seemed, at least not where God's will was concerned.

"But if love has nothing to do with marriage," I whispered to Sunshine one night just shortly before her wedding, "what's the real purpose of marriage, anyway?"

She sighed loudly, then answered, carefully. "I asked Sky that same question, Rainbow. And he said that God's sole purpose for marriage is procreation."

"Procreation?" I let the strange word roll around my mind for a few seconds, deciding whether I wanted to reveal my ignorance once again or not. "Okay, what's that mean?" I finally asked, throwing my pride to the wind.

She giggled. "It means having babies, silly."

"Oh." Well, I suppose that made sense. After all, both Breeze and Moonlight had rapidly swelling bellies (in fact, it seemed as if Moonlight was expanding in all directions!). And while this all fascinated me, a little, I had no desire whatsoever to become pregnant myself. In fact, the very idea of having a child of my own nearly scared me to death. And I even momentarily wondered if I shouldn't be thankful and relieved that I wasn't the one getting married after all. "Do you *want* to have a baby, Sunshine?"

After a long silent pause where I almost thought she'd fallen asleep, she answered. "No, not yet."

"But what will you do?"

"I don't know. I've been really praying about it, Rainbow, but I still don't know what to do. Sky says it's sinful to withhold our bodies from the Lord. He said that it's God's will for us to procreate, that this is how he'll increase our population in 'The Promised Land.' But I'm still worried."

"Have you talked to Stone about it?"

She laughed. "What good would that do?"

"I don't know."

"Rainbow." Her voice grew hushed now, and I couldn't tell if it was with warning or just plain fear. "You know that no one questions Sky's authority here."

An uneasy feeling swept over me, kind of like the way you feel when you get to school and realize that you forgot to study for a test that day, only this was more unsettling. Much more. Still, afraid to respond to Sunshine's veiled confession, I said nothing. And that was the last time we talked about such things for quite a while. I sensed that she, or maybe I, had closed that door, and we were not to open it. But the next day, as I was canning freestone peaches, Stone slipped into the kitchen.

"Do you have a minute, Rainbow?" he asked quietly.

I shrugged without looking up as I slipped a freshly peeled peach into a canning jar. "I guess so."

"Rainbow?"

I sensed he wanted my full attention, and so I rinsed my hands in the sink, then turned to face him. "Yes?"

"This is hard to say, but I really thought that you were going to be the one for me." He spoke quietly, glancing over my shoulder, out the window (I suspect keeping an eye out for Sky since this was not the kind of conversation our leader would appreciate or approve of).

"Oh, Stone," I said, forcing a lighthearted laugh. "That's awfully sweet of you, but I can see that God has other plans for you. And Sunshine is a truly wonderful person."

His brow furrowed and he bit into his lower lip. I sensed he wanted to say something more, but I wanted the conversation to end right there. Finally he spoke. "Do you ever wonder if this could be wrong?"

I swallowed hard, then looked away from him, forcing my gaze down to my hands clasped tightly around a faded tea towel. How red and cracked they had become lately, a reward from my constant kitchen work.

Yes, I did wonder. But to admit such a thing would be considered pure heresy by our leader (something punishable, and punishment was becoming more common within our little society). And so I said nothing.

"Sorry," he said, turning toward the back door. "I shouldn't have said that."

My heart pounded within my chest as I considered stopping him right then and there and telling him how I really felt. How I sometimes felt worried that Sky was just making it all up as he went . . . how I sometimes felt like a little child pretending to be grown-up, but all the while being treated like a child . . . how I felt concerned that we were all runaways, had performed illegal marriages and funerals, and had even taken over a dead woman's farm. But how could I ever begin to express all those things? And if I did, wouldn't it be sin? Wouldn't it be a lack of faith? And what would happen when Sky found out? Surely I would be punished. And so I kept my mouth shut.

And I continued to keep my mouth shut as I watched the solemn marriage ceremony of Stone and Sunshine. From then on, I just worked in the kitchen and kept my mouth shut.

It was during this time that I first began to nurture some serious doubts. First off, I doubted myself. Next, I doubted Sky. And finally, I doubted God. And it was during the golden month of September that I actually considered leaving "The Promised Land" altogether. I think if ever there was a time when I could've willingly walked away, even though I felt circumstantially trapped, it was in September. But then something sneaked up from behind me, something that locked me in.

During those days following the September wedding, I kept mostly to myself. I worked alone, slept alone, prayed alone, cried alone. What else could I do? With everyone so neatly paired off, and me feeling like that proverbial old fifth wheel, what did they expect me to do? Whether in my bedroom or my kitchen, I did not wish to be disturbed, and I made it clear to any who came near me. Even when Breeze sweetly asked me to help her start making some baby clothes (although her baby wasn't even due until December) I simply brushed her off, rudely telling her I had too much to do just then to think about babies! I knew I was pushing it when I started taking my meals by myself in the kitchen, separate from the group. I knew I was treading on thin ice. But I just didn't care. I'm sure I was hoping it would simply break and let me fall, going down . . . down . . . down.

And yet, despite my silent rebellion, I remember feeling uneasy and even nervous when Sky came into my kitchen one evening after supper. I was at the sink scrubbing the scorched bottom of a saucepan with a vengeance when he tapped me on the shoulder. I jumped, nearly dropping the pan.

"Rainbow," he said quietly. "I've asked Sunshine to clean up in here tonight. I want to talk to you in private."

I blinked in surprise to see Sunshine standing in the doorway. I realized then that I hadn't actually seen her, really *seen* her, for days, maybe weeks now, and as I looked at her standing there, her countenance dark and gray, she honestly seemed a mere shadow of her former self. She didn't even smile at me. I didn't know if it was because she felt guilty for abandoning me by marrying Stone, or maybe she was actually worried for me. At that moment, I don't think I even really cared. I shrugged, then flipped my braid over my shoulder as I set down the stubborn pan. I slowly removed my apron and handed it to Sunshine. "Have fun."

Sky opened the back door and led me out into the autumnal night. The air was just starting to get a slight chill to it, but the smell was still that of summer—the last tomatoes ripening on the vine, the heaped compost pile decomposing, remnants of overlooked fruit now lying rotten on the ground. We walked in silence and I could sense a seriousness in Sky's step—nothing new, really. It was almost as if he wore his sobriety, his spirituality, over his shoulders like a thick, heavy cloak for all the world to see. But for once I didn't quite care, and I realized as we walked that I wasn't even scared.

For days, I had known that Sky would eventually call me aside to reprimand me for my willful and disrespectful ways. (I'd even stopped coming to Bible class of late.) He might demand that I show contrition by kneeling down before the group and begging their forgiveness and then waiting for my punishment (it might be extra chores or an extra hour of prayer or maybe even corporal punishment—we hadn't actually seen that yet, but Sky had alluded that it could happen). But wouldn't he be surprised when I refused to submit to his rules? How would he react when I told him that it was all over—that I was finished with the game? Would he even care? Or maybe I wouldn't get the chance. Maybe he planned to publicly shun me now—to excommunicate me from the group. Perhaps he would send me from "The Promised Land," out into "The Wilderness" to wander for, say, forty years? Well, maybe that would be just fine and dandy with me. Surely anything would be better than this.

"Rainbow, I don't know how to say this," he began.

Waiting in silence, I offered him no help. I said nothing. Felt nothing. Was nothing.

"This isn't easy, but I need to tell you something."

Again he paused, and now I grew slightly irritated. I drew in my breath and held it inside my chest, preparing myself for the worst he could give me. I would welcome his judgment, his stinging words, his chastisement, and even his exile.

Then he turned to face me and gently placed both hands on my shoulders. And suddenly I felt disoriented by this strange turn, and the breath I'd held in now escaped in a long, slow sigh—I was deflated.

"Rainbow, I need to ask you to forgive me."

I shook my head in disbelief. I must've heard him wrong. I couldn't ever remember having heard Sky ask anyone to forgive him. *"Forgive you?"* I repeated almost inaudibly.

He nodded, and in the faint light of a half-moon just cresting over the eastern hills, I could see a glistening on his face as a tear streaked down his cheek. Was Sky actually crying? "I have made a grievous mistake," he said. "Rainbow, I—I—"

I clearly heard the break in his voice. "What?" I asked him as I strained my eyes in the semidarkness to better see his face, to study his expression. Was this for real? Was he really upset? Or was I simply imagining this whole thing?

He collapsed onto the bench, and holding his head in his hands he sobbed like a child. I sat down beside him and placed my hand on his back. "What is it, Sky? What's wrong? Please tell me. I don't understand."

After a long moment, he sat up straight. Then taking both my hands into his, he looked directly at me and said, "Rainbow, you were the one I truly wanted to marry. You were the one that I loved. But you were so young. And Moonlight—she enticed me with her—her ways—and—and—" His head slumped down again.

My heart pounded against my chest and I could hear a high-pitched buzzing in my ears, getting louder. I felt sickened and confused and just slightly faint. I didn't understand what he was saying, whether he meant it or not, or even if I'd heard him right.

He looked up. Placing his face close, just inches from mine, he said, "Rainbow, I don't know what to do now. I'm married. But you need to know that I love you. I have since the beginning."

I just nodded, still too dumbfounded to speak.

"And every day I notice how you're so beautiful and so truly spiritual, but each day you look sadder and sadder, and I don't think I can bear it for another day. Can you ever forgive me?"

Still unsure as to whether I could form words, I simply nodded, a multitude of conflicting and indescribable emotions tumbling and whirling through me like a tornado.

Then I felt his hand cup my chin and he gently pulled my face to his, and I felt the warmth of his breath and the stiff prickle of his beard . . . and then he kissed me! Not a brotherly kiss, but fully on the mouth.

And perhaps most humiliating in this memory is that I kissed him back. Certainly I was tentative at first, but as he continued pressing his mouth against mine, I responded—eagerly and hungrily. I don't know how long we kissed, but I do remember feeling dizzy and dazed when we finally stopped. And again I thought, *I must be imagining this.*

He then pulled me into his arms and held me tightly against him, stroking my hair as he spoke the kindest, most comforting and soothing words to me. He promised me that he would look out for me especially now. That I was to be set aside like his precious jewel, and that I would never be forced to marry anyone.

And somehow, despite my earlier resolve to walk away from that place, I now knew I wouldn't. I simply couldn't. That door was bolted for good.

More than anything, I wanted love, and I swallowed Sky's words of love with a fierce hunger. I bit right into them—hook, line, and sinker—and he began to reel me in.

chapter nineteen

HOW IS IT POSSIBLE TO FEEL totally hopeless and worthless one moment and then higher than the sun and the moon in the next? When Sky finally opened up to me, revealing his humanity, his broken dreams, yes, even his sin, I fell in love with him like I'd never imagined possible. Of course he warned me our relationship was to remain strictly top secret. But he also told me that just because it was secret didn't mean it was sinful. He said that sometimes God has reasons for making us keep secrets. The Bible is full of them, he said.

Then he carefully explained that he was like Jacob (in the Bible). He even read the story to the whole group the following night, but I knew he was reading it for my benefit. And I'm sure I sat there gazing up at him with real stars in my eyes.

He had already told me how Jacob had been in love with the beautiful Rachel, but after working hard to earn her for his bride, he'd been tricked into marrying her older sister, Leah. But Jacob didn't give up, no, he worked for another seven years and was finally allowed to marry the lovely Rachel. And although he had to keep Leah as his first wife, Rachel had always been his one and only true love.

"And that's just how it will be with you," he secretly promised to me later.

"Does this mean we'll get married?" I asked.

"In due time," he told me. "Just be patient."

And so I was. Incredibly patient. But it wasn't that hard, really. To be honest, I didn't feel any great hurry to be actually married. It was enough for me to simply be *loved* by our admired leader.

Instead of being jealous of Moonlight, I almost came to pity her, for she seemed to grow more unhappy and even fatter with each passing day. And it wasn't just the natural weight that comes with pregnancy. Supposedly Breeze's baby was due before Moonlight's, but she wasn't nearly as enormous as Moonlight.

Of course, I was privileged with information about the real due dates. Sky had confessed to me that Moonlight had enticed him into her bed several months before their marriage. He explained how he'd been in a weakened state just then, feeling concerned that he'd forced River and Breeze to marry and worried that it might've been a mistake. And Moonlight had offered him her "comfort" and naturally that led to other things (sinful things). And even though they'd "only sinned once" according to Sky, Moonlight had missed her following period, and then her next, and that's when the sudden July wedding became necessary. Somehow this all made perfect sense to me back then, and I felt greatly comforted in my newfound knowledge.

Now I felt happy to work and to wait—more a part of the family than ever. And it was amazing how just a smidgeon of Sky's attention could take me a long, long ways. How I loved it when he pointed me out to the group as such a good and willing servant. He often used me as an example of how we all should live, and I know I took exceeding pride in all this (even though I had to repent of it later). But repenting, for us, was just a normal part of daily life—

and in some twisted way I'm sure it almost gave us pleasure. We would get down on our knees before the group and confess to all sorts of sins, everything from impure thoughts to picking our noses, and then we would sob or beat our fists on the floor and beg forgiveness from God and everyone.

The only one who never seemed to have much to repent of was Moonlight. I found this interesting, especially in light of my suspicion that she was stealing food from the kitchen. I first noticed food missing in the fall. I'd go into the cupboard to get something, like a bag of chocolate chips for making cookies (this was before all forms of sugar were outlawed) and the bag would be gone—not just some chips, but the entire bag. Or maybe it'd be a jar of peanut butter or homemade jam (and that really made me mad because I'd sweated over a hot stove putting up that jam!). At first I thought it might be one of the brothers—and they worked so hard it was understandable that they might get the munchies and come foraging (even though it was forbidden). But when none of them confessed I became suspicious.

And so I decided to set a trap. Mindful that things most often went missing following a grocery trip, I waited till Sky and Stone returned from shopping in town. (The brothers were the only ones allowed to leave the farm.) As usual, I had given Sky a very detailed list of what was needed for the kitchen. I ran on a very tight kitchen budget since our income was limited to whatever we could sell off the farm—like old antiques found in the attic, Sunshine's car, and even produce. (It was starting to become slim pickings, but we had high hopes for the upcoming year, when we planned to have even more produce and perhaps some hand-crafted items to sell.) I unloaded the groceries as usual, but when I got to the chocolate chips, the cheap kind that came in a bright red bag, I carefully "painted" over the red plastic surface with red food coloring and then set the "bait" in a visible spot in the food cupboard.

The rest was simply child's play. I listened until I heard footsteps, right around midnight, then slipped downstairs in time to spy Moonlight in the kitchen furiously trying to wash the red food coloring off her fingers—I'd caught her literally red-handed! Then I went to Sky's room and told him about the problem. I knew I was being a snitch, but this behavior was expected within our group. It was our responsibility to hold one another accountable.

Moonlight was punished by having to wash dishes for a week—quite a nice little vacation for me, but I must admit to feeling just a little guilty as I watched her straining past her extended stomach to reach the sink. Still, I figured the exercise might do her good.

Sky was going into town on a fairly regular basis these days, sometimes to sell things, and sometimes to pick up supplies. But to my surprise he traded an old dresser for a bunch of used guns.

His rationale, he explained at dinnertime, was that he and the brothers might need to do some hunting during the winter (for food). Plus, he said, who knew when we might need protection?

"Protection from what?" I asked as I set a bowl of potatoes on the table.

"Now I don't want you to be afraid," he said in an authoritative voice, "but we live in strange times and there are people out in the world who don't like us." He looked around the table and I could feel a lecture coming. "We are not of the world and so the world questions our ways. And the world will persecute us for our beliefs—we don't know what they might do to hurt us. So it's best to be prepared for anything. Besides, as I've been teaching you from the Scriptures, this present world will soon come to an end. But first there will be a holocaust and plagues and warfare, and we

must be prepared, my children. We must be ready for anything."
He smiled then. "But don't be afraid."

Well, it was hard not to be fearful when you thought about all
those things, and I suppose it was our fear (in a way) that kept us in
submission to Sky's authority. He was like our big daddy, our pro-
tector. Under his spiritual roof, we believed we would be safe from
all outside harm. We never considered the harm within our own
gates.

When Sky drove around town in his colorful van (decorated
with crosses and fishes and doves) he occasionally met up with
other Jesus freaks, and they were always interested in who he was
and what he was doing. As a result, he sometimes invited folks to
come out and visit our farm. These were special times, and we
always worked hard to get everything all spruced up for our visitors. And it was fun seeing a fresh face—almost like a holiday
(which were of course forbidden).

We all knew it was Sky's plan to eventually increase our
numbers—but only with the right people, he'd said, the ones God
revealed to him. Naturally, we couldn't adopt just *anyone* into our
special circle. But before long, we took in a new couple. I can't recall
their original names, but during our "adoption" ceremony (the first of
its kind) Sky blessed them with new names: Venus and Mountain.

Venus was vivacious and pretty with long, curly, auburn hair.
And Mountain was a big, somewhat serious sort of guy. In a way he
could've seemed like a threat to Sky, but for some reason he wasn't.

In fact, Mountain really seemed to respect Sky and became
one of his closest friends, if not bodyguard. And while I'm sure Sky
appreciated the friendship, I don't believe he was ever *really* close
to anyone (not in the way of a healthy give-and-take mutual relationship). But I'm sure everyone, including me, thought they were
close to Sky.

Venus and Mountain were older than most of us and had recently dropped out of Stanford, saying how they had decided to focus all their energy on spiritual growth instead of the wasteful accumulation of worldly knowledge. They were both from families with money, and so, to start out with, they were able to contribute generously to our little farm. And of course Sky made them feel very welcome. To do this, Sunshine and Stone were asked to move their things out to the barn and take up residence in the old make-shift bedroom in the loft. And then Venus and Mountain moved into their old bedroom.

Earlier in the fall, Sky had picked up a secondhand book on nat-ural childbirth and this became mandatory reading for all the sis-ters. And although I found it slightly disturbing, I read the whole thing from cover to cover (mostly because books were extremely limited and I missed reading). And so, in a way, I became something of the local expert (a remnant of my old academic ways). But as I reread the chapters on prenatal care, I grew somewhat alarmed.

The book warned not to neglect things like regular obstetric exams, blood tests, vitamins, proper weight gain, and more. So far neither Breeze nor Moonlight had seen a doctor. And according to this book, Moonlight's excessive weight gain in her first pregnancy placed her and her baby at great risk—especially for natural child-birth!

I mentioned my concerns to Sky, but he said that, as with everything, we just needed to trust God with this, and that God would see that the babies were born safely. And so instead of wor-rying, I tried to trust God more, praying that he would watch over our expectant mothers' health. However, I did encourage Moon-light to eat less and exercise more (which she didn't appreciate at all—especially in light of our earlier "red-handed" confrontation. I'm sure she secretly had it out for me more than ever just then). All the same, I carefully studied the chapter on nutrition and did the best I could to prepare sensible and balanced meals for our two mothers-to-be.

It was a great relief to everyone when the days grew cooler and shorter and the farmwork decreased. Thanks to all my long hours in the sweltering heat of summer, our pantry was fairly well stocked against winter (although I knew we couldn't survive on it alone).

With more free time on my hands, I could do more sewing. Sky regularly visited a Goodwill store in town where he purchased inexpensive clothing items that could either be mended or altered to suit the needs of our group. And I began making things for the two babies who would soon join our family.

Breeze got involved in helping me and showed real talent at creating some sweet little items for her soon-to-be baby. My favorite was a bright-colored patchwork quilt with all kinds of embroidery. As a result of all this sewing, Breeze and I grew closer. And while I enjoyed her companionship, at the same time I worried that Sunshine seemed to be withdrawing more and more. Not only from me but from the entire group as well.

One day in late October, I confronted Sunshine while she was helping me prepare supper. I asked her what was wrong, and why had she been so quiet lately? I actually wondered if she might be pregnant and perhaps depressed about it.

At first, she studied me closely, as if determining whether or not she could trust me. "Oh, Rainbow," she finally said with a deep sigh. "I don't know . . ."

"Are you unhappy?"

She shrugged uncomfortably. "Oh, I don't know . . ."

"Is it your marriage?"

She glanced over her shoulder to see if anyone was around. "Maybe."

"Are you and Stone getting along okay?"

She shrugged again. "I don't know . . ."

I stopped stirring the biscuit batter. "Sunshine, *talk* to me. What's wrong?"

I could see tears building in her eyes, but she pressed her fist against her mouth as if trying to keep the words inside.

"Come on, Sunshine," I urged. "It's me, Rainbow. You can trust me."

She looked me straight in the eyes. "I don't want to be here anymore," she whispered, then turned her attention back to cleaning a head of cabbage.

I took in a sharp breath. A confession of this sort was just barely short of treachery. "But, Sunshine," I began, "we're a family—we all love you."

She rolled her eyes as she shook the water from the cabbage head. "Yeah, Rainbow, but some of us want to 'love me' a little too much."

I studied her. "What do you mean?"

She forced a laugh. "Oh, you wouldn't understand, Rainbow. You're so pure and innocent—almost like an angel really." She raised the large knife and brought it down with a loud bang, splitting the cabbage head in two.

Now I knew I could take her words as a compliment, but somehow it just didn't feel like that to me. "What exactly do you mean, Sunshine?"

She let out an exasperated sigh, then lowered her voice. "I mean . . . that just because Sky is our *highly exalted spiritual leader*, it shouldn't give him the right to sleep with anyone he likes."

I felt my eyes open wide, and now I glanced over to the doorway, but no one appeared to be anywhere near the dining room. "What are you saying?" I hissed at her.

She put her face close to mine and with wild-looking eyes said, "I'm saying that I've had enough of this place. I didn't come here to be a *sex slave*, Rainbow." And then she stabbed the knife into the old kitchen table and the point stuck right into the wood.

I couldn't believe what I'd just heard. Had she lost her mind? "Sunshine—" I tried to speak soothingly— "you don't know what you're saying."

"Oh, don't I?" She turned and glared at me. "Well, just wait, *little one*, it'll happen to you too sooner or later. Sky plans on fathering a child with every one of the sisters."

"Sunshine!"

"Oh, I knew you wouldn't believe me, Rainbow. You're too good and innocent—and *naïve!*"

I just stared at her and shook my head, and I'm sure my horrified expression must've really frightened her, making her regret her terrible confession.

She grabbed my hands. "Please, Rainbow, don't tell Sky what I said. I'm sorry, it was wrong to say those things. I'll repent of my sin, I promise, I will. But please, please don't tell Sky. I'm so sorry."

I just stood there in silent shock. Sky was our spiritual father, our ruler, our leader. How could I not tell him?

"Please, Rainbow, I'm begging you. Promise me you won't tell."

I nodded dumbly, anything to shut her up—to put an end to her blasphemous heresy before someone overheard us and we both got called in to confession.

She went back to quietly chopping cabbage for a while, but then turned and spoke in a calm voice. "Rainbow, if I leave here, do you want to come with me?"

I firmly shook my head. "No, Sunshine, of course not. This is my home. This is my family. I'm safe here."

She nodded. "Yeah, I figured that's what you'd say. And that's okay. But please, I'm begging you, don't mention this to anyone."

For two days I kept Sunshine's admission to myself, waiting for her to come forward and confess her sinful thoughts, to break down before the group and fall on her knees and beg their forgiveness. But she did not.

When I woke up on the third day, I decided I'd waited long enough. It was time to speak up and inform Sky about Sunshine's false accusations. I surely didn't look forward to betraying her trust like this, but I knew in the long run it would be for Sunshine's best. You just can't hide sin like that and not expect to suffer the consequences—and according to Sky, sooner truly was better than later.

But as it turned out, I didn't get the chance. Sunshine had left during the night.

Strange as it may seem, Stone didn't even notice her missing until she didn't show up for lunch. He hadn't seen her all morning and had assumed she'd risen early, but upon checking further he suspected she'd packed up a few things the previous day and then slipped out of bed during the night.

Apparently she'd left on foot, since Sky had long since sold her little car (for just a few hundred dollars since he couldn't provide a title). Stone was worried for her welfare and wanted to go look for her, but Sky wouldn't let him. Instead he called us all to a meeting.

I could tell by the white line around his lips that he was upset, maybe even angry, but he kept his voice controlled, calm and even. "Unfortunately our sister Sunshine has made a very bad decision," he informed us. "She has broken our trust and betrayed God by abandoning her spiritual family. So according to Scripture, as of this date, Sunshine is hereby separated from fellowship with us. If anyone should see her, you are not to speak to her."

Stone raised his hand. "But what if she wants to come back?"

Sky considered this. "If she wants to come back, she must first come to me. And she must confess her sin and ask forgiveness, and then she must submit to my authority and accept whatever form of punishment seems appropriate."

And so it was agreed. Sunshine was "separated from fellowship." Not that it mattered much since she never came back anyway. Much later I would learn that she had simply walked to town, used a pay phone to place a collect call to her mother, and by late that afternoon was on a jet, bound for home.

That same week, and two months before she was due to deliver her baby, Breeze began feeling sickish. Her hands and feet became quite swollen and she had severe headaches. According to the natural childbirth book this could be the warning signs of preeclampsia or toxemia ("a very serious illness that endangers both the baby and mother and should be treated by a trained obstetrician").

Concerned, I went to Sky with this medical information, interrupting what appeared to be a very intense conversation between him and Venus and Mountain.

"I'm sorry to bother you," I said quickly, "but I think Breeze needs to see a doctor."

Sky looked up from the open Bible lying on his lap. "What is wrong?"

I described the medical conditions, hoping to convince him that it was serious.

"Have you anointed her yet?" he asked in the kind of tone one uses with a very ignorant person.

"Uh, no—no . . ." I stammered.

"Well then." He lifted his brows with a slightly amused smile.

"Maybe I can be of help," offered Venus.

Sky sighed heavily, then waved his hand in dismissal. "Yes, Venus, why not go see what you can do for our ailing sister."

Venus and I anointed Breeze with vegetable oil and knelt down to pray for her healing, then Venus followed me back to the kitchen, where I started to heat up a can of chicken noodle soup that I hoped might entice Breeze to eat. Her appetite had been quite poor lately.

"I don't think you need to be too worried," said Venus. "I'm sure God is healing our sister. And if it's any comfort, I took some health and nutrition classes during my first year of college, and if I remember correctly her condition is really quite common."

"Really?" I looked at her hopefully as I stirred the soup.

"Yes. She just needs to stay off her feet for a few days and eat healthy food." She cleared her throat now—in that way a person does when they wish to say something but don't quite know how to begin. "And speaking of healthy food, I asked Sky if I might not be able to give you some tips here in the kitchen."

I turned and looked at her. "What do you mean?"

"Well . . ." She made a funny little face. "I know you're doing the best you can in here, Rainbow. And I know you haven't had any formal nutritional training. But it's just that I think we could all be eating a lot better with a few changes. And as Mountain and I were just discussing with Sky, God wants us to keep our bodies in holy condition since they are his temples. We don't want to be filling our temples up with poison—"

"Poison?" I turned down the heat on the soup. "I have never given anyone poison—"

Venus laughed. "Of course not. Not knowingly anyway. But there are things you cook with that are not healthful."

"Like what?"

"Oh, things like white sugar and bleached, white flour instead of whole grains. And then processed food and red meat and . . . well . . . all sorts of things." She laughed again as if I should get the joke.

I poured the soup into a bowl and then turned to Venus. "You know, I've been handling the kitchen for nearly a year now. If you think you can do better—"

She placed her hand on my shoulder. "Oh, no, dear. I don't want to take over your job. But maybe I can just help you with the menu planning." She picked up the empty soup can still sitting on the counter. "For instance, do you realize that this is mostly a bunch of chemicals?"

I shook my head, but I could feel a large lump growing in my throat. Who was she, this newcomer, to come in here and criticize my cooking? "Excuse me," I said.

I took Breeze her "chemical-laden" soup and told her I hoped she'd take it easy for a few days. Then excusing myself once again I went up to my bedroom and cried. And lying prostrate across the cold wooden planks of my bedroom floor I cried for the duration of the afternoon.

I wasn't even sure exactly why I was crying. I knew I missed Sunshine, and I was concerned for Breeze, and I didn't like what Venus had said about my cooking. But I suspected it was something more too—I just couldn't quite put my finger on it. And as I cried, I begged God to help me to deal with this . . . this spirit of whatever it was that had come upon me so recently and now seemed to be chasing me down like a pack of rabid dogs.

chapter twenty

FROM SOME REASON I've always harbored an aversion to the month of November. I'm not sure when my phobia first began—perhaps in childhood when I fretted over the onset of the cold weather that would most likely keep me indoors more often than not, or maybe it was just that familial celebration of Thanksgiving that always left me feeling empty, alone, and forgotten. But despite our relocation to California, the dismal foreboding of November followed. And it was only the first week of that ominous month when Breeze became very sick and went into premature labor.

I tried to help her as best I could, but I knew her needs were far beyond what I could give, and although I stayed in the bedroom with her, kneeling beside her and praying, I felt completely helpless. Just after dark, despite Sky's warnings and threats, River wrapped Breeze in a blanket and carried her out to the barn, then hijacked the van and sped straight to the local hospital where the emergency room doctor just barely managed to save her life. But the baby (a tiny girl) was born dead.

Breeze later told me (confidentially) that the doctor had said that if she'd only come in for help at the first signs of preeclampsia the baby might've survived. Brokenhearted over their loss, she and River briefly considered not returning to the farm at all, but then realized they had no money and, they felt certain, no one else to turn to. And so they came back—broken, dejected, and in trouble.

They both knelt down on the matted living room carpet and confessed their transgressions (rebellion in the form of stealing the van and seeking outside medical help) and contritely asked Sky's forgiveness—which he granted (along with a short sermon on the importance of obedience and submission).

All things considered, I think they were warmly welcomed back into the family. I'm sure everyone felt truly sorry for their loss. Even Moonlight, who had quite recently become much more cautious with her eating and exercise habits, expressed her sympathy over the lost baby.

"I'd been looking forward to having our kids grow up together," she told Breeze the next day. "They could've been playmates, you know."

Breeze had simply nodded and said nothing. But the following week, she gathered up all the sweet baby things she'd created in previous months. Tying them into a neat bundle, she quietly set them outside of Sky and Moonlight's door. All except for the colorful quilt. That she kept on the foot of her bed (and sometimes, when she didn't know I was looking, I would spy her hugging it tightly to her chest and crying quietly).

I must admit now (although I never confessed it back then) that I felt just slightly chagrined at the unjustness of all this. And I wondered if this might not be God's way of laughing at us, right in all our religious faces, because if the truth were known, Breeze had worked hard, been honest and good, and yet she lost her baby. And then there was Moonlight, who had sinned many times over (without ever confessing hardly a thing—at least nothing that was real, and not to the group) and yet she always seemed to come out on top!

First off, she had trapped Sky into marriage. Then she had stolen and lied and cheated. And she never did her share of the work. She didn't even take proper care of her health or her body, but so far she'd never suffered any problems in her pregnancy. And now she (who had never sewn a single stitch) was rewarded with a great big pile of lovingly hand-sewn baby clothes. Where was the justice in that?

I suppose I might've brought these concerns to Sky during one of our little private and intimate talks—because for a time there (back before Venus and Mountain had arrived and Sunshine had left) Sky and I had spent a fair amount of time together. And it had been nice. I'd always looked forward to our moonlit walks and chats. But as fall turned into winter these times became few and far between.

Venus, as promised, began to do all the menu planning for me. As a result, and for the first time ever, Sky allowed a woman to accompany him into town (only because Venus was the expert when it came to health foods and the best places to get them, he explained, plus we all knew she was contributing financially just then . . .). Venus said they had found most items at the Farmers' Market (a place where she said you could find anything).

I didn't know what to think when she began to unload all these strange things in my kitchen. Things like soy powder and tofu, wheat germ and brown rice and whole wheat, raw honey and sprout seeds and yogurt and goat cheese. To be honest, some of these things didn't even look edible to me. There were new pieces of cooking equipment too, and suddenly I realized that cooking, as I had known it, was over. From now on it would be a very complicated affair indeed.

Venus was a fine one to tell me exactly what to cook, but that's about as far as she went with it (sometimes I wondered if she even knew how to cook at all!). And although I'd been demoted from head chef to kitchen hand, it still fell to me to make her menus succeed. If I tried one of her new recipes, and it didn't turn out (even though I'd followed it to a T) she would blame me—right in front of everyone.

Oh, she always did it in a funny, clever way, like, "Poor Rainbow, she didn't know that whole wheat kernels have to be ground first to make whole wheat flour. Ha, ha, ha." But despite her merry smile, her words stung and in many ways reminded me of old Sally Roberts (from back in my school days). It seemed strange to me to think that Sally Roberts would only be in her senior year of high school. After all, I felt completely grown-up by then—as if I'd been out on my own for years now (although we were only just approaching our one-year anniversary).

During this "transition" period in the kitchen, Sky did come in occasionally to give me a few little pep talks. Perhaps Venus felt worried she might actually have to don an apron if I became overly discouraged. Sky would rub my back as he told me that God would reward me for my servant's spirit, and that he knew it wasn't easy for me to make these changes, but they would be for the best, just wait and see. And then he would kiss me, soundly. And suddenly all would be right as rain with my little world again.

Just before Christmas we had three new members inducted into our family, making us a total of eleven altogether. The new members had originally been introduced to Sky by Mountain and Venus. The two new brothers (also dropouts from Stanford) went out to the barn to bunk with Stone. And a young woman (one of Venus's childhood friends) became my new roommate. Sky had given her the name of Cloud during the "adoption" ceremony.

I think that may have been the first time it occurred to me that all the sisters in "The Promised Land" had names that were somehow connected (Moonlight, Sunshine, Rainbow, Breeze, Venus, and now Cloud). Celestial-type things, I thought to myself, and all related to the sky—*Sky*—just like our leader!

I know I didn't really allow myself the luxury of thinking too much about this odd coincidence, not at the time anyway (although Sky always was quick to say, "There's no such thing as a coincidence—everything comes from the hand of God"), but it did catch my attention. On the other hand, all the brothers had very earthbound names like Stone and River and Mountain. Curious indeed.

As expected, we didn't celebrate Christmas (other than the reading of the first Christmas story for our evening devotions) and so "Christmas Eve" passed quietly for us, with a plain supper of soybean "meatless" meat loaf and rice and beans and whole wheat "rolls" that could have doubled as hockey pucks. The word *bland* came to mind, but I knew better than to criticize Venus, and so kept my thoughts to myself. But I couldn't help but notice how our family didn't seem to be thoroughly enjoying their meal, not in the way that I remembered them doing in the past. At least I didn't think so. And afterwards, as Breeze and I were cleaning up in the kitchen, she mentioned that the meal had been a little lackluster. As a result, we decided to sneak into the pantry and open a jar of peaches. Together we forked right into the jar and gorged ourselves on the sweet, golden, juicy peaches—allowing the sugary syrup to run right down our chins as we giggled with glee. Our secret Christmas Eve treat!

"I don't see why Venus won't let you serve fruit with our meals," said Breeze as she dropped her fork into the now-empty jar.

"It's because of the sugar, but I'm hoping she might eventually change her thinking." I glanced proudly over my still fully stocked shelves (lasting longer than expected due to Venus's stringent menu planning). I loved the look of those bright-colored jars. They reminded me of a string of beautiful jewels or maybe even those colorful glass balls some people hang on Christmas trees. In fact, the pantry had quite a festive, almost partylike feeling. And I suppose Breeze and I were feeling just slightly giddy—that is, until the door burst open.

"What are you two—" Venus stood in the doorway, staring at the two of us in wide-eyed horror, as if we'd both just been caught making a sacrifice to Satan, or something equally abhorrent.

Breeze smiled innocently, the empty peach jar still clutched in her sticky hands. "Uh, we were just having some—uh—fruit."

Venus scowled at both of us in disgust. "Don't you know that's full of *sugar?*"

"Well, it's not *that* bad," I said in defense. "Actually it was mostly full of peaches that grew right here on our farm."

She grabbed the jar from Breeze, and after swiping her finger through the remaining syrup, she stuck it into her already puckered mouth. Then, making a horrible face, she groaned. "Ugh, that's *pure* sugar!"

"But we only ate the peaches—"

"You two are as bad as children." Then she smiled. Not a friendly smile though, more of a superior smile, like she knew something we didn't, and I figured we'd both find ourselves kneeling on the living room carpet confessing to gluttony before bedtime. Oh well, what else was new?

"Go on with you now," she commanded, closing the door behind us.

We finished cleaning the kitchen and to our relieved surprise, not a word of our peach-snatching episode was mentioned during our evening devotions, and Sky didn't even give an invitation to confession time. So I think Breeze and I were feeling borderline cocky when the group broke to go to bed. I remember winking at her before heading up to my room.

The following morning was Christmas Day, and although we weren't "observing" the holiday, I still wished I could fix something special for breakfast. But naturally the menu was already set for oatmeal and whole wheat toast (this made from the really dry whole wheat bread that I'd baked on Monday and which would become even drier once made into toast). And this toast was to be consumed without the help of any of the delicious jams and jellies I'd so lovingly made last summer.

Tempted to sneak out a jar of jam for myself (that I thought I could smuggle up to my room and enjoy later) I opened the door to the pantry. But to my stunned amazement, the shelves had been stripped clean of more than two-thirds of my beautiful, colorful jars. All that remained from all my home canning were green beans, corn, and tomatoes!

I blinked and stared again, thinking maybe I was seeing (or not seeing) things. But it was all too real. Every single fruit jar had been removed. I knew this must be Venus's doing, but where had she taken them?

Dismayed, I went over to my kitchen window and stared blankly outside. And there I saw Venus and Sky, right next to our big compost pile. Beside them was a wheelbarrow filled with jars of canned fruit, and at their feet was a quickly growing pile of empty canning jars. I watched in disbelief as, one by one, they popped open each tediously sealed jar and dumped its precious contents onto the stinking compost pile.

I felt dizzy and sick, and honestly thought I might pass out, right then and there, and hopefully lie unconscious for hours on my freshly scrubbed kitchen floor.

"Need some help?" asked Breeze, coming up from behind me.

Mutely I looked at her, then pointed toward the unsettling scene outside.

She just shook her head, then placing her hand protectively over her abdomen, she simply turned and walked away without saying a word. And I realized that my sacrifice must seem small compared to hers. And yet it hurt. It hurt horribly. So badly, in fact, that I couldn't keep it in. And so, after brewing all day, I finally confronted Sky.

I waited until after supper, when I knew we could be alone for a while. I told him I had an urgent matter to discuss with him, and, as usual, he invited me to take a little stroll around the farm. And despite my lack of a warm coat and the winter chill in the air, I didn't refuse.

"Do you realize how much time and work I spent putting up that fruit last summer?" I finally demanded once we were seated on the bench beneath the oak tree. I glared at him, not overly concerned that he'd notice my seething expression since there was only a pale sliver of moonlight to illuminate my face.

He nodded. "Yes, Rainbow, I know. And I can see that this troubles you greatly."

"You're right it troubles me. First of all, we may not have enough food to make it through the rest of winter now."

"Oh, ye of little faith." He tilted his head upward. "Don't you know your Father in heaven can take care of you?"

I bit my lip and thought for a moment. "Well, what about the waste then? We could've at least taken the canned fruit and sold it at the Farmers' Market in town. Venus said they sell things like that there."

"Yes, isn't that just what Judas said when Mary anointed Jesus' feet with her precious oil? He said they should've taken it and sold it for money. But the Master corrected him, didn't he?"

I nodded, properly chastised and yet thoroughly confused. What did Judas have to do with my fruit preserves?

"Can you understand why it's so important to submit, little one?" He ran his hand over my cheek.

"Yes," I murmured. "I suppose you're right. I guess I wasn't being very submissive just now. Will you forgive me, Sky?"

He put his arm around me, then drew me close, pulling me into the warmth of his heavy wool coat. "It's okay, little one. As long as you see the error of your ways and repent, everything will be just fine for you."

And then we kissed for a long while, and quite passionately too, and suddenly everything seemed much better (at least, in a blurry sort of way). Sky and I met again the following night, and this was the first time he suggested we might do more than just kiss (not in so many words, but the insinuation was clear). And yet I pretended not to understand what he was talking about. (Hadn't Sunshine called me "naïve"?) And so we played like that, and I teased him for a bit, but then finally I squirmed away from his embrace and ran back into the house, giggling loudly as I went.

Why didn't I give in to him? To this day, I still wonder. Maybe it was because I still held out for the old promise that he would make me his wife someday—maybe I actually believed that we were going to have an "official" ceremony, right there under the old oak tree, in front of God and everybody. Or maybe it was simply God watching out for me after all, and despite myself. Maybe I'll never know all these things for absolute certain.

During that week following Christmas (while I was enjoying Sky's "attentions" and playing coy and hard to get) a strange and unexpected visitor came to "The Promised Land." By then we had locking security gates so that no one could just drive right in (although we didn't have the barbed wire or guard dogs yet— these would come later). But this visitor just parked his car right out there on the road and somehow (I'm still not sure how) scaled the front fence and walked right up and knocked on the front door.

I remember hearing the commotion from where I was working in the kitchen, and with dish towel still in hand and my long gingham apron tied snugly around my waist, I came out to see what was going on. And there, to my utter amazement, stood my dear old friend Joey Divers.

chapter twenty-one

"JOEY!" I CRIED OUT in delighted surprise. But then I stopped myself as I noticed how Sky was scowling darkly at our unexpected "guest."

"Cass!" exclaimed Joey, a big smile breaking across his face. Then he turned to Sky. "I thought you said she wasn't here."

"I said she wasn't *here*," Sky waved his hand around the room. "I didn't say she wasn't in the kitchen."

"Whatever," said Joey, turning his attention back to me. "I came to see if you'd like me to take you home."

I blinked. *"What?"*

"You know, break you free, get you out of here." He turned and grinned defiantly at all the faces now staring at him. I could see Mountain sizing him up, probably taking in his slight build, his leg brace and cane. Joey was dressed neatly, collegiate as usual, and I'm sure the brothers and sisters thought he looked like an establishment nerd. "Hey, Mitch. Hey, Cindy," he said as he noticed River and Breeze standing over by the sofa. "How are you guys doing?"

"Their names are River and Breeze," said Sky in a serious, almost seething, tone.

"Oh yeah, I forgot about your name-game thing." Joey turned back to me. "What's your name now, Cass?"

"Her name's Rainbow," said Sky, taking a step toward Joey. "And I'd like to ask you to leave. Maybe you didn't notice, but we have our road gated for a reason, and you're on private property."

"I didn't see a warning or a sign or anything stating that," said Joey in a matter-of-fact voice. "However, I did see the sign that said 'The Promised Land,' and I thought, hey, that sounds like an open invitation to any believer. Besides, I wasn't planning on staying on, Sky. I just thought I'd drop by and say hey."

"How did you find this place?" asked Sky with narrowed eyes.

"Sara told me all about it." I sensed by the crease in Joey's brow that Sara had told him a lot. "And she gave me directions. She's doing just great, by the way."

He turned and studied me again. I could tell he was curious about our strange homemade dresses and bare feet. (We never wore shoes in the house, and only wore them outside during the cold months.)

"Maybe I could just take you for a ride, Cass. Maybe we could drive into town and get a burger or something—and just chat." He looked hopeful.

"Well, I—"

"Rainbow," said Sky in a calm but firm tone, "you know you are free to do as you choose. But if you choose to leave us right now, even to take a little ride, then you are choosing to disobey. And as a result you separate yourself from our fellowship. And you know what that means."

Then he stepped over and placed his arm around my shoulders and pulled me close to him. It was the first public display of affection he had shown to me (or any other sister, for that matter—besides Moonlight, that is) and I suppose in some way it felt like a small victory to me. Okay, a very mixed and messy sort of victory.

"I appreciate you coming, Joey . . ." I stopped, finding myself staring into his earnest and familiar brown eyes. It was funny how they looked just slightly bigger behind the lenses of his wire-rimmed glasses. And suddenly I couldn't even remember what I'd been about to say.

". . . but why don't you just be on your way," finished Sky in a cold tone.

"Is that what *you* want, Cass?" Joey's eyes locked with mine.

I'm sure I must've looked like that old proverbial doe who was caught in the headlights just then. Should I run to the left or to the right or freeze and take whatever was hurling in my direction? Which way should I go?

Then Sky gave me a gentle squeeze and spoke in an understanding tone. "It's okay, Rainbow. I'm sure that this visit is very upsetting to you."

I swallowed and nodded, searching for words.

"Cass?" said Joey again, still standing his ground, although I could see that Mountain was moving in closer to him, a show of force perhaps, or maybe just getting ready to escort him out the door.

"This is my home, Joey," I said in a small voice that didn't even convince me.

"Then why don't you just come out and take a quick little ride with me?"

I felt tears in my eyes then, and I seriously considered accepting his offer. I could bolt out the door with him . . . but when it was all said and done, where would I really go? What would I do? Joey was still in college, had a life of his own—did he think he could take care of me and continue his schooling? "Thanks anyway, Joey—" I choked on the words and looked down at my bare feet.

"Which means, 'No thanks,' " said Sky firmly. "Now we won't keep you any longer."

And that's when Mountain pushed open the door and escorted Joey outside and down the path and onto the road and past the gate and into his blue car, which finally drove away.

It only occurred to me much later that evening, as I cried silently in bed, that Joey had driven a very long way just to come and find me here. I knew he must be on his Christmas vacation, home from college for a couple weeks.

To think he had wasted his time and gasoline on a useless cross-country trip, and on me.

chapter twenty-two

JUST BEFORE THE NEW YEAR, Sky made an announcement. "All sisters must be present during the birthing process," he told us as we gathered around him one evening. "For this is God's way of showing each one of you what you can expect when your time comes."

All the sisters nodded in agreement, and all seemed fairly convinced that their time would indeed come. All except for me, that is. I wasn't sure about the idea of having a baby just yet, and besides that, I knew how my own mama had died as a result of childbirth, and according to the natural childbirth book, daughters often had birth experiences similar to their mother's. That alone was enough to put the fear of God (or was it man?) within me.

As a result of my diligent study of the natural childbirth book (I knew it both forward and backward by then) I was deemed the "official" midwife shortly before Moonlight was due to go into labor. I felt a mixture of emotions about my new responsibility. Part of me wanted to run screaming in the opposite direction, but another part was just slightly curious as to what an actual human childbirth might be like. (During my short stint at the Crowleys' I had witnessed the birth of a calf and had found this experience grotesquely interesting and somewhat exhilarating.) Naturally, I knew it would be different with humans, but sometimes I almost forgot that Moonlight was human. Now this is not to suggest I wished her any ill during her birthing process, and I did try to control my thoughts when I would unexpectedly envision her dying during childbirth (this is what jealousy can do to a person).

Moonlight's contractions started around four o'clock. "Just strong enough to interrupt my afternoon nap," she told us nonchalantly at dinner. As usual her appetite was unaffected. Shortly after dinner her water broke and the sisters gathered in her room, ready to witness the special event. Some of us sat on the bed, others on the floor, but an air of excited anticipation filled the air. Even Breeze, although she seemed uneasy, participated in the prebirth chatter. After only a couple hours of what seemed only mild discomfort accompanied by some general groaning and complaining, Moonlight said she thought it was time to push.

"But you haven't been in labor long enough to start pushing yet," I argued.

"Look, Rainbow," she said between clenched teeth, in the midst of a strong contraction. *"I'm* the one having this baby—" She took in a breath and glared at me with fiery eyes. "And if *I* say it's time, then it's *time to push!"* And then she let loose with a whole string of expletives and swearwords that I hadn't heard used in almost a year. I wondered if she'd have to get down on her knees and ask forgiveness afterwards.

"Let her push," said Venus, as if she knew all about birthing babies.

"Fine," I snapped. "Go ahead and push. Just don't forget to do your breathing when you're pushing. And don't blame me if you get yourself all worn out before it's really time."

Moonlight was wearing an old flowered housedress that I'm sure Sky must've picked up at some thrift shop in town. When she started to push she hiked the dress up in order to grab hold of her knees, thus exposing her enormous rotund abdomen to all. I don't know about the other sisters, but I'm sure my jaw must've dropped several inches when I saw that huge, white belly come out—why, it looked just like a full moon! And I suppose that's when I began to giggle.

"Shut up!" screamed Moonlight as her eyebrows came together and her face went from red to magenta. Then she gave another big push. Breeze punched me in the arm, and I immediately got control, reminding myself that this was serious.

Focusing my attention on the contractions, I continued to coach Moonlight, trying to get her to wait until each contraction was at its peak before she pushed. And just before nine o'clock, with Moonlight now screaming and crying and cussing like a sailor, she managed to push out a slippery, wet mass of life that proved to be an actual living baby!

I'm sure I was in shock as I caught the infant in the towel that I had ready for it, and my hands trembled as I wiped the squirming baby's mouth and nose clean with a damp washcloth. But when the baby began to howl with what sounded like a fairly healthy set of lungs, I must admit to just totally losing it. My earlier cool was completely lost as tears poured down my cheeks. Maybe it was pure relief or emotional exhaustion or just plain amazement. I think we were all crying by then, and it seemed a natural reaction. I reckon it's just something about the birth of a baby that gets to you like that. To this day, I still cry at a birthing, and I still believe it's one of God's most amazing miracles in life.

As I was wiping my hands it occurred to me that, fair or not, Moonlight had once again been "blessed" with a relatively easy labor and the uncomplicated delivery of Sky's firstborn son. *Just another one of those many injustices of life,* I thought to myself as I observed Breeze staring blankly at the healthy newborn.

And so, on the second of January, just one year to the day since we'd first embarked upon our journey to "The Promised Land," the first child of the second generation was born into our unusual family.

I felt almost light-headed as I left, relieved to escape that metallic smell that permeated the birthing room. I discovered Stone and River sitting nervously in the living room (a world away from the claustrophobic confines of Moonlight and Sky's bedroom) both anxiously awaiting the news. With pride I told them Moonlight had just delivered a healthy baby boy and they both lifted their hands and praised God. I saw River's face visibly relax, and I felt sure that (like Breeze) he'd been reliving their unfortunate birthing experience only two months earlier.

"Where's Sky?" I asked as I glanced around the corner and into the empty dining room. I'd expected to tell him first.

"I think the rest of the brothers are working on something out in the barn," said Stone. Clearing his throat, he returned to reading his Bible.

And so I went out in search of our new "daddy," anxious to share this good news. But when I pushed open the barn door, I noticed a blue cloud of smoke in a dimly lit corner and I was about to scream "Fire!" when I heard Sky's voice calling to me.

"Rainbow?"

I peered through the haze to see Sky and Mountain and our two new brothers all sitting on hay bales in the smoke-filled corner. A kerosene lamp barely illuminated their shapes. "What's going on?" I asked as I cautiously moved toward them. "It looks like there's been a fire or something."

Then they just laughed. And I mean, *really* laughed. Like I had said something outrageously funny. But as I got closer I could see they were smoking! And I immediately recognized that almost putrid, sweet, green smell. It wasn't tobacco, but marijuana! At first I felt confused like maybe I'd just gone back in time, but then I realized where I was and who I was with, and then I felt betrayed—like another part of my little world had just been drop-kicked and was now spinning totally out of control.

"You—you guys are smoking pot," I finally said.

"Yeah," said Mountain. "Want a drag?"

I shook my head. "Isn't that sinful?"

Sky stood now, waving me over to him. "Come here, little one." He looked slightly off-balanced and placed his hand on my shoulder, probably to help steady himself. "Listen, Rainbow," he said slowly, as if I were a half-wit who might not fully understand. "We've studied this. And marijuana is not a sin. You see, there's a verse in the Bible that says everything that grows on this beautiful earth has been put here by God and is to be used for our benefit."

"Yeah," said Mountain, "and we happen to think grass is pretty beneficial."

Everyone just cracked up over that. Everyone but me. I didn't know what to say or even to think. It's as if everything had just been turned upside down. Finally, I remembered why I had come out to the barn in the first place. "Sky," I said soberly, hoping to get his attention. "Moonlight just gave birth to a healthy son."

Then they all began to whoop and congratulate themselves, as if each one there had been personally responsible. I just shook my head and left. I don't know when Sky finally came into the house to see his newborn son that evening, but I knew I'd had enough for one night. I sneaked off to bed without waiting up for devotions (which were already running late anyway due to birthing babies and pot parties).

As I lay in my bed that night, I still remember being unable to say my prayers. And for the first time in a long time, I seriously began to doubt God. At first I doubted that he really cared about any of us. Then I doubted that he had actually led us to the farm. And finally I began to doubt that he even existed at all. It was a dark, sick feeling, taking root inside me, invisible perhaps, but real just the same.

I'd like to be able to say that it was then and there—at that particular moment—when I came to my senses. That I finally woke up and realized that coming to "The Promised Land" had been nothing but a great big stupid mistake. But unfortunately, some of us don't learn our lessons quite that easily. And the life I'd lived as a young child may have instilled a certain stubborn quality into me—a downright bullheadedness that wasn't too easily knocked out. Besides, where would I go anyway? No Joey Divers was going to show up to rescue me now.

Had it only been a week ago that he'd come by? Had he really even come, or had I just imagined the whole thing? And if he had come, why hadn't I been smart enough or strong enough to go with him, despite what Sky had said? What if Joey really had been God's escape route for me? What if I had blown it?

Suffice it to say that I lived and moved in something of a trance during the next couple months. Perhaps it was simply a survival mode, a remnant of those ever-important skills I'd learned so early in life: *Do your chores, keep a low profile, don't rock the boat—and maybe, just maybe, you'll make it through this thing called life. Or not.* And so I became the great pretender, working hard in the kitchen to placate Venus and Sky and putting on phony "spiritual airs" whenever necessary, but the cold, hard truth was, I was dead inside.

It was during this era that I began to really fear Sky—or maybe the power he seemed to hold over me and everyone else. And I knew that I'd somehow fallen down in the pecking order. For whatever reason, I was low woman on the totem pole now (and women were already so much lower than men at the farm).

By springtime, he had a whole houseful of women to choose from. And unlike me, none of the others seemed to mind the way things were going. I guess that was my main problem—when you got right down to it, I minded.

Perhaps our most unlikely member came in the form of a has-been movie actress by the name of Helen Knight. To be honest, I'm still not completely convinced she'd ever really been an actress (at least not on the silver screen) but she assured us that she'd been quite a hit in her time, and there was certainly no disputing that this woman had a certain theatrical flair about her.

Her name was quickly changed to Star (fitting, since she'd supposedly been one once). Star reminded me of Bette Davis (in her later movies) with her exaggerated mouth and sagging expressions. And contrary to Sky's early decree in regard to women's modest adornments and appearances, Star was allowed to wear whatever she pleased, including flashy costume jewelry and garish makeup that I'm sure she must've salvaged from the stage. And to be honest, I liked her a little at first. She seemed the odd exception to so many of our ascetic rules. In a way I suppose she gave me hope. But of course it was short-lived.

We immediately began to experience Star's more spiritual side, always cast in a flamboyant and dramatic package. And she in turn became Sky's closest confidante and, I'm sure, biggest influencer. Yes, it finally seemed that Sky was under the spiritual influence of another. Star was what some might call a "spiritualist," meaning that she was (or was supposed to be) greatly in touch with the spiritual world. She had been to India to study under gurus, to the Himalayas to converse with Buddhist monks, and claimed to have once dined with John Lennon (I highly doubted this). Without warning, Star might go into a trance right in the middle of oatmeal at breakfast time. She would moan and groan, rocking to and fro, as she held her wrinkled hands, palms up and trembling so much that her rings would clink against one another like finger cymbals. It was so unsettling (the first time I witnessed it) that I was unable to finish my meal. But as time went on it became more of an everyday occurrence.

More and more I wondered where God and Jesus were in all this. Our original spiritual direction had changed drastically. Oh, sure, we might hear those names mentioned here and there, along with a bunch of others. But somewhere, somehow, things had definitely changed. And I found it hard to believe that I was the only one disillusioned by all this. And yet, no one questioned these changes. Everyone seemed pretty laid-back and happy, and I suspect this was a result of the influence of the marijuana. It's as if pot and Star had cast a spell over the entire farm. I think that's when I began to think of "The Promised Land" as the Funny Farm.

I'd been disturbed to see first the brothers, but then later on, the sisters as well, using and then growing marijuana. One of Mountain's friends brought in a big truck with a bunch of plants, and presto, we were in business. And while I'll admit that I never observed anyone becoming violent or mean-spirited while under its influence, it troubled me deeply just the same.

Somehow it reminded me of my daddy—and everything else I'd tried to escape from since the earliest memories of my life. Not only that, it seemed to strip away everyone's initiative and creativity. They just didn't seem to have an ounce of "spizzerrinktum" as my grandma used to call it. It's as if their motivation had just gotten up and walked right out the door. Now it seemed all anyone cared about was growing, protecting, and eventually selling more marijuana plants—and then of course, getting high.

But as if pot and Star weren't enough, it had also become more widely known and accepted (though never openly discussed) that Sky was in fact sleeping with all the other sisters. In fact, other than me and Breeze (because for some reason, she and River had some sort of exemption) I'm sure Sky slept with every sister there. And so it seemed quite obvious now that poor Sunshine had been exactly right about her accusation last fall. Why hadn't I believed her?

Breeze and I carried the bulk of the household chores, and that bulk was increasing with each new resident. My roommate, Cloud, only lasted for a few weeks, until she got married to one of the brothers. After that it seemed my roommates changed with the regularity of "weddings."

Surprisingly, Sky still hadn't attempted to match me up for a marriage. I couldn't quite figure this out, but I didn't really care since I didn't want a loveless marriage anyway and I couldn't bear the idea of watching my stomach swell into the full moon I'd seen on Moonlight before she gave birth. In fact, as time passed, I felt fairly certain, and somewhat hopeful, that Sky had forgotten all about me. I was just that girl who worked in the kitchen.

And yet, despite all my isolation and misery and hopelessness, I still loved the farm. I can't fully explain or understand it—maybe it was a love-hate sort of thing. But I did love that clean smell of the sweet dewy earth in the morning, and seeing the small tender seedlings beginning to sprout in the vegetable garden in the spring, and the fruit trees in full blossom. And even though I no longer believed in "The Promised Land" per se, I knew it would be hard for me to leave this place. Not that leaving was an option any-more.

With the progression from simply smoking marijuana to sell-ing it, our farm had turned into a very tight security establishment. Under the management of Mountain, much of the profits from the high-quality marijuana were quickly reinvested into tall chain-link fences encircling the land (with electrical current running throughout). This was the only project that year where I noticed the brothers really throwing themselves into it, but then, why would that surprise me? And if that imposing fence wasn't enough, the property was also patrolled at night by two trained German Shepherd guard dogs by the names of Michael and Gabriel, our "angelic" protection. So even if I'd wanted to escape, how could it be done?

One day in early spring, as Breeze and I were outside hanging up laundry (I often tried to repay her help in the kitchen) I decided to tread on some somewhat shaky ground.

"Are you and River happy here?" I asked as I pinned up another diaper (naturally, despite three more babies on the way, we'd never have dreamed of using disposables).

"Happy?" she mumbled with a clothespin stuck between her teeth.

"You know." I glanced around for eavesdroppers. "Do you think you'll be here for—well, forever?"

"I don't know where else we'd go." She sighed.

Now I was fully aware that River, and sometimes Breeze, smoked pot occasionally, and while this had disturbed me some at first, I tried not to hold it against them. Especially since, out of the whole group, they were probably my best friends, and to my relief their use of pot had not greatly impaired their ability or willingness to do their share of work. "But do you ever want something more than this, Breeze?"

She looked me straight in the eye. "Rainbow, I think I'm pregnant again."

I wasn't sure how to respond. Was this meant to be good news? "Are you glad?" I finally asked.

She smiled. "Yes, I really want a baby. And River's happy about it too. And I think everything's going to be okay this time."

I wanted to ask her how she could be so sure and what would happen if she was wrong, but just then Moonlight walked up and fingered a damp diaper on the line. "Aren't there any dry diapers here?" she asked with irritation. "Thunder just messed his last one and I can't find a single one in the house!"

I still couldn't believe that Sky had actually named his firstborn son Thunder. But apparently I was the only one who thought this slightly strange. Certainly, I never thought he'd name him something ordinary like John or Mike. But it just seemed that as time went by, Sky became more extraordinary and even weird (in my opinion this was greatly due to Star's influence). Now, following her lead, he'd begun going into these long "trances" where he'd be meditating and hear "spiritual forces" speaking to him. I must admit that it was all pretty convincing, if you were into that sort of thing (which I felt less and less inclined to be). Mostly I just thought both Sky and Star were great big phonies.

The really weird thing was that Sky's influence steadily grew. People all up and down the coast, from all ages and walks of life, were strangely drawn to him (or was it simply his pot?) and as a result our commune was growing steadily. By that spring we had over forty members.

Gram wouldn't have recognized her property by then. And I hoped she couldn't see it for I'm sure she would've rolled right over in her grave, or more likely she would've simply laughed from the heights of heaven. But now her once somewhat serene (albeit slightly run-down) farm was a strange conglomeration of make-shift buildings, wildly painted hippy buses (also being used as houses), and old trailers that people had pulled onto the property. And here and there were little outhouses and outdoor showers.

Children (we had quite a few now) as well as a motley assortment of dogs (besides our guard dogs) ran freely. And constantly in the background of all this hubbub was the rumbling growl of several gas-powered generators.

I remembered when Gram had asked if we were a traveling circus. It seemed she was just about right. Between Star's theatrics and Sky's lengthy sermons we had some pretty interesting acts going. But for the most part I think we were more like a bunch of sideshow freaks. We were the outcasts, the unloved, the misfits. I remembered my little misfit club from childhood, and suddenly Joey and I (despite our handicaps both seen and unseen) seemed incredibly normal in retrospect. At least we'd had our hopes and dreams. The people on the Funny Farm had nothing. I had nothing.

I realized my little conversation with Breeze had gotten me nowhere, and could possibly get me into trouble if I pushed it any further. Although she was my closest friend, I knew better than to trust anyone by then. Not even myself.

More and more I longed for a way to escape. I just couldn't figure out how it could be done. First of all, no sisters (not even Venus anymore) were allowed to go into town, since it would be "sinful" for any man outside of our family to "look upon" us (as if our long, dowdy dresses would tempt those unwitting men out there to lust!). And then with our tightened security, there seemed no way to simply walk out (as I might've done a few months earlier). It seemed I was trapped.

I suppose I had almost resigned myself to this hopeless fate, until one day, something I'd seen happen on an almost daily basis caught my attention in a new way. Perhaps this was my answer.

chapter twenty-three

As I was doing the breakfast dishes (since none of the other sisters had offered that day) I was blankly looking out the window over the kitchen sink when, as usual, I observed the little mail jeep drive past (really only a small white dot on the distant road, but one you could almost set your clock by). Of course we had no mailbox out on the road, for we neither sent nor received mail (although I'd heard Sky kept a postal box in town, which of course no one was allowed to use but him). But suddenly I wondered if there might be some way I could get the mailman to stop and take a letter from me.

It seems silly now that something as simple as posting a letter could've proved such a challenge for me, but the truth is, I didn't have paper, envelopes, or stamps. And even if I did, I wasn't sure where or to whom I could send a letter. I considered my Aunt Myrtle, although I didn't know her address and I seriously doubted that she would help me anyway. Of course Joey came to mind almost at once, but I didn't have his college address. However, I did remember his home address, so I decided I would attempt to send a letter in care of Mrs. Divers to be forwarded to Joey.

I knew the chances of its even making it off the farm were rather slim, and to make it to Joey seemed a pure impossibility.

And supposing it did, I wondered what Joey could possibly do? After all, he'd already used up his whole Christmas vacation to drive to California, and I'd stupidly refused his help. What could I expect from him now?

Still, this crazy idea kept me going for almost a week as I secretly worked to write Joey a letter (on a piece of a recycled brown paper bag) asking him for help. This I enclosed in a home-made envelope (also made from a bag). And then I wrote another brief note (this time to his mother) asking her to forward the enclosed letter to Joey. I placed both these items into an even larger paper-bag envelope. I'm sure my bulky, oversized brown letter looked slightly ridiculous, but it was the best I could do under the circumstances, and at the time I felt proud that I'd managed to do so much. Then I wrote a note addressed to the mailman, apologizing for not having the postage, but telling him I was desperate, and begging him to see that this letter was sent. Then I wrapped the whole thing up in another piece of brown paper and wrote "To the Mailman" in big, bold letters on the front and on the back.

Then on a Thursday morning in late April (when another sister took a turn at washing up after breakfast) I tucked this package into the front of my apron, picked up my basket, and went outside under the guise of picking wildflowers (something I was commonly known to do). Feeling like someone in a spy movie, I zigzagged my way across the front field until I reached the gate. Pausing there just briefly to make sure no one was looking my way, I tossed my precious package out onto the road, then quickly turned and walked away, bending now and then to pick wild daisies and asters.

My heart pounded with excitement (and perhaps fear) as I slowly made my way back toward the house. What if someone had observed me by the gate? Or what if the mailman didn't notice my package on the road and simply drove right on past it?

Suddenly it occurred to me that if the mailman failed to pick it up, it would most likely be spotted by Sky as he opened the gates before he went off to town. I felt a knot of horror in my stomach, for surely Sky would open it and read the whole thing! And what would happen to me then? Suddenly I felt very stupid and foolish. Why hadn't I thought this through more carefully? I'd been so caught up in getting everything just right, thinking I was so clever, it had never occurred to me that the mailman might not even pick it up.

And so with heart still pounding and beads of perspiration gathering across my forehead, I made my way over to the stand of pines where we had buried Gram less than a year ago. Kneeling down before her grave, I actually began to pray. Not in the phony way that I could put on for the sake of the group, but this time I prayed for real!

I begged God to somehow get that mailman's attention and make him stop and pick up my package. Yet even as I prayed these words, I realized how unlikely this would be. The mailman usually drove by our farm quite fast, and the color of my brown package blended well with the road. It probably looked like a piece of trash. But nonetheless, I prayed—fervently! And I even asked God to work things out so that I could leave this place once and for all. And I promised that if he got me out of here that I'd make up for all the stupid things I'd done and I would always—

My prayer stopped instantly as I noticed Sky's van heading slowly down the driveway toward the road. Of all the impossible timing, how could it be that Sky was going to town today? He never went to town in the morning, and rarely on a Thursday. I'm sure I must've stopped breathing as I watched the van stop before the gate. A brother hopped out of the passenger seat to open it. I couldn't tell who it was from the distance. But as he swung the gate open toward the road, he paused, then stooping briefly, he appeared to pick something up, and I knew my plans were ruined. I was ruined.

And I knew that God had let me down—again!

I think I understood what it meant to "die a thousand deaths" as I sat in the shade of the pines, next to Gram's grave site. I fretted and cried for several hours, waiting in fear for Sky's colorful van to reappear in the driveway. What would he do to me after having most certainly read my pitiful little letter to Joey? Of course I would be punished, but how severely? And would it be in public?

Perhaps it wasn't even the threat of punishment that troubled me so much. Maybe it was simply the death of all hope. The letter had been my best—and now, I feared, final—attempt at an escape. I had even gone so far as to think that God might have inspired me to do it—that he might've really cared. I had even prayed—for real (not like during our meetings where I'd gotten pretty good at faking it).

But look where my faith and sincerity had gotten me. How could I have been such an idiot? I probably deserved whatever punishment Sky would dish out. Maybe not for sinning so much as for being a perfect fool.

Sky had recently been quoting Scriptures about removing whatever part of your body caused you to sin. I stared down at my hands. My fingers had written that letter. Did that mean he might consider cutting them off? Besides sounding painful, I didn't know what I'd do without my fingers. Small and insignificant as they might appear, they seemed to hold all of my creative ability in them. They drew and played the guitar, cooked food and sewed clothing. Surely Sky wouldn't be so senseless as to cut them off. Would he? Yet behavior around here had become strange and unpredictable in these last few months. And Star's influence seemed to be everywhere.

I studied the electric fence line, and like that old POW with too much time on his hands, I began to imagine other ways that I might escape. Perhaps dig my way out? But the fence line was so easily visible and checked daily for signs of intruders (primarily of the law-enforcement type). Having done some digging in the garden, I seriously doubted I could dig a tunnel quickly enough to escape without notice.

Then I remembered how our generators occasionally went out. Perhaps I could use this opportunity to scale the fence. But then I wasn't even sure which generator powered the fence, and even if I was, what if they kicked the power back on just as I was straddled atop the barbed wire (which seemed enough of a challenge in itself)? Would I become toast up there? I could just imagine how they might let my charred and lifeless body hang there for a day or two as a sign to all—a reminder of what happens when you disobey! Perhaps they'd allow the vultures to pluck at my flesh (as we'd seen happen to a neglected ewe that had died with a stillborn lamb just a few weeks back).

I even considered simply ending my life. As I lay back beneath the pines I imagined how I might find a rope of some kind, and then climb up one of those tall trees (perhaps the one right over Gram's grave) and although I didn't know how to tie an actual noose, I could probably make some sort of knot that would hold and do the work.

And to be perfectly honest, the thought of a permanent escape like that was somewhat tempting. If only there hadn't been the spring sun shining in the clear blue sky and the feel and smell of soft green grass beneath me. How could I leave all that? And maybe that was God's way of lulling me back to life again—his gentle reminder that there might be something more. Nature is often like that for me.

I knew by the position of the sun that it must be nearly noon by now, and I was sure that Venus was frantically wondering where her kitchen slave had gotten off to, and I figured as long as I was going to be in trouble, why not just go for the big prize? And so I showed up in the kitchen quite late and then informed Venus that I was feeling ill and would spend the remainder of the day in bed. And without giving her the opportunity to question or protest, I went directly to my room and closed the door.

Remembering the days when I used to lock my bedroom door against my daddy's drunken rages, I once again longed for a lock that could keep them all out—and away from me. But I knew it was useless. I thought I would just lie down and cry myself to sleep, but to my dismay no more tears would come.

I remember thinking, *You are really hopeless, Cassandra Jane.* Yes, I used my given name, and from that day on, I began to think of myself as Cassandra Jane again. Because, to my way of thinking, Rainbow died that day, and she was buried right next to Gram beneath the pines. And if I was lucky (or if God was listening) then maybe, just maybe, Cassandra Jane would survive.

I remained in my bedroom throughout the dinner hour, surprised that Sky hadn't been up there by then to drag me out, kicking and screaming, to receive my humiliation and punishment before a crowd of circus sideshow freaks (as I now thought of all of us). But I didn't hear a knock on the door until the sky was completely dark. With heart pounding, I opened the door and squinted out at the lighted hallway beyond, but instead of Sky, it was Stone. Perhaps Sky had sent him to fetch me.

I said nothing but just looked at him with mild curiosity. Then I noticed a plate of food in his hand. "I thought you might be hungry," he said.

I stared down at the plate.

"Can I come in for a minute?" he asked, glancing over his

shoulder to make sure no one was around to witness this, because despite the general acceptance of Sky's regular adulterous and fornicating habits, no one else could get away with such sinful behavior (and unmarried brothers and sisters were not allowed to be alone together in a bedroom). I stepped aside and let Stone in. He closed the door behind him and I flipped on the light.

"What do you want?" I asked as I took the plate and sampled what appeared to be whole wheat pasta with some kind of cheese sauce. It tasted, not surprisingly, a little dry and bland.

"I just wanted you to know that I found your letter."

I felt my eyes flash up at him, revealing, I'm sure, too much emotion to be safe. I looked back down on the plate and picked up a green bean (one that I had canned last summer) and although I don't particularly care for green beans, I pretended to like these. I took a bite of the bean.

"I just wanted you to know that I didn't tell Sky."

I looked back up at him. "You didn't?" This was like a confession of conspiracy. Was Stone telling the truth?

He shook his head. "I noticed it when I opened the gate. I don't know why, but I just picked it up, then shoved it inside my jacket while I was still bent over. I never showed it to Sky."

"What did you do with it?"

"I peeked inside to see who it was addressed to, then I dropped it into the mail slot while Sky was checking his post office box."

"Did you see that it had no postage on it?"

He nodded. "Yeah. Sorry I couldn't help you out there. But you know I don't have any money to buy stamps. And even if I did, I'm sure Sky would've caught me."

I peered into Stone's eyes. I hadn't really talked with him in ages, it seemed, probably not since last fall when he and Sunshine (no, it would be Sara now) had been forced to marry. I wondered if I could really trust him with this. Was he really telling me the truth? Or had Sky sent him up here to conduct some sort of search-and-destroy game?

He stepped closer to me, then lowering his voice asked, "Do you want out of here, Rainbow?"

My eyes flashed again, this time at the sound of that name. "Rainbow is dead," I announced in a flat voice, knowing full well that I had stepped over some sort of imaginary line here. There would be no going back now.

He looked slightly confused.

"My name is Cassandra."

A look of understanding crossed his face. "Okay. But do you want out of here, Cass?"

I swallowed hard, then nodded.

"I thought so."

"Is it that obvious?"

"Well, I suspected as much. Then when I saw the name on the envelope, I guessed it must be Joey's mom, and I know he's a good friend of yours, and I remember last winter when he came to get you."

I bit into my lip and closed my eyes tightly.

"And now you wish you'd gone while you had the chance?"

"Yeah."

"Well, I just want to warn you, Rain—" he stopped himself, then lowering his voice again, continued. "Cassandra . . . Sky is get-ting pretty paranoid about anyone leaving the farm. He's afraid that if anyone defects they'll turn him in to the authorities and this whole place will come crashing down around his ears."

"I wouldn't do—"

He raised his hands. "It doesn't matter. If Sky thinks it's true, then—"

"It's true," I finished for him.

"Yeah. And so I'm warning you, be real careful. Play your hand close to your chest. If you've got some kind of plan, don't tell anyone—not even Breeze."

"But what about you, Stone?"

He smiled. "You can call me Skip."

"Do you want out?"

He nodded. "But I'm in a better position than you. I could leave almost anytime I like. I could've left today. I could've just hopped out of the van and walked off."

"Why didn't you?"

He shrugged. "I'm not sure."

"Maybe it's because you know you're free to go."

He shrugged again. "Kind of free. But not completely. I mean, I don't know what I'd do. I don't have any money. I don't even have a high school diploma. I doubt if my parents will help me. They were pretty messed up when I left. I'm just not sure what I'd do or where I'd go."

I looked into his eyes. "But, Skip, there's a whole world out there. I'll bet if we stuck together we could figure something out that'd be a whole lot better than this. I'd be happy to get a job in a restaurant cooking or washing dishes or anything. And you're really good with the carpentry stuff, you could probably get hired doing something like that. I'll bet we'd be okay." I could hear the pleading in my voice. "We could do it together."

He looked hopeful. "You really think so?"

"Yes, Skip, I really do. If you can help get me out of here, I'll do everything I can to make sure we make it out there. I promise."

He smiled. "Well, if anyone could do it, I'm sure it would be you."

"Can you really get us out?"

"Let me do some thinking about this. In the meantime, you better start acting normal again so no one suspects anything. The worst that can happen is that Sky starts suspecting us of wanting out. Then we'd really be in trouble."

"Right. That makes sense." I smiled up at him. "Thanks, Skip."

"Just don't call me that out there." He opened the door and glanced down the hallway, then quickly slipped out. I finished up the food on my plate, then turned off the light (not wanting to face the questions of my roommate) and for the first time in a long time I went to bed with a tiny glimmer of hope in my heart.

Skip and I didn't speak again for nearly a week. But true to my word, I acted just like normal—cheerful in fact (and that wasn't an act because I felt more hopeful than ever). Even Venus commented on my changed demeanor and I told her that it was probably simply because spring was here and that always made me happy. This answer seemed to suit her just fine and she even suggested "we" try out a new recipe for spring asparagus soup, which didn't even turn out too badly either.

When Skip finally approached me, it was in public. In fact, Sky was only about ten feet away. It was in the early evening, shortly after dinner. "Hi, Rainbow," he said with a smile. "I've been thinking about you lately."

I immediately grew flustered, wondering what he was doing. Why was he blowing our cover like this? I could feel Sky's eyes upon me and I knew it wasn't good. Still, I forced a smile to my lips. "What kind of thinking?" I asked, hoping I sounded normal, although by then I hardly knew what normal sounded like anymore.

"I wondered if you'd like to take an evening stroll with me?"

I glanced nervously over toward Sky and I knew without a doubt that he was watching us, and then it seemed as if he nodded just slightly—as if giving his blessing. Without showing too much surprise I turned back to Skip. "Okay, why not."

After we were outside, in the safe privacy of the night, Skip quickly explained his plan. "I've been telling Sky that I'm interested in you, saying that I'm lonely after losing Sunshine. Today I asked him if we could get married."

"*Get married?*" I tried not to raise my voice. But this was not what I'd intended.

"I don't mean for real, Rainbow—I mean Cass. I just thought we could pretend to be married. That is unless you want to—"

"I'm not looking to get married right now."

He chuckled. "Well then, neither am I. But I thought if we pretended to be married, it would be easier to get you out of here. We could probably get away most easily at night. I have a couple of ideas, but I won't go into all that just now."

"Okay, I think I get it, and I can see how that would make it easier. But, honestly, Skip, as much as I like you, I'm just not ready to get married for real right now."

He raised up his hands defensively. "Believe me, I won't force anything on you. I already know what it's like to be hitched with someone who doesn't love you. Sunshine was miserable. In fact, we both were. But despite everything we remained friends. She even invited me to run away with her."

"So you knew she was going?"

He nodded. "But for some reason I wasn't ready to leave just then. Although I'm still not sure why I wanted to stick around."

"Probably because you never felt as trapped as we did."

"Maybe." He started walking us back toward the house now. "We don't want to be gone too long. Don't want to give anyone reason to accuse us of anything."

"Good thinking."

"Oh, by the way, I think Sky has plans for you for himself. He suggested that if you and I got married, that it would improve his relationship with you, and I think we both know what that means."

I groaned. "Then we better not get married until we're ready to get out of here. I don't want to take any chances with Sky."

"I don't think we'll have much say about the date. Sky, as usual, said that he thinks sooner is better. So if I come back tonight and tell him you said yes, you can expect that we'll be hitched within a week or so."

"And that means we'll be out of here shortly thereafter?"

He nodded.

By now we were within the light of the front porch and I suspected we were being watched. I stuck out my hand and shook his, as if we were just sealing the deal.

"A handshake instead of a kiss?" he teased.

"Under the circumstances, I think it's more believable, don't you?"

"Yeah, you're probably right."

And so it was I became "officially" engaged.

chapter twenty-four

WHAT LITTLE GIRL DOESN'T DREAM of becoming a beautiful bride someday? And I suppose I am no different.

My first "wedding" took place on a perfect day toward the end of May, with a few fluffy white clouds wafting over a powder blue sky. A gentle breeze caressed the warm afternoon air, and everyone from the Funny Farm (all of us looking uncannily like circus freaks) gathered together beneath the green canopy of the old oak tree to witness the "blessed" event.

The bride (being me) wore a somewhat tattered patchwork skirt of many clownlike colors (my preference over my everyday prairie dress of drab blue calico). And into the waistband of my bright skirt I had tucked a threadbare, off-white, lace-trimmed blouse that had seen better days (a castoff from one of the newer sisters). My feet, as usual, were bare and dirty. But I had unbraided and vigorously brushed my hair, allowing it to fall freely down my back. My black tresses (which I believed to be my best asset) now reached well below my waist and were quite thick. And I'd taken the time to weave daisies, buttercups, and purple asters into a small braid that I wrapped around my head like a crown.

The shaggy and bearded groom wore faded bell-bottom jeans that were well frayed at the hems and an old chambray work shirt that had been mended many times over. His feet were also bare and dirty. I'm sure we must've made quite a pair.

Naturally, Sky officiated the ceremony. He wore a fine-looking homespun shirt of white linen and loose-fitting drawstring pants, also of linen. And, as usual, his feet were shod in a pair of heavy brown leather sandals (and I think he fancied himself to look a bit like Jesus that day). Sky didn't always dress this nicely for weddings, but maybe he thought this one was special. Perhaps it was simply because the bride had not yet slept in his bed—or any man's, for that matter. I'm sure that alone made him feel quite pleased as he stood before us and recited the words (his own poetic version of wedding vows).

Sky looked directly into my eyes with an intensity that actually brought a lump to my throat, and I briefly wondered if he didn't imagine that he was the groom, the one marrying me, and perhaps he considered Stone (Skip) to be only the best man. After what seemed an exceedingly long ceremony, and to my great relief, Sky finally pronounced us husband and wife, and everyone cheered with enthusiasm (or so it seemed).

As usual, no cake or punch or photos or reception followed, but I did get out of dinner detail that night, and I suspect everyone else used this "blessed occasion" as another good excuse to go get stoned. Dinner that evening was prepared by a couple of the newer sisters and was served rather late, but no one seemed to notice or even mind much, just another sign of the changing climate around the Funny Farm.

I must say it was nice not to be stuck in the kitchen, and I almost wondered if my life on the farm might've gone differently if I hadn't been subjected to all that exhausting kitchen work day in and day out. Sitting in the dining room and eating food prepared by others wasn't so bad. Perhaps this was just one of the reasons that everyone else seemed so content to be cooped up on the farm like that. Well, that and the pot, of course.

And, okay, I'll admit it, I think some of the people may have been honestly searching—maybe it was for God or spirituality or maybe just family or an escape from the modern day rat race of the exterior world. Or perhaps like for me it was all of those things.

Anyway I saw things in a slightly different, more gracious, light that night—if only for a moment. And it didn't hurt that I thought this might possibly be the last time I'd dine with these people. Or at least I hoped so.

Still it bothered me that all throughout dinner, and then during our evening devotions time, Sky seemed to have his eyes on me. And I honestly don't think I was imagining this, either. I felt certain that he must've already been counting the days (or was it hours?) until I would become another one of his little conquests. I had already told Skip that I was ready to leave at the first possible moment, and I secretly hoped it might even be tonight.

After devotions, Skip and I slipped out into the night and took a stroll around the grounds. We were hoping to appear romantic to any casual observers, but it was actually his way of showing me "the plan." He had discovered which generator fed electricity to the fence, but he wouldn't shut it down until the last possible minute. Prior to that, he explained, he would feed the guard dogs a specially prepared dinner of leftovers mixed heavily with a ground-up mixture of marijuana.

"Are dogs affected by pot?" I asked as we walked past the pen where the "guardian angels" were kept during the day. The dogs lunged at the fence as we passed by, barking and growling and baring their teeth.

"I don't know why not," he answered. "The trick will be to time it just right. I'm thinking just before bedtime." Fortunately for us, bedtime or "lights-out" still happened fairly much like clockwork, usually right around ten o'clock when all but one generator were shut down for the night. "I figure if I time it just right, the dogs will have eaten the pot but not be showing any signs when Mountain lets them out at ten. Hopefully they'll take off like usual and then after a while just start slowing down."

"And getting high?"

"Yeah, hopefully they'll be a couple of mellow fellows. I know this is kind of experimental, but I think it'll work. I'll hang around and keep my eye on them, just to be sure." He then showed me the route he thought would be best for exiting. He'd discovered a place where the barbed wire gapped just slightly, plus he'd found a pair of wire cutters. And escape really seemed possible! I began to feel slightly giddy with anticipation.

We continued walking and talking until we finally reached the barn where he and I would share the original annex bedroom that had been built for the brothers up in the loft of the barn. He'd already told me about the window he and River had frequently used to climb out of at night when they needed to relieve themselves and didn't want to disturb others inside the house. A shed roof was only a few feet below, and from there you could easily jump down to the ground.

The plan was that we'd hang out in the room until just before ten. At that time Skip would slip out on the pretense of using the outhouse (where he'd already stashed the "dog goodies"). We were like two excited kids waiting for Santa to come as we talked in hushed tones, carefully going over each detail of the plan one final time. We would only take what we could carry in our pockets (and luckily I had dug out my old overalls where I could stick several mementos into the many pockets, including my mother's photo and a few other things I'd managed to hold on to over the years—

unfortunately I'd have to leave my guitar behind). Just shortly before it was time for Skip to leave, I threw my arms around him in a good-luck hug. "Thank you so much for doing this with me, Skip. I know I couldn't do it without you."

He hugged me back. "I feel the same way, Cass. But you know, even more than that, I don't think we can do this without God's help. I've really been praying today, and I believe that God is going to deliver us tonight."

It was the first time I'd heard Skip personally speak of God since our early idealistic days when we'd come to the farm. And I felt a little surprised by his strong words of faith. I guess I'd assumed that, like me, he'd become something of a cynic when it came to religious things. "So you really still believe that God exists?" I asked.

He laughed lightly. "You mean just because a bunch of us crazy kids made some stupid mistakes, you think that makes God any less than he was before?"

"I'm not sure what I think anymore."

He gently pushed a strand of hair away from my face. "Cass, I believe in God and Jesus as much and maybe even more than I ever did. I just don't believe in all this." He waved his arms as if to encompass the entire farm. "Maybe we started out all right—" he shook his head— "or maybe not. But somewhere along the line we began to go way off track. We quit thinking for ourselves and just totally allowed Sky to lead us. But I sure don't think that's God's fault. And I made a decision this week. When I get out of here, I plan on serving God—not a man who *thinks* he's God."

I considered his words. "Yeah, maybe you're right."

And then he kissed me on the cheek and set out on his mission, and I was left alone with only his words to ponder. I had never realized that Skip was so deep. And suddenly I wondered if perhaps I was interested in more than just this pretense of a relationship with him. Maybe he was the kind of person I should hold on to. Maybe, as strange as it seemed, God had put us both here, and through all this, so that we could be together—maybe forever. This unexpected thought was exciting to me and I started to grasp a whole new perspective on God. Could he take something as messed up as the Funny Farm and bring something good out of it?

With growing hopes and eager expectations, crouching by the opened window, I waited for Skip to return for me. He had firmly instructed me to stay right there until I literally saw the whites of his eyes. "Just in case anything goes wrong," he'd warned. We knew that was a possibility. Maybe the dogs wouldn't be hungry. Or perhaps someone could be hanging around and prevent him from feeding them or turning off the generator. And we knew if I went out wandering around and looking for him we could really wind up with a mess on our hands. And so I waited by the window, ears and eyes tuned into the night, my heart pumping with adrenaline and anxiety as the minutes slowly ticked by.

Lights-out came and went, but still Skip didn't return. I listened hard into the darkness but only heard what seemed like the normal sounds of people heading off to their various beds, doors slamming, people saying good night, dogs barking, a baby crying. Just the regular stuff.

Slowly the farm grew more quiet. And still I waited . . . and waited. It took every ounce of my self-control (which had been fairly well developed by then) not to climb out the window and go see what was up. But I took Skip's warning to heart and stayed posted.

When Skip didn't return after what I felt certain must be several hours—I guessed it was well past midnight—I began to feel sick and panicky inside. What if something really big had gone wrong? What if they had caught Skip and were now onto us?

Suddenly I realized that to protect Skip and myself I should appear to be asleep in bed, just in case someone came looking. So I stripped off my overalls, rolled them up, and shoved them back into my bag, then jerked on a T-shirt Skip had tossed on the floor and crawled into bed, shivering from both an icy fear and the chill of the night. My body as rigid as a board and my heart still thumping against my chest, I waited and waited, barely breathing. I knew beyond a doubt now that something had gone wrong.

Please, help us, dear God, I prayed silently and desperately (for the second time in two weeks). *Okay, God, I really do believe you're the only one who can get us out of here. So, please, please, help us. And watch over Skip.*

Just then the door to my room opened and there standing like an ominous shadow was Mountain, a kerosene lantern in his hand. "Get up!" he demanded.

I leaped up and scrambled for my skirt, still lying in a heap by the bed. I barely had it buttoned before Mountain grabbed me by the arm and pulled me out of the room and down the steep, ladderlike stairs.

Soon we were standing before Sky and two of the newer brothers in the living room of the farmhouse. The generator to the house had been turned back on, making the room bright and garish. And although it appeared that only Sky and the three brothers were present, I sensed others were around, watching us, listening in hallways or from behind partially closed doors.

"Where is your husband?" asked Sky in an eerily calm voice.

At first I didn't know what he meant. Then I realized I was a married woman now. "I don't know," I answered honestly.

"When did you last see him?"

"Tonight," I said, glancing back and forth at the brothers, wondering what was going on and whether or not they had discovered Skip. "He went down to use the bathroom just before lights-out."

Sky slowly nodded, pressing his fingertips together. "And you weren't concerned when he didn't return?"

"I guess I fell asleep." I looked down at the floor.

"Yes, I'm sure you've had a very tiring night . . ." The way Sky said it sounded more like a question than a statement.

"Where is Stone?" I asked, looking up and meeting Sky's gaze.

"He's gone." Sky's eyes held mine, as if to test me.

"*Gone?*" I made no attempt to conceal my confusion and horror. "What do you mean?"

"I mean he left."

"He *left?*" I shook my head in disbelief. "But why? How?"

"That's what we want to ask you."

"But—but how would I know?" I felt real tears filling my eyes at the thought of Skip abandoning me here like this. It seemed inconceivable, unbelievable.

Sky continued gazing at me, evenly, as if discerning the inner secrets of my heart. And to be honest, I wasn't sure that he couldn't.

Totally defeated, I collapsed onto my knees, my colorful skirt billowing up around me like a parachute, then slowly shrinking to the ground. I fell forward and just sobbed uncontrollably—the whole while wondering, *Why, why, why?* Why would Skip do this? Why would he leave without me? Why would he put me through this? I had trusted him. He had seemed so real, so sincere. What about that stuff he'd just said about God tonight? I'd believed him! Oh, was I really such a fool?

Finally I felt someone gently tugging on my arm. I looked up to see Venus hovering over me. "Come with me," she said solemnly.

And I was taken upstairs, back to my old room where I was placed under what I assumed to be "house arrest." Venus informed me that I was not to leave that room under any circumstances.

For the next day I stayed in my old room, by myself, in something of a daze or maybe even shock. Meals were brought to me, but I had no appetite. By late that evening, someone knocked on my door. I didn't bother to get up or even to answer. I knew they would simply walk in. To my surprise, it was Star. Although it was dark, I could sense her presence by the jingling of her jewelry and the smell of heavy cosmetics and cheap perfume.

"Please come with me, child," she said kindly.

I stood, physically weak and emotionally drained, still wearing the same rumpled clothes as yesterday. I followed her down to the living room where it appeared the "council" awaited me.

It's not that we had an "official" council per se, but there were always certain people who were in the higher echelons—Sky's inner circle, I suppose. At that time, his circle consisted of Mountain and Venus and Star.

"We've come to a decision," said Sky after Star was seated. I remained standing before them, like the convicted felon about to go to the electric chair. "Do you have anything to say to us first?"

I looked from face to face, trying to determine what it was they were thinking. How much did they know? What did they want from me? But, as usual, their faces were impossible to read.

"I don't know what to say," I finally said. "I don't know what to think." I sadly shook my head. "All I can do is ask for your mercy." I looked directly at Sky, knowing this was exactly the penitent sort of behavior he thrived upon. It made him feel both powerful and benevolent.

He smiled, then nodded to the others. "See? I told you she has great potential."

I tried not to register surprise at this unexpected compliment, but merely looked down—humbly, I hoped—at my bare toes poking from beneath the hem of my skirt.

"Yes, I have always sensed Rainbow to be a deeply spiritual child," said Star dramatically.

"And for the most part she's been a good servant in the kitchen," added Venus. "She has worked harder than most of the sisters."

I stared at Venus in disbelief. Was she mocking me? But her expression appeared sober and genuine.

Mountain said nothing, just studied me carefully, and for some reason, of the four I feared his discernment the most. "I'm not so sure," he finally said.

"Come now, Mountain," said Star in a melodic voice. "The child is an innocent. Can't you see this by observing her countenance?" Then Star stood and walked toward me, raising her arms in the air as she came near. She moved her hands slowly in an arch over my head and then back down to my shoulders, again and again, as if she were feeling the air around me. "I sense truth and peace in her aura," she proclaimed in her theatrical voice, full of authority. Then finally, as if exhausted, her flabby and wrinkled arms fell limply to her sides and she sighed deeply.

"I believe Star is right," confirmed Sky. "Rainbow, you are hereby released from all accusations. You may rejoin the family and return to your regular duties." He smiled at me. "Have you anything to say now?"

Knowing full well that he expected me to fall to my knees and express my gratitude, I didn't disappoint him. I knew I'd been spared from something—something ominous and probably horrible. And although I had no idea what that something was, I knew I should be thankful.

The next few days passed uneventfully. I quietly resumed my role in the kitchen. I worked in silent competence, like a well-trained zombie.

It's as if something in me had died the night that Skip had abandoned me. Not the old Rainbow me, for she was already dead and buried, but something more. The real me, Cassandra Jane, fighter, survivor—she had given up. The only energy I possessed now was to peel and cut and slice and boil and wash and chop and stir and bake . . . and that was all.

Then toward the end of the week I overheard a conversation that, like a jolt of electroshock therapy (the kind they once used to stimulate mental patients) jarred me back into consciousness—back into reality!

I had walked out to the pigpen to dump the slop bucket of kitchen scraps—a job one of the sisters had neglected for two days. Not appreciating the accumulation of flies the bucket brought into the kitchen, I had decided to rid the back porch of this nasty business myself. But as I crouched in the shadow right next to the pigpen, carefully pouring the slop into the trough to avoid splashing it on my bare feet, I overheard two brothers talking quietly, with the kind of emotion that makes your ears prick up and listen. The small metal building separated us, but their voices carried with clarity.

"Stone had it coming," proclaimed one man. I recognized his voice as one of the brothers who'd been with Sky that night when Mountain had taken me to stand before them, that night when Skip had escaped without me.

"I'm not so sure," said the other. "There could've been another way."

"What, just let him go? What if he'd gone to the police or the FBI? What then?"

"He promised he wouldn't."

277

"But how could we trust him?"

"But it would've been better than—"

"Like Mountain said, we had to do what was best for the group."

"But it feels wrong."

"Look, you'd better just forget all about it. It's over and done with. And what's done is done. Now don't keep bringing it back up."

I squatted there on the ground as if frozen for what seemed a long time but was probably mere minutes. Flies swarmed about me, and the smell of rotten food drifted up to my nostrils. Yet I hardly noticed. As realization fully hit, I began to shake and tremble, and a fresh fear washed over me to think they might discover me eavesdropping.

I felt sickened by what I'd heard, what I now suspected had happened. Skip had not escaped after all. He had been caught. Deep down inside of me, in some hidden place in my heart, I knew with a cold certainty that Skip was dead.

Somehow I managed to stand and stumble back into the kitchen, and then, just barely grabbing the edge of the counter in time, I threw up in the sink. Crying and gasping and choking, I continued to vomit again and again before I finally collapsed onto the floor in sobs, curled into a fetal position, just hoping to die. Venus found me like that and called in one of the sisters to clean up the mess I'd created while she escorted me up into my bedroom.

There she helped me to lie down on the bed and then looked me over carefully. I didn't know why, nor did I care. I simply lay there, helpless and limp, thoroughly beaten. I closed my eyes and tried to shut everything out. I must've fallen asleep because when I finally awoke it was dark all around me. Somehow, perhaps only by

God's grace, I had managed to sleep for hours, but now I needed to use the bathroom.

Tiptoeing out my door and down the hallway, I paused when I heard voices. I could tell at once that it was Sky and Venus in the middle of what sounded like a serious and heated argument.

"Listen to me, Sky. I know what I saw."

"But she *can't* be pregnant," insisted Sky.

"She has all the symptoms," said Venus in her I-know-every-thing voice. "I found her vomiting this morning, she's been sleeping all day, she has those dark shadows beneath her eyes—"

"But Stone said that was why he was leaving," interrupted Sky. "Because she refused to sleep with him. He said after what happened with Sunshine he just couldn't take it all over again."

"But you didn't believe him, did you?" injected Venus. "Remember, Sky, you called him a filthy liar."

"That's not the point."

"The point is, I think she may be expecting Stone's baby. And if she is, that means you were all wrong."

"I am not wrong," he said firmly. "I know Rainbow is still a virgin. *I know.* I could see it in her eyes that night."

Venus laughed lightly. "Oh, Sky."

"Do not mock me."

"I'm sorry, Sky. But, really, just think about it."

"I don't need to think about it. God has already shown me that she's *the one.* Our promise child *will* be born through Rainbow— that's what her name means, you know, it means promise. And she *will* bear my promise child."

At that point I knew I could stand no more. I feared I might actually explode with words and rage and accusations that would only put me into worse trouble, and so I bit into my lip and tiptoed back to my room. And despite my resolution just days ago (when

I'd believed Skip had abandoned me) when I had sworn that I would never, ever pray to God again, I now fell on my knees next to my bed and prayed. It was all I knew how to do just then.

I prayed and prayed and prayed—all kinds of things. It was just like opening Pandora's box—everything just started flying out! I asked God why he'd allowed all this to happen. I asked him if Skip was okay. Was he alive? Was he with God right now? I just prayed and prayed, like I've never prayed before. And when Venus walked into my room, that's how she found me.

"Rainbow," she said quietly. "I need to talk to you. And I need you to be totally honest with me. Okay?"

Unsure of how best to answer, I simply nodded, then stood. "What is it?" I asked as I sat down on my bed, feeling surprisingly calmed and strengthened.

She sat next to me and took my hands into hers—a strange gesture for her. But I didn't resist her act of kindness. "When I saw you getting sick down in the kitchen I thought it might be because you're expecting a baby. Do you think this is possible?"

Now in what was probably just a split second, I wondered what the safest answer might be. If I lied and told her I was pregnant, it would make it appear as if Skip had lied to Sky about our wedding night and that would naturally put me in greater suspicion regarding his botched escape plan. But if I told the truth that I could *not* be pregnant, Sky would most likely try to force himself upon me before too long. And so I shot up a quick and silent prayer, and to my surprise felt an answer: to simply tell the truth.

"I am not pregnant, Venus. That would be an impossibility."

"Are you positive?"

"Well, I believe in order to become pregnant you must first have sex. And since I have not, I would have to assume that I'm not pregnant."

She nodded. "Okay. Well, I was just wondering since it seemed you had all the symptoms."

"Oh, that," I said dismissively. "I had just emptied the slop bucket and I think the pigpen smell got to me." I looked down at my hands lying limply in my lap. "And I suppose this whole thing about Stone running away is still pretty upsetting to me. It makes me feel like a real failure as a new wife, you know." I turned and looked at her, hoping for some sympathy, although I knew it was a long shot.

She nodded. "Yeah, that must've been hard. I don't know what I'd do if Mountain pulled something like that." She started to stand, then stopped. "And if you don't mind me asking, Rainbow, when did you have your last monthly cycle?"

I paused for a moment to remember. "Actually, I think it's been nearly a month right now."

"So you should have it any day then."

"Yes."

I could see the wheels spinning in her head, as if she were mentally calculating (and I knew from reading the natural childbirth book exactly what she was adding up—it should be about two weeks before I would become a good, fertile baby factory). "Well, good night then, Rainbow. Sorry to bother you, but I was just concerned. Now you sleep well."

I don't think I slept a bit that night. I felt more at peril than ever, and so once again I began to pray in earnest. It seemed that prayer was all I had. And as strange as it sounds, it's as if I could feel Skip leading me through this horrible thing, telling me that everything was going to be okay, that he was just fine now, and that I could trust God. And somehow that sustained me.

I always feel slightly hypocritical when I tell people I found God while living in some crazy cult-commune better known as the

Funny Farm out in California. But I think that's pretty much the truth of things. Oh sure, I may have given my heart to Jesus some time before that. But I believe I truly *found* God when I discovered I could *really* talk to him (and say absolutely anything—good or bad or ugly) and believe that he was still there, still really listening to me during those long, dark hours after I learned of what I felt certain must be Skip's death. And so as I continued to keep to myself in the following days, still grieving the loss of Skip, I also clung to my new lifeline with God—a line I firmly believed Skip had tossed to me. Had he tossed it to me while still here on earth, or from heaven? I can never be fully sure. But I clung to it all the same. For it was all I had. And to this day I am thankful.

Did I fret over the strange conversation I'd overheard between Sky and Venus about me becoming the mother of their "promise child"? More than likely, but at the same time, I tried to bring these worries and fears and anxieties to God—my lifeline. And somehow I believed that God was going to provide me a way to escape.

Days passed with nothing. And by early June, I felt my spirits sagging some. But still I prayed.

Then one afternoon, just after I'd gone outside to pick leaf lettuce out in the kitchen garden, a very strange thing happened. First, and not so unusual, I noticed Sky's van pull up on the road (he'd probably been running errands in town). But behind him was a black-and-white police car.

I stood and watched with interest as both vehicles paused at the gate, and then once it was opened, the patrol car slowly followed Sky's van up toward the house.

I don't quite know what came over me just then, but for some reason I just set down my produce basket and began to walk out toward the driveway, slowly at first, then faster, almost running. I had no idea why a policeman had followed Sky inside the compound (or why Sky had even allowed it—for all I knew he was going to sell the officer some pot!) but it didn't matter. I knew I was going to be leaving in that police car. By the time the two vehicles had pulled to a stop, I was only about ten feet away from the patrol car, and that's when I saw Joey Divers sitting in the passenger's seat right next to the uniformed cop.

He opened the door and climbed out, and I ran straight toward him.

chapter twenty-five

I FELT SKY'S EYES ON ME as I ran toward Joey, and I knew this could be dangerous, foolhardy even. Sky was still king of his little domain, and I was behaving in a way that was intolerable. But I simply didn't care. I was leaving. This time, there was nothing Sky could say to pressure me into staying. Dead or alive, I was getting out of this place.

By now the officer had gotten out of the car, and I noticed his hand poised just above his revolver. "Is that her?" he asked, nodding toward me as he warily eyed Sky and Mountain. The two had just climbed from the van and looked extremely ill at ease.

"Yes," said Joey as I fell into his arms. "This is her." He looked at me earnestly. "Do you want to come with me now, Cass?"

"*Yes,*" I said, clinging to him with both hands. *"Right now."*

"Do you want to get anything first?" he asked as he looked over my shoulder.

I would've liked to have retrieved my mother's photo and my guitar and a few other things, but I glanced at the crowd that was quickly gathering and knew there was no time to lose. I looked into Joey's face, still incredulous that he'd actually come for me. After all this time and all that had transpired—after I'd given up all hope, here he was standing right before me. I felt my fingers dig hungrily into his arms and yet he didn't even flinch.

"Cass?" His face was close to mine now, a sense of urgency in his eyes. "Do you want to get any—"

"No," I interrupted him. I had suddenly remembered the guns on the Funny Farm, and after what I believed had happened to Skip, I just didn't know what Sky and his bodyguards might do if we gave them half a chance. The policeman was clearly outnumbered. "I think we should just go, *now*."

The officer nodded at me as he opened the back door. "Get in, then, both of you."

I wasted no time as I grabbed up my full skirt and climbed into the backseat with Joey climbing in next to me. I remember how it struck me as funny—despite the threat of danger—that there were no handles on the interior of the doors and that Joey and I were locked in just like a couple of common criminals. And yet this was the first time in ages that I finally felt safe. Joey slipped his arm around my shoulders and I leaned into him with relief.

I didn't even look back as the officer quickly turned around his car, then sped down the driveway, away from the Funny Farm, his tires spewing gravel as he went. I closed my eyes, welcoming Joey's arm around me, and prayed for our safety. I didn't care if I ever saw the place again.

Once we were safely beyond the gates, I turned to Joey. "*You came!*" I cried, throwing my arms around him. I started to shake, even though the danger was behind us. "Thank God, you came!"

He looked into my eyes, his expression full of concern. "My mom sent me your letter, and it sounded pretty desperate. I came just as quickly as I could." He glanced at the officer, who was focused on the road. "After the 'warm welcome' I got the last time I came, I thought I'd better bring some help this time."

"Good thinking," I said, nodding. "And you didn't come a moment too soon." I exhaled deeply.

Joey took my hand in his. I clung tightly, savoring the warmth and strength of his touch. What had I ever done to deserve this kind of a friend?

"Are you okay, Cass?"

I wasn't sure where to begin, but I began to pour out my story, words piling on top of words, stopping just short of what had happened to Skip. I wasn't sure if I could talk about that yet.

The officer, completely stunned by my words, said, "You're kidding! Everyone in town thought that group was a bunch of nature-freak hippies. We had no idea about all that other stuff. Are you willing to make a statement, miss?" He glanced into the rear-view mirror. "And to press charges?"

"A statement? Charges? I—uh—I don't know." Everything was happening too fast. I needed some time to figure out what to do next.

As if he had read my mind, Joey spoke up. "I think we need to give her some time to relax first. She's been through a lot."

So we stopped just briefly at the police station. There I answered some preliminary questions. "I think that's enough for now," said Joey, who was sort of acting as my attorney even though he was barely into his own prelaw classes at the time. "Cass needs a chance to rest and recover from all this. We'll be in touch."

After leaving the police station, Joey took me out for dinner. I can still remember my utter amazement at being in an actual restaurant where you could order anything—absolutely anything—you wanted. I just sat staring at the plastic-coated menu, unable to make a decision. Finally, after the waitress came back for the third time, Joey offered to order for me. I simply nodded in relief. He ordered a bacon cheeseburger with fries and a chocolate shake for me (food that had long since been banned by Venus) and I slowly consumed it all. I felt Joey watching me as I ate, and I knew I should attempt to make some sort of conversation, but the embarrassing truth was I was so completely fascinated by the forbidden food that I could only focus my attention on each delectable bite.

Finally I dipped my last fry in ketchup and looked up. "Thanks, Joey."

The waitress picked up our plates and Joey asked me if I wanted coffee.

"Coffee?" I remember saying the word slowly, letting it roll off my tongue as if it were something exotic or foreign. Then I nodded.

After she brought our coffee, I began to talk. The whole story of Sky's oppression, the drugs, the rules, and even Skip's disappearance came pouring out of me. Joey just listened in silence, but I could see the pain and concern in his eyes. Finally, in a lowered voice, I told him that I believed that Skip was dead—had been killed. And that's when I saw tears filling Joey's eyes.

"Skip was a good friend of mine, too," he finally said. "We both became Christians at the same time." Then he slammed his fist down on the table, making the silverware jump. "They have to be stopped, Cass. Do you think you can make a statement?"

I swallowed hard. "I don't know. I just want to get as far away from them and this place as possible."

He reached over and took my hand. "I know. But think about Skip. Can you do it for him? And what about the others? It's possible that someone else will want out too! Maybe even right now. And what then?"

I thought about Mitch and Cindy (River and Breeze). She was expecting another baby. What if she had complications again? I couldn't bear to think of her losing another baby . . . or worse. I closed my eyes and forced myself to say, "Yes, I think I can do this."

chapter twenty-six

DURING THE NEXT FEW DAYS I was amazed that Joey could afford two rooms at the Holiday Inn. We spent most of our time discussing what would become of me. Although he wanted to take me back to Brookdale, the local police wanted me to stay in California so that I would be available to offer testimony as needed when the case eventually came to court (we knew it could be a while). And I knew he had enough to worry about without adding me to the list.

And so we finally worked it out for me to live in a small California town, just a couple hundred miles away from the Funny Farm, where there was a community college that Joey thought sounded good. His suggestion was that I get my GED and then take college classes.

Joey drove me to the campus, then walked me around, making inquiries as he went and acting very much like my guardian, which I suppose I greatly needed just then. And somehow Joey found Elizabeth Jones, an academic counselor who was a strong Christian, and I think he asked her, maybe even begged her, to keep me under her wing for a while. At the time I was still somewhat oblivious and I think fairly overwhelmed. But I trusted Joey. His instincts were good, and his track record far superior to mine.

Joey helped me to secure housing in a dorm right on campus, a private room, even (he'd explained how this was easier accomplished in summer than in fall). And then he took the time to drive me downtown to do some quick shopping, just some jeans and shirts and personal things, but enough to get me by for a while. Finally he drove me to the bank right next to campus and explained to me that a small trust fund had been set up to cover my college and living expenses, and so I wasn't to worry about money.

"But how?" I asked. "Who—"

He waved his hand. "Don't worry about it, Cass. It's like when Jesus said not to be anxious about what you eat or wear, but just remember how God takes care of the flowers and the birds."

I rolled my eyes at him. "Oh brother, Joey, that sounds like something Sky might say."

Joey reached across the car and put his hand on my shoulder. "Cass, the problem with Sky was that not everything he said was a lie. He always mixed some truth along with it, so that it was easier to swallow."

"I suppose so." I looked down at my lap. "But I feel like a fool just the same."

"Don't, Cass." He sighed deeply. "The only reason you got sucked into all that was because you have a good heart and you wanted someone to take care of you. But I know you, and I believe you were really trying to follow Jesus."

I looked up at him. "That's true, Joey. I did believe I was following Jesus. I really did."

He nodded. "I know. And for a while I even tried to believe that you guys were okay out here. I mean, who was I to judge your choices? Even if Sky was a little off base, aren't we all a little off sometimes when it comes to spiritual things? But I figure God can usually set us straight. I guess I hoped that's how it would be with Sky and you guys. But I never stopped praying for all of you."

"Really? I thought maybe you'd written us all off as a bunch of crazed fanatics."

He laughed. "Well, I did think you were a little fanatical. But then there were times when I was working so hard and felt so pressured and stressed out that I actually felt slightly envious of your little commune, and I even wondered if you guys didn't have the right idea after all."

Now it was my turn to laugh. "You've got to be kidding!"

He'd parked the car by now, and we got out and sat down on a shaded cement bench situated on the edge of campus. "Maybe, but there is something to be said about a slower, quieter kind of life." He glanced at his watch and groaned. "Speaking of the rat race, it's almost time for me to get going again."

I felt a tightness creep up into my chest, almost as if I wasn't going to be able to breathe. And suddenly everything in me wanted to grab on to him, to fall on my knees and to beg him to stay with me, or to take me with him—anything!

But I bit my lip and took in a deep breath. I knew I had no right to make such demands. I also knew that Joey had such a good heart that he might have given in to my hysteria. No, I had to be strong. "Well, I wish you didn't have to go so soon, but I understand."

"Cass, I'm sorry."

I felt tears slipping down my cheeks, but I didn't want him to see, so I bent down and picked some dandelions that had crept into the flower bed surrounding the bench. I remember wondering why they considered them weeds as I studied their sunny, yellow faces, slightly blurring around the edges due to my tears. "I know you need to go, Joey. And I really appreciate all you've done for me. Really."

"I'd stay longer if I hadn't already registered for summer classes, but even as it is I'll have missed a few by the time I get back.

I think I mentioned to you how I'm trying to pick up some extra credits this summer. I want to get all the electives that I can in the next two years, so I'll have a better chance at getting into law school."

"I still can't believe you're halfway through college already." I shook my head in amazement. "It just doesn't seem that long ago since we were both in the same grade back in Brookdale. And look at me, Joey, I don't even have my high school diploma yet." I forced a pitiful laugh. "Here you have it, once again, ladies and gentlemen, Joey Divers sprints ahead, leaving Cass Maxwell back in the dust."

He squeezed my hand. "You know it's not like that, Cass. Whether you can see it or not, you've had some real-life education that could be more valuable than college."

I blinked at him. "You've got to be pulling my leg."

"Really, Cass. I'll bet the things you learned at the commune will be with you for a long, long time."

I moaned. "Oh, I hope not. I'd like to forget the whole thing."

"No, Cass. You need to remember what you've learned— things like how you need to follow Jesus and not a person, no matter who he claims to be." He peered down into my face. "Not even me, Cass."

"But I can trust you, Joey. I've always—"

"You need to trust God, Cass. And yourself."

I nodded. "I suppose you're right."

Then he reached inside his jacket pocket and pulled out a small leather-bound Bible. "I know you didn't get to bring anything out of the commune with you, and I thought maybe you could use this."

I fingered the cover of the book, soft and worn from use. "But this is yours, Joey. I can't take your—"

"I want you to keep it for me, Cass. And promise me you'll read it every day. I've underlined some verses that have been especially meaningful to me. Maybe they'll mean something to you, too."

I thanked him and we hugged briefly. I no longer tried to conceal my tears, since it was useless anyway. "I know you need to go now. I'll be fine, Joey. Please don't worry about me."

I waved and waved, tears streaming down my face, until his car was completely out of sight. And despite my relief at being free from the Funny Farm, I'd never felt so completely alone in my entire life. Even though I knew that God was with me.

I can still remember the metallic taste of fear in my mouth as I walked across the campus to the counseling center a couple days later, on my way to take my GED test in Elizabeth's office. I had spent the previous days in the cloistered security of my little dorm room, almost afraid to venture out. Only a week ago I'd been living out at the farm, and suddenly everything on the "outside" felt big and overwhelming and scary to me. Not only that, but I felt like an imposter here, like they would soon find me out and send me back to the Funny Farm to go peel potatoes in the kitchen or have Sky's baby or something.

But of course that didn't happen. Instead I passed my GED, with flying colors just as Joey had predicted, and then spent an hour talking with, or mostly listening to, Elizabeth. At first I felt uncomfortable and somewhat intimidated by this tall, attractive black woman. She seemed so together and I felt like such a loser. But she was kind and supportive. And she encouraged me to take general studies courses for now, until I could decide what I'd like to major in for my bachelor's degree (although I wasn't even sure I wanted to, or could even afford to, attend four full years of college).

"Your friend told me a little of your previous circumstances," she said as we were winding down the interview. "I want you to feel free to call me if you need to talk to someone. I used to have a private practice as a counselor before I came on staff here, and I'm not all that busy, at least during the first part of summer anyway."

And so it was arranged I would meet with Elizabeth twice a week to start with (we later changed it to weekly as her schedule grew fuller). By the second week, she helped me to find work—not in a kitchen!—but as a part-time receptionist in the psychology department that was run by a good friend of hers.

"You'll probably need to dress more traditionally for work," she said, glancing down at my jeans. "I have a daughter a little older than you, who's just about your size, and she's always cleaning out her closet—" Elizabeth pressed her lips together. "Oh, I'm sorry, dear. I shouldn't be offering you hand-me-downs."

I laughed. "Don't worry. I've worn them all my life and it really doesn't bother me much anymore."

By the following week I was wearing Yolanda Jones's hand-me-downs (which were really the nicest clothes I'd ever had in my life) and working in a quiet office environment. Well, who would've thought? And to look at me you might've assumed, *Now there goes a normal, ordinary girl.*

But that's not how I felt on the inside. I could tell, as I continued to meet with Elizabeth, that I had what she called "issues" to resolve. And while her counseling was helpful and good, I realized these were things I'd have to work out for myself, and over time (and hopefully with God's help, since I still continued to read Joey's Bible and pray a lot). I found, probably as a result of living the past eighteen months in a fairly "restricted" society, not to mention the earlier years of my life, that I had become somewhat fearful and careful and even suspicious of others. When classes started in the fall, I found myself pulling more and more into myself and more and more away from others.

Elizabeth invited me to visit her church, but (as ridiculous as it sounds) I was afraid of getting swept up in some crazy religion that might suck up what little remained of my spiritual self-preservation and then render me completely brain-dead. And so I politely declined.

Instead I just faithfully went to my classes, worked at my reception job, did my homework, read the Bible and prayed, and regularly wrote letters to Joey (although I never told him about my personal struggles and phobias—I tried to sound healthy and normal and happy). And thankfully, despite Joey's full load of classes, he wrote to me regularly too. He even wanted to come visit me during Christmas break, but his mother became quite ill and he had to go home instead.

By spring the legal trials against the commune were scheduled. My teachers were understanding and allowed me to make up for things that I missed. I found giving my testimonies, plus seeing Sky and the others in the courtroom, to be highly stressful. I think that's when my hair began to fall out. Elizabeth assured me this was normal and encouraged me to cut it (so I wouldn't get too freaked when I saw huge dark globs of hair piling up in the shower). So I did. But then, more than ever, I started to feel like I had lost myself, or lost my soul, or lost something (besides my hair) and that's when I began having confusing and frustrating nightmares that made me afraid to sleep at night.

Finally, while meeting with Elizabeth shortly after the trials had ended (with numerous convictions for everything from selling a controlled substance to statutory rape to second-degree murder—somehow the DA managed to convince the jury that Skip had been killed during a scuffle) I told her that I was afraid I was losing my mind. Once again, she assured me that I was having a normal response to all that had happened in my life, and to just give myself time. I really tried to believe her. I hoped she was right. But just the same I began reading psychology books in the office where I worked.

Before long I thought I might have every mental disorder in the book. Or perhaps, and worse, I was simply a mental hypochondriac. All this obsession with the mind finally convinced me that if I should continue my higher education, perhaps I might consider majoring in psychology.

This is not to make it seem that I gave up on God during this time, because believe me, I did not. I still prayed and read the Bible every day, and I know this was my greatest lifeline, but even so I can see now that I was still floundering. And yet I seemed to get a little better each day. I'm sure I gained some satisfaction from my careful daily routine of going to classes and work. But I never engaged in any sort of social life to speak of, and I didn't attend church or any other kind of religious functions. I'm sure everyone who knew me thought I was odd or a hermit or (because of the newpapers) "that crazy girl who'd lived in a commune." But I tried not to think about these things too much.

chapter twenty-seven

Joey came to visit me just after spring-term finals ended, almost exactly one year since he'd rescued me from the Funny Farm. Once again, he only had a few days before he had to return to his own summer classes and part-time job. And on his last day there, we sat down together on the same cement bench on the edge of campus, his old blue car parked on the street nearby. We were just talking and joking and enjoying the sun and our last few minutes together, when Joey suddenly suggested it might be time for me to move back home.

"Home?" I echoed. "Now where would that be?"

"I mean, you could transfer to the university. Maybe we could get you housing near mine."

I considered this, briefly. And for a moment it sounded almost possible, but in the next instant I felt flooded with complete horror. How could I possibly just pack it up, pull up my roots, and move on—just like that? "I—uh—I don't know, Joey. I mean, I've sort of started to feel at home here."

"Yeah, Cass, and that's great. I can tell how much you've grown in the last year. You seem so much more confident and at ease—"

"But that's just it, Joey, if I have to start over—well, I just don't know if I can handle that. I mean, I've got my room here and my job, and there's Elizabeth—we're still doing counseling sessions, you know, and . . ."

". . . you're just not ready to leave," he finished for me.

I wanted to say that I was too frightened to leave, that the mere idea of moving completely overwhelmed me and threw me into a complete panic. But the problem was, I had enjoyed that brief experience when Joey said he saw me as more confident and mature. And as silly as it seems now, I just didn't want to shatter that image.

It's not that I ever felt him look down on me, but on the other hand he was so together and successful that I always felt a little flaky in contrast, like I could never quite live up to him. And just then, I really wanted him to see me in a better light, even if it wasn't a true light. To admit I was terrified would undo all that.

"Well, like I told you before, Cass, it's your life and you've got to make your own decisions. The only one who should ever direct you is God, and I can tell by your letters that you're leaning on him more and more."

I nodded. "Yeah, it's been a hard, uphill climb this past year, but I really believe things are changing for me. And I know God is seeing me through this."

"Have you been able to go to church yet?"

"Well . . ." I sighed. "No. But maybe I'll do that this next school year. Elizabeth keeps inviting me."

"You should really give it a try, Cass. It's not good to be too isolated, you know."

I could hear disappointment laced through his voice, and I wondered if it was because I hadn't gone to church or because I didn't want to move yet.

"Now, you're sure you don't want to reconsider moving back?

Maybe think about it for a while? I have to admit it'd be great having you live closer to me, Cass. It would really shorten the commute." He smiled and his dark eyes glowed warmly.

Suddenly the idea of living near Joey became very tempting, but at the same time I felt worried that I would become too dependent on him. I hated the idea of becoming a helpless, cloying female, literally sucking the life out of my best friend. I knew I didn't have the strength to just pick up and leave all that had become familiar this past year if I had to completely stand on my own two feet. As it was, I could barely make it through a week if Elizabeth was forced to cancel on me for some reason. The whole idea of giving all this up just scared me witless. "I can't explain it very well, Joey," I said, now fighting back tears. "But I just think I need to stay here."

"But, Cass," he tried again, "we could spend more time together. It'd be great."

"I can't do it, Joey. This is my life right now, it's all I have, and I just can't leave."

"But, Cass . . ." He looked right into my eyes. "What if I said I love you and that I'd like to marry you?"

Shocked, I studied his face. Was he serious? Or was he just doing this out of pity? Perhaps he could see right through my wimpy façade—maybe he knew that I was barely holding on, ready to tumble into pieces at any moment.

But how could I allow him to rescue me, yet again? And especially with a marriage proposal that from all appearances seemed motivated by pity.

"Joey," I said slowly. "You can't mean that. I know you feel sorry for me and you've been a wonderful friend and everything. And I know you want to help me. But you don't have to—"

"Oh, Cass!" His head dropped and he stared down at the

ground, thumping his cane into the dirt with what seemed anger, or maybe just pure frustration.

"Joey," I tried again, "I really do appreciate your help and all. But this is a decision I have to make for myself. I can't keep letting other people tell me what to do all my life. Can I? You've said yourself that I need to think for myself and not let anyone else tell me what to do. And the fact is, I feel I need to stay here." I clasped my hands tightly in my lap, as if to show my firm resolve, when really it was to hide my trembling.

And so it seemed it was settled. Joey didn't try to convince me that his proposal (if it truly was such a thing) was really motivated by love. He simply gave me a quick hug and climbed back into his car and drove across the country again. How many times had he done that for me? I wondered. Three? Perhaps this would be the last.

And then I went to the safety of my little room and cried. I think I cried for a couple of days. Elizabeth thought I was having a breakdown. And maybe I was, but I told her I was just tired.

Looking back, I'm not entirely sure how I survived that summer. In many ways I felt more alone than ever before. And yet I suspected that God was with me. More than ever I found myself reading from that little Bible Joey had given me the previous year. And I remember how one particular line (one that Joey had underlined in red) seemed to literally leap off of the page at me. It was actually the second half of a verse in Matthew. It was something Jesus had said: "Lo, I am with you alway, even unto the end of the world." And although I would admit it to no one at the time (not even myself) I suppose a part of me just clung to those words, hoping that somehow I would discover them to be really true.

I continued my second year of college, living it out very much like my first—quiet, controlled, safe. Strangely enough, my little "trust fund" remained intact, and for some reason it never occurred to me to wonder what kept these funds flowing. During the first year, I had simply assumed that the state had provided for my expenses (in exchange for my testimony) but why would they still keep it coming? Still, I told myself, perhaps it's like Joey said, it comes from God, so why question it? And so I continued my education and my part-time job that helped with the little extras of living and I tried not to think too much about what the future might bring.

I enjoyed my classes and did quite well. I had been on the dean's list since my first term there, and toward the end of my second year, Elizabeth suggested that I start making plans to transfer.

"Transfer?" I echoed, a rise of fear catching me by the throat.

She smiled patiently. "Yes, Cassandra, you know we're only a two-year college."

"Oh."

"Where would you like to get your degree from? I think you could get into almost any school—and probably with scholarships to boot."

"I don't know if I want to leave."

"But, Cassandra, why would you stay here?"

"Maybe I could just work full-time at the psych office and stay in my room and . . ."

She frowned. "Cassandra, you're an intelligent young woman, and you need to continue your education."

I took in a jagged breath. "But what if—what if I don't want to?"

She firmly shook her head. "I think you're allowing your past to hold you prisoner again, Cassandra."

And that's when I just totally broke down and told her how deathly afraid I was to make a change (any change). I told her how much I clung to my daily routines, how I hadn't made a single friend, and other than Joey and God (and maybe her) there was no one in the entire world who really cared about what happened to me.

We went back to meeting twice a week again after that. And by the third meeting, Elizabeth helped me to decide it would be best to transfer to the university where Joey was going to school. She assured me they had a fine psychology department, and I would be in somewhat familiar territory, only about a hundred miles from where I'd grown up. Still, I wasn't completely convinced and wondered if I might not chicken out at the last minute anyway.

Naturally, I didn't inform Joey of this decision, since I felt so unsure of my ability to carry it out. And I continued my receptionist job throughout the summer, taking a few art classes (which I enjoyed immensely) just to fill in the time. And then at the end of August, Elizabeth drove me to the bus stop (in her little red Porsche) and hugged me good-bye. Then she held on to my arms with both hands and said, "You're going to be just fine, Cassandra. I know that underneath all this fear and anxiety that's been dogging at your heels, there lives a highly spirited girl who's going to come out on top of it all."

I blinked at her choice of words but thanked her for all her kindnesses during the past two years. Then, finally, I made myself turn away from her (the closest thing to a mother I'd had since my grandma died) and I woodenly climbed the steps to the Greyhound (feeling like a convict scaling the platform he'd soon be hanging from). Then I turned and, forcing a smile to my lips, waved good-bye.

With blurry eyes I made my way down the aisle until I found an empty seat at the back of the bus. And there, as the bus began the first leg of its cross-country journey, I sat and mulled over Elizabeth's parting words. Wasn't that exactly what my grandma used to say? That I was a "highly spirited girl"? And didn't that usually come right after someone else (like my daddy) had just come down upon me, maybe even saying something like I "had the devil" in me?

And that's when it began to hit me. All this fear and anxiety I'd been experiencing during the past few years. Certainly *that* wasn't from God. No, I had learned about fear from people like my daddy and Sky. That kind of fear had nothing to do with God—not the God I now knew and prayed to daily. And for once I thought that maybe my daddy was right. *Maybe I did have the devil in me!*

And so for the next two days (while riding nonstop on that old Greyhound bus through the sweltering heat of August) I began to pray that God would just "beat the devil outta me." I sat with my knees pulled up in front of me, praying that God would help me to escape my fear-filled, wretched, little life, all the while devouring page after page in Joey's little Bible as I searched out every verse I could find that made any reference whatsoever to fear.

The best thing I found was a verse way in the back of the Bible about how there shouldn't be any fear in love because God's love should completely obliterate our fear. And while I wasn't completely certain what it meant at the time, I knew that there was power in it, and I could see it was in direct opposition to what I'd been taught at the Funny Farm.

As a result, by the time we rolled into my home state, I was feeling somewhat calm and at ease. Call it Greyhound Bus therapy or what have you, but somehow God used that long, hot cross-country trip to just set me free. And I'm sure it was the first time I'd been truly happy in years!

chapter twenty-eight

AS MUCH AS IT SEEMED like it, and as much as I wished it were so, all my fears and apprehensions had not completely vanished into thin air. But there was no question about it, I had definitely changed. For the first time in a long time I now felt I had some sort of control over my life.

I climbed off that Greyhound, caught a cab over to the university campus (which was much larger than the community college) and spent the afternoon exploring. And to my relief, I wasn't nearly as overwhelmed as I'd imagined I'd be.

And somehow being only a hundred miles from Brookdale was strangely comforting. I'm not sure why. It's not like I had anyone back there who I thought gave a hoot about me. I felt certain my Aunt Myrtle probably thought I was dead and gone by then. And I figured my daddy probably didn't give a whit one way or the other.

To be honest, I hadn't really given him much thought over the past few years. I had enough issues to deal with, and my feelings toward him were so conflicted and confusing, it was simply easier not to think of him at all. And yet I suppose if I'd been perfectly honest, I'd have to admit that I'd reached that desolate place where more and more I secretly blamed him for all the mistakes and misfortunes that'd come my way. And it only made sense that I did, for aren't parents supposed to nurture and protect their young from such mayhem?

I found that on those rare occasions when my daddy did come to mind (like on his birthday or if I happened to see a man walking down the street who resembled him) I would feel my jaw and my insides tightening up and, well, he was just someone I didn't want to think too much about. Did that mean I hated him? I'm not entirely sure. But it was a strong emotion that closely resembled hate, although I'm positive I never admitted this much to myself. It's as if the space my daddy should've occupied inside of me had become a big, black hole. And I was afraid that if I went down there to poke around, I might simply fall in and become lost in it forever. And I was tired of being lost. Especially when I was just starting to feel found. Besides, I knew that God had become my daddy now. I knew that he was the one who would see me through.

Elizabeth had called the university, getting me all set up in a dorm that I suspected wasn't too far from where Joey lived. She'd written all this information down on a little three-by-five card that she'd tucked into my purse at the train station. (I'm surprised she didn't just pin it to my chest, since I was acting like such a baby about then.) And so it was all arranged that I'd have a roommate, and I felt ready for that.

To my relief the dorm room didn't look all that much different than the one I'd occupied during the past two years. I could see my roommate hadn't yet arrived, which was in itself a relief. This gave me time to unpack and settle in and sort of catch my breath.

And after spending that first afternoon just walking around the campus and checking things out until I felt somewhat secure and almost knew my way around, I knew it was time to call Joey. Suddenly I couldn't wait to see his face and to tell him I was here.

"Hello?" said a guy's voice on the other end. It wasn't Joey.

"Hi, is Joey there?"

"No, didn't you hear the news?"

"What news?"

"Joey got that Harvard scholarship he'd been trying for. You just missed him. He took off yesterday. Man, was he ever jived!"

"Oh . . ."

"Do you want his address?"

Somehow I managed to scribble down the lengthy address that sounded so strange and much too far away; then I stuck it in a drawer and leaned my head down onto the built-in desk with a thud. *Joey was gone.*

Suddenly I felt completely alone again, depressed and slightly frightened. I guess I hadn't realized exactly how much I'd been counting on being near Joey, how much I looked forward to seeing his face again. I couldn't even admit to myself just how much.

But taking a deep breath, I remembered my resolve on the bus. I remembered that God was my daddy. And just because Joey was gone, I would not give in to fear and anxiety. I would continue to trust God. I would live my life fully. And I would make it! I would.

At least I hoped I would.

My roommate, Billie Jean Duncan, turned out to be a home ec major—a senior who'd just transferred from a small private college in Georgia. Now, I tried not to show how strange I thought her major was (in an age where women had long since burned their bras and Gloria Steinem reined supreme) because Billie Jean really seemed quite pleased with her vocational choice.

And besides, she had told me on the first day we met, "I'm a born-again Christian, Cassandra, and I sure hope that doesn't bother you any." I told her that was fine with me, and that, as a matter of fact, I was too (at least I thought I was, although this "born-again" talk still made me slightly uncomfortable). And I made it perfectly clear to Billie Jean that I had no desire to attend any organized churches and had a slight phobia when it came to fanatics or fundamentalists. Billie Jean said that was just fine by her, but she'd probably look around for some sort of fellowship group or Bible study to attend on campus.

She also told me that she'd been in 4-H "since forever" and that she'd always loved cooking and sewing, and that she even dreamed of becoming the "perfect little wife someday" (I swear those were her exact words!). Naturally, I tried to conceal my horror and didn't tell her of my own slightly disastrous domestic experiences out west on the Funny Farm, or how I'd just as soon leave all that behind me, thank you very much!

But I did have to tease her just a little about her name, since Billie Jean King had become something of a feminist icon the year before when she beat the pants off of that bigmouth Bobby Riggs. But, oh, did that ever irk my conservative roommate. She was what you might've called an antifeminist, and did not appreciate sharing her name with an outspoken celebrity such as Ms. King—not one little bit.

Then strangely enough, as fall term progressed into winter, I did notice that Billie Jean seemed quite happy (maybe *passionate* is a better word for it) about her home economics studies. She'd bring home various projects, throwing herself into some complicated creation of a historical wedding gown or some international cooking project that required more pots and pans than I'd want to wash in a week. (Although I never complained while sampling her various experiments—far tastier than Venus's "health food" recipes back on the farm.)

But what Billie Jean forced me to come to grips with was that I didn't have this same sort of passion and excitement for my own major in psychology. And although I found my classes interesting, informative, and even intellectually challenging, I just never felt quite "taken away" by my studies. At least not like Billie Jean appeared to be. So one chilly night in February I told her about my dilemma.

"Well, what do you *really* love to do, Cassandra?" she asked with pins protruding from her lips like a porcupine and elbow-deep in the construction of a colorful Amish quilt.

I studied the neatly cut shapes of teal and fuchsia and gold that she was carefully assembling into a star and thought for a moment. "Well, there was a time when I actually enjoyed sewing—well, maybe not sewing so much, but creating things, using fabric and ribbon and beads and colors and stuff."

"Kind of like a designer, maybe?"

I shrugged. "I suppose, but I'm not really sure."

"So did you, like, actually *enjoy* making clothing? Or was it just the creative process that fired your engines?"

I thought about her question. "I suppose I mostly liked the creative process. And you know, I did take some art classes last summer, just for the fun of it and to pass time, but the fact is I really enjoyed them—the creating part."

She pointed her scissors at me. "There! You have it, Cassandra. You should think about becoming an art major. Maybe you could just minor in psychology."

"An art major?" I toyed with the idea for a moment. "But how would I ever support myself with an art degree?"

"You can do like me. Just teach it until you get married."

I laughed. "I doubt I'll ever get married."

Now she laughed, sputtering pins everywhere. "Oh yeah, sure. That's what all my girlfriends say; then the next thing you know they're asking you to be a bridesmaid in their happy little June wedding and forcing you to wear some hideous pink dress that makes you look like a fat jar of Pepto-Bismol. Good grief, I've been in three weddings already."

I considered telling her about my own circus "wedding" but couldn't bring myself to do so. (It seemed a dishonor to Skip's memory to just toss something like this out for others to hear and perhaps laugh at.) And as much as I liked Billie Jean, I just couldn't imagine how someone as normal and perky as her would ever understand or even appreciate a crazy tale of such grim woe. So far I hadn't told her anything about my little stint on the Funny Farm. Although I'd considered it a couple of times, if for nothing more than just pure shock value. But I suppose I was saving it.

The next day I phoned Elizabeth (in California) and told her I was considering changing to an art major. "Good for you, Cass!" she exclaimed with what sounded like sincere enthusiasm. "You should do what really makes you happy, and then just wait and see how the rest of your life will just fall right into place. You know, that's usually how God works."

And so by spring term I was an art major (with a minor in psychology). And Billie Jean and Elizabeth were right, I absolutely loved it. Whenever I was creating (whether it was with clay or oils or block print or watercolor or sketching or just whatever . . .) I found myself completely carried away by the process.

It's almost as if Cassandra Jane Maxwell just disappeared altogether, as I became lost in the creative process. But it was a good kind of lost—the kind of lost where when you finally come to and wake up, you are found. And as I created I became even more mindful of God, the Creator, and I felt more in touch with my spirit than ever before. It was amazing, really! So freeing and fulfilling and, well, just plain fun! In fact, it was so much fun that I almost felt guilty about it, but I figured that was probably just an unfortunate remnant of my days spent under Sky's authority and not worthy of an actual thought or response.

Joey and I continued to write letters throughout this year, but not with nearly the regularity as before. And over time his letters became shorter and more impersonal, as if they were quickly jotted down, sharing information and activities, but lacking in feeling. I suspected that he was quite busy with law school and his part-time job. Or maybe he'd found something else to distract him—like a girlfriend perhaps, and he was trying to slowly wind down his relationship with me.

And it seemed only natural that some intelligent girl would snap him up. Joey Divers would be quite a catch! I tried hard not to think about that time he'd asked me to marry him (at least I think he did, but part of me thought I might've simply imagined the whole thing since I'd been in such a truly fragile and vulnerable state just then). And even if he *had* actually offered to marry me, I'm sure it was merely a kindhearted act of sympathy on his part, his way of rescuing me once again.

So even then, I felt thankful that I'd controlled myself back then (and not accepted his rescue efforts) because I could see now how that most likely would've ruined all his chances for that great scholarship at Harvard. And I knew that going there must be like living out his greatest dream. And I must admit I was extremely proud of him.

But I did miss him just the same. Considerably. And then, due to his job, he hadn't been able to come home for either Christmas or spring break. Not that he'd promised to come see me, but I had hoped he might visit his folks, and maybe stop by the university. . . . But he explained in his letters how important it was for him to work all the hours he could. (He worked in the security office on campus, where he could study at night.) He said he needed those extra hours to help cover his living expenses, which I suspect were considerable.

I think it was during spring term that it occurred to me that I should find out just how much money was actually left in my "trust fund," which was still somewhat of a mystery to me. And although I had a full scholarship at the university and lived like a very frugal church mouse, I knew the funds couldn't last forever.

And I suppose I had begun to worry that since Joey had set the whole thing up, perhaps he was actually the one helping to contribute—and that made me feel absolutely sick inside. What if he was up at Harvard working himself to death just to put me through school?

I wrote him expressing this concern, but what he wrote back to me was even more mysterious. He informed me that I had a "secret benefactor" and not to worry because it looked like funding would continue until I graduated. Still not convinced it wasn't him, I decided to take a job during the summer when my class load was lighter (that way I could contribute to my own support). And so I got a reception job at a travel agency just a block or two off campus, and it went so well that they invited me to continue part-time in the fall.

Billie Jean opted to do one more year, getting her master's degree, which would enable her to teach at the high school level (and since her Prince Charming had yet to show up, she figured she'd better be ready for the long haul). As a result, I wasn't forced to adjust to a new roommate during my senior year, and I must admit I'd become rather fond of Billie Jean and her sensible, domestic ways.

Somehow, she enticed me to start going to her nondenominational Christian fellowship group that year, and I was surprised to discover a fairly normal group of kids who just wanted to hang out and study the Bible together without going over the deep end. In fact, it seemed we only spent a small amount of time actually studying the Bible. Mostly we just talked and laughed and did ordinary things like bowling and eating pizza. And so I wasn't too worried.

And I had to admit, the teaching seemed sound and lined up with what I'd been learning myself in my daily Bible reading. It was refreshing to be part of a group where we could talk freely about Jesus without getting all big-eyed and putting on spiritual airs. It was more like knowing Jesus was just an everyday part of an everyday life. And I must say I liked that.

But as a result of this new "social" outlet, I was faced once again with the guy problem. Now, Billie Jean could not for the life of her understand why I perceived this as a problem, and I couldn't even begin (without going into all my embarrassing history) to explain it to her. And finally one day she just confronted me and asked me quite blatantly if I was, in fact, a lesbian. Her normally plumpish, pink face had become all red and splotchy and I could see that the possibility of my questionable sexuality had given her no small amount of stress and vexation.

I just threw back my head and laughed. "Of course not, Billie Jean!" Then I absolutely howled with laughter. "Good grief, Billie Jean, were you afraid that I had fallen in love with you or something?"

She was totally mortified and actually speechless for a few moments; then she sputtered, "Well, no, no—but I—well, you know, I just didn't know what to think." She folded her arms across her chest and scowled. "Think about it from my perspective, Cassandra! First you go on about Billie Jean King and all that women's lib stuff. And then, here's this nice Paul Copeland, and he's just a-calling and calling, and you just keep making up your petty little excuses. Good night, I'd jump at the chance to go out with some-one like him."

"Well, then why don't you?"

She made a face. "Because he hasn't asked me, you big nin-compoop!"

And so we settled that matter. I was not, and never had been, nor did I want to become, a lesbian. But it did worry me some that she had thought so.

I suppose it was true that I didn't put much care into my appearance. But I enjoyed wearing jeans and work shirts and over-alls, and besides, this kind of clothing fit in well at the art depart-ment, where the dress code was definitely casual. But when I took a jewelry class during winter term I made myself some long, dan-gling earrings that I hoped gave me a more feminine look.

Although I must say I'd never noticed any problem with *guys* thinking I was a lesbian. In fact, it seemed I had no problem attract-ing guys, probably because I just didn't care that much and they felt at ease around me. But for the time being I just wanted to be friends. Somehow I knew I wasn't emotionally ready for anything more. And I explained this to "that nice Paul Copeland" and so we kept things low-keyed and went out for coffee or sodas occasion-ally, and we even went to a concert and a movie together. But that's all there was to it as far as I was concerned.

It was during that year, my senior year in college, that Joey all but quit writing. Just a card at Christmas, and then one again at Easter. I kept writing to him (thinking he was just swamped with classes and work) but I slowed it down some when I began to think maybe this was his way of cutting himself free from me. I sure didn't want to be some kind of ball and chain tied around his one good leg.

But toward the end of the school year (just before my graduation) I decided to send him an announcement (just a little home-made one since I saw no need to send out more than two—one for Elizabeth and one for Joey). I honestly didn't expect him to come, but I suppose it was just my way of saying, "Hey, look, I did it!" And thanks, of course.

Elizabeth sent me a beautiful bouquet of yellow roses, but to my surprise Joey actually showed up! You could've knocked me over with a sneeze when he stopped by my dorm and invited me out for lunch before the ceremony. Unfortunately he said he had to leave right afterwards (to get back to his job on campus) but I was deeply touched that he'd driven all that way just to watch me march down the aisle and pick up my diploma.

We went out for a quick cup of coffee before he had to hit the road, and I told him that I was following my roommate's example and going for my master's too. But I explained that I planned to live off-campus next year. (I'd found a cozy studio apartment that didn't cost any more than my dorm room.) Naturally, I would continue working at the travel agency (full-time during the summer, except for the two-week tour of Europe that I had booked at an incredible rate).

"You're going to Europe!" he exclaimed as he set down his cup.

"Why, yes," I stammered, suddenly wondering if he might've been, after all, my "secret benefactor." (And then who else could it have been? Joey had given me some complicated explanation about why he was taking four years to finish law school instead of the usual three, but I was still afraid he might just be working too hard and putting all his extra earnings into my trust fund.)

"That's great, Cass." He looked slightly unhappy, though.

Suddenly I felt like I needed to explain what might be perceived as extravagant. "You see, I've been putting a little down every month and it was such a great deal that Marsha—the woman who owns the agency—said I couldn't afford to pass it up and it works well with my art major and—"

"Cass, you don't have to defend yourself. Really, I think it's absolutely fantastic. I wish I could go too."

"Do you think you—"

"No, no . . . I'm . . . too busy right now. But maybe someday."

"I could get you a good deal, Joey."

He smiled. "Yeah, I'll keep that in mind." He glanced at his watch. "It's about time for me to go, Cass."

"I wish you could stay."

He shrugged, then started to stand, arranging his cane to help balance himself, but the look on his face made me wonder if his leg was giving him pain. "Say, I hear that you and Paul Copeland are going out."

"You know Paul Copeland?"

"Yeah, he was a friend of my roommate."

"Well, I wouldn't exactly call it going out, Joey."

"Oh, you don't have to explain anything to me, Cass." He began walking to the door, but I could sense something was different about him. Almost as if he were hurt or something, but it just didn't make any sense.

We stood out on the sidewalk for a few minutes. "I'm so proud of you, Cass," he said, his old smile returning and warming me all over. "I knew you could make it."

"Not without your help, Joey." I reached over and touched his arm. "I couldn't have done any of this without you. You know that, don't you?"

"Oh, you're a survivor, Cass. You always have been. And there's always been greatness in you. I knew you'd come out on top."

I could feel a big lump catch in my throat. For some reason this felt like one of those final good-byes—kind of like Bogie and Bacall in *Casablanca*—the ones where you never see that person again, or at least not in the same way. "Joey, I just want you to know that you are the closest thing to family to me."

He reached out and pulled me into a big hug that felt more intimate than usual. But then he said, "You've always been like a sister to me, Cass."

So, it was a brotherly hug then. Well, I could accept that. But when he finally let go of me I'm sure we both had tears in our eyes, although we didn't speak of it.

And quite honestly I wasn't even sure why I felt so broken up, almost forlorn, even. I really didn't know what was going on inside me. Was it that our lives were finally just going in two separate and totally different directions now, and perhaps this was his way of telling me, "It's been nice"? Maybe he did have a serious girlfriend back at Harvard, and why not? Or perhaps he had some big, important plans that could never include someone like me. Or perhaps it was just his way of saying that this was the last time he'd be able to simply drop everything and run off to check on poor old Cass again.

And of course I understood completely. I knew better than anyone how Joey had gone above and beyond what any other ordinary friend might've done. I'd never expected this much from him, not ever. Still, I could barely see through my tears as his old blue car drove away.

chapter twenty-nine

THE FUNNY THING ABOUT A RUT is that you never notice exactly when or quite how you got yourself into one. I guess it just starts slowly, but the more you keep going along those same old lines, the deeper your rut becomes until one day you're just totally entrenched and you begin to wonder if you will ever find your way out again. I think that's what happened to me after graduating with my master's degree in art.

Oddly enough I got my first teaching job right back at old Brookdale High—the same school I never graduated from. And to add to the strangeness of that, some of my old teachers were still there—just a-teachin' away like no time had ever passed. Maybe they were in a rut too, although I'm sure they didn't think so. I suppose it was just me. And I know I should've been thankful that old Mr. Rawlins had decided to retire from teaching art just as I was needing a job, and that my supervisor Bev Jacobs at the university had possessed the foresight to do some checking around for me before graduation time.

But I couldn't help but think something was wrong about this whole setup right from the get go. Me, back in Brookdale? What would people think? And what if, of all things, my daddy happened to live there and was still working down at Masterson Motors during the week and being the town drunk on the weekend? It would be just too humiliating for words. But as it turned out my daddy was nowhere to be seen in that town, and as far as I knew he hadn't shown his face around there since the last time he'd gotten himself into such trouble by trying to kill his only daughter.

Aunt Myrtle still lived in town though and had managed to get herself another bank job, which seemed to please her. Not only that, she'd finally found herself a man! His name was Burt Flanders and he owned the Shell station on Main Street. So in some ways my little family was gaining a tiny bit of respectability (although I'm sure that lots of folks still whispered when they saw me or my aunt passing by).

It's not like Aunt Myrtle and I had become all warm and cozy living there in the same town together, but at least we were on speaking terms now, and I didn't mind driving into the Shell station when it was time to fill up my little Datsun, because I liked Burt just fine. In some ways I was even a little bit worried for him, afraid that he might be just a little too good for my aunt, but he didn't seem to mind her somewhat prickly and persnickety nature. And I think they were happy, in their own way. I was only up to their house a couple of times, but when I was there they both treated me just fine. And my aunt even dug out another photo of my mother for me to keep. It looked just exactly like the other one, and yet something seemed different too. Or maybe it was me that had changed. She'd found the photo tucked away in my grandma's things—things I never really got to look at much or handle.

Aunt Myrtle seemed to be protecting them from something, keeping them all shut up in an old trunk that she kept shoved into a corner of the back bedroom. Now, if they'd been my things I'd have taken them out and enjoyed them some. But as it was Aunt Myrtle never gave me the option.

Sometimes I'd go over and visit Mrs. Divers. I knew she'd had some serious health problems and didn't get out much anymore, so I'd take her some flowers from my garden or some sort of home-made goody I'd whipped up. I suppose I felt I owed her my eternal gratitude for that time she'd forwarded that strange-looking letter I'd sent from the Funny Farm on to Joey. She could so easily have thrown it away.

We'd sit there in her front room and just visit a spell, and I started to realize she really was a very nice woman. Surprisingly, she seemed to actually like me now that I was a grown-up and not leading her son astray and getting into trouble all the time. And after the first couple times, she even learned not to inquire about my family (or rather my daddy). I'm sure she hadn't meant any harm by it, probably just being social and friendly and all, but I did not appreciate anyone bringing up my daddy to me, and I never attempted to hide my feelings about this either. And so in time she caught on.

Mostly we'd talk about her health (she suffered from what women called "female problems" back in those days). But she also loved to go on and on about Joey, which I never minded a bit. She'd talk about his fine scholarship and his graduating with honors, how he could work in any law firm in the country—on the planet, even!

Yes, it seemed Joey Divers had the world by the tail now. Not to sound jealous, of course, because I most certainly was not. But it just seemed that once again my old buddy Joey Divers had left me far, far behind. And the sting hurt some. Perhaps that was why I felt sort of stuck in a rut back here in Brookdale. But then I'd have to remind myself that things could've been worse, far worse.

Just think, I could've still been back on the Funny Farm, bare-foot and working in the kitchen, bearing "promise children" for

Sky to "raise up in the way they should go." But as far as I knew Sky and Mountain were still doing time (unless they'd been paroled) in some California state prison. I wondered if they might not be recruiting new cult members from in there. I'd heard that Charles Manson had something like that going from within the prison, although his cult group sounded much more evil than the Funny Farm. But who knows?

Speaking of the Funny Farm, I was quite relieved to find out that my old friend Sara (Sunshine) was doing just fine now. Like me, she'd gone on to college. And after graduating with some kind of business degree, she was now living in Nashville and working in the music industry (where she'd met her husband). And according to her mom (who told me all this in the canned-food section of the supermarket) Sara was expecting her first baby in the fall. I told her how glad I was for her and to give her my love and my best, and if she was ever in town to drop by or give me a call. Of course I didn't really expect Sara to do this, and I'm not even sure what we'd say to each other if she did. I know that I'm still not entirely comfortable talking about that whole scene—our time on the Funny Farm. But I wouldn't mind seeing Sara and her baby. And I was happy for her that she'd gotten on so well with her life. In fact, it seemed she'd progressed better than I. Which brings me back to my rut.

Every day (except weekends) I would do the exact same thing. I got up at seven, made coffee, read the paper, got dressed, went to school. There I taught all day—and while I really liked my students (and sometimes even forgot that I was the teacher and they were the kids because sometimes I swear we all seemed about the same age) still I just didn't *love* teaching art. And that surprised me. But I kept on going just the same.

I think it was mostly the students who kept me going, because I truly did care about them (especially the "down-and-outers" that reminded me of what I'd been like back then) and I tried to reach out to them, to help where I could, to encourage, and to listen. But the times spent doing that were so short, and there were so many kids to interact with—more than a hundred and fifty each day. Sometimes it was a little overwhelming, and really, I knew I was there to teach art. But I do think it was those moments of connecting with kids that really kept me going. Still, during the rest of my little life, I felt just like that poor old hamster just stuck on a silly, old treadmill, just peddling away but getting nowhere fast.

Now, I suppose it might've seemed less like a rut if I'd gone home at the end of the day and pursued some art interests of my own (since I'd always loved creating) but after spending the whole day around clay and ink and charcoal and paints and all those other art supplies, I just didn't have any desire to smell those smells anymore.

Oh sure, I did some decorating in my rental house and a little cooking and I puttered in my garden some, but mostly I was just lonely and, I'm ashamed to say, bored. And yet I never did one single thing about it. I did visit several of the churches in town (since I was nearly over my religion phobia by then) and while they were okay, and I met some nice folks, I just never seemed to find one that quite fit. And although I felt guilty about it, it was so much easier to just sleep in on Sunday. And as a result, I'm sure that my rut just kept getting deeper and deeper. And I wasn't really sure how to climb out.

The one thing I really did look forward to, and something that almost got me out of my rut, was getting an occasional letter from Joey. We'd finally gotten back into the habit of writing again after I'd sent him a Christmas card the previous year. I knew he'd be graduating in June (with honors and offers, according to the *Brookdale News* and his proud mother). And I was proud of him too and had actually wished he'd invite me to attend his graduation. I knew due to his mom's health that his family wasn't planning to go. But as it turned out, no invitation came for me, and I figured he might be just as happy not to have some old Brookdale "nobody" up there to distract him while he was enjoying his big day in the sun.

Okay, I didn't exactly think I was a "nobody," but old habits are hard to break, and I figured Joey was in a league of his own by then. Besides that, something about being back in my hometown seemed to bring out all my insecurities again.

For instance, I'd see Sally Roberts (now Sanders) driving around in her brand-new red 1978 Corvette and I'd feel like she was still queen of the prom or homecoming or the town or whatever . . . don't ask me why. She'd married Brad Sanders straight out of high school (he was one of those jocks who hadn't been nearly as nice as Jimmy Flynn) and then she'd gone right to work as a teller in her daddy's bank. Brad worked down at the tire shop, not actually changing tires, but up front at the desk. When Sally saw me downtown or at the grocery store, why, she'd just point her little nose up in the air and step aside as if I had scabies or lice or something equally contagious. It all seemed rather unnecessary (not to mention juvenile). I simply pretended not to notice or care.

Just the same, it was those kinds of things that tended to drag me down, I suppose, and maybe that's why I became such a homebody. Yet even when I'd try to putter around with my art, I never seemed able to finish anything. Call it a rut or a slump or maybe just the blues, but it seemed like my little life was going absolutely nowhere—fast! I was almost twenty-four and lived the life of someone twice (no, make that three times!) that age. And I didn't even own a cat!

But at least I still read my Bible and prayed. And that spring I began to pray fervently that God would do something—something big that would just jerk me right out of my rut. And, deciding it was time to grab the bull by the horns, I even started going to church regularly!

It was the middle of June, and school had been out for a week. To fill my time, I'd started doing some volunteering with the park district, setting up an "Art in the Park" program to help reach out to "underprivileged" kids (yes, it was another attempt to escape my rut). But to be honest, I was really enjoying the work, and I felt certain that God was using this. Anyway, it was late in the afternoon and I'd just come home, clad in my paint-splotched overalls and my hair (getting long again) held back with a red bandana, and there sitting in my driveway was Joey's old blue car! I knew that he'd just graduated, but hadn't had time to visit Mrs. Divers lately and get the latest lowdown.

"Cass!" he called out as I hurried toward him carrying a heavy wooden crate of art supplies (I also provided the materials for the classes). "I'm so glad I caught you!"

"Hey, Joey." I forced a smile, careful to disguise my complete shock at seeing him pop up so unexpectedly on my doorstep. I tried not to mentally calculate just how long it had been since I'd actually seen him—face-to-face. He looked pretty much the same though, only older, more mature and dignified somehow. I brushed a loose strand of hair from my eyes, determined not to do anything to reveal my true feelings or the childish hurt I'd experienced when I'd realized how he'd moved on without me. "What's up?" I asked in what I hoped was a casual tone.

His face grew shadowed. "It's your daddy."

"My daddy?" I set the box down on the porch. "What're you talking about, Joey?"

"It's a long story, Cass. But do you have time to come with me? Over to Radner?"

"Radner?"

"Yeah, your daddy lives there."

"In Radner?" I studied him carefully. "But how do you know?"

"Like I said, it's a long story. But can you come with me?"

"Gee, I don't know, Joey . . ." I reached for my house key. "I don't really have any desire to see my daddy right now—or maybe ever." I opened the door and let us both in. It was cool inside and smelled of the rose and lavender potpourri I'd mixed up just the other day.

"Nice place, Cass."

"Thanks." I set the crate on the floor in the hallway, then stood back up looking Joey straight in the eyes, trying to figure out what this was all about. How would Joey Divers know anything about my daddy? "What's going on, Joey?"

"Look, Cass, you're daddy might be dying, even as we speak. And he wants to see you—you know, it's only an hour's drive from here. I can take you right now.".

I pulled the bandana from my head and shook out my hair, then shrugged. "I don't know, Joey . . . I'm not so sure I want to see him."

Now Joey reached over and put his hand on my shoulder, not in a way so as to comfort, but more like a vise grip, like he was about to give me a real firm shake and bring me to my senses. "Cass!" he said urgently. "You *need* to go. Can you just trust me on this?"

Suddenly I remembered the many times Joey had helped me, rescued me, bailed me out. And even today, he'd driven all the way here from— "Where did you drive from, anyway?"

"From Harvard. I was just finishing some things up there. But I'm done now." He looked impatient. "Can you come, Cass? *Now?*"

"Do I have time to clean up and change?"

"Can you hurry?" His brow was furrowed and his eyes full of concern.

326

So I ran down the hall and quickly scrubbed the paint off my hands, then pulled on a sundress and some sandals, taking a few seconds to rip a brush through my hair and apply some lip gloss, then dashed out again.

"That was quick."

"Well, you said to hurry."

As we drove, Joey told me how he and my daddy had stayed in touch somewhat over the years. And while I found this extremely strange, I couldn't bring myself to ask Joey why in the world they had done this. I mean, how could I explain why I went to visit his mom? Maybe it's just something friends do.

"Cass, you need to understand that your daddy's been on the wagon for the last eight years."

"You really believe that, Joey?"

"Well, okay, he admits himself that he's fallen off a time or two. But then he gets right back on. And for the most part he's been clean and sober. He goes to church and AA every week."

I folded my arms across my chest and scowled. "I don't believe it."

"Well, that's your prerogative."

"Why hasn't he been in touch with me?"

Joey shrugged as he turned onto the interstate. "I think he's a little afraid. And he feels guilty too. I suppose he remembers those times when you returned all his letters when he wrote to you from prison. Mainly, I suspect he thinks you're better off without him."

I looked straight ahead and nodded. "It's true. I am."

He shook his head. "No, you're not, Cass."

"How can you say that, Joey?" I turned and looked at him.

"Because you've gotten bitter."

"*Bitter?*" I heard the edge in my voice, but at the same time I was angry that Joey would accuse me of such a thing.

"Not so that most people would notice, Cass. You're pretty good at hiding it. But it's there. I can see it. And I can tell it's hurting you inside."

"Bitter?" I said the word again, slightly louder this time. "How can you call me bitter? I mean, here I am, just living my life, minding my own business." I felt my chin quiver. "You really think I'm bitter, Joey?"

He nodded, his eyes focused on the road, lips pressed firmly together.

"Joey, here I thought you were my friend and all this time you've been thinking I'm some horrible, old, bitter person?"

He laughed. "Well, it's not as bad as that, Cass. But I do think it's taking its toll on you. I think it's hurting you. And I've wanted to bring it up, but to tell you the truth I only just really began to understand it myself."

"And how's that?"

"Just recently I heard this guy at my church preaching about bitterness and how it can get a hold on you."

"You go to church regularly?"

He smiled. "Yeah, don't you?"

I shrugged. "I've been trying to lately. But it's not easy. It's like something keeps me from it."

"Maybe it's bitterness."

I made a growling sound. "Okay, let's not keep talking about that right now. Now, tell me, Joey Divers. Why is it so doggoned urgent that I see my daddy all of a sudden?"

"Like I said, he might not make it. He's had a pretty bad heart attack and he's in serious condition."

I shrugged again. "But does he really *want* to see me?"

"I think so."

"You *think* so?"

"Oh, Cass, maybe we should just talk about something else until we get there. I can see this is only upsetting you." He paused for a moment, tapping his fingers on the steering wheel. "Say, how about if I tell you about my graduation?"

I leaned back into the seat and sighed deeply. "Yeah, sure, why don't you just tell me all about it." I still felt slightly aggrieved that I'd never received an announcement.

He glanced over at me as if reading my mind. "You know, Cass, I almost sent you an invitation, but then I thought you'd still be having classes and I didn't think you'd want to come all the way up there just to see me walk down—"

"Joey Divers!" I exploded. "I would've gladly missed school for a whole week and paid for a first-class plane ticket just for the honor of watching you graduate from Harvard, you big idiot!"

"You would've?"

"Of course, you ninny!" Now I actually felt my eyes misting up and I wasn't sure if it was due to Joey or my daddy. "But you never even gave me the chance. Now if I wanted to become bitter, Joey, there's something I could get pretty bitter about real easy."

He turned and glanced at me. "I'm sorry, Cass. Really." And I could tell by the tone of his voice, he meant it.

"I'm sorry too, Joey. I didn't mean to yell at you like that. I guess this whole thing about my daddy is kind of upsetting to me." I could feel my stomach already tied into all sorts of tight little knots.

"Just try to relax now, Cass. It won't do any good to fret about it."

"Oh, Joey, I haven't spoken to my daddy in years, not since that last time—" I felt the tears coming now. "Oh, what in the world am I going to say to him?" And then I did start crying, just a little at first, and hopefully not enough for him to notice. But when Joey reached across the front seat and clasped my hand, instead of feeling comforted (or maybe because of it) the dam just broke and I just burst into hot tears. And I'm sure I must've cried all the way to Radner.

chapter thirty

ONLY "IMMEDIATE FAMILY" were allowed into the intensive care unit, and I think Joey used this as an excuse to send me in there all by myself. I'm not sure what I expected to find, but for some reason I felt surprised when my daddy didn't look all that much older than the last time I'd seen him. Just worn-out and tired was all.

I think I'd expected him to be an old, wrinkly, white-haired man, but then he was only in his late forties at that time—not so old, really. His slate-colored eyes met mine and our gaze just locked there for a long moment. Part of me wanted to turn and flee, but instead, I walked up closer to his bed.

"Hi, Daddy," I said, suddenly feeling timid and like a little girl again. But it wasn't a good "little girl" feeling; no, it was one of frustration, compounded with confusion, as if I were being held down and trapped by someone with more power than I. Still, I tried to shake it off, reminding myself that he had no power over me anymore. At least I thought he didn't.

"Hi, baby," he spoke quietly, barely moving his head. But I remembered how he used to call me "baby" sometimes. And back when I was young I liked it because it usually meant he was in a good mood and not intoxicated. But as I grew older I hated it, for it smelled of hypocrisy and denial.

I looked at the tubes and monitors connected here and there. "Are you in pain?"

"A little. But it's not too bad if I don't move around much." He closed his eyes and took in some slow shallow breaths.

"Maybe I should go and let you get some—"

"No." His eyes fluttered open and I could see the desperation in them, almost as if he were the one who was now being held down, trapped and helpless. Perhaps I now held the power. "Cassandra," he whispered pitifully, "please don't go."

"Okay." I pulled a chair over to his bedside so that I could sit down and see him at eye level. "I just don't want to make you overdo. I know you're pretty bad off and all."

"Thank you for coming. I don't know how . . . I didn't expect . . ."

I could see tears forming in the corners of his eyes now, and suddenly I wished there was something I could say. Something kind and comforting, but I had nothing to give him. No words. Nothing. Just the emptiness of that big, black hole that he'd left inside me.

He swallowed. "I know you've been through a lot, Cassandra. And it's all my fault. I've put you through—" His words were choked with a sob, but he continued. "I won't blame you if you never forgive me. I was a stupid, good-for-nothing—"

He broke down, and I just sat there dumbly watching him cry. I didn't say a word, I didn't reach out, I offered no consolation. I just sat there in numbness.

Oh, I'd seen my daddy cry before, usually after a particularly bad spell of drinking and meanness. And I'd learned not to take it too seriously. And despite the years that had passed, despite his fragile condition, seeing him crying like that just brought it all back to me, as if it were yesterday. Why, I could almost smell the soured whiskey on his breath. I closed my eyes and inhaled deeply, praying for strength.

Just then I felt a hand on my shoulder. "I think you'd better go, miss," said the nurse. "Your father needs to rest."

And so I walked out of his room, knowing full well that he might actually die right then and there, and knowing that I hadn't forgiven him.

It seemed incredibly cold and harsh and not even like the person that I had thought I was. And yet it was like a part of me just didn't give a rip. I think I believed that my daddy was simply getting what he deserved from me. The same thing he'd given me— *nothing*.

"How is he?" asked Joey.

"He doesn't look too good."

"Did you talk?" He looked at me intently, probing me with those big dark eyes, made larger by the lenses of his glasses.

I shrugged. "Not really."

We went to the cafeteria to get some dinner, but the food tasted like sand in my mouth, and I just sat there staring at my plate, wondering who in the world I really was and what I was doing here. Finally, I looked up at Joey. "I need to be alone," I said as I pushed back the chair and stood.

"Sure, Cass, whatever."

I walked out of the stuffy cafeteria and then outside, continuing on down the sidewalk, walking quickly away from the hospital. I didn't know or care where I was going, I just wanted to get away— far, far away. Was I running from my daddy? Or from myself? I couldn't even be sure.

As I walked my eyes blurred, and even as the tears streaked down my cheeks, I didn't know who I was crying for. Was it for myself, the little girl who'd been beaten and betrayed by the one living relative who should've protected and provided for her? Or was I crying for him, the poor, sorry man, lying on his deathbed, who couldn't even get the comfort of forgiveness from his only child? Maybe I was grieving for both of us, two lives caught in the twilight between love and hate.

The sky was just getting dusky as I found myself in a tiny city park, which was thankfully deserted. I sat down on the only bench there and leaned forward, clutching my arms around my middle, and allowing the pain to envelop me as I sobbed loudly. "Oh, God," I said over and over, again and again. "Oh, God!" It was a prayer, a desperate wordless kind of prayer, that I didn't even know the full meaning of myself. But I believe, I truly believe, that God understood my cry perfectly.

And then, just like the rainstorm that floods the earth then is gone, it was over. I stood up and dried my face with the backs of my hands and turned around and walked back to the hospital. It was dark by the time I reached the hospital's entrance, and in the same moment that I walked into the brightness of the lobby, I knew. I knew I must forgive my daddy. It was in that flash of an instant, just as my foot hit the carpet. It was as if God himself had spoken to me. And I knew what I had to do.

I rushed to the elevator, suddenly concerned over my daddy's welfare. What if his tired heart had simply stopped beating after my unsettling visit? What if he was already dead? What if my bitterness had killed him? Inside the elevator, I punched the third-floor button again and again, waiting impatiently for the doors to finally close and for the elevator to sluggishly make its ascent, stopping on the second floor to wait for a man with a cart of medications to slowly maneuver himself on.

As the elevator climbed from the second to third floor, a parade of all those I had known and loved (and who now were dead) filed across my imagination. My mama, my grandma, Mr. Crowley, Gram, Skip. And suddenly I knew that death is simply a fact of life—

it just happens and we have no control over it. And it was quite possible that it had already happened to my daddy. I might've waited too long.

When the doors finally opened, I burst out and ran down the wide hallway toward the intensive care unit. Joey stopped me just before I reached my daddy's room.

"Wait a minute, Cass," he said. "They're in there with him right now."

"Is he alive?"

Joey kept holding on to me, then nodded soberly. "Barely. I think he just had another heart attack."

I leaned my head into Joey's shoulder and felt his arm holding me (only one arm because the other hand held firmly to his cane as he managed to balance for both of us). "Let's go sit down, Cass," he whispered quietly.

We sat down on a hard molded vinyl seat and he put his arm around me and drew me close, and then quietly, and in a way that sounded incredibly genuine and sincere and not quite like anything I'd ever heard before, Joey began to pray—really pray—for my daddy to get better. I just sat there and listened in amazement. How was it that Joey had learned to pray like that, without sounding religious or frantic or poetic or desperate or long-winded or empty-worded or foolish, but simply *real*?

"I didn't forgive him," I finally told Joey after he stopped praying. "At least not when I was in there with him anyway. But now I have—it just happened—kind of miraculously. I need to tell him. I can't let him die thinking I never forgave him, Joey, because I did. I really did."

Joey grasped my hands in his. "Cass, even if your daddy does die, he'll know that you forgave him."

I eyed him suspiciously. "How can you be so sure?"

"I just can't believe that God would keep something like that a secret from him."

"You mean in heaven?"

Joey nodded.

"Oh, Joey, do you honestly think my daddy will go to heaven?"

He nodded again. "Based on all the conversations I've had with him, I'm fairly certain he'll be there."

Then Joey and I sat and talked and talked that night. Mostly about God. And I was amazed and impressed with his maturity, his understanding of the Bible, and what I can only describe as his steadfastness. Because more and more I could see how Joey's faith had never wavered over the years. He'd given his heart to Jesus back in high school, and after that he'd just steadily moved forward.

And it's not like his life was easy either. He had his own battles to fight, his personal struggles to conquer. But all the while he never gave up, and he never got swept up by some sensational doctrine that seemed to offer all the answers in one easy lesson. No, Joey Divers just kept trusting God one day at a time and moving steadily forward.

My life, on the other hand, looked like some kind of a carnival ride—the roller coaster or Tilt-A-Whirl. Anything but steadfast. And yet Joey could still find the good in it all, and once again he told me that he was proud of the way I'd come through. And not for the first time, he called me a survivor.

"The Steadfast and the Survivor." Sounds like the title of an old movie that never was. Anyway, a lot of things about Joey and me and God became clearer to me during that long night. And when we could think of nothing more to talk about, we simply put our heads together and prayed—mostly for my daddy to get better.

To the doctor's amazement, and my great relief, my daddy

didn't die that night. And by the following morning I was able to go back into his room and talk to him once more. And while I didn't do it terribly eloquently or perhaps even all that coherently, I did tell my daddy that I'd forgiven him.

His eyes misted up and it looked as if he were about to cry again, but thankfully he did not. "Thank you, Cassandra," he said in a quiet voice. "I know I will never deserve your forgiveness, but it means everything in the world to me. I just wish I could forgive myself now."

"Maybe you will in time," I said, not even knowing exactly why, but the words seemed comforting somehow. We weren't allowed to talk much longer because the nurse came in again and I could see that even after such a short visit, my daddy was weary and needed rest. "I've got to go home, Daddy," I told him as I stood.

I was surprised at how sad his eyes became when I said this— as if he really didn't want me to leave him. Could it be that he actually needed me? Suddenly I realized that he had no one else on earth—not one other living blood relative, that he knew of any-way—nor did I, for that matter. All we had was each other, and that seemed to be slipping away fast.

"But I'll just go home to take care of a few things," I told him quickly, as if this had been my plan right from the start. "And then I'll drive back over here in my own car and I'll find a place to stay for a while, until you get better."

"You can stay in my apartment, Cassandra," he offered, his eyes hopeful.

I nodded, feeling uncertain. "Yes, I suppose I could do that."

"When will you be back?" His voice reminded me of a small child's.

I looked at my watch. It was just before noon. "Maybe by early evening," I said. "Would you like that?"

His smile was weak, but I could see a faint light glowing in his eyes. "Yes, if it's not too much trouble. I'd like that."

I reached over and gently squeezed his hand. "No, it'll be just fine. You take care now, Daddy."

On our way back to Brookdale, Joey and I talked about our parents and Joey mentioned how he'd been growing more concerned about his mother's bad health lately, and how he wanted to spend some time with her this summer, to make sure she was getting all the proper medical attention.

"My dad seems almost oblivious to the whole thing," he continued. "It's like if he pretends it's not there, it'll just go away. Kind of like when I was a kid—with the polio, you know."

"Maybe that's just his way of protecting himself, Joey. Maybe it's like a shield so he doesn't get too close, so he doesn't get hurt."

Joey nodded. "Yeah, despite his tough-guy exterior, I'm pretty sure there's a soft heart underneath it all."

"And you know how his generation is—big boys don't cry and all that macho stuff."

"Yeah. But it'd do him some good to cry. I looked at your dad lying there in the hospital bed and I got worried that my dad might be next. He still smokes like a chimney and my mom says his blood pressure is sky-high."

"Isn't it strange how our parents are getting old?"

"Yeah, and it's kind of ironic too."

"What do you mean?" I asked sleepily as I leaned back into the seat, fighting to keep my eyes open after our long sleepless night.

"Well, here we are both concerned about our parents right now, we're trying to help them and—"

I sat up straight. "And you wonder where were they when we needed them?"

He laughed. "Well, sort of."

"Yeah, part of me is still struggling with this whole thing, Joey. I mean, I truly believe I've forgiven my daddy. Really, I can feel a change in my heart. But I guess I'm wondering why I need to do more. I mean, should I really get involved in his life again? Part of me wants to know why can't I just say *adios* and wish him well, and then move on. What would be wrong with that?"

"Hanging around might be more for your benefit than his, Cass."

I nodded, closing my eyes again. As usual, I figured Joey was probably right.

chapter thirty-one

I QUICKLY PACKED A FEW THINGS as I phoned Ashley Romero (my best high-school art student) and invited her to oversee my "Art in the Park" project for the rest of the week. Ashley agreed and even refused to let me pay her, saying she wouldn't be doing anything anyway since she hadn't gotten a job for the summer yet and didn't know if she even would.

Ashley reminded me a lot of myself back when I was her age, not her home life so much because she had two parents (albeit two fairly absent parents) but more because she was sort of an outsider with her peers. But she was an artsy girl, with her own ideas about things, and someone I would also describe as a survivor. I smiled as I hung up the phone, thinking I wouldn't mind having a daughter like that someday.

As I drove back to Radner, late that afternoon, I wondered what in the world I'd gotten myself into. Playing the devoted daughter to a man I hardly knew felt like such a foreign and even phony role to me. And yet how could I not?

I felt uneasy at the idea of staying in my father's apartment by myself and almost opted to get a motel instead. But he seemed so hopeful that I'd take him up on his hospitality that I took his key and then drove by the little complex where he lived (not far from where he'd been working at the Volvo dealership downtown).

Although nothing fancy, I found the exterior of the apartment building in fairly good repair and decided it might be worth a look even if I decided not to stay. When I opened the door to his apartment, I felt mildly surprised. I'm not entirely sure what I'd expected to find—probably something reminiscent of the shabby dives we used to inhabit during my childhood—but this little place was nothing like that. The rooms were neat and clean and orderly, yet almost painfully frugal, without the least sign of extravagance.

Now, this seemed highly curious to me, especially because I remembered how my daddy had always had this habit of spending his earnings wastefully on things like fancy clothes or expensive gimmicks in addition to alcohol. As a result, it never failed that we'd run short on the common necessities. We'd be all out of things like food or laundry soap or toilet paper, but my daddy would walk into the house wearing a fine new pair of leather shoes or a sharp new hat. It seemed that somewhere over the last ten years (probably when he gave up drinking) my daddy figured these things out.

As promised, I stayed in my daddy's little apartment for the next couple days, spending most of my time at the hospital, visiting with him or his friends from work or AA or church (he seemed to have a fair number of good friends). I'd converse with his caregivers and get the latest details of his prognosis, and it seemed his health was improving steadily.

On the third day, he was moved from ICU to a room he shared with a cantankerous old railroad man who smoked about two packs a day (those were the days when they still let patients smoke in the hospital). But since my daddy had given up smoking a few years back I knew he found the smell offensive (although I could tell he didn't like to make a fuss). So I went ahead and asked the head nurse if there was any hope of changing his room, but she said not for a day or two. Then I asked how soon he could be released to go home, and she said she'd check with his physician. Later she told me he could be released by Saturday morning if he had someone to stay with him.

I knew it would be a tight squeeze with both of us sharing his little one-bedroom apartment, but I offered to stay there and sleep on the couch if he wanted to come home from the hospital, that is, unless he had someone else he'd prefer to stay with him. But he said he didn't think any of his friends would be able to help out that much, and desperately wanting out of the hospital, he seemed to sincerely appreciate my offer. Although I'm sure it made him nervous. And I could understand that because I felt uneasy myself.

So far we hadn't talked too much about the past. He'd told me about his job selling new, not used, Volvos at the dealership, and how he'd been there long enough, and performed well enough, that he'd made it up into a managerial position (and I could see he was proud of this accomplishment). He also told me about the little church he attended that was only four blocks away, but how he felt he'd never really gotten to know the people there too well and admitted to being slightly surprised when a couple of them paid him a visit.

Then he talked a bit about his AA friends, and his face lit up. He explained how they had been instrumental in overcoming his "addiction." That's what he called his drinking problem—he either referred to it as his "addiction" or his "illness," and it didn't seem to bother him to call it such.

I'd heard these terms before in school, but they sounded strange coming from my daddy's lips. Still, I appreciated that he didn't try to bury his past problems or pretend like these things had never happened. His approach seemed truly humble and fairly straightforward, and he was always the first one to admit that it was alcoholism that had, for the most part, ruined his life. And mine. Although I tried to make it clear to him that I had survived and was doing just fine.

Anyway it was decided that on Saturday, I would drive my daddy home to his little apartment (which thankfully was on the first floor so there were no steps for him to climb). So in the meantime, I changed sheets on the bed, did laundry, got a few groceries, and generally freshened things up. But as I was straightening the counter in the kitchen, I noticed a small stack of recent mail, and found it interesting that my daddy had a bank account in the very same bank that I used, the same bank I'd been using since going to community college in California.

And suddenly I knew, I'm not even sure how, but I just knew. My daddy had to have been my secret benefactor. I wondered if I should mention it to him, or might that make him uncomfortable since for whatever reason he'd asked Joey to keep this information private? So for the time being I decided to just hide it away in my heart. But I have to admit I was starting to see my daddy in a whole new light.

I helped my daddy into my little car and then drove carefully across town, making small talk about the weather and the traffic. As I helped him from the car and up the walk to his apartment, I suddenly felt worried and apprehensive. What had I gotten myself into? But as one slow step followed the next, I tried to give these anxieties to God, and when we finally made it inside I felt better. I helped him to take off his slippers and get settled into his own bed, and I could tell the familiarity of his own things brought him some comfort as he leaned back into the pillows.

"I'm sure you must be all worn out now, Daddy," I said as I stood up and pushed a strand of hair from my face. "I think you should get some rest."

"Do you know how much I hate being a burden to you, Cassandra?" he said sadly as I pulled the thin blue blanket up over him.

"Daddy," I said with real conviction, "you're not a burden to me. You're my own flesh and blood. And as Grandma used to say, blood *is* thicker than water!"

He smiled. "Yeah, but I never did get that one. Who cares about thick blood anyway?"

"Well, I think it just means that family comes first," I said as I closed the curtains. "Now, I want you to get some rest and then maybe you'll be able to get up in time for a light dinner."

Fighting off feelings of strangeness, I went into the little kitchen and began making preparations for dinner. It seemed like a hundred years since I'd cooked dinner for my daddy, and I hoped he'd think my skills had improved some since then. I hadn't told him about my stay on the Funny Farm yet and didn't even know if I could. But for some reason I wanted to. For some reason I felt he needed to know. Although for the life of me I wondered how someone of his generation could possibly understand such craziness.

I'd already told him of going to college (not realizing at the time how he probably had a lot to do with that). And then I'd told him about my teaching job back in Brookdale, trying to paint a cheerful, happy picture. I almost convinced myself that my life was perfectly wonderful—and maybe it wasn't that bad, all things considered. Besides, hadn't this whole episode with my daddy really jerked me out of my rut, at least for the time being?

That night, we sat down together at his little table and ate dinner. Following doctor's orders, I'd prepared a plain, low-salt meal of white fish and rice and a green salad with light dressing, but I'd taken care to arrange everything just so and had even placed a couple of pink geraniums (snipped from a planter by the parking lot) into a water glass for decoration.

"This is just lovely, Cassandra." My daddy looked approvingly at everything, then bowed his head and said a short blessing.

We ate quietly, making small talk about whether Carter would win again, the general deplorable state of our country, and the world at large. And then I served us each a small bowl of orange sherbet along with some of the instant Yuban coffee I'd found in his cupboard.

"Cassandra, when I got that heart attack last week, I was so worried that I'd never get a chance to talk to you—to tell you things . . ." His voice trailed off slightly.

"Tell me things?" Suddenly I wondered if he was about to tell me about the trust fund, and part of me longed for him to keep this a secret. Just the same I waited for him to continue.

He took a sip of coffee. "Yes, I had put some things together to give to you. Some time back, I'd asked Joey to act as my attorney if anything were to happen to me." He set down his cup. "You see, I'd had these twinges of chest pains a few times, off and on, during the past year, and well, I just had this feeling . . ."

I nodded. "You knew you were going to have a heart attack?"

"Not exactly. But I felt uneasy, somehow. Anyway I had some things for you—things that belonged to your mother."

"My mama?"

"Yes. Long ago, I'd put some things in a storage place at Masterson Motors. It had been ages, and I'd almost forgotten about them. But then Mr. Masterson got ahold of me and I drove on over and picked them up. A lot of it was just junk. But there were a few things I thought that you should have. And—" He stopped himself.

"And?"

He sighed heavily. "Oh, I don't know how to rightly say this, Cassandra, but I suppose there's some things you should know about. I'm just not sure you're ready to hear them yet, or if I'm even ready to say them. And seeing as how you've only just barely forgiven me, well, I just hate to put too much on you all at once."

I picked up the empty dishes and took them into the kitchen. "Oh, Daddy," I said, hoping to sound light. "You'd probably be surprised to find out that I've been through some rather hard things during my lifetime. And I don't break very easily. In fact, I think I'm made of some pretty tough stuff."

His brow grew concerned. "I know you've been through a lot, Cassandra. I must've put you through some horrible nightmares—"

"Oh, you can't take all the credit; I've put myself through some nightmares too."

"Yes, Joey told me about some of the crazy stuff you went through in California. But believe me, Cassandra, I blame all that on me. You wouldn't have done what you did if I hadn't made so many stupid mistakes back when you were a kid."

"But I made my own choices, Daddy."

He shook his head. "I had a lot to do with those choices, Cassandra. In fact, I'll bet I could take the blame for every single bad thing that's ever happened to you."

I blinked. "Well, that's a whole lot of blame to heap on yourself."

"Nothing more than what I deserve."

I sat back down and laid my hands on the table. "Look, Daddy, I don't claim to know too much about these things, but I'm learning more all the time. And the thing is, I think you need to give all that blame stuff to God."

He nodded. "I know. And I try to."

"And I think you need to forgive yourself."

He pressed his lips together. "I know you're right, Cassandra, but I guess I just don't rightly know how to do that."

"To be honest, I don't completely know how to either, but I'm working on it. And I think if God can forgive us for all the crud we do to ourselves and to others, well, then we ought to be able to forgive ourselves too."

He didn't say anything after that, and I began to suspect he was getting a little worn out. And so I helped him back to his room and then returned to clean up in the kitchen. But just as I finished drying the last dish, he came back out, this time wearing a dark red flannel bathrobe. "Cassie," he said as he eased himself down onto the sofa, "there's something I need to tell you—just in case."

"In case what?"

"Well . . ." He touched his chest. "I'm not sure how long this ticker is going to last me. Even the doc said he couldn't give me any guarantees. And who knows, I might just up and go in my sleep tonight. But there's something I've never told you—or anyone else, for that matter—and it has to do with your mother."

Interested, I sat down in a chair across from him, the dish towel still in my hand. "What is it?"

He exhaled slowly. "This isn't an easy thing to tell, and there was a time when I thought I'd take this to the grave with me. But since then I've learned a few things that make me think otherwise. And now I feel that since you're her daughter, and all grown-up, you have a right to know the truth. And knowing all that you've been through, Cassandra, I reckon you can probably handle it now."

"Sure, go ahead," I leaned forward, eager to listen to anything he could tell me about my mama. In my mind, she'd always been just a step away from sainthood, and anything I could find out about her was of the utmost interest to me.

"Well, right after you were born, your mama, well, she wasn't quite herself." He rubbed his chin. "Always before, she'd been cheerful and happy and a real go-getter. And . . ." He paused and studied me. "A lot like you."

I smiled.

"In fact, you remind me of her in so many ways."

"Thank you."

He nodded. "Your mama was a good woman. And what I'm about to tell you, I don't want it to diminish in any way how you think of her, because your mama was fine and decent. She was smart and pretty and kind, the pick of the crop, really and truly. All these years later, I still can't believe she agreed to marry me. I didn't think I had anything to offer her—except my undying love, that is. Oh, I loved her with my whole heart, Cassandra. Believe me, I did. And you may not know it, but I didn't have a drinking problem back then—that only came later, afterwards. And anyway I promised your mama that I'd make her proud of me, and that I'd work real hard and make us rich someday. And I think I would've, too . . ."

"But what happened?"

"Well, right after you were born, your mama got what you might call the blues. Only in a real bad way. She would just cry and cry and cry. And I couldn't understand why, because you were a fine, healthy, beautiful baby. But your mama was just plain miserable. I tried to do everything I could think of to help her. Why, I even fed you and changed your diapers during those first couple of days, thinking your mama was just worn-out. But on that third day, I had to go back to work, if we were going to eat." He sighed. "And well, when I got back home that night, I found her."

"But I thought you'd been out drinking." The words came out of my mouth before I could even stop them, but instantly I regretted them. Not because I thought they were untrue, but because of my daddy's delicate heart condition just then. But to my relief, he took no offense. He just nodded sadly.

"I know that's what you were told, Cassandra. But that story only came along later—after I started turning to the bottle for relief. You know how stories go. Sometimes they change and get worse with the passing of time."

I nodded, although I wasn't entirely sure.

"Anyway, when I got home, I could hear you crying in your crib and I ran in there to see what was wrong. I could tell that you'd probably been neglected most of the day. And when I went to find your mother—" He stopped now and wiped his hand over his brow as if the memory were still fresh in his mind. "Well, she was in the bedroom, in a pool of blood and already dead." He looked across the room at me, straight into my eyes. "But she didn't die in the way that I told everyone, from complications of the birthing. No, your mama had been so distraught and depressed that she'd slit her own wrists with a razor blade." He looked down at his lap and sighed heavily.

"No!" I gasped. "No, she couldn't have done that. She wouldn't have—"

"I'm sorry, Cassandra. I hated to have to tell you, but I've done some reading up on this whole thing and I know—"

"No," I said, standing now, tears filling my eyes. "No, I can't believe it, Daddy. Are you honestly saying my mama killed herself?"

He nodded. "I never would've told you this before, Cassandra, but I talked to someone who knows about such things, and then I did some reading up, and I've learned that your mama had an illness that affected the way she was thinking . . ."

I sank back down into the chair, trying to take in his words, trying not to appear so skeptical, so confrontational. But at the same time, I wondered if he was making all this up—just to make himself look better.

"I can't think of the name of it just now, but your mama had a kind of depression that some women get after giving birth."

"You mean postpartum depression?"

He looked at me in surprise. "Yes, that's it. That's what the book called it."

Well, I remembered that name from the natural childbirth book as well as my psychology classes. "Yes, Daddy, that's a real condition, brought on by hormonal imbalances after giving birth, but women don't usually kill themselves." I studied his face carefully, suspiciously.

"No, I don't expect they usually do." He sadly shook his head. "And for years I blamed myself for her death, and well, to be honest I guess I blamed you too." He looked up at me. "I'm sorry, Cassie. I know it was completely unfair, and it makes no earthly sense. It was nothing but pure craziness on my part. But, the fact is, I was crazy back then. Losing your mama like that just pushed me right over the edge. And even though I'd try and try to get back again, and sometimes I'd even think I'd made it, well, then off I'd go—back to the bottle." He leaned over and buried his head in his hands. "It shames me to remember those years, and yet, to be perfectly honest, I'm sometimes still thankful that the alcohol's poison blurred a lot of those bad memories for me."

"But why are you telling me this?" I still didn't know if I believed him or not. I still couldn't imagine that my sweet mama would've killed herself when she had a dependent little baby girl who needed her—needed her *badly!*

"Well, in the box I saved, there's a note written by her—on that day—the very day she did it. And I didn't want you to read it and not understand what she meant. She couldn't help how she felt. She wanted to be a good mother. She loved you, she really did. But she was just so sad and hopeless that she couldn't hold on. She just gave up. And I was afraid that if I died, then you'd get that box and you'd read that letter, and well, you'd be so shocked and hurt that, and oh, I don't know . . ."

He was right. I did feel shocked and hurt—and now more abandoned than before. "But why didn't you just throw that letter away, Daddy?"

He sighed again. "You know, I considered doing that. And the truth is, I'd never intended to tell you at all. But lately, I'd come to think that you had the right to know about these things. You know how I grew up not knowing a thing about my own real family. And I used to pretend that it didn't matter none, that I didn't care. But the truth is, Cassie, it does matter. And I felt you had the right to know what really happened to your mother, not to diminish her memory in any way, but just so that you could have all the pieces to your puzzle—so you could figure things out for yourself. That's why I didn't throw the letter away."

I looked right at him then, and suddenly I could sense how hard this whole thing was on him, how it would've been much easier to have just destroyed the letter. "Thanks, Daddy. I'm sure you did the right thing. And now, if it's all right with you, I'd like to see the letter, and those other things, too."

His smile was heavily laced with sadness. "I'd hoped you would." Then he pointed to a small chest of drawers right beneath the window with several cactus plants neatly arranged on top. "It's all there, in the bottom drawer of that old chest." Then he slowly stood. "I'll leave you to look at it as you like, but I'm feeling pretty worn-out just now."

I went over and took his arm and helped him back to his room. And then I did something that surprised even me. I gave my daddy a hug.

"Thanks, Daddy," I said again, and this time with more meaning. And I came very close to saying "I love you," but somehow I just couldn't do it right then. I couldn't form those words just yet. Not without sounding phony, that is.

And I decided that if and when I first told my daddy I loved him, I wanted to mean it with my whole heart. And so I simply said: "Good night, Daddy, you take care now."

chapter thirty-two

NO ONE EVER SAID there wouldn't be any bumps on the road of life, and there's no denying that my growing-up years had plenty of lumps and jolts and thumps to go around, and then some. This is not to suggest that I think I have somehow "paid my dues" and will consequently get off easy from here on out (because who's to say what's around the next bend anyway?) but I must admit that the following installment of my life story progressed much more smoothly than even I would've expected. Not that everything's perfect, by any means, but maybe it's just the contrast that makes it seem so good to me now.

Naturally, I was brokenhearted for a brief period after learning of the tragic circumstances of my dear mama's death, but then as my daddy had predicted, it all began to make sense to me, over time. For you see, I finally began to understand that my daddy, while clearly a mess, hadn't been after all quite the "evil man" that I'd imagined during all my painful growing-up years. And I finally began to see how he'd been hurting inside—badly. But unfortunately for him (and for me) he turned to the bottle for comfort back then. Now, thank goodness, he turns to God—and his family.

For you see, we are a family now. A real family, like I'd always longed for. In the same summer that I was reunited with my daddy,

Joey Divers, once again, asked me to become his bride. And this time I took him seriously. I looked him right in the eye and said, "Do you really mean that, Joey Divers? Because I swear if you're just toying with me, I'll take that pretty cane of yours and just beat you silly!"

Well, he answered me soundly (in the form of a kiss) and of course, I knew he meant it, and I knew I couldn't possibly say no this time. Because when in my entire life had I *not* been in love with Joey Divers? And how could I possibly manage to spend the rest of my life without him? To me, the one truly amazing thing in all this was that he actually loved me!

Fighting back my disbelief in the following weeks, I asked him over and over—was he absolutely, positively sure that he really loved me? Or was he just feeling sorry for me again? Because no matter how I loved him, I still didn't want his pity! And I'd ask him if he was completely sure there wasn't somebody else who would be better for him. Someone with more education? more brains? more class? But he would just laugh and say that the only one for him had always been and would always be Cassandra Jane Maxwell. And who was I to argue with a highfalutin Harvard-educated lawyer anyway?

My daddy got himself well enough to walk me down the aisle that fall. And I don't even think the Diverses were too terribly embarrassed to, at long last, welcome me into their family (or at least not so they'd show it).

After a blissful honeymoon in the Florida Keys, Joey and I moved up to New York City where he joined an impressive law firm and I taught art in an alternative high school full of troubled kids who reminded me a lot of myself when I was their age. Joey didn't disappoint his associates one little bit, and before long his name appeared right along with theirs in big, shiny, brass letters. And I went back to school for my counseling degree, which led me to become something of a pioneer in the field of art therapy (actually, it was God who did the leading). Before I knew it I was teaching classes to other counselors, writing grant proposals, and setting up clinics to help young people deal with their problems by expressing themselves through art. And I just totally loved it!

But after about ten years in New York, both Joey and I became seriously homesick. And while we had maintained close contact with our parents, we knew they weren't getting any younger, and so we decided that our first child should be born back in our hometown of Brookdale.

Our first child turned out to be twins, of all things! And so these days our time is mainly divided between two very active daughters, Joey's thriving law practice, our church, my counseling center, our extended family, and our small farm (complete with horses, chickens, and a trout pond). And, of course, I still make time for my own artwork and a women's Bible study that I've led for the past several years. But I honestly think one of life's greatest thrills occurred for me just this week when one of my clients (a troubled adolescent boy named Shawn) found real help in the creation of a mural painting.

Shawn's parents' hostile divorce, along with a few other stress factors, had triggered a fierce rebellion and subsequent depression in him that had culminated itself in a very real suicide attempt that was narrowly averted by the Brookdale police. After his release from the state hospital, Shawn was sent to me for counseling and treatment. Subsequently, Shawn and I spent six very intense weeks painting an enormous mural that I had previously promised to the city library more than a year ago. It was to be of a stately looking Cherokee Indian chief (that I secretly imagine resembles my dearly departed grandfather whom I never knew). And at the end of our time together (a long, grueling stint of creation mixed with counseling) Shawn finally arrived at the place where he feels in control again. And even better than that, he actually believes that God has a plan for him, and wants to pursue a career in art!

But here's what really sets this case apart. You see, his mother came to visit me at the center today. And I could see she was pretty uncomfortable in here. Up until today, she'd never set foot in the place. She'd simply drop Shawn at the door and then zip away in her faded, old, red Corvette. For Shawn's mama is none other than old Sally Roberts! But today she just walked right into my center and stood there right in front of a group of "mentally challenged" kids who just stared at her hot pink miniskirt and watched with wide-eyed fascination as she apologized for the way she'd treated me back when we were kids, growing up. And then she graciously thanked me (with real tears in her eyes) for helping her son Shawn. Because the fact is, and I can see it now, she really loves that boy! Of course, I realize now that I still need to apologize to her for that time when I informed her that her daddy was cheating on her mama, but since she just signed up for my Beat the Blues Pottery Class, I'm pretty sure I'll get the opportunity before too long.

I think it was Sally's little visit to my center that finally convinced me that Joey's and my dream has really and truly come true. We're no longer just the ex-members of the Misfit Club who've taken up residence in Brookdale again, but now I really believe we're a vital part of this community. And despite our crooked and seemingly small and insignificant beginnings (and because of the mighty grace of God) we have ultimately grown up straight and strong. And nowadays when the good folks of our fair town look upon us as we're walking down the street, they might actually say what we'd always hoped to hear: "Yep, I remember when I knew them two, way back when."

ABOUT THE AUTHOR

MELODY CARLSON is the award-winning author of more than seventy books for adults, teens, and children. In other words, she loves to write! But more than an author, she considers herself to be a storyteller, and feels that the power of fiction can be as life-changing as anything. After all, Jesus himself utilized stories to make some of his most valuable and memorable points.

Melody's most recent novels include *Blood Sisters; A Place to Come Home To; Everything I Long For; Looking for You All My Life; Someone to Belong To;* and for teens, the Diary of a Teenage Girl series.

When not writing, Melody likes to spend time with her husband and her Labrador retriever, enjoying the natural beauty and outdoor activities so readily available in central Oregon.